THE ILLUMINATION

THE NEW WORLD SERIES
BOOK ONE

ASHER D. PAYNE

For the dreamers, the seekers, and the outcasts,

This one's for you.

CONTENT WARNING

The New World Series is based in a fantasy, post-apocalyptic world where the government holds the reins and survival is sought no matter the cost. Each book within the series contains dark elements such as—government corruption, graphic violence, death, murder, torture, betrayal, explicit sexual scenes, explicit language, and referenced sexual assault.

If you read those and still feel ready to buckle in, I welcome you to the complex story of *The New World.*

PROLOGUE

It was August when everything changed.

Six months into the pandemic, the virus escalated to an unimaginable tragedy. With the abrupt shift, the government tightened its grip on society, turning minimal lockdowns into strict curfews where defiance granted the death penalty.

As a reward for following their rules and demonstrating 'good behavior,' they paid out ration cards, which were the insurance for our survival. With implemented laws and obliging citizens, those in power cast out the individuals deemed Infected once medical supplies dwindled, coercing them into the world beyond our sanctioned regions.

As cities fell, the administration's higher-ups ordered the erection of Walls around the infrastructure that was once the United States. Cities that harnessed militaries before the outbreak became our last bastions of safety, forming the three Regions we'd become acquainted with throughout the years.

Region One spanned what had been known as Fayetteville, North Carolina. Region Two occupied the southern portion of the continent where Killeen, Texas, reigned before the destruction. Region Three, where I'd come to take up residence, hunkered down along the West Coast and took up space in a once-thriving Lakewood, Washington.

There was no method of selecting where Uninfected survivors ended up. Most flocked to where safety was most attainable, some staying in cities they'd grown up in and others finding themselves elsewhere. Even though each location was familiar, those in power forbade the use of the city and state names, and their elected titles were the only acceptable way to refer to them.

With the sanctions' complete establishment and the President's declaration, the unrelenting war between the Uninfected and the Infected began, marking the official start of what the remnants of society would know as the Fall. As those in power worked to protect the Uninfected from those beyond the Walls, an exploration group known as the Venturers was established. Those bearing the title were responsible for transporting materials to other walled communities and hunting down and executing those living in the Wilds—the Rebellion.

Those who survived interactions with Rebel members were slim, but those who did shared horrific stories involving the recognition of the symbol they'd painted as both a warning and significance of their opposition. Because of the teachings and warnings from remaining Venturers, the Uninfected saw Rebellion members as untamed beasts with uncontrollable abilities that had once been nothing more than fairy tale ideology. Even with the spectrum of power they held, one fugitive, in particular, became known across all three walled cities for his defiance and capabilities.

He was the Most Wanted.

His reputation spread like wildfire, and every story shared about him signified unimaginable abilities that placed him at the top of the totem pole of power. The President and his right-hands worked tirelessly to eradicate our world of the male who did everything he could to destroy it, yet behind the scenes, those in power kept dark secrets of their own.

Tests were conducted in hidden facilities alongside the mysterious evolution of the outbreak. No information had been provided on how the virus started, but many questioned the truth behind the claim. Even with unease, restricted areas within the Walls remained unquestioned by the public and even those wearing the badge of protection. We all turned a blind eye to the intricacies of what occurred behind closed doors because we believed they held our best interests in mind—safety and survival.

Then everything I thought I knew was spun on its head when I met *him*.

At twenty-four, I never thought I would support the government or join the Venturers in a post-apocalyptic world.

The badge sewn into my uniform solidified my unique role in a fractured society built upon control and refuge. The design featured a prominent compass. Its sharp cardinal points radiated outward and represented our duty to traverse beyond the Walls and into the Wilds. A shield encircled it, symbolizing our vow to ensure the survival of the Uninfected population.

I sat by the wincowsill of my makeshift apartment, where I had remained in Region Three for the past three and a half years, finding sanction along the West Coast. With my knees pulled to my chest and my back against the worn, faded wallpaper, I buried myself in a copy of *The Great Gatsby* I found on my last excursion beyond the Walls. The book's wear was evident, with pages practically falling from its decaying spine.

As I ran my fingers across the textured pages, the abrupt interruption of the announcement speakers distracted me, ringing a message throughout the community's streets.

"The public execution of Layonheart, Marksworth, and

Pagway will occur in the courtyard in ten minutes. You may join if you wish to witness them face the consequences of their actions for going against protocol. Refreshments are available for those who attend." Before the announcement could begin its second and third loops, I drowned it out entirely and shifted my attention back to reading.

Thankfully, the three names weren't ones I recognized, but they still indicated another day of public executions. Each roll call that drowned out through the speakers served as yet another gut-churning reminder of the intentional thinning of the Uninfected population.

I turned to the next chapter as someone drummed their knuckles against my door, the intrusiveness just as agitating as the advertised broadcast. Exhaling deeply, I folded the corner of the page I was on—cringing with the act of further harming valuable literature—and pushed myself up off the ground.

"Who is it?" I called, my boots hitting the wooden floor.

"Is that even a question?" a comforting male voice replied from the other side.

Pulling the lock to the right and twisting the knob, I yanked the door open to find Radley in his uniform. The dark-colored military-style suit hugged his lithe figure, his frame dwarfing mine. The mid-morning sun from my open window caught his light blonde, near-white hair, highlighting its stark hue. As his vibrant blue eyes met my gaze, he smirked.

"I should've figured you'd be swinging by about now. If it were any later, I would've thought—"

"What? That I died? That they hauled me away for questioning?" He chuckled, shaking his head. "No, not today, Miss Carnell. I hate to inform you, but you are stuck with me for yet another dusk till dawn."

"Oh, gods, Radley." I grinned, rolling my eyes. "Is it that time already? For our patrol route? I thought we had the later shift tonight?"

"Yeah, they've requested us for a debriefing about a new assignment. I hate to put a hole in your..." He shifted his body to glance past me to the book I'd abandoned on the ground. "...twenties commemoration."

"Give me shit about the book I found, and I will steal your rations for the next two weeks," I said, a soft smile spreading across my face.

"As if you haven't done that already," he flicked my forehead, a genuine laugh leaving him as I swatted at his hand. "You've got to work on your threat if your goal is to intimidate me."

"Would you like me to lay you out on the sparring mats the next time we are in the training yard?"

The corner of his lip curled upward into his renowned cat-like grin. "Sounds like a date."

I kicked his booted foot with my own, rolling my eyes. "Let me grab a few things, you flirt, and I'll be out, alright?"

He shook his head as the awaiting laugh finally rolled off him. "Yeah, take your time, sweet cheeks. I'll wait right here."

I briefly shut the door behind me to gather the rest of my gear before opening it again and stepping outside. Once I secured the lock, my attention landed on Radley, who stood with his back to the wall.

Standing around 6'5", he made my more petite frame of 5'7" seem miniscule. Being as tall as he was, he often intimidated others within the community we'd come to know as home. Even with the stone-cold mask he wore, I knew Radley better than anyone else in Region Three. He was far from what they believed him to be, which became frequently mentioned when he conversed with people when his persona faltered and illuminated his outgoing and fun-loving personality.

Yet every kind-hearted person held a darker side, and for him, losing his younger brother to the Rebellion shaped his temper and protective nature. Revenge weighed heavily on his mind, as it would for anyone with the same circumstances. While I never met his brother, I related to that level of loss in my own magnitude.

Every story Radley shared about his brother made me reminiscent of the close familial bond I'd lost as well, the personalities between his and my brother uncannily similar.

They had both been hard-headed and stubborn, rarely listening to others' concerns and often occupied with the worries of protecting those they loved. Both of our siblings' deaths had the same impact on the two of us, stitching us together in ways that seemed to be fated by some pre-determined destiny—one I was still attempting to uncover.

We swiftly traveled from the housing facilities to the epicenter of the community, where most of the business took place. Watching a group of individuals make their way toward the announced execution, I exhaled deeply.

"I know how you feel." It took me a moment to realize Radley was talking about my exasperated sigh. "I never understand how people can go to those things and watch while those in power deem innocent lives forfeit. Despite other horrific tellings shared by other Venturers, those occupying our city are still curious about what exists beyond the Walls."

I glanced back at the path before us as we approached the building entrance, sympathizing with those entrapped by our rulers. "Yeah, I mean, if they had assigned me some other form of labor, like housecleaning, cooking, or anything else, my mind would have wandered toward the possibilities. I guess what I don't understand is—"

"Well, well, if it isn't Radley and Astrid. The duo of the century."

The sense of a looming threat had consumed me before the words left my mouth, yet I'd spoken them even though everyone within the Regions knew that any conversation about disagreement with government policy, especially from those holding titles, could lead to immediate questioning. Depending on the severity deemed by higher-ups, it could even lead to public execution for treason.

I glanced over my shoulder, my stomach pitting, and found Gael glancing between us. His lips pulled into a snarky smile.

His dark hair, highlighted with streaks of mahogany, reflected many shades in the sunlight and hinted at his varied personality. The Venturer uniform clung to his broad shoulders and muscular figure, the various emblems speaking of accomplishments I never bothered to note.

"Gael. Figures you'd be out here. I presume you're heading to gather orders for the day?" Radley quickly interjected.

Gael threw an arm over my shoulder, smirking as he peered at me. "Yeah, something like that. I'm assuming you two are as well. Likely heading outside the Walls today?"

I attempted to shrug him off, but it was useless as practically all his body weight pressed into me. "Likely, yes." My voice displayed immense annoyance, which usually drew people away.

But not Gael.

Never Gael.

"You both seem to have made dear friends with our higher-ups." Mockery filled his tone as he finally pulled himself away from me.

"I wouldn't—" Radley began, but I quickly cut him off.

"Maybe it's because we efficiently execute each assigned job, so they rely on us because of the incompetence of others. Ever think of that?" I went to add onto my retaliation, my blood searing with decreasing patience, only to be interrupted by his aggravating chuckle.

"Ah, the snarky Astrid Carnell. Why should I expect any other response from someone known for running their mouth as if their words actually hold any weight?" His emerald eyes bounced between us, humor lacing every corner of their unnatural hue.

Gael's superiority complex was a frequent experience, especially during our six months of training. Dealing with a cocky asshole who forced himself into every conversation and always got the last word was exhausting. And regardless of us no longer sharing a classroom with him, the constant battle remained.

"Hey, Gael!" A female voice broke through the apparent tension from a distance, drawing our attention.

I didn't know her name or care to find out.

"Oh, would you look at that? Our time has come to a close. As always, it's been a pleasure chatting with you both." He stepped forward, stopping mid-stride to glance over his shoulder. "As a friend looking out for a friend, I'd suggest keeping your conversations surrounding any disagreement with our lovely over-seers private. You never know who's listening or what their intentions might be."

WE CONTINUED to the outpost in silence. Gael's unwanted engagement rocked us both, and we knew it was far from a minimal interaction. He was renowned for getting what he wanted no matter what it took. Even if it required sacrificing lives, he remained unbothered as long as he stayed on top. Radley and I were just another hurdle in his marathon, and if he wished, reporting our conversation to the higher-ups within Venturer operations for negligence and verbal declaration of opposition would result in our downfall.

Out of the corner of my eye, I noted Radley's tight-lipped expression. I knew his thoughts aligned with mine, contemplating our fate and what Gael's convoluted threat meant before he strolled off as if the words had never left his mouth.

We arrived outside Dylan's office sooner than expected, our minds distracted by the contemplation of what Gael's intentions could be and how deep the underlying warning of his words went. Radley raised his hand to tap his knuckles against the door before pushing it open to reveal the well-acquainted space.

Dylan always kept her space put together, solidifying her importance within the ranks. Her desk remained tidy despite being consumed by paperwork. The neatly organized bookshelves lining the eastern and western walls constantly made me envious, my fingers itching to get my hands on pristine reading material. Considering the interior of most other buildings, the deep oak of her office was a breath of fresh air—with resulting apocalyptic conditions came dwindling interior design. The living quarters and other facilities were no exception, lacking aesthetic appeal. Yet, in contrast, buildings tied to government work remained pristine.

Dylan glanced up from a thick packet of paper. Her blonde hair, secured in a tight bun, aligned with the uniform ideology in the Walls. The glasses resting on the bridge of her nose highlighted the light dusting of freckles along her cheeks, and the sunlight streaming through the windows seemed to illuminate them further.

"Well, hello, you two." She smiled softly, setting the papers down.

"Good afternoon," Radley greeted her first, and I followed with a nod. "You wanted to see us?"

"Yes. We need a team to go outside the Walls today. A handful of men spotted Rebels further west and closer than their last reported location. We're unsure if they're planning an attack or desiring to stir up unrest." She swiveled her chair and pushed herself upright. "This is not an order for active engagement or ceasing, but recon. We need to gather information and attempt to determine their next moves."

"Simple enough," I shrugged, looking at her and then Radley, who nodded before I returned to Dylan.

"Perfect. I appreciate your flexibility." Her tone abruptly shifted from gratitude to sympathy, her gaze never leaving us. "I understand these last-minute excursions can be tiresome."

Excursions outside the Walls filled our last three weeks, reminding me of the statement I unleashed on Gael about our capabilities. It was a paradox that our skills, which earned us favor, also put us at risk.

"What about rations?" Radley asked, slicing through my train of thought.

"Since it's recon-based, the two of you know the compensation won't be as high as other delegations. But given your hard work, I've put in a good word for both of you. I was able to score you both fifty rations each, considering it's so last minute."

Every Venturer expected a breakdown before accepting to determine if the valued ration cards rewarded upon completion were valuable enough to agree to the terms. When drafting a recon assignment, the operations group offered close to twenty-five ration cards depending on what they gathered during the outing—similar to what someone within the Walls would make for general contributions.

Based on the predetermined danger, the payment for cessation requests increased to thirty or forty. Meanwhile, the expected return for capture and elimination orders skyrocketed because of the likelihood of irreversible consequences. Most people who accepted missions in that regard lost their lives or returned gravely injured after actively engaging with the Rebellion. The award, if survived, ranged from one to two hundred ration cards, depending on the exposed danger and what they returned with—information, prisoners, or bodies.

Then, the most tempting reward came with apprehending the Most Wanted Rebel alive, offering nearly five hundred ration cards and providing a comfortable life without requiring another day's work to survive. If a designation to that individual came through as an elimination order, and the assigned Venturers pulled off a successful execution instead of a capture, the payout jumped to nearly eight hundred.

"You've got yourself a deal," I replied with a smile. "We'll make our way to the gates and plan to be back just after sundown with enough intel to make our trek and your willingness to put your neck out for us worthwhile."

"I appreciate your commitment to humanity. Every sacrifice and contribution you make for Region Three is invaluable."

Dylan stood, her small stature fully revealed as she moved around the desk to shake our hands before leaving us with one final statement. "Remember that the Runners become more active once the sun sets. Remain on the lookout and mindful of your surroundings. We would hate for anything to happen to either of you."

CHAPTER

TWO

Before the Fall, the land was rich with vegetation along the West Coast. Now, outside the Walls after civilization's collapse, Mother Nature swiftly reclaimed what was once manmade.

Once bustling with life and vehicles, the streets were a tangle of plants and wildlife. Birdsong and the rustling of leaves had replaced car horns and engines. The noises of daily life faded, leaving only the occasional thud of boots on concrete to remind us of human presence. Vegetation even swallowed the cars that clogged the roads. Trees towered over transportation paths, their roots breaking through the pavement unchecked by human hands. Vines and weeds crawled up the sides of buildings, progressing their internal growth.

The cities' post-apocalyptic landscape provided an eerie yet fascinating reminder. Each step we took toward desolation welcomed a journey into a world both dead and alive—a clash between humanity's past and nature's future.

Exhilaration clung to the air, my stomach flipping with the enjoyment of being outside the Walls. Constantly anticipating an ambush by Rebellion forces or a pack of Runners kept my senses sharp. But the breath of fresh air that came with it—unfiltered and wild—was worth the risk.

I positioned myself at the opening of a street we frequented, admiring a café on its right-hand side. It was void of light, human interaction, and protection from the elements, with shattered glass from its rectangular holes littering the ground.

At the start of the outbreak, everyone frantically worked to protect what was rightfully theirs, boarding up establishments and blanketing themselves in a false sense of security. Even with active attempts to safeguard, most people who'd locked themselves in merely crafted their own inescapable tomb, and with an inability to flee came the inevitable doom that would've snuffed them out regardless. If the virus didn't successfully escort them to their doom, the Rebellion waited on the opposite end, chasing them toward death with their bloodthirsty willingness to kill.

Radley kicked some wooden boards around inside the café, his gun in hand, finger on the trigger. He disappeared into the back, his silhouette quickly fading from view.

My attention returned to our surroundings and how much had changed in just four years; the barren streets made me feel at peace, even if only temporarily.

Nature had flawlessly executed her artistic plan, painting the bricks of the building with a light layer of moss. There was something beautiful about how the plant life had taken over, and I would never tire of witnessing it. It completed a broken piece of me that had been robbed of living life as it once was. Even though stepping outside the Walls granted an immediate ticket to danger, I reminisced about our previous life.

The café's interior, on the other hand, had seen better days. From where I stood, I could see tables toppled over in disarray, bullet holes riddling the walls, and the once-ornate glass decor behind the barista counter shattered—vines wound around the remaining tables.

It was once a space of functioning liveliness where friends shared laughter, patrons engaged with one another, and all savored delicious food and the bitterness of coffee. Now, deafening silence replaced it, a haunting reminder of what was lost.

"The place is empty. Let's head further north." Radley's voice snagged my attention. I turned to watch him step out of the building and move his hand to his holster.

"So, no action for two days, huh?" I crossed my arms, my crossbow slung across my back.

Was Dylan's tip just a bluff?

I mentally checked my weaponry after watching Radley adjust himself, the weight of the twin pistols on my thighs greeting my fingers. My fingers grazed over the hilt of the hunting knife on my left leg before bouncing across the untouched throwing knives and ammunition clips with a mental count. Saving the most critical piece for last, I wrapped my palm around the cold steel of the electric baton that extended down my left leg, reassuring myself that it was still, in fact, on my body and prepared for emergency use.

"Yes, a mere two days." Radley chuckled, his boots scuffing against the concrete with palpable tease.

I sighed dramatically as he approached, knowing my words would yield more banter between us. "Another trip outside the Walls with no action."

"Are you saying you want to run into someone or something?" He cocked a brow, shaking his head. "You consistently label me as the crazy one, but here you are, wishing to greet Death with open arms."

"There's nothing wrong with a little excitement," I smirked.

"Excitement? Is that what we're calling it?" He laughed as we continued down the street.

Shrugging at his question, I scanned the surrounding buildings. An uneasy stillness flooded the streets, providing the perfect moment for an ambush, yet nothing stirred from the shadows.

I glanced over my shoulder, spotting nothing but the massive and suffocating Walls in the distance. We had to be about three miles from Region Three, and with the freedom that came without confinement, a part of me desired to be further.

Turning back to the path ahead, I kicked a rock on the ground for brief entertainment. It danced across the pavement, bouncing twice before rolling to a stop. As I went for another, Radley beat me there, sending it sailing down the street and into uncharted territory.

"Hey, you stole my rock, asshole. Get your own." I groaned, playfully shoving him as we continued to walk side by side.

He chuckled, returning a light nudge that made me stagger. "You're not the only one who gets to have fun. Didn't anyone teach you how to share?"

Rolling my eyes, I went to retort, but the snap of what seemed to be a branch cut me off. My head swiveled, and I lifted my hand to Radley's chest, signaling for silence before turning my attention toward the source. A side alley, separated by an old barbershop and restaurant, greeted me, undeniably concealing whatever awaited us.

I conscientiously unfastened the holster on my thigh, making as little noise as possible before withdrawing my knife. Given the potential threat's lack of engagement and sudden presence, I assumed it was a Runner.

Before I could step forward, Radley's hand wrapped around my arm, pulling me into him. "Didn't you request entertainment?"

Smiling at him, I suppressed a laugh. He loosened his grip, and I continued with softened footsteps before a low growl greeted us, confirming my suspicions.

A Runner.

Peering around the edge of the building, I spotted the decomposing frame hunched over a body and occupied with consumption. Its back remained to us, obscuring its features but still decipherable enough to be a man. He wore a collared shirt, messily untucked from tattered jeans, his curly brown hair matted and streaked with dried blood, but those were the only slivers of humanity that clung to him.

Black veins spread throughout his ashen skin, some portions occupying holes that I assumed belonged to a spray of bullets. Inky blood spilled from every laceration, highlighting the virus's significant influence on those whose DNA failed to keep up with the mutation. With every movement came a sickening grind of bone on bone, signaling the internal destruction that would have once been deemed detrimental. Yet he kept functioning, unbothered by injury and solely focused on satiating a hunger that would never cease.

As I watched, I imagined the life he might have lived before the Fall—perhaps a father, a brother, a man with a simple, beautiful life.

The body beneath him remained covered, save for a limp hand visible around his legs. It was impossible to tell if the person had been a Rebel, a Venturer, or someone from the Walls who wandered into the Wilds.

Exhaling slowly, I tightened my grip on the hilt and inched forward, Radley close behind. Before the Runner could turn, I took a deep breath and raised the blade, swinging for the base of its neck. Its serrated edge severed his spinal cord in one fluid motion, and his body slumped over the person he had been devouring.

Another life ended as quickly as it had fallen apart.

I sheathed the knife and proceeded down the alleyway.

Radley stepped past me, grabbing the Runner's shoulder and pulling the corpse off the body feasted upon. The person beneath was a woman, her eyes staring vacantly past us. A deep bite mark on her neck revealed the tendons beneath her skin, crimson red pooling beneath her. With parted lips and pale skin, it became immediately notable that she was past the point of saving—her life force drained entirely.

Her reddish-orange hair draped across the pavement, still vibrant despite her lifelessness. I scanned her for any identifiers of belonging—she wasn't in a Venturer uniform, and her features didn't draw up any recognition from within the Walls. I glanced at Radley, who shook his head, suggesting his lack of familiarity.

"A Rebel?" I asked, bending down to search her for any identifying marks. The only thing I found was a magazine of ammunition for the gun still strapped to her thigh.

"Possibly." Radley knelt beside me, pointing at the weapon holstered on her thigh. "But *that* doesn't add up."

It didn't. If a Runner actively attacked her, she would have drawn her weapon in defense. The fact it remained untouched suggested a far different story.

I scanned her again, searching for clues when a deep stab wound in her abdomen greeted me.

"Someone attacked her." I pointed to the lethal injury and looked at Radley. "But the question is, who?"

He cocked his head to the side, examining the stab wound just below her bulletproof vest—so much for adequate protection. Concern filtered through his expression as he pushed himself up, his figure towering over me as I still crouched by the body.

"You don't think another Rebel did this, do you?" My question came with an anxious edge as I peered up at him.

Radley's blue eyes filled with caution as he considered my question. I held his gaze as he ran a hand down his face before responding.

"We have a limited understanding of the Rebellion. Every Rebel we have captured has sworn a level of secrecy that resulted in execution. They haven't disclosed their operation tactics or further information, and we've been ineffective in digging it up. But it's not impossible. Maybe she wasn't with the Rebels local to the area. Or maybe she was and betrayed them, which resulted in this attack. It seems like the Rebellion is far more complex than we realize."

He glanced down at the lifeless woman before finalizing his statement with an undercurrent of unspoken knowledge. "There's a real possibility they're not all allies."

WE VENTURED DEEPER into the city, the hours slipping away unnoticed.

I raised my hand to gauge the sun's position; it hovered in the center of the sky, signaling late afternoon. We had left the base around mid-afternoon, and clearing the first section of our route had taken longer than expected. The unexpected encounter with the Runner hadn't helped our time constraints. Though we deduced that the young woman we found was likely part of the Rebellion and, therefore, Immune, Radley still put a bullet between her eyes.

Lowering my hand, I spotted Radley emerging from another building he had just searched.

No gunfire, no yelling, no signs of life.

Nothing.

None of it made sense. I wondered if someone had attacked the woman while we cleared the café. But we had heard no screams or cries for help, let alone any sign of struggle. Then again, was there any point in screaming out here where survival was a solitary struggle?

Especially if what Radley said was true about the Rebellion—maybe they weren't all allies.

"Nothing." Radley approached, exhaling deeply. "None of this makes any sense, Astrid. She was—"

"Fresh," I cut him off, squinting against the slowly sinking sun that symbolized our countdown. Dropping my gaze, I continued. "No, it doesn't. Someone must have attacked her while we were in town. But there was no sound, not a single noise to indicate anything. How is that possible?"

"If a Rebel attempted to murder her, anything is possible, right?"

I nodded. If a Rebel had targeted her, they could have done it in several ways. Using abilities we could barely comprehend—a clean, quick attack with no trace left behind.

"Wait." I looked back at him, the sun blinding me again. "That makes sense. If a teleporter targeted her, they could have stabbed her and then fled without a trace. Which would explain why the knife used in the attack was nowhere to be found."

"So, what is this now, Sherlock Holmes? Nancy Drew?" He chuckled as I punched his shoulder. "Come on, as much as we'd love to solve the mystery, we need to clear the rest of this street. It'll probably take a couple more hours, so long as we don't encounter any other surprises. Then we have to head back before it gets dark. We don't want to be stuck out here past sunset."

I sighed and followed him down the street. The smell of decay and abandonment clung to the air, mingling with the distant scent of something burning in the distance. If a Rebel had attacked the girl, they couldn't be far from where her body was.

Or could they?

We'd grown accustomed to the unease of exploring the city, the radar in the back of my mind constantly scanning for the possibility of danger lurking in the shadows. During the past three and a half years as a Venturer, I had only encountered Rebels a handful of times, and none had been in these streets. Yet every time we patrolled them, I couldn't shake the gut feeling that someone watched us.

Radley groaned ahead of me, turning his head to the right as a loud pop sounded from his neck. "Oh, thank gods. I've been waiting for that."

Laughing, I became eager to engage in conversation, unaware of how long my contemplation had kept me prisoner. "Sheesh, that was loud. You drew me out of my disassociation. Feel better, old man?"

"Old man?" He glanced over his shoulder, smirking. "Ma'am, last I checked, I'm only a couple of years older than you."

"The key word is older." I smiled, playfully lifting a brow.

He was about to respond when a sudden voice caught our

attention. Radley raised a finger to his lips and pointed to his ear. *Be quiet. Listen.*

I nodded, scanning the building to our right. Its destroyed windows created an accessible entry point.

Gesturing for Radley to head in that direction, I followed tightly behind. I turned toward the voice, trying to spot anyone as Radley stepped over the windowsill. Before I could pinpoint where it came from, he tapped my shoulder, offering his hand to help. My boots hit the ground inside, and broken glass cracked underfoot.

"Come on, get down," Radley whispered, gently pushing me beside the window.

I sank beside the empty frame, Radley sliding down next to me. We stayed out of sight, listening for any conversation and trying to catch a glimpse of whoever was approaching. While crouching, I focused on the brick wall before us, where a bold image caught my eye—the unmistakable Rebellion insignia.

Vibrant reds and deep blacks painted the symbol with striking clarity—an opposing entity watching over the area. The eye's gaze felt piercing, almost as if it could see right through us. It was a constant reminder of the Rebels' vigilance in this territory, a stark warning to anyone stepping into their world.

"You just had to jinx us, didn't you? Not once, but twice," Radley whispered beside me, his attention landing on the symbol. "You wanted action. Is this what you had in mind?"

"Shut up," I hissed, my brows narrowing.

A Runner and an unknown, potential Rebel wasn't exactly the combination I had in mind.

I closed my eyes, focusing on our surroundings. My breathing grew louder, and I struggled to steady it.

Was the voice we heard from one Rebel or a group of them?

I leaned my head against the rough brick wall, and once the connection happened, I heard a female voice.

"Oh, stop. I'm fine. I'll be back; don't get all worked up."

Radio static followed her voice, suggesting she used a walkie-talkie for accessible communication.

Peering over the edge of the windowsill, she came into view.

Pulled back into a ponytail, her dark, tightly curled hair accentuated her golden-brown skin, which glinted against the fading light. She walked confidently, her light-wash jeans and loose orange T-shirt catching the sun's last rays. A backpack hugged her shoulders, and her black Converse thudded softly against the ground as she moved through the streets.

I would have thought she was ordinary if I hadn't known better. Two red flags stood out—she seemed entirely unarmed and was very much alone, except for her radio companion, who remained unseen.

Before I could study her further, a male voice crackled through the walkie-talkie. "Imelda, I swear to the gods, if you don't get your ass back here—"

She pressed the button, cutting him off. "Onyx. Take a chill pill, alright? I'll be back in...fifteen minutes?"

"I told you not to leave the bunker. Not alone. Not without me. You're smarter than that and know about all the city mutts scouring the Wilds. Especially lately."

Despite his harsh words, his voice had a protective undertone —a deep, husky sound that was both captivating and stern.

Who was he to her? Who was *he*?

"And you know what? I haven't run into a single one of them. I told you, fifteen minutes." She sighed into the speaker before releasing the button.

"Fine. You've got fifteen minutes. But if you're not back by then, I'm coming to you, and you know what that means." Onyx's voice cut through the static again, and she shook her head with a soft smile.

Even with his clear threat, comfort laced her expression, and I couldn't help but understand.

Seeing that we weren't in immediate danger, I shifted to lower myself from the window and out of sight. My left foot slipped on the glass shards, sending me skidding. I grabbed the windowsill to stop my fall, but a shard of glass sliced deeply into my palm, and foreboding seeped through every pore of my body. Pain shot through my hand, spreading quickly down my wrist, followed by the undeniable warmth of my blood.

I inhaled sharply, biting my lip to stifle a cry, but the crunch of glass and my boot sliding against it proved loud enough. I glanced at Radley, who looked at me with widened eyes.

Her footsteps halted.

"I'll give you five seconds to show yourself." The softness in her voice from before vanished.

Radley exhaled, dropping his head before pushing himself up. He slowly stepped into view through the broken window, raising his hands in surrender.

I pulled my hand from the glass, my life force coating my palm and trickling down my forearm. With a pained sigh, I pushed myself up and stepped into view through the window on the opposite side. Mirroring Radley's stance, I began to feel warm crimson droplets slither from my elbow to greet the glass-covered floor.

Imelda narrowed her dark brown eyes at us. My assumption was correct—no weapon in her hand, just the walkie-talkie. Now that I could see her more clearly, her petite frame became notable, which made me question her age. The sun caught her face, revealing a deep scar over her left eye and another across the bridge of her nose, likely from a past encounter with a Venturer.

"Listen, kid—" Radley began, but she cut him off sharply.

"Uh, uh. Shut the hell up." She shook her head, raising the walkie-talkie. "I'm guessing you heard that conversation. I'm not alone, so if you try anything, I promise all hell will break loose."

"That's not our intention," I quickly interjected, catching Radley's glance from the corner of my eye. "We don't even have to acknowledge this happened. We never saw you. You never saw us."

She laughed softly, narrowing her gaze. "How stupid do you think I am? Every Venturer is a liar. It's in your blood. You're all brainwashed government puppets sent to execute every Rebel out here, regardless of age. Why would I believe you wouldn't just turn around and kill me the moment we agreed?"

Radley sighed deeply. "You're not entirely wrong. But we're not as mindless as the others. There are things—"

He was about to expose our doubts, and I would have shut him down, but we needed to gain her trust. Somehow.

"That the government has been doing and blah, blah, blah..." She shifted her glower between us. "As if I haven't heard that same sob story from every Venturer I've encountered. Why would you go back there if you disagreed heavily with what's happening inside the Walls?"

It was a valid question but one-sided. She didn't understand the complexities of betrayal or the near-impossible odds of surviving out here as a known Venturer among Rebels.

"It's not that simple." I looked at her sympathetically, feeling my brows draw together.

Neither of us wanted to hurt her.

My mind wandered to her conversation with the unseen male. He'd given her a time limit. Fifteen minutes. The clock was ticking.

"Who were you talking to?" I asked before she could speak again.

She stepped back, glancing at the walkie-talkie in her hand, then back at us. "And why would I even answer—"

Radley drew his weapon, and my stomach dropped. I knew he desired vengeance for his brother's death, but she hadn't threatened either of us, the reaction belonging to a side of him I didn't know. It was his darkness, the shattered pieces of him, that had been put back together throughout the years of us knowing one another, and I couldn't but fear that his rage-induced mindlessness would force him to pull the trigger and take an innocent life.

"Radley!" The gunshot rang out, cutting off my plea before slamming through my eardrums to violate my skull. The ringing quickly subsided—something I'd become accustomed to with time.

I held my breath, glancing from Radley and his drawn pistol to Imelda, fearing I'd see her lifeless body on the ground. But she stood there, unharmed, her eyes widened in shock.

Then I saw it—the walkie-talkie, blown to pieces on the ground beside her.

Radley had destroyed her only method of communication with the unknown male.

Before I could fully process what it meant, a snide grin spread across her face as she slowly scowled at us. The death glare in her eyes was unmistakable. "That was probably the stupidest mistake you could have made."

"Radley, for hell's sake! He gave her a time limit, and now she cannot contact him!" My brows narrowed as I snarled, "Did you even consider the potential outcome of your brash decision?!"

"You're naïve to think she would've told him to stand down. Either way, we're screwed, Astrid." He snapped back, sliding his weapon back into place. "Better that we destroy her means of communication so she can't give him her exact location or tell him about us. We're in a city. He'll have to search before he finds her. Did you think *that* through?"

Exhaling in frustration, I glared at him as the tension swelled between us.

"I mean," Imelda broke the silence, her mocking tone unmistakable. "Theoretically, neither of you is wrong. If that helps you feel better."

Radley turned to her, but before he could respond, a massive blast of fire erupted in our direction. The heat was intense, even with the structural barrier separating us.

He pivoted quickly, slamming into me and sending the two of us to the glass-covered floor. The breath left my lungs on impact, and I grunted in pain.

"Ah, shit," Radley muttered, pushing himself up, his face hovering above mine.

The attack—could it have been the male she was talking to? Could he have arrived that quickly?

"Are you okay?" Radley's anger was gone, replaced by concern, as he gazed down at me with a softened expression.

He straddled over me, careful not to put weight on me, his right hand cradling my head to protect it from the hard ground.

Before I could answer, the rapid drum of footsteps on pavement came—but only one set.

She was still alone.

Radley realized it, too, and he pushed himself off me. He helped me up as we watched Imelda sprint to the right of the building and out of sight. The blast of fire had come from her, confirming the depth of risk the Wilds contained.

Radley's expression darkened with reactivity before he bolted after her, driven by the need to look after me. He hurtled over the windowsill and took a sharp left down the alleyway, the repercussive thunder of his footsteps drowning out with distance.

"Radley!" I called after him, pushing myself up and through the windowsill, having no choice but to follow.

His pace and long legs gave him a head start, and I struggled to keep up, remaining a decent distance behind him. The sun caught his whitish-blonde hair, its golden hues seeping into its starkness, making it easier to track him.

Ahead, Imelda climbed a fixed escape ladder on a building, glancing down at us as she hurried to the rooftop. Radley reached the ladder seconds later, pulling himself up its bars with a rapid ascent. He had always been athletic, and even in his Venturer gear, he moved with a swift ease.

I reached the ladder, gritting my teeth as I wrapped my injured hand around the unforgiving metal. The throbbing pain increased, but I forced myself to ignore it. I climbed quickly, pushing through the agony, and finally swung my legs over the lip of the structure, dropping onto the gravel-covered roof where Radley and Imelda were.

She stood on the edge of the building, Radley only a couple of feet away.

"Did you really think you could outrun us?" His voice cut through the early evening air, the sunset casting long shadows across the city.

"Maybe that wasn't my plan." Imelda glanced over her shoulder at us and jumped before we could react.

I gasped, and we rushed to the edge of the building.

Instead of plummeting to the ground below, Imelda rolled onto the rooftop of the neighboring structure. We watched as she instantaneously pushed herself up and, without missing a beat, turned around and raised her middle fingers at us.

"She's something else," Radley groaned before pushing himself onto the lip of the building.

After knowing Radley throughout the years and his dedication to ensuring those he loved remained untouched by harm, I knew the chase wasn't over until he caught her.

I watched him hit the ground next, rolling out of his dismount and immediately continuing the pursuit. Following, I pushed myself onto the next rooftop right as Radley slammed into Imelda, knocking her down face-first.

"Get off me!" she screamed with an unexpectedness of our company, struggling against him.

He quickly flipped her onto her back as she squirmed beneath him, trying to break free. She was small, not just in height but also in stature. With Radley straddling over her, pinning her arms above her head with one hand, she looked almost childlike.

"Let me ask you again," Radley said, his voice cold as he stared down at her, his grip on her wrists firm. "Did you *really* think you could outrun us?"

Instead of a snarky comeback or an answer, she spat in his face, a trail of saliva running down his nose.

"Fuck you!" she yelled, thrashing beneath him, but it was useless.

Radley groaned in annoyance, running a free hand down his

face to wipe off the bodily fluid that had sprung from her mouth. A deep exhale followed, signaling his attempt to keep himself level. He teetered on a fragile edge, his patience rapidly dwindling.

I stood behind him with my arms folded, unfurling them when he reached for his pistol and retrieved it from its holster.

"Radley, what—" I began, but he elected to answer with actions, not words.

I watched in horror as he pressed the barrel of his gun against the center of her forehead, my breath catching in my throat.

"We sat and talked with you calmly, with no intention of harming you," Radley hissed through gritted teeth, pressing the weapon harder against her skull. "We made that clear, but instead of listening, you tried to kill us. If you'd just run away, fine. But you tried to kill us. And the moment you put us in a life-or-death situation, mercy goes out the window."

"You would've killed me anyway," Imelda shot back, her voice laced with defiance despite the fear in her eyes. "Every Venturer is a murderer!"

"You want to know something?" Radley lowered himself closer to her, his voice a harsh whisper. "You Rebels and us Venturers—we're not that different. We're all trying to survive, and we've all killed. There's no innocence left in this world. The apocalypse brought corruption and made us do whatever it took to survive.

"Yeah, Venturers are murderers. We've killed countless Rebels —because we had to. And your people have done the same. It wouldn't surprise me if you also have a record of killing. I lost my younger brother to the Rebellion, so don't sit there and call us vile when you're just as guilty. We're all in this for survival; when someone threatens that, we fight back. Even if it costs someone else their life."

Imelda continued to struggle, but it was clear she was listening now. Fear rolled off her in waves, even as she tried to hide it. And Radley wasn't wrong. Everyone was trying to survive with those they still had left. Most of us had already lost the people we loved, and the rest of us clung to the new families we'd found.

"Yeah? So, are you going to do it?" Imelda's voice wavered slightly. "Are you going to put a bullet between a fourteen-year-old's eyes?"

The realization hit me hard. She was much younger than I'd thought.

"I'm afraid that when you attacked us, you left me no choice, kid." Radley sighed, releasing the safety on his gun.

His finger slowly moved to the trigger, but I could sense his hesitation.

Imelda, sensing it too, threw out a final taunt. "Do it! You coward!"

She stopped struggling and scowled at him defiantly. Despite her fear, she tried to push and make him hesitate, and she succeeded. Conflict clouded Radley's eyes and became more noticeable in how his hand trembled.

She didn't want to die. I knew that, just as Radley didn't want to kill her.

Stepping forward to rest a hand on his shoulder and pull him back, the sudden arrival of a fourth pair of boots on gravel cut off my stride.

It was as if they had jumped from the neighboring building and landed behind us, but the gap and height made that impossible. There were no other access points to the rooftop we stood on, which meant only one thing.

They appeared out of thin air.

Imelda's face softened, and a smile formed on her lips as she glanced past Radley and at the person who had arrived. The fear rolling off her seconds ago vanished, and I didn't need to turn around to know who it was.

"I will give you three seconds to drop your fucking weapon." The words delivered behind me were raspy but carried a weight of authority that was impossible to ignore.

It was the same voice I'd heard on the walkie-talkie earlier, warning Imelda about the dangers of being out alone. Now, without radio static interference, it sounded even more defensive —and somehow, even more captivating.

"Radley," I spoke slowly, keeping my eyes on the back of his head, watching as Imelda's sneer grew. "I suggest you listen to him."

Radley exhaled, his hesitation evident. He seemed to weigh his options and chose refusal, the barrel of the gun remaining pressed against her forehead.

The male behind us spoke in a tone that should have been enough proof to Radley that he wasn't here to negotiate. Neither of us knew what kind of threat he posed, but it was clear he wasn't someone who would hesitate if actions became necessary.

Radley shifted slightly, his body tensing. Then, in one swift motion, he pulled the gun away from Imelda's head, spun around, and fired.

The gunshot echoed across the rooftop, and Imelda screamed.

Everything slowed.

I promptly turned, and my hair whipped around me with fluidity, my breath halting once the sight came into view.

The bullet from Radley's gun hovered mid-air, spinning as if it had hit something solid. But there was nothing there.

Standing before me was the man who had spoken to Imelda over the walkie-talkie, warning her of the dangers. His glowing powder-blue eyes narrowed in annoyance, their intensity framed by dark brows and his porcelain complexion.

It was *him*.

THREE

Three Years Prior

I quickly made my way down the halls of the Venturer outpost building, rounding a corner as I headed toward the recovery rooms as anxiety flooded my veins. Word had spread fast—Quinn had returned from the Wilds, injured and without her teammates, but alive. The rumors stated she had several encounters with the Rebellion on her cease-and-capture mission.

One encounter, in particular, would provide valuable information.

She had run into the Most Wanted Rebel alive.

Pushing the door to the recovery hall open, I sidestepped a nurse, nodding apologetically as I nearly collided with her. Continuing my route, my eyes scanned each passing room until I found Quinn's.

Room seventy-eight.

Finding it would have been an uphill battle if I didn't already have someone on the inside feeding me information.

I knocked once before pushing the door open.

Radley, my mole, stood in the corner of the room, his arms

folded over his chest. As soon as I entered, he looked up, his vibrant blue eyes meeting mine. Relief greeted me once our gazes locked, a soft smile of mirrored emotion sprawling across his lips.

I glanced at the other three individuals in the room—a higher-up from the Venturer mission designation group and two of the President's secretaries. The first had a cropped a-line hairstyle, her vibrant orange hair resting just beneath her chin and complimented by her ruby lips and chartreuse eyes. The other's hair was longer and blonde, her persona clashing the harshness of the first as her doe brown eyes glanced between us.

I knew they were here to gather information and nothing more—that's how it'd always been with the higher-ups within the President's inner circle.

"Ms. Hart," the female secretary began, her voice soft and laced with mock kindness. "Can you tell us a little about what happened?"

A pained expression crossed Quinn's face. She swallowed, clearly struggling to relive the nightmarish hell she experienced. I scanned her, noting the extent of her injuries—her left arm sat in a sling, a bandage tightly wrapped around her chest and shoulder, and visible bruising covered her face. Her dark pixie cut appeared tousled as if she'd just got back, and not much time had passed since the medics had finished cleaning her up. Her light grayish-blue eyes moved from the woman who had spoken to me.

I offered a weak smile to try to encourage her it would be okay—even though I knew it was far from the case.

Quinn and I weren't particularly close, but we had trained together in the same Venturer graduating class. We had interacted a few times, and while we didn't harbor bad blood, we weren't exactly friends. Still, I hoped my presence might comfort her, knowing she had lost her entire team—her recon partners.

As I considered the possibility of losing Radley, my stomach dropped. A pang of the same nausea that was evident on Quinn's face washed over me.

"Quinn," Radley said, shaking his head, ensuring his voice

remained steady. "You don't have to go into heavy detail. Just give them some insight as to who you encountered and what happened. Keep it basic, alright?"

"He's right. You can simplify as much as you need," the higher-up from the Venturer designation group added, his adenoidal voice grating my nerves. His dark black eyes evoked a sense of dread, and his ashen skin and dull hair didn't grant him any more sense of liveliness. "We're not here to make things worse for you. We just need some intel to help keep everyone within the Walls safe. That's our goal."

His words came off as far from empathetic. I knew they didn't mean any harm, but coming in and questioning someone fresh from the horrors of the Wilds felt far from understanding.

Quinn looked down, her fingers twiddling as she tried to distract herself from the memories. "We were out on a cease-and-capture mission—me and my partners, Rowan and Elias."

I knew them both. Rowan was a light in any room, always supportive and wanting to see everyone succeed. Elias was more brutal and relentless but cared deeply about the people closest to him, mirroring Radley's demeanor—an immense care for others because so much had been lost.

"Things were going smoothly, and honestly, it was probably one of the least problematic missions we'd been on. We cleared the territory and started searching for the person we were supposed to capture, working our way through the middle of the city. It wasn't even a Rebel we were after—just a traitor who had escaped from within the Walls."

I closed my eyes in recognition, knowing the implications that came with hunting down other community members. Nausea burned the back of my throat, and I forced myself to swallow, trying to bury all the burdens I carried. Settling on Radley, we exchanged an understanding glance before turning back to Quinn.

"We found and cleared the area where they were last spotted, but there weren't sufficient signs of them still residing in the reported area. Eventually, we found them, but they were already dead. Since we strive to keep disease out of the Walls, we decided not to bring the body back and concluded that our mission was complete. The first thirty minutes of our return were eerily quiet, but then they ambushed us."

She paused, her fingers stilling as the memories flooded back.

"It was a group of what we assumed were four Rebels—two older males and two younger individuals, a male and a female. We defended ourselves, drew our weapons, and a firefight broke out. We took out the three men and thought we were in the clear. I'd already taken a bullet to the shoulder. Then, out of nowhere, a younger female tackled Rowan. She had a knife and stabbed him, but he fought back. When she tried to retreat, Elias raised his weapon to kill her, and that's when *he* showed up...."

Her voice trailed off, her fingers no longer moving, the memories too vivid to escape.

"Can you describe this man? The one who showed up?" the dark-eyed secretary asked. "Even if you don't have a name, a description would be beneficial."

"He's the one everyone speaks of and warns about..." Her voice was soft and breathy, as if saying the words aloud might make it all too real. "He was tall, probably near Radley's height. Broad-shouldered, muscular. His hair was jet black, a little past shoulder length, with a slight wave. His dark brows contrasted with his pale skin and amplified his ghostly blue eyes that seemed to glow even in daylight. A scar spanned his entire face, starting above his right eyebrow, crossing his nose, and ending on the right side of his lips, but it wasn't a recent injury."

A tear slipped down her cheek as her voice cracked. "He forced his way into Elias' mind first, made him turn the gun on himself instead of the girl. Then Rowan cried out in agony, clutching his head before blood started pouring from his eyes, nose, and ears. And then...he just collapsed, lifeless. I-I don't know why he let me live. It doesn't make sense..."

The three officials had heard enough of the gruesome

details, their faces pale, as if the horrors she described were too much for them to handle. They had gotten what they came for —a rough sketch of the man's features based on Quinn's description.

Thankful for her openness in answering their questions, each of them stood and offered a weak wave, wishing her a swift recovery before leaving the room to distance themselves from her trauma. Only the one with the soulless gaze lingered longer than the others, placing a hand on her shoulder and giving it a gentle squeeze. The gesture seemed to be an attempt to extend gratitude for her sacrifice before he trailed after the others—part of me was precarious about why he, out of all the others, offered to stay behind.

And then they were gone.

They wouldn't have to deal with the aftermath of what Quinn had witnessed, and the horrors other Venturers spoke of would never touch them in the same way. They only cared about the information they'd gathered and the rough sketch they'd produced from her description, not the agony we were forced to live with, and that ignited a fire in me that burned far deeper than surface level.

Shortly after their visit, they plastered Wanted with his image across the regions, making him a known target for every Venturer.

The Most Wanted Rebel alive.

PRESENT

The once-spinning bullet dropped to the rooftop with a soft clink, cutting through the deep silence. My gaze slowly lifted from it to the man standing before me.

Onyx.

His black henley clung to his athletic frame, emphasizing the defined contours of his biceps. Loose-fit black military pants ran down his long legs, complemented by tightly laced black combat boots. A single pistol sat strapped to his left thigh, the only visible weapon on his otherwise unarmored body—a clear sign he didn't need more. His infamous scar from every Wanted poster within the Walls etched a path from his brow, across his nose, and down to the corner of his lips. His loose, wavy dark hair caught the breeze, tousling with the wind. The distinct look of annoyance that marked his face became more accentuated the instant his arms folded over his chest.

He was ready to kill both of us.

"I thought I told you to drop your weapon?" Onyx questioned, the raspiness in his voice emphasizing the harshness of his tone.

I watched as Radley tried to fire another round, unsure of what he hoped to accomplish when the first attempt had failed. The bullet from the chamber now sat between me and the man who was no longer a mystery.

Onyx stood there, wholly untouched—resounding proof of his capabilities.

Before Radley's finger could pull the trigger again, the gun in his hand collapsed, crumbling into pieces before our eyes. My heart stopped, sinking in my chest and making it difficult to breathe with the display of his abilities that existed as mere stories up until now.

"The next time you try to draw a weapon on me, I'll make sure you turn it on yourself. And I *will* be successful in doing so." Onyx barked at Radley, his eyes glowing in the setting sun's light. "If you don't want to be responsible for your own death, open your damn ears and listen."

Imelda pushed herself out from beneath Radley, taking advantage of his distraction. Gravel rolled underfoot as she stood, glancing at Onyx. "I was going to be back in fifteen minutes until—"

"I don't want to hear it." He shook his head, his voice monotone as he looked at her. "Didn't I tell you there'd be military dogs out here?"

"Yeah, but I didn't run into—"

Onyx cocked an eyebrow at her, and she fell silent, knowing she couldn't justify her actions.

Judging by Onyx's build and how he interacted with Imelda, I guessed he was in his late twenties or possibly early thirties. His protective nature toward her was evident, and it was clear he wasn't someone capable of being harmed, let alone someone who would allow those he safeguarded to be endangered.

His gaze shifted to me. Our eye contact was brief before I looked away, the intensity of his presence overwhelming.

"Care to explain what the hell you're doing in our territory?" His query was sharp, marking his scrutiny.

"What do you think we're doing? Sightseeing?" Radley's snarky retort came from behind me, and given Onyx's abilities, I had to admire his boldness.

Imelda suppressed a laugh at Radley's blatant disrespect, turning away to avoid getting herself into more trouble.

Onyx's sudden arrival made it clear he came to protect her, just as Quinn had described. The scars on her face told a story of previous battles, which were now definable with the recollection of Quinn's story. Imelda had been there, as was the one Onyx had come for, and his immediate presence before us on the rooftop showed he would surely go to war for her.

"We were out here on a recon mission. Our intentions weren't hostile, and we never planned on hurting her," I whispered, hoping to defuse the tension. "It was a misunderstanding. We tried to reason with her, but things escalated, and here we are."

Onyx's tongue traced his bottom lip, crossing his scar before he cocked his head, rubbing his chin in consideration.

"Are you proposing that finding your mutt over there holding a gun to a fourteen-year-old's head is nothing more than a mere misunderstanding?" Onyx stepped forward, narrowing the gap between us. "Help me understand how that doesn't show ill intent."

"The bitch tried to kill us," Radley snarled, his voice dripping with defensiveness.

Immediately, his insult proved to be a grave mistake.

Within seconds, he cried out in agony, clutching his head as he collapsed to all fours, struggling to stay upright. Droplets of blood trickled from his nose, and a scream followed closely behind that rocked me with instantaneous horror.

Quinn's account of her encounter with Onyx flooded my mind—how he had been capable of crushing a man's brain without a second thought.

Fear and anger surged through me at the thought of losing one of the few people I had left. I reacted without hesitation, pulling a knife from my utility belt and launching myself at Onyx to break his hold. To my surprise, it worked, and the two of us tumbled to the rocky rooftop.

Radley sighed in relief as he collapsed to the floor, still breathing. With size comparison alone, I knew I didn't stand a chance in a fight against Onyx, but I would take every second I could to protect the white-haired male who'd fought endlessly for me.

Straddling Onyx's large frame, I shifted my weight, aiming the knife between his third and fourth ribs. Before my weapon could make any forward progress, an unseen force halted my path. Onyx lay beneath me, his arms at his sides, utterly unbothered by the threat I posed.

I clenched my jaw, holding back tears of billowing agitation. A smirk spread across his scarred lips, joined by a deep, mocking chuckle.

"And look at that. The lioness attacks," he sneered, his voice dripping with disdain.

My body shook, not just from the strain of fighting his mental hold but from the rage pulsing through my veins.

Before I could respond, Onyx thrust his hips upward, throwing me off him and onto the floor. The knife slipped from my grasp as he disarmed me, and I found myself pinned beneath him, our positions reversed.

He loomed over me, his glacial blue eyes glaring down as he held my wrists above my head with one hand. The cold steel of the knife pressed against my throat with a tightness that hinted at the comfortable ease of ending my life.

"You see, here's the thing," he began, his voice dangerously calm. "If your pup had followed my instructions and kept his mouth shut, we wouldn't be in this situation. You realize that, don't you?"

I inhaled sharply, realizing that any struggle would be futile. "Yeah, I get it. He can be a hothead, but he intended to protect us, just as you did with her."

As much as I wanted to berate him for attacking Radley, I knew it would only make things worse and likely end with inevitable repercussions.

Onyx's stare shifted, perhaps recognizing the comparison between us. A glint of sympathy flashed through the deeper blues in his eyes. Maybe we weren't so different despite living in a world that pitted us against each other.

He pulled the knife away from my throat and moved off me, pushing himself up from the ground. His standing position obscured the setting sun, casting a long shadow over the rooftop. My mind raced with the possibilities—would his next decision be to shoot me or attack with another method?

Instead, he extended a hand, offering to help me up.

I hesitated before grasping his roughed palm, and he pulled me to my feet in one fluid motion.

Imelda kicked a rock toward us. "So, uh, now what?"

Onyx sighed, his brows knitting together as he glanced at the rapidly setting sun. "The hordes will be out as soon as darkness hits." He looked over at Radley, unconscious on the ground, and scoffed. "You two should come back with us. You'll never make it to the city before sunset. No Venturer has."

"Wait, what?" My words came in tandem with Imelda's.

"Woah, woah, woah. What the hell, Onyx?" she looked at him, concern lacing her tone as she glanced between me and her taller counterpart. "You've lost your mind. Venturers staying with us? Did you even weigh the consequences of that?"

"Don't speak to me like I am incompetent," Onyx replied firmly. "They deserve a place to sleep, considering the situation we put them in, don't you think?" He held her gaze, his tone leaving no room for argument.

Imelda's expression shifted, a flash of guilt briefly appearing as she nodded, acknowledging her role in escalating the situation.

Onyx turned back to me. "The offer stands. Where we stay isn't fancy, but it'll keep you safe for the night. You can head back to the Walls in the morning."

Moments ago, he had been ready to kill with his display of undeniable power. Now, he was offering us refuge for the night.

"Yeah... I mean, that would be great," I replied, my voice shaky but relieved at the sudden shift in the situation. No part of me trusted them, but I knew we wouldn't survive a night in a city crawling with Runners and other Rebels.

"I'll carry him back." Onyx motioned to Radley, who lay limp on the ground, his chest rising and falling softly.

I nodded, watching him cross the space. He grabbed Radley's arm and hoisted him off the gravel rooftop without a hint of struggle. "He'll be fine," Onyx reassured. "The pressure I applied was similar to a brief cutoff of oxygen flow to the brain. It's just a simple loss of consciousness. Once he wakes up, he'll be good as new."

Radley's limbs hung with a near-lifelessness that forced me to remind myself he was still breathing. Dried blood flaked under his nose and by his earlobes. His whitish-blonde hair molded against his forehead was tousled with a mix of sweat and his having been lying on the unforgiving gravel. His head hung limply to where his chin came to touch his chest.

Onyx looked over at Imelda, who had distanced herself from

us, whistling softly to grab her attention. "Imelda, we need to move now."

"Don't tell me we have to hike back," she pouted.

"Usually, I'd say yes. But since we're this close to sunset and have an unconscious visitor with us, you're in luck." Onyx smiled down at her, rolling his eyes slightly with her immediate excitement.

Once everything leveled out, the playful nature of their relationship became apparent, marking a relationship that seemed similar to siblings—perhaps even parent and child. While I didn't know the confines of the length of time they'd known one another, the natural ease of their connection seemed to point to years.

The man so feared within the Walls had proven himself deserving of his title, but there was something more. He had every opportunity to kill Radley and me the instant he appeared on the roof, but he didn't. While there was a moment when I thought he might take my counterpart's life, I realized something deeper motivated his actions.

Every risk Onyx took was for one reason and one reason only —to protect the young woman beaming up at him. The stories shared about him and the encounters people disclosed suddenly seemed one-sided. Yes, he had killed people in the past, but so had every Venturer who had spoken about him. As Radley had mentioned to Imelda, there wasn't a single person alive who hadn't taken another's life.

Onyx was no exception. Sure, he housed a level of power that was unimaginable. Still, like anyone else, he was trying to survive the apocalypse—working to defend himself and the only person he had left in a difficult-to-navigate environment.

We were at least safeguarded from the Runners in the Wilds inside the Walls, which created a sense of safety. We had places to sleep, food to eat, and community connection. But in Onyx and Imelda's case, there was nothing safe about free-roaming outside the Walls—guilt nearly consumed me with our distinct differences.

Imelda crossed the gravel rooftop toward us, glancing at me with a soft smile. The loss she had witnessed living in a collapsing society for the past four years encased her expression. Yet, there was comfort behind it.

Onyx looked over at me as he kept a tight hold on Radley's limp body. "I need you to grab hold of my arm," he said, throwing me off momentarily with the request.

"To avoid any run-ins with Runners, he's going to teleport us back to our bunker," Imelda explained, grinning to the point lines etched into her cheeks.

"Teleport?" I looked from her to Onyx, and he shook his head, a smile tugging against the corner of his lips.

"Yes, teleport. If you don't wish to be left behind, I'd suggest you grab ahold of my arm."

I did as he instructed without further prodding, gently wrapping my hand around his forearm. The warmth of his skin surprised me, clashing with his demeanor. His size became irrefutable as my fingers struggled to close around his arm. Glancing over at Imelda, I watched her do the same.

Before I could contemplate what teleportation might feel like, a strange sensation washed over me.

The air hummed with electric energy, and my vision blurred as if I were looking through rippling water. A sudden pressure followed, creating a dizzying sense of weightlessness. My ears popped, and my stomach flipped while my body struggled to process the simultaneous feelings of falling and being pulled outward.

In the blink of an eye, we were in a new reality, my balance wavering as I struggled to adjust to the new surroundings.

We stood in what I presumed to be a living room; a few small lounge chairs sat around a wooden coffee table in the middle. A rifle leaned against it, suggesting it had been left hurriedly. Only a few cracks in the boarded-up windows let the last light of day filter in. Wooden window sills accented the olive green walls, though some portions lacked paint, and ceiling sections clung to a discoloration.

I continued to scan the room, noticing a map on the wall where a television might have been in another life. Pins scattered across it, with marked circles denoting something significant. Backpacks slumped beneath the map, a box of supplies beside them. In the entryway behind us, I spotted what looked like a kitchen, a shovel leaning against the wall, and stacked cases of water. The wooden floor had seen better days, some boards giving way to reveal clear holes.

"Welcome to our humble abode," Onyx said from beside me as he watched me absorb the sudden shift. "It's nothing fancy, but it works for the two of us and has kept us safe for the past few months."

Imelda sidestepped us and ran down the hall, disappearing into what I assumed was her room. Onyx's eyes softened briefly until his focus returned to me.

"We have a spare room for the two of you to share. There's a mattress and a couch, both untouched during our stay here." He adjusted his grip on Radley before making his way down the hall, passing Imelda's room and progressing to the one at the end.

The hallway walls were the same olive green as the living room, and the notable blemishes appeared to be a continuing theme. I followed him, each of our footsteps creating varying creaks of protest. The breadth of his frame seemed to fill the narrow passageway, making it impossible to mark the path ahead. He halted suddenly, and I had to keep myself from running into him.

Onyx nudged open the door at the end of the hall, the wood groaning loudly. As he dropped his hand from the frame, the room came into view. It was nothing like the rooms inside the Walls, which I'd expected given the vastly different conditions.

Tipped-over bookcases hinted at prior chaos; their contents splayed across the corner of the room. The books, papers, and random items cluttering the small desk near the door pointed to an occupant long gone. The single mattress tucked in the corner came equipped with a bedframe, blankets, and pillows—all highly sought-after items. Across from the bed sat the couch Onyx had mentioned, a few red pillows in the corner. The boarded-up windows let only a faint light filter through the cracks, casting the room into near-darkness as the day's light faded.

Onyx dropped Radley on the bed carelessly, his decision to lift his legs onto it catching me off guard. "When you two wake up tomorrow, you can head back."

"Thank you," I whispered, surprised by the genuine gratitude in my voice when all I felt was apprehension.

He turned, dark hair framing his face, the sharpness of his features drawing me in. But as he approached, his expression changed to an undeniable and searing hatred. His boots thudded against the floor, and the distance between us closed. My back met the wall as I stepped back; a flood of nervousness and betraying excitement greeted me.

Onyx's hand thudded against the surface above my head, vibrating down my spine. He narrowed his gaze, his face inches from mine.

"I want to make something clear," he said, his voice low with warning and his breath warm against my skin. "Just because I let you into our space doesn't mean I won't hesitate to kill you if you give me a reason to. Understand?"

I swallowed, nodding.

"If either of you alerts any level of government forces about your location, neither of you will live to see another day. Don't make me regret doing something kind because I can promise the number of men I have killed easily laps the two of your kill streaks combined. And unlike you, I have no issue adding to that list. Both you and Sleeping Beauty over there are lucky I didn't leave you on that rooftop for the night to fend off not only Runners but other Rebels simply because I could have. Or better yet, I didn't snap his neck in front of you only to end you shortly afterward.

"This is your only warning. If I sense any betrayal from either of you, I will kill both of you without batting an eye." His jaw feathered, "I can also promise that if you send anyone out here after us once you return to your bullshit safety net inside the Walls, I will hunt the two of you down until I find you. Even if that means having to cross walled lines to do so. Don't think that just because a cement barrier exists, you are by any means safe. Is that clear?"

His threat was direct and full of resentment, making me unsure how to respond. A surge of frustration built, the build of energy having nowhere to go, considering anything aside from pure agreement would only cause further turbulence.

I forced my voice to level. "Understood."

"Good." He pushed away from the wall, something rough pressing against my chest. I looked down to find a bundle of first-aid supplies in his hand.

"Clean yourself up," he said gruffly. "I don't want your blood all over the floor as a reminder of your presence once tomorrow rolls around."

He spoke about the wound on my hand, which I'd forgotten amidst the disarray. I dipped my chin once and promptly took the supplies from him. Our fingers brushed, and we held the position until he pulled back.

He turned on his heel before I could express gratitude for providing them or allowing us to stay. The door slammed shut behind him with a finality that left me breathless.

I glanced over at Radley's limp frame on the bed. He seemed wholly unharmed, aside from the likely possibility of a headache when he woke up.

Exhaustion tugged at me, and the weight of reality settled in as I crossed the room. Sinking into the mattress, I dropped the medical supplies beside me before looking at my hand.

A persistent throb racked through it, accompanied by a sharp sting. The wound was deep, and the skin flapped over the vertical cut. Light bruising surrounded the edges, and a few particles of dirt and gravel clung to my torn flesh.

Grabbing the alcohol pad, I tore it open with my teeth and brought it to the gash. I dabbed the wound, hissing sharply.

A groan from Radley caught my attention, and I turned to see him stirring, his brows furrowing as his eyes fluttered open.

At first, he appeared dazed, confusion coloring his features as he digested the unfamiliar room. But then his gaze found me, and relief magnified his dulled stare.

"Astrid...?"

"I would say good morning, but that feels counterproductive," I said, attempting to steady my voice amid the pain. "We're in their bunker for the night."

Radley inspected the room, irritation flaring. "What happened?"

"Before I tell you, I need you to promise me you won't lose it," I warned, knowing how close we were to another explosion. "We can't afford any more conflict."

He groaned, rubbing his head with one hand as he used the other to push himself up. "You're making me promise not to kill that—"

"Radley," I snapped, cutting him off. "I'm not repeating myself."

He met my stare, resentment apparent, but nodded. "Fine. What happened?"

I took a deep breath, choosing my words carefully, leaving out any details I knew would spark his anger. "After Onyx downed you, we talked things out. We're staying here for the night because we wouldn't have survived out there alone. He let us in, gave me supplies to clean my hand, and provided a place for us to sleep."

"What's the catch?" Radley's voice dripped reluctantly.

"The catch is that we don't report this or send anyone after them," I answered firmly. "We leave tomorrow and let him live."

Radley shook his head. "You're telling me we are just going to let him walk after everything he's done and the damage he's caused?"

"Yes, we are. Because if we do anything different, he will kill us," I stated, irritation building in my voice.

"He threatened you?"

"He threatened *us* and meant every word." Our eyes met again, and I clenched my jaw. "Think about what we experienced on the rooftop—his level of ability, how quickly he got there, and what he did to you. Gods, Radley, please explain to me why he hasn't made his way into the Walls and killed everyone if his goal is destroying the remnants of humanity as they preach."

His anger sizzled from his face, replaced by contemplation.

"We can't go back. We can't tell anyone what happened. We can't send a team after him because he'll come after us," I continued, trying to drive the point home. "He can *easily* breach the Walls. His threats are not empty. We have to leave him alone and let them live."

Even though the government claimed Onyx was targeting the Uninfected population, intending to eradicate those remaining, he was reacting solely to survive. The realization came to me upon his arrival and only grew exponentially the longer I was around him, making me question everything those in power had taught us.

If he had intended as they declared, the Walls wouldn't have been standing, and the number of Uninfected would have plummeted to zero years ago. We both knew that the government was hiding information, but his demeanor solidified it.

Finally, Radley sighed, defeat etched into his features. "My hell. I get it. We'll let him walk."

Relief washed over me, my shoulders sinking with the safety we'd been granted—for now.

"Now that's settled," I said, turning to him. "Can you help me clean my hand?"

He nodded, a soft smile creeping across his face as he took the supplies from me. "Yeah, gladly."

He worked carefully, his touch gentle as he cleaned and dressed my wound. The tension between us eased, and I watched him closely as he positioned the adhesive makeshift stitches over my wound, pulling each side of the torn skin back toward the other.

We sat silently for a moment before a faint smile crossed his lips. "So, does this mean we are sharing a bed?"

I laughed. "Yeah, I guess it does."

FOUR

The sterile walls and metallic tables greeted my subconscious once more. Forcing myself from my sleep, I sat up abruptly, continually reminding myself that it was just a nightmare.

Running my fingers through my hair, I forced myself to gulp down the oxygen that seemed to assault my lungs. Sweat beaded across my forehead and neck, working down my chest from the heightened terror attacking my subconscious.

Reaching out, my palm gently touched Radley's arm. It wasn't a movement intended to wake him but to confirm that he was still alive beside me. I exhaled deeply, my eyes lifting to the boarded windows.

The cracks that had cast the moon's illumination last night now welcomed the sun's rays with open arms. A cool breeze blew through the sliver of a gap, bringing the smell of late spring. Time had become an anomaly, with no notable detection aside from the positioning of the radiating ball of light in the sky. Based on the angle of the sunlight streaming through the window, I guessed it was early afternoon.

The snap of splitting wood disrupted my appreciation of the silence. Another crack followed shortly after. Its repetition confirmed that at least one individual in the space was awake, and based on the rhythmic sound, it was undoubtedly the male who had threatened me last night.

I moved from beneath the comforter, placing my hand on the bed to work out of it as silently as possible. The sharp tinge of agony that followed brutally confirmed my wound and everything else that had happened the night before. I hissed, pulling my palm away from the mattress and rotating my wrist.

The reality of my run-in with Imelda, which had led to an unexpected encounter with the man I never thought I would know, all came flooding back, and I couldn't help but find myself intrigued. The same interactions had pulled us away from the Walls and into the bunker they called home. While a part of me had desperately desired escape from the community that had confined us, another part regretted coming back with Onyx and Imelda because of the dangers our presence wrought.

My feet connected with the cold wooden floor as I grabbed my socks and boots from beside the bed. I glanced down at my Venturer uniform, still on my body, and shoved my foot into the first shoe, fastening the laces with practiced ease. Anxiety and resentment rolled through me, matching the bitterness in my throat. Placing my uninjured hand on my leg, I stood up.

I glanced at Radley, the only man I trusted in our dystopian reality.

The heightening sun and the chopping of wood outside hadn't stirred him from his sleep. His eyes remained closed, lips slightly parted, his face peaceful. The sight drew a rare smile from me as I made my way to the door, wrapping my fingers around the knob and stepping into the hallway we had traversed hours ago.

I quietly latched it behind me and pivoted down the hall with equal caution. Each footstep was softer than the last as I passed the various closed doors. Imelda's was the only one that reserved any familiarity, but like the others, it remained shut—she must have still been asleep.

Rounding the corner, I entered the living room. Everything

remained untouched except for the repeated snap of wood just outside the front door.

The sound awakened horrific memories from the confines of my mind, my inner world beginning to spiral while my surroundings remained almost eerily calm—a deceptive serenity in a troubled world.

I inhaled deeply, every part of me screaming to go back to the room and stay with Radley. No matter how much I tried to deny it, there remained a lingering fear of the man outside. Not only because I knew what he was capable of but because of his volatile and unpredictable actions.

Forcing myself to breathe, I brushed off the rising apprehension and gripped the handle. The springs of the front door protested as I pushed it open, the noise enough to draw the attention of the man standing outside.

The sun caught the shades of his dark hair, highlighting the near-blueish tint hidden in its darkness. A single elastic held it in a messy bun, tied back and up at the base of his skull. Sweat had soaked his long-sleeved, light gray compression shirt, which differed vastly from the black henley he had worn the day before and brought more life to his near-porcelain skin. The material clung to his torso, outlining the defined muscles that moved fluidly with each swing of the axe.

"I figured you'd sleep all day."

Without turning around, he threw the comment in my direction, interlaced with underlying annoyance.

And just like that, we were off to a great start.

"With your continual audible display of male dominance?" The question slid from me with distaste as I held my position outside the front door, leaving the opportunity to turn back inside if desired. "If you wanted to mark your territory, you could just lift your leg and go piss on a tree like an obedient mutt."

He chuckled as he shifted to face me, the haft spinning between his fingers as he tossed it with careless ease. The action hinted at his ability to handle weaponry proficiently, an open acceptance of the battle I had thrown his way. Sweat glistened on his forehead, calling attention to the well-known scar on his face. The sharpness of his desolate blue eyes, which locked on me with no intention of pulling away, deepened.

"I apologize for disturbing your slumber, *Sweetness*." He grinned, tipping his chin upward in mockery to glare down his nose. "Unlike you, some of us live by utter survival, not just gifted opportunity."

His demeaning comment made my blood boil as its intended bite sank in. My knuckles turned white, and my fingers curled into tight fists at my sides.

"The naivety." I spat, my ears roaring with searing rage. "Why am I not surprised that you're a grade-A asshole?"

His tongue swept across his teeth as his sneer grew. "I figured that you'd wake up in a better mood after getting some needed rest, but it seems we are both disappointed with one another, aren't we?"

"It's hard to be disappointed when you already anticipate the received outcome." I folded my arms over my chest and swallowed the response I desired to deliver.

"I suppose I could say the same." His lips pulled together tightly, the smirk remaining as he shrugged. "You came out here with venom on your tongue and ready to fight. I will even go far enough to applaud you for your decent retort. But then, as soon as I matched your energy, you tucked your tail between your legs." He lifted a finger, his lips forming an open-mouthed smile. "So, let me ask you this. Since we are throwing demeaning labels around and you have selected mutt for me, what exactly does that make you?"

"My recollection entails that you selected the terminology first." I lowered my forearms onto the patio railing, displaying my refusal to leave. "Apologies for using your own ammunition against you. Your usage just happened to stick with me, and I couldn't help but find it rather inspiring."

"Ah, verbal retaliation with material that isn't your own." His brow raised slightly, and the monotonality of his voice remained. "It's understandable, as none of you can handle your own conflicts since our *lovely* overseers have consistently pampered and shielded you."

"You think you're the only one who has dealt with loss?"

"The context of that question would influence the answer. Are you talking about an equal level of loss?" He mused, huffing in amusement before swinging the axe again, splitting the wood perfectly down the middle.

"You speak to me like I have no idea what I'm talking about."

"Do you?"

I bit the inside of my cheek, my brows narrowing. "Just because you have survived in the Wilds doesn't mean those within the Walls don't know what survival is."

"Right, Ms. Astrid Carnell, the twenty-four-year-old who—"

I froze.

What did he know?

"How do you know my name?" The query practically fell from me as I pushed myself upright, trying to block off the horror that weaved itself through each word. "And age?"

"Information finds its way to me." He tapped the side of his head, "Especially when it pertains to those who stray outside the Walls. You Venturers think you're so secretive, but secrets are a currency I rule over out here."

My mind struggled to understand how he'd obtained intricate details in such little time. It was an unsettling realization but also a reminder of our societal positions. Every move and decision we made felt like it was being observed under a microscope.

"I'm not going to divulge what you're suggesting," I finally replied. "But I suggest you stay the hell out of my business."

"Oh, but your business is my business now," he said, his eyes never leaving mine. "You see, out here, alliances are everything. If you and your friend wish to survive, you'll accept that whether or not you like it. Once you left your falsified idea of sanction, you stepped into a treacherous world in which I hold a lot of sway."

His words hung in the air, serving as both a challenge and a warning. Refusing to back down, I held his gaze, but the accuracy of his words was indisputable. We were deep in enemy territory, and that was just the beginning of our fight for survival and freedom.

The corner of his lips quirked upward in recognition—a shark scenting blood in the water. "Your naivety proves that you don't understand the scope of my capabilities. It's either that, or you've stupidly assumed the reports you've heard about me didn't contain factual information."

I swallowed my unease, folding my arms across my chest as I attempted to regain my footing. "The reports that state you're a mindless, murderous bastard?"

"Mindless?" His lips curved in a near-feline manner, not denying the latter half. "I would watch who you label as mindless when you blindly follow those responsible for death and destruction while claiming innocence. You realize that makes you no different from them, no matter how much you pretend it does?"

The roaring built in my ears as I pushed myself from the patio, my feet drumming against the two steps that separated the fabricated structure from the foliage below. Between the insults and the prying into personal information through beyond-intrusive methods, I had reached the pinnacle of my willingness to listen.

As I approached him, his eyes flared in interest, a near-taunting beam circling each pupil. Each step was louder than the last as the distance between us shortened and suddenly became inches, the comfort of the door to the bunker no longer at my back.

I lifted my chin and locked onto his beckoning gaze, which spoke of nothing more than ridicule. My hand lifted before he could offer another bold assumption about my character or allegiance.

The audible slap lowered the heightened rage that had drowned out any surrounding noise, planting my feet back in reality.

"*Never* speak to me again like you know a damn thing about me just because you took information without permission." My words came through gritted teeth. "I refuse to be someone you merely take advantage of whenever you please because of your inability to control your emotional lows. So, until you sit down and have a civil conversation with me, not as some taunting sadist, you can shove your assumptions straight up your ass."

He turned his head back toward me as the words tumbled from my lips, his brows hooding over his near-suffocating glare. Between the building glint in his haunting gaze and the tight-lipped sneer he extended, his mind appeared to revel in how he could break me.

The silence between us grew with each passing second as I waited for my life force to cease.

I clenched my jaw as my stomach tumbled, realizing I had put my hands on the Most Wanted Rebel—the man who could end life without the blink of an eye or the lift of a finger.

The hardness of his gaze stuck, but his lips lifted again, just as they had when extending verbal lashings in my direction. His eyes remained locked on mine, squinting slightly in response to the growing smirk.

"If you decide to stick around, I think you and I will get along just fine."

I stared at him, his words sinking in and catching me off guard. He was no ordinary man—he was a predator sizing up his prey.

And I refused to be anyone's prey.

"You have no idea what you're dealing with," I said, my voice steady. "I'm not here to play games."

"Oh, I'm well aware of who and what you are, Astrid," he replied, his grin never faltering. "And that's exactly why I offered you a space to stay."

I took a step back, the weight of his gaze following me. "I'm not here to be used by you or the Rebellion."

"Everyone is used by someone. The trick is to ensure you're

getting something out of it, too," he said, continuing with something that encased a chilling underlying meaning. "Trust me when I say that we aren't that different."

A PULSATING, orange light radiated from the hands that cupped my palm. I pulled my attention from the intricate work and landed on the youthful female sitting before me.

Imelda.

Her brows pulled together in attentive focus as the gash wove itself back together, the skin connecting as if being stitched by an invisible thread. Deep in concentration, her tongue poked out from between her lips as their corners turned upward.

The breeze rustling the surrounding trees sent her tight brown curls into a dance, her ebony skin radiating beneath the afternoon sunlight. She had swapped out the orange T-shirt she wore during our initial run-in for a light green one, which highlighted the speckle of freckles on her cheeks.

"There." She pulled her hands away, and her tongue slid from view.

She moved back to let the overhead beacon light my palm and her completed work. Her bounced step marked the pride that rolled through her in response to her success. The deep laceration that had existed was gone, a light scar taking its place—the only physical reminder of our run-in.

I lifted my gaze, looking at her. "You're a healer?"

"Fire user first, healer second." She beamed cheek to cheek, her finger lifting in correction.

I nodded, smiling. "Well, your abilities are amazing. Thank you."

Her renowned smile lines carved deeply into both cheeks as she dipped her chin, curtsying. "You are welcome."

The gratitude I extended wasn't solely for the healing she had provided, ridding me of the bothersome pain that continuously radiated up my wrist with minor movement. It had also been for interfering after my palm had undeniably connected with the side of Onyx's face with enough force to leave a glaring red mark. She had barked at him for being an 'inconsiderate asshole' for speaking to me how he had. Once she turned to me, there wasn't a single verbalized disapproval extended in my direction for slapping her protector.

The engagement had been humoring enough, seeing a fourteen-year-old rip into a full-grown and hardened male as if she ran the place, and it became very evident that was the case.

"I promise he's not always a jerk." She responded as if able to read where my mind had wandered to.

"Just occasionally?"

She giggled as she nodded, her curls bouncing more than the wind had provoked. Her hand lifted as she brought her thumb and pointer finger together, narrowing the gap between them as an attempted demonstration.

I laughed, and hers heightened to join with mine in a joyous symphony.

"I hope what you're talking about is as funny as you both think it is." The level voice came from behind us as Onyx rounded the corner. "Considering our food is nearly prepared, and the corn won't shuck itself, I'm beginning to think that the two of you are better off separated."

Imelda groaned, rolling her eyes. "Boo, you're no fun."

"We can swap." He shrugged, glancing down at the petite girl in front of him. "Do you want to chop wood?"

"I would rather die." She lifted a dramatic hand to her forehead, swaying slightly.

My lips pulled together in a tight-lipped smile as I raised my gaze to the broad-shouldered male before us. "You've got yourself a handful."

"You have no idea." He moved past me, our shoulders

connecting as he headed toward the bonfire to make the first meal of the day.

Even with his extended offer of sanctuary, the tension remained. I knew he deeply hated the government, which rippled to us because of our affiliation. Still, part of me was unsure what resulted in the continual shift between level-headedness and animosity.

Imelda nudged me with her elbow, clearing her throat once Onyx had moved far enough away from the two of us.

I glanced down at her as I lifted a brow in question. "Hm?"

"So, are you staying?" She questioned, her growing smile tugging at my heartstrings.

It was a plea.

The world's cruelty clung to her dark brown eyes. It was the gaze belonging to a girl who had seen too much, far too young. There was a silent, unspoken desire beneath them to help save the man—who loved her deeply—from himself before she lost the person she cherished the most. The man who stood in front of her as a battering ram, willing to destroy the world for her, no matter the cost.

And gods be damned, I contemplated staying. It was beyond tempting to escape the constant brutality that encompassed the Walls and the fears that a single misstep or an overheard conversation encasing disagreement could land you swinging from the gallows. We'd all learned to survive, and I was no exception. The skills I'd developed during my time as a Venturer, and even beforehand, could potentially convince Radley of our benefit in joining them, even if Onyx was a grade-A asshole.

Guilt washed over me as I realized I was considering upending everything I knew without discussing it with the man who'd walked alongside me for so long.

"I'll talk to Radley," I replied, hope radiating through my words.

The silence was suffocating.

Radley's eyes lifted slowly, brows hooded as he locked onto the male across from him. His fingers tightened around the cob of corn, knuckles whitening, as his leg bobbed with barely contained energy beneath the table. Every fiber of his being screamed a desire to lash out, yet he held back, the tension in his body notable.

I inhaled deeply, the atmosphere heavy with unspoken words. Lowering my cob, I glanced between the raven-haired male and his youthful companion. "Thank you for cutting firewood this morning and making us a meal, by the way."

Onyx's tongue moved across his teeth, his icy eyes landing on me with a predatory gleam. His elbows rested on the table, the breadth of his chest becoming the forefront of my attention, and I kicked myself for finding an intrigue in it.

"You're welcome." His response was curt, dripping with a disdain that bordered an outright insult.

A loud thud reverberated through the room as Radley's knee struck the underside of the table, his frustration boiling over at the lack of respect in Onyx's reply.

He exhaled sharply, a slew of muttered curses barely audible but thick with anger.

"Care to speak up, Heroux?"

Radley's head snapped toward Onyx, his gaze settling on the Rebel with a wrath that hinted at implosion. The glint in his eyes overlapped with another emotion I couldn't quite identify, something raw and personal.

My thoughts drifted to the intrusive methods Onyx had used to gather information on us. Radley's reaction was valid; it mirrored my vexation from earlier, intensified by our shared history.

Onyx smirked, lowering his elbows to the table, a brow arched in amusement. "Is there something wrong? Perhaps we could discuss it."

"What happened to enjoying our meal peacefully?" Radley's jaw clenched. "Isn't that what you said before we sat down?"

Onyx leaned back, folding his arms with a look of utter disinterest. "I guess it was an assumption that you had something you wanted to share, considering the current dynamic."

"There isn't anything I am interested in discussing with a Rebel."

"You sure about that?"

"Onyx."

"Radley."

Their names left Imelda's and my lips simultaneously, our voices sharp with urgency. It was a desperate attempt to defuse the situation before it erupted.

"Tell your damn attack dog to sit down," Radley hissed at Imelda, his grip crushing the cob in his hand, kernels spilling onto the table.

Onyx chuckled, his tongue sweeping across his canines. "That's bold, considering—"

Radley exploded from his chair, the wooden structure clattering to the ground as he lunged across the table. The sounds echo seemed to reverberate endlessly, amplifying the chaos.

Onyx moved with lethal precision, his hand seizing the knife beside him. He was up from the table just as fast, his boot connecting with the chair, sending it skidding behind him as he spun the knife expertly between his fingers.

Their movements were a dance of opposition—a trained government soldier and a powerful, Wanted Rebel.

Radley's hand clamped onto Onyx's shirt, yanking him closer even as the blade hovered near his throat. Their teeth gritted in a snarl as their faces came inches from each other, lips tightened with fury.

It was as if they had been enemies for centuries. Their hatred was palpable, and each second escalated their desire for violence.

"Enough!" I hissed through clenched teeth, my eyes darting between them.

Onyx's glare remained fixed on Radley. "I suggest you remember where you stand with me before I remind you."

Radley's jaw tightened, nostrils flaring in response.

"Now, get your filthy hands off my shirt before I butcher you like the damn pig you are," Onyx whispered dangerously, his cobalt eyes gleaming with dark anticipation.

Radley slowly released his grip, stepping back with deliberate slowness. The knife lowered from his throat in response, and for a moment, the room clung to the thick silence and unspoken threats.

Radley turned to me, his eyes filled with an apology but underlying rage. Without a word, he bent down, retrieved the fallen chair, and set it upright before storming out of the dining area toward the front door.

His booted footsteps echoed loudly, stopping briefly as his hand met the wood. The door protested as he shoved it open, slamming shut behind him with a force that rattled the frame.

Imelda groaned, rubbing her eyes with her palms. "Can it ever not be death and destruction, even for a few minutes?"

I inhaled sympathetically before I turned to the male who had nearly executed Radley for a second time. "Are you this way with everyone you meet?"

His shoulders bobbed with a shrug. "If they live long enough."

Imelda cursed quietly, the vulgarity enough to temporarily catch Onyx's attention.

"You must have a lot of friends then," I replied, sarcasm infusing my remark.

He sneered, "You have no idea."

"Onyx," Imelda growled.

My impatience grew as I looked at the ebony-skinned girl. "How do you put up with him?"

She remained in her chair, attempting to finish her food as she glanced up at me. Her dark eyes sang of sorrow and sympathy, the look nearly bringing me to my knees.

Her words came hushed, "He's not a bad man, I promise."

The phrasing and selection spoke loud enough.

I promise.

I swallowed, my throat bobbing as my aggravation retreated. "I'm going to go talk to him."

Onyx refused to look in my direction with the brief comment, but Imelda dropped her chin in acknowledgment.

I turned, walking behind her chair as I reached forward, extending a gentle and apologetic squeeze to her shoulder before making my way to the door Radley had stormed out of.

I stepped out not only to converse with the male who walked alongside me but also to provide them with the space to come down from the heightened emotional state and tension that smothered their haven.

It was an attempt to extend them a peace offering amidst chaos.

As soon as I passed between the interior and exterior and stepped onto the porch, the warmth of the late afternoon spring day embraced me. A gentle chirp from a few birds became detectable, along with the soft rustle of leaves as a cooling breeze slithered through the area.

I inhaled, savoring the connectivity and grounding that followed before progressing to the white-haired male who stood a few feet away.

My boots thudded against each step before colliding with the earth as I walked to the tree line and one of the larger trunks that Radley leaned against.

The question that I posed was simple. "Do you want to talk?"

He turned to look over his shoulder, the tension on his face remaining. "If you want to hear me vent about how big of a prick he is, then sure."

I sighed as I folded my arms over my chest. "For just having met each other, you two are the definition of oil and water."

His gaze lifted, sweeping over me with refusal to offer his remark.

"To be frank," I positioned myself beside him. "I'm not picking sides, nor do I find him necessarily enjoyable to be around."

"That's a fact stated too kindly." He huffed.

I smiled softly, shaking my head. "However."

"I knew it was coming."

My hand landed on his arm, nudging him to the side. "He offered for us to stay here."

"And you want to stick around?" He asked, his query packed full of disapproval.

"We have been discussing our disagreement with government operations for months, Radley." I squinted as the sun broke through a few leaves. "Now that we are outside the Walls, we can rid ourselves of it."

He groaned, his pointer finger and thumb digging into his eyes. "I understand that, but we are talking about aligning ourselves with the Most Wanted Rebel alive."

"I would prefer that for survival in the Wilds." The words came from me without hesitation. "The government is going to retaliate over our shift in alliance, and those banished from the Walls likely won't be thrilled about it either."

"You think he would protect either of us?"

"Isn't he already?" I exhaled. "He's letting us stay here. In the safe space crafted for him and Imelda—their home."

"Aside from that, Astrid."

"I don't know," I snapped. "All I know is that I can't go back there, Radley."

There were so many things the two of us had seen.

It had been a range, from executions for opposition to the hand-offs of power wielders to higher-ranked Venturers. There were too many questions, holes, secrets, and lies that even the two of us remained uninformed about.

The man we were staying with was one of the biggest mysteries of them all, both because of his temper and the depth of his abilities.

He growled, his arms folding over his chest tightly. "You're staying here regardless of what I say, aren't you?"

"I told you I could not go back there." My gaze met his as I continued, "I can't stomach being in those Walls and being responsible for all we had in the past, not anymore."

He released the breath he had been holding, and a deep sigh followed. "Gods."

"You don't have to—"

"Stay here?" He loosened a chuckle of incredulity. "So, what, I leave you here alone with him?"

"I am simply stating that you're not obligated to stay here if you don't want to." My arms dropped to my sides. "I will not force you to."

"I understand that." The sternness in his voice seemed to vanish. "You aren't the only one who doesn't want to go back."

My tongue moved across my lips. "I'm waiting for the but."

"The but is that I can't stomach our new roommate, or whatever the hell you want to refer to him as." His cerulean eyes remained on me. "I also refuse to leave you here alone with him, just as I recognize the advantage that aligning with him brings."

I raised a brow, my lips lifting with it.

"Don't look at me like that."

"Like what?" I laughed, shaking my head.

"Like you've won a battle or something." He groaned, his shoulder blades bouncing against the trunk.

"I would equate it to that," I grinned, tipping my head to the side as I extended a lighthearted look in his direction. "Convincing you to stick it out with a man you can't stomach is a win."

"I'm staying here for you—no one else." His shoulders dropped with his acceptance of defeat.

I lifted an arm, placing it over my chest. "Aw. What an honor."

"Alright, enough." He shook his head, smiling gently.

I rolled my eyes, leaning against the tree, and hummed victoriously.

Nature's movement filled the silence between us. The trees continued to ruffle against the afternoon breeze, the audibility of the brush of leaves a clear sign of Mother Nature's refusal to stop —no matter how badly we wished time could slow.

Even just momentarily.

"Thank you," I muttered as I turned to look at him.

"You're welcome." He nodded briefly before continuing, "I know you're doing it for her. Mostly."

Imelda.

"She deserves to experience things differently." I looked forward. "The Fall wasn't just a loss of humanity but of innocence."

"She's a good kid."

"And he's a good man."

His head snapped in my direction, a scoff following. "Says the one who just said she can't stand being around him."

"Correction," I lifted my finger. "I said that he isn't very enjoyable."

"Same shit."

"Different shit." My eyes completed another rotation. "He is an asshole. That is undeniably accurate. But he is also a good man who cares for those he holds close. He just has built a fortress around himself. There isn't anything wrong with that."

His brows lifted as his tongue traced his teeth. "I suppose."

"I say we give him a chance." I pushed away from the tree with my foot. "We hold assumptions about him because of our prior affiliation, but I believe he deserves the opportunity to show us who he really is."

"We already know who he is."

"No," I shook my head. "We know what they've programmed us to believe he is."

"Fine," he lifted his hands in front of him. "I will give him a chance, but I will not make any promises that we won't disagree with one another."

"Or that fights won't happen?" I prodded playfully, tipping my head back to savor the sunlight's kiss.

"That too."

"That's fine." I smiled, turning my head over my shoulder. "All I ask is that you try."

He nodded, his attention moving forward as he gazed at all that surrounded us in admiration.

"I'll be inside," I spoke gently as I recognized the look setting on his face, watching the wind rustle his sun-infused white hair. "Take your time."

He didn't turn toward me or say another word as I pivoted from where I stood and headed in the direction I'd come from.

We would stick around whether or not our decision enthused Onyx.

CHAPTER

SIX

The few days that followed the altercation were eerily quiet.

Onyx seemed to vanish intentionally anytime an engagement with Radley and me arose. His presence in the space remained unaccounted for most days unless he was involved with Imelda. His absence had been both a blessing and a curse dipped in a thick layer of irony, considering he had been the one who suggested our stay. Although another had likely been responsible for influencing that offer.

I sighed as the thoughts swarmed my mind. The floorboards creaked, a sign of another body entering the makeshift living room. I lowered the book in front of me, my eyes peering over the pages in anticipation of finding the usual glaring male standing there with apparent annoyance on his face.

Instead, Imelda beamed at me as she lowered her chin. "Whatcha reading?"

My fingers pinched the dystopian novel I found under the bed in the room Radley and I shared closed. "A boring book that you likely would've had to read in your later high school years."

"If it's boring, then why are you reading it?" she posed, her head tipped to the side in clear contemplation.

"Has anyone ever told you that you're too smart for your own good?" I winked, earning a harmonious giggle from her.

"Sometimes, yes."

The corners of my lips soared upward at the light flush that crossed her cheeks. "Well, I think it should be more often."

Her chin tucked downward, and a shyness cast over her expression before her eyes returned to me—a level of anticipation hidden in her gaze.

I pushed myself from the lounge chair, leaving the novel behind. "Is everything okay?"

She nodded, her curls bouncing with the movement. "Yes, but I figured you'd want to see this."

I lifted a brow as she waved me forward and grabbed my hand. Her small fingers wrapped around mine. She wiggled them, checking her grasp before pivoting from where she stood and rushing down the hallway as if whatever it was were urgent.

Her bare feet padded against the floorboards as she progressed toward her bedroom, and my booted footsteps nearly swallowed her gentleness. Questions flooded my mind, specifically around what her use of 'this' meant.

We waded through a sea of olive-green walls before coming to the room she occupied. Her space was bare, similar to the room Radley and I had shared for the past few nights. Two windows framed the twin bed in the corner, with a light purple comforter neatly positioned on top. I couldn't help but wonder if it had come with the room or if they had scouted it out per her request. A light gray dresser butted up against the wall closest to the door, and a few knickknacks—a carved wooden turtle, a bundle of dead roses, and a stack of broken CD cases—lingered over the top of it. There was a small desk in the corner, and a map nearly identical to the one in the living room rested over it. The worn paper contained a similar pattern of circles in various colors drawn by the man responsible for the documented methods that covered the bunker walls.

My heart ached at the sight—a key depiction of her admiration for the male who worked to keep her safe.

She turned, her mocha-brown eyes lifting in my direction as she lifted her finger to her lips. At the same time, she extended the gesture and tugged me toward the window to the right of her bed.

We landed in front of it as she adjusted her attention to the gap between two boards. I followed, eyes scanning the open field and all-encompassing greenery that acted as a protective barrier around their home. And then I caught what she had been referring to.

The sun beamed down on Onyx, emphasizing his chest, abdomen, and forearms. Their shadows projected against his tight-fitting navy blue long-sleeve shirt. His expression was impossible to read, with no frontal emotion present as he engaged with the man across from him in a basic conversation.

Radley moved as he stated something that earned a nod from Onyx, his Venturer uniform hugging his body. His lithe frame contrasted against the breadth of the raven-haired male who faced him, the span of their shoulders displaying the difference in build between them.

"They're talking," Imelda whispered, the smile marked in her tone.

I watched, waiting for one of them to detonate. "Indeed, they are."

Words continued to flow between them in a manner that seemed to display explanation, at least on Radley's side. Onyx remained unphased as my counterpart continued, his lips pulled in their usual taut line and brows hooded. His typical expressions ranged from disinterest to anger to understanding, making the variance between them nearly impossible to decipher and his emotions an immovable mask.

"And," Imelda's soft voice came from beside me. "They haven't killed each other."

I choked down the laughter that lunged forward; her added smirk not helping. "How long have they been talking?"

"Hm, I'd say twenty minutes or so."

"What?" I turned my head toward her. "And you waited until now to get me?"

"Well, I figured it wasn't a big deal since blood and weapons weren't involved," she snickered. "Then I figured you'd want to know that they can talk to each other like normal human beings."

My lips pulled together as I shook my head, the grin growing. "Lords, I would pay money to hear you say that to Onyx."

"Would you?" The query came from the doorway behind us, the graveled voice sounding the warning bells of my subconscious.

I shifted, glancing over my shoulder at the stern-faced male who had been outside engaged with Radley just seconds ago. He leaned against the doorframe as his eyes danced between us.

I exhaled, blowing a piece of hair from my face. "Gods, I forget that you're intrusive."

"Says the one crouched in front of a window with a fourteen-year-old girl and partaking in the act of spying on me." His brow lifted as he folded his arms over his chest, his thumbs pressing against his biceps.

"Last I checked, it wasn't just you."

"Right." The word accentuated as his tongue crossed his lips, his gaze hardening and remaining on me.

"It must have been an important conversation, considering you left the house for it." I leaned back against the barren wall behind me, matching his demeanor.

"Perhaps." The corner of his lip twitched before continuing, "There are some things we need to discuss. We'll be waiting for you both in the living room once you finish with whatever game you were playing."

Before I could retaliate, he shifted and moved back through the door frame, his shoulders nearly filling it.

Imelda pushed from her position beside me, rushing after him as the thunder of her feet proceeded down the hallway once she had slipped from view.

I groaned, running a hand through my loose hair before

following the two of them. My footsteps progressed as I worked down the hallways before stepping into the living room.

Radley lifted his chin in my direction, having taken the position in the lounge chair to the right of the one that my book occupied. "It would seem that you got caught red-handed."

I threw a vulgar gesture toward him and bent down to grab my book before sinking back into the seat I should never have left.

"Sit," Onyx directed the statement at the young girl, who remained at his side.

She moaned, turning away and walking toward the seating arrangement while dragging her heels across the floor. "Boooooring."

I watched as Radley's lips lifted to a smile with her reaction and the pushback given.

Imelda dropped herself into the chair to my left, releasing a heightened sigh. Her arms folded over her chest as she slouched into the material, glancing at the male who'd ordered her to do so.

Onyx ignored her verbal displeasure and moved to sit in the last chair, his icy blue eyes trailing over me before he lifted a booted foot and placed it over his knee. "There were a few things that I wanted to address."

"Does this pertain to your super-secret conversation outside or something else?" I drummed my fingers over the book cover as I held his gaze.

"Both." The length of his fingers swept down his leg before landing on his ankle. "Since you two have elected to stick around, I feel it's about time we scored you some new attire."

"It's nearly been a week, and you're just now deciding this?" A bite harsher than intended filled my query.

"I didn't want to waste time securing supplies for two people who were going to vanish as soon as the opportunity presented itself." His forefinger tapped against the leather of his over-the-ankle boots with growing impatience.

My nails halted in their strum as I shrugged, a nonverbal

demonstration that I understood without giving him the satisfaction of hearing me say it.

"We will head out tomorrow morning for the city to scavenge. If you're planning to walk alongside me and, as an inarguable addition, the Rebellion, there is no way in hell you'll continue to wear government-assigned clothing."

"Understood." Radley nodded at him, the reply nearly throwing me for a loop.

What had they discussed to yield such an abrupt shift in demeanor?

"It's equally important to discuss dynamics since we now directly influence one another's survival." His gaze seemed to darken as soon as the words left his lips, sweeping between the two of us seated across from him.

"Valid," I muttered, keeping my attention pinned on him. "What are your expectations for us?"

"Communication," Imelda interrupted from the shell she had curled herself into. "He's heavy on communication, especially if you're going out alone."

Onyx rolled his eyes at the reference to her trip to the city and the banter they had engaged in. "I expect direct communication, yes."

"Likewise." I jutted in his direction. "Engagement with you beyond a single word would be incredible."

"I think I can make something work." He smirked as his eyes scanned me with one fluid sweep. "On top of that, contribution."

"Helping around the house and out looking for supplies," Imelda added for him.

His head bobbed, approving her statement: "I expect there to be equal give and take from all parties. If you want to survive with us, uphold that end of the bargain. And when I speak of give and take, it doesn't solely pertain to finding supplies, food, and other beneficial survival items—it also applies to protection."

"With how things are out there, we have to be prepared to protect one another if it comes to it." Imelda kicked her legs from where she sat, watching them glide over the wooden floor beneath her. "It's not just the Runners, but other fully functioning humans that could pose problems for us."

"I can handle myself," Onyx intercepted before she could delve further. "But the two of you will be equally responsible for watching over Imelda and ensuring that she remains out of harm's way—Runners or not. In return, since this is equal give and take, we will keep the two of you safe if either of you becomes endangered."

"Simple enough," I replied with a shrug. "Your expectations are valid and something that we have no issue respecting. But I also place responsibility on you to uphold them on our side."

He bit his cheek, his tongue circling his canine. "An intelligent negotiator."

I swallowed, trying to shove down the surface-level compliment he extended. "I'm simply informing you that since you speak on equal give and take, we will expect you to reciprocate whatever you ask of us."

"Understood." His chin dipped as a wave of gentleness passed through his gaze before desolation consumed it.

The momentary flicker between the two served as a window to his soul and a view of the trust he was about to extend, the consequential wrath of what we would face if we betrayed him dusting over it.

"Then I think we have a deal." I leaned forward, extending my hand to him.

He bent over his knee, his hand meeting mine as his stare remained pinned on me. His hand, calloused yet surprisingly soft, embraced mine as the length of his fingers encased the backside of my palm.

"It would appear so, Carnell."

"Astrid." I slowed our shake before pulling away. "You can call me Astrid."

Even though he already knew, I extended permission and a hint of trust in allowing him to use my name. His following sentence radiated into my core and sent a far-reaching heaviness over me as if I had desired this moment for far longer than I expected—not only escaping the Walls but coming to join with a powerful Rebel. What it meant to align with *him* and all that meant for me. For *us*.

"Welcome to the Rebellion then, Astrid."

SEVEN

I walked down the dimmed hallway, my book tucked under my arm. With every thought violating my mind, I intended to go to my room for some needed isolation—even if only for a few minutes.

The wooden floor creaked beneath my bare feet, but it wasn't its squeal that caught my attention. Instead, the laughter seeping through Imelda's partially cracked bedroom door drew me in. Her snicker was contagious, immediately causing a smile to form on my lips. I slowed my movements to remain undetectable, positioning myself against the wall and basking in the late evening light that crept from her room.

Her petite frame came into view, and she swatted Onyx's hand from where she stood. "Stop it! Let me show you!"

In any other instance, I would've presumed the two were arguing solely based on Onyx's demeanor, but I knew that was far from the case—the two were enjoying each other's company.

"That requires you to unpin it from the wall, and I think it makes for good decoration," Onyx responded, the unforeseen smile present in his words.

Imelda extended a middle finger in his direction, a deep

chuckle his only response. "I've worked hard on it, asshole. Now, for five seconds, can you give me the limelight?"

"Clocks ticking, kid," he teased, earning another vulgar gesture.

"Since you're so adamant about me keeping it to frame my intelligence, I will lecture you like a teacher." She pointed toward her bed. "Sit."

I awaited another opposing tease from him, but the squeak of springs followed. His body undoubtedly moved to occupy the place she instructed, the essence of her soul cradling his heart.

"Since you were so stubborn about me nailing cartography, that's what I've spent the last few months doing since we left your boyfriend's community."

"He's not—"

"Aht." She clapped, her tongue clicking against the roof of her mouth with disapproval. "I don't believe you raised your hand to ask a question, but since you want to argue the claim that he isn't, I will add that the keyword is *yet*."

Onyx splayed his legs in front of him, leaning back on his hands, a casual position I hadn't witnessed before. "Proceed, Ms. Jefferson."

Without skipping a beat, she did exactly that, her fingers trailing between each point as she spoke. "I've chosen each pin color for a purpose. Red points to potential hordes or other threats in the area. Yellow marks places we've been before, saving us the time and energy that comes with arguing," she jutted him a look, and he shrugged, drawing a huff from her. "Essentially, it keeps us from backtracking. Green pins are the safe zones where we could set up camp if needed. And blue marks freshwater sources—simple enough."

"As for the black lines drawn in Sharpie?" Onyx poked glee-fully. "That use of material seems to be—"

The marker he spoke of sailed through the air, colliding with his forehead. I bit my lip to prevent my laughter, watching as he lifted his chin in her direction. His expression wasn't one he'd graced me with before—hinting at a desired violence—but one that spoke of a lively retaliation that made me slightly jealous.

"Don't look at me like—"

Before her threat was complete, he vanished from where he sat and appeared behind her. The abrupt shift reminded me of the depths of his abilities and all the damage he could innately accomplish if he wished.

She screamed merrily as he wrapped his arms around her, picking her up off the ground. Her limbs flailed as she struggled against him before he tossed her onto the mattress. She bounced once before he was there, his fingers clutching her sides and drawing her infectious giggle.

"I'm sorry! Okay! I'm sorry—Onyx!" Her laughter mixed with his, a symphony of happiness in a world blacked by sorrow.

He grinned, pulling his hands away before jolting toward her. She jumped back before he could grab her, lifting her leg to defend herself from the tickle attack if necessary.

Silence encased the space, and neither moved from where they were, creating a need for their connection to continue filling the growing void. A sadness of realization followed—our reality allowing minimal moments of simplicity and robbing us of all we'd taken for granted before we could fully appreciate it.

Onyx opened his arms, ushering for Imelda to join him without threat. She crawled across the bed and into his lap, his embrace making her seem far younger than she was. He trailed his fingers through her curls, dropping his chin to kiss the crown of her head.

His eyes lifted to the map again. "I'm proud of you and incredibly impressed with your accomplishments."

She clung to his shirt desperately, as if she feared the moment she let go would be the last touch they shared. "I just want to help in any way I can. You do a lot, Onyx, for so many people."

His scar highlighted his melancholy smile. "You do plenty, Imelda. For me and many others."

She was his saving grace, keeping him grounded in tumultuous times. Her soul served as his grounding cord in a world he despised, and his presence provided a safety net that our apocalyptic society robbed her of. They needed one another more than those living needed oxygen to survive.

"You know," she started, changing the subject before either could sink further. "I learned something from a special someone."

"Yeah?"

She nodded, leaning back to look at him. "Mapping things out is invaluable. It's more than just a tool. It's our story and path forward. Every mark is a decision, a choice that can change everything."

He winked in response before saying, "It seems you've memorized a quote from someone."

"Or a few." She smiled, mirrored lines digging into her cheeks. "It's about understanding the world, about seeing beyond what's in front of you. The map helps, but it's your instincts, your experiences, which guide you."

"Or a few," Onyx repeated, following her repetition of what I presumed was another extension of the knowledge he provided her.

He pulled her back into him, cradling her in another silent embrace. The constant exchange of touch between the two displayed how much her presence meant to him—a man who seemed put off by the idea of intimacy.

She nuzzled into him, burying her face against his chest and muttering, "I love you, Onyx."

"As I love you," he responded softly. "There will not come a time where I'm not proud of you for all you are and continue to be. You are a radiant beacon of hope in a world of suffocating darkness. You are the future, Imelda—our future."

Unshed tears burned my gaze, their deep connection stirring something buried inside me.

Imelda wiped her eyes and sniffled. "You saved me that day, and I can't even express how grateful I am to know you."

Onyx's thumb trailed beneath her lash line, wiping away the

tears she shed. "For you, Imelda, it's an honor. There isn't a thing I wouldn't do for you."

She laughed again, the sound broken by the influx of sudden emotion. "Like visit a library? Do you remember when we came across that decrepit one?"

He chuckled, rolling his eyes. "Be mindful of how you use that word, young lady. Libraries were a hot commodity when I was your age, and believe it or not, I had a library card."

"You know how to read?"

He shook his head. "Your elected insults are becoming far too similar to mine."

"Okay, let me try again with a little touch of authenticity." Mischievous glinted in her eyes as she continued, "As an owner of a library card, you are definitely *ancient*."

He shoved her lightheartedly, her laughter echoing throughout the small room. "Maybe it does, but that isn't the point. To answer your question, my *youthful* counterpart, how could I forget? You spent hours pouring your heart and soul into reading those *ancient* books."

"Maybe I admired them so much because they made me think of someone specifically *ancient*," she grinned, earning a playful pinch from the man who refused to let her go. "Ow! Okay, no, but seriously, it was like we found a piece of what once was— something that somehow remained untouched by the destruction."

Onyx nodded. "The calm those moments bring are precious and serve as a reminder of all we fight for and hope to rebuild."

While the world labeled him as a monster waiting to destroy the remaining innocence of life, he pushed forward to ensure her vision was attainable.

His words drew my attention back to the map. It became notable that each line Imelda drew held far more than a literal meaning. They represented steps forward and symbolized their relentless pursuit of creating a world she desired.

EIGHT

I rolled over for the fifth time, a soft groan escaping my lips as I stared into the darkness. The only light came from the stars outside, confirming it was still the dead of night. Radley's steady breathing beside me was a comforting reminder he was undisturbed by the turmoil in my mind. His arm wrapped securely around my waist, holding me close even in sleep.

Slowly, I loosened his grip, careful not to wake him. He instinctively turned away, exhaling deeply. I sat up on the edge of the bed, rubbing my palms over my eyes before standing. There was no point in staying in bed when sleep had become elusive.

I moved silently across the room, mindful of the floorboards, but a single squeaky section betrayed me. I froze, glancing over my shoulder at Radley. With adjusted eyes, I could see him clearly.

He remained undisturbed, his messy hair splayed across his forehead, his lips parted in a deep sleep.

A soft smile tugged at my lips before I turned back to the door, carefully wrapping my hand around the knob and easing it open. The hinges groaned, a low echo in the bunker's quiet, but soon, tranquility reigned again.

Navigating the dark hallway by memory, I followed the faint light filtering through the boarded windows, leading me to the living room. As I passed Imelda's room, I noticed the tightly shut door, the stillness behind it comforting.

Despite our extended stay and new understanding, I still didn't know where Onyx slept. Every door remained closed, a silent sign that while he extended trust, privacy was something he held dear.

Entering the living room, my gaze fell on the coffee table first. My eyes scanned the space, landing on the cases of water stacked near the kitchen entryway. I debated taking one when a throat cleared behind me.

Pivoting, I spotted a figure leaning forward in one of the chairs, features obscured by darkness.

"What are you doing?" Onyx's raspy voice cut through the quiet, my shoulders relaxing in relief.

"I couldn't sleep," I whispered, unsure how he would react to my presence.

A lighter flicked, and a small flame illuminated his face briefly before he snapped it closed. "Looked like you were contemplating stealing a water bottle," he muttered, a hint of humor in his tone.

I hesitated, more interested in why he was awake than in thieving a drink. His earlier harshness seemed to have softened, replaced by something more human, more weary. I stepped forward, but his eyes snapped open, locking with mine.

"Why are you up?" I asked, curious despite the tension between us.

"Does that concern you?" His response was predictable, but his tone lacked the usual bite.

"So, you can't sleep either?" I pressed, stepping closer.

"Something like that," he admitted, his voice lowering as he glanced away. "I'm lucky if I get a couple of hours. Between taking care of her and—" He paused as if catching himself from revealing too much.

I waited, wondering if he was about to share something personal, something that might explain the hard exterior he always wore. But the moment passed, and his words remained undisclosed.

"Yeah, I get it," I said, trying to keep the conversation alive. "It's hard to sleep with the constant threats of the outside world. I'm still adjusting. I don't know how you've done it all this time."

"Because I don't have any other option," he replied, his voice turning cold. "Unlike some people, I can't crawl back to a confined cage for safety. So, no, you don't fully get it. Not yet."

He was right. I'd never fully understand what it was like to live in the Wilds, exposed to danger every day for four years. While we had the Walls for protection, Onyx had been fighting to survive with only his wit and abilities to protect himself and Imelda.

"Is it just us?" The question slipped out before I could stop it, driven by the remembrance of the woman we'd found in the city before we initially met the two we now shared living quarters with.

He frowned, not understanding my question.

"Venturers," I clarified. "Is it just us that you all have to worry about out here? Or do other Rebels pose threats alongside the Runners?"

Onyx huffed, a low, humorless chuckle escaping him. "Fear?" He questioned mockingly as he leaned forward, his eyes piercing through the darkness. "The government isn't something I fear. Not a single Venturer could last a night out here. The two of you staying with us as long as you have proves that."

I cut him off before he could continue, biting down the desire to reiterate his offer of letting us stay. "Let me rephrase. Is there anything else out there that opposes you besides the expected?"

He went to respond, but a sudden crack outside caused us to halt our engagement immediately. Onyx stood, his large frame blocking the faint moonlight. The lighter's flame vanished, plunging the room into darkness as he moved toward the window, listening closely to whatever was about to greet us.

Then, a voice shattered the silence, snapping through the night like a whip.

"It doesn't look empty to me," a male voice sneered, and my blood ran cold.

I recognized the voice instantly—Lyons, one of Gael's partners.

"Well, no shit, Sherlock." Briar's authoritative tone filled the room, making my stomach sink further.

Then came the voice I dreaded the most.

"They've got to be somewhere around here. Tracking devices never lie," Gael's smugness tore through the peaceful night, a wave of nausea washing over me.

Tracking devices? Since when did they use those? My mind recalled Onyx's warning about betrayal when we arrived. Despite our agreement, I suddenly realized the extent of the danger we were in with their arrival.

Onyx's gaze turned deadly as he looked at me, suspicion flaring. His muscles tensed, and I shook my head, whispering, "We didn't alert anyone, Onyx. I swear on my life—"

He held my gaze a moment longer, then signaled for silence, his distrust clear but overridden by the situation's urgency. His focus shifted entirely to Imelda's safety, leaving Radley and me as mere afterthoughts.

"Once a traitor, always a traitor, huh?" Gael's pointed laughter echoed in the darkness.

"I've been waiting for this moment," Lyons added, his smirk discernable. "I knew they'd been sleeping with the enemy."

"And now that the higher-ups know, we can put those two in the ground with the other traitors," Briar said.

"Honestly, they get what they deserve," Lyons sneered, their footsteps nearing the once-safe haven. The rustling of dried leaves underfoot pinpointed their location, and I knew Onyx was already calculating their every move.

Dread gripped me as I realized they were hunting us—Radley, me, and now, unintentionally, Onyx and Imelda.

Onyx's eyes narrowed, his agitation palpable. But there was no time to argue.

"Are we engaging? It's so quiet; they're probably asleep." Briar's voice was suddenly too close.

Suddenly, I saw something out of the corner of my eye bounce across the ground near the window—a small, flickering red light illuminating the wall.

Before I could fully comprehend what it was, Onyx reacted, his voice a sharp command cutting through the darkness.

"GET DOWN!"

He moved faster than I could react, his arms wrapping around me. The world tilted, and the next moment, my body slammed against the cold tiles. A clicking sound registered, marking the second until the explosion.

A grenade.

The blast engulfed the space we were in moments before, wood splintering and bowing to the detonation and consuming flames. Debris rained down, and I struggled to decipher our surroundings through the thick smoke and disorientation. The overwhelming sound caused my ears to ring, its intensity blurring my vision, but I could vaguely make out Onyx's form as he shielded me.

He moved off me, and I struggled to push myself off the ground, my senses sluggish to return. Smoke billowed from the living room, filling the kitchen with an acrid stench. The orangish-red hue of the spreading fire reflected off the tiled floor, casting flickering shadows on the walls. The chaos was suffocating, but Onyx's protectiveness cut through the disturbance. Even amid this hell, his priority was clear—Imelda.

"Astrid!" Radley's voice pierced through the war zone, the sound of the grenade waking him violently from sleep.

"I'm alright!" I called back, glancing at Onyx.

The moonlight filtered through the kitchen window, highlighting his scar and those hauntingly blue eyes now blazing with fury. Ash clung to his skin, adding to the ferocity of his expression. I could see the questions burning behind his gaze, but we lacked the time for interrogation.

"We need to—" I began, but something clattered with the kitchen floor, abruptly cutting off my suggestion. The metal echoed off the barren walls, bouncing before rolling to a stop, the oddly shaped object stopping between us.

Onyx reacted instantly, shoving me back harshly. I lost my footing, crashing to the ground just as the device released its assault. An electric net shot out, ensnaring Onyx's legs as a scream of agony tore from his throat.

"Onyx!" Imelda's voice came from the hallway, laced with fear and desperation. Flames had devoured the wooden floors, effectively trapping her and Radley in the hallway, separated from us by a wall of fire.

"Shit," I muttered, scrambling to my feet.

I needed to free him from the electric net that now held him captive. I tore through the kitchen drawers, searching frantically for something to assist in his freedom. My fingers rifled through various utensils, but not a single knife greeted my touch. My palms wrapped around every handle, tearing apart the kitchen to rescue the man capable of demolishing everything.

A boot greeted the door with a harsh kick, solidifying our reality—they were forcing their way in.

Onyx writhed on the floor, his body convulsing as electricity coursed through him, amplifying his anguish. The net dug into his legs, the effect more potent than I imagined. Realization hit me—Onyx's immense power made him more susceptible to a voltage-based attack. The very abilities that made him formidable now rendered him vulnerable.

The door splintered and caved inward, time evading us. With thunderous steps, all three burst into the bunker, their boots echoing on the wooden floor. Smoke and burning wood filled the air as the fire crackled with a sinister appetite that mirrored their intentions.

"Surprise!" Gael taunted down the hallway, the beam of his flashlight slicing through the smoke to light the kitchen walls.

Onyx grunted, ripping part of the netting from his legs even though touching it worsened the voltage's intensity. He cursed under his breath, reaching forward again in another fleeting attempt at freedom, biting down the affliction consuming him.

I yanked open the last drawer, my hand closing around a large chef's knife. Its cold steel felt solid in my grip, proving to be a lifeline in the chaos. I glanced at Onyx, my heart pounding as two decisions presented themselves—cutting him free or leveraging the blade for something else.

I chose the latter.

With a deep breath, I clutched the knife, my resolve hardening. My reflection in the blade highlighted my hazel eyes, burning with a vengeance. It had been months since I'd looked at myself in a mirror or any other reflective surface, the horrors of our predicament illuminating the golden ring around my irises. The ash from the explosion streaked my face, accentuating the scar above my left eyebrow. My hair was a tangled mess, but none of it mattered when lives were on the line.

Gael's voice, thick with malicious glee, floated through the smoke. "Make your way to the back rooms. There's an accessible path through the flames."

"Copy that," Lyons responded, his footsteps moving toward the hallway.

"Dead or alive?" Briar asked, her footsteps halting just outside the kitchen.

A sickening chuckle rumbled from Gael's throat. "Alive. So we can have a little fun."

The implication behind his words caused my stomach to churn. I knew exactly what he meant by 'fun'—torture, suffering, and breaking the power wielders in the space, especially once he realized who one of them was.

I pressed my back against the cold wall, drawing in a breath as Gael's footsteps grew louder, closing in on the corner that shielded us. Onyx gazed over at me with a mix of agony and question. As he went to speak, I shook my head, silencing him before he gave way to my location. Seconds later, Gael's arm came into view first, holding what appeared to be a pistol, but its design was unfamiliar—deadlier. I knew what that meant.

It emitted an electric charge.

"If you think I'm going to put you out of your misery with any ounce of mercy, you're sorely mistaken," Gael snarled, unaware of my presence.

"Funny," Onyx replied, his voice strained but laced with dark amusement. "We both know the only reason you're still breathing is because of this net. You're pathetically weak, and that fact alone maddens you."

Gael's jaw feathered and a tight smile tugged at my lips. Onyx hit a nerve, Gael's superiority complex proving to be a flimsy veil for his insecurities.

"Because I came prepared?" Gael's chuckle sharpened. "This won't be anywhere close to our prior engagements. I'll kill her in front of you and then drag you back to the Walls' prison where you belong. The only thing you deserve is a miserable, endless life. It's a far better punishment for you than death will ever be."

Prior engagements? Why hadn't any of the higher-ups informed the Venturers of his experiences?

"You're right. It won't." Onyx's voice dropped to a menacing rasp, his laugh chilling. "I'm done holding back with you and your little squad, and I promise none of you will leave here alive, Gael."

A sneer twisted Gael's face as he tightened his grip on the weapon. Before he could fire, I pivoted from my position and drove the knife into his exposed bicep. The blade tore through muscle and flesh, pinning his arm to the doorframe. The electric pistol clattered to the ground between us.

His emerald eyes locked onto mine, burning with rage. "You bitch," he spat, pain filling his words.

I reached for the fallen gun, but before my fingers could close around it, Gael's knee collided with my sternum. Air dissipated from my lungs as I inhaled a sharp gasp, the force of the impact lifting me off the ground. Pain violated my chest as I hit the floor harshly, attempting to gather my barrings.

As I struggled to push myself up, Gael ripped the blade from his arm, tossing it to the ground. The successive drum of blood dripping from his wound drowned the knife's clanging beside me. I planted an arm beneath me and rolled onto my back, gazing up as his frame came into view, looming over me.

He clutched his arm with his left hand, crimson staining his fingers. A cruel smile played on his lips as he shook his head. "We knew you were here, Astrid. I hate to say it, but this level of reunion feels rather reminiscent, doesn't it?"

I wheezed, meeting his glowing emerald gaze. "You're a pathetic excuse of someone to fear."

The smile vanished, replaced by a snarl. His angered steps drummed against the tiles, closing the distance between us. His boot found home against my throat, cutting off the air I had struggled to find. Instinctively, I reached for his leg, attempting to pry him off me, but I knew it was useless. He responded to my effort by pushing down harder, his sole digging into my windpipe.

"That'll change soon enough," he growled, leaning in, increasing the pressure.

A stinging pain spread across sensitive skin as his weight bore down, my lungs burning from the lack of oxygen. Dark spots danced along the edges of my vision, the outskirts blurring with each passing second. I was fading fast, slipping into unconsciousness. Desperately, I turned my head, searching for Onyx.

The spot where the net had pinned him down was empty. It lay discarded on the floor, but Onyx was gone. My heart sank. He'd left—escaped while he had the chance, leaving me to die.

I was his distraction, a means to an end. And honestly, I couldn't blame him.

Radley and I had pursued his partner and nearly killed her. We were Venturers, hunters of Rebels, and responsible for countless deaths. We had no right to expect mercy from any of them after the horrors they'd witnessed. And despite seeking refuge with the Most Wanted Rebel, we had unintentionally endangered them, going against our agreements.

Defeat washed over me as I dragged my eyes back to Gael, his face twisted in a mocking grin. He shifted, grinding his boot deeper into my throat. My vision dimmed further, the tingling in my fingers and toes spreading as the blood struggled to reach my brain.

"Nice knowing you, bitch," Gael taunted, his voice growing distant as the world around me faded.

I made one last feeble attempt to free myself, but my strength was gone. My body refused to obey, too weak to move or fight. My eyes fluttered, and I surrendered to the darkness as it swallowed me whole.

I accepted my fate.

CHAPTER

NINE

I never realized what they claim about your entire life flashing before your eyes as Death reaches for you would be true.

In mere seconds, memories consumed my mind—snapshots of my childhood, teenage years, and early adulthood played out like movie scenes. Family trips with my parents and brother stood out, each moment vivid and warm. Reliving those days was serene, and being greeted by their presence one more time was something I'd craved for years. But along with the beautiful memories came the dark ones—a reminder of life's cruel balance.

Every mistake, every hurtful word spoken in anger, came rushing back with stinging clarity. The guilt of my brother's death before the Fall, a less that still haunted me, hit with brutal force. Then came the faces of those I'd killed—their lifeless eyes, the blood staining my hands. The recollections lingered, serving as a cruel reminder that the consequences of my actions were inescapable, even in my final moments.

"Astrid!" A voice echoed through the haze, interfering with the influx of emotions that came with the echo of my past.

I stared at the body of a Rebel, his chest soaked with blood that spread across the ground in a dark, widening pool. He stared dully past me as a single tear fell from his cheek to mingle with the crimson beneath him.

I killed him.

"Damn it! Wake up!" The interruption came again, urgent and familiar, dragging me back from the brink.

I shook my head, closing my eyes to try and avoid the gruesome scene. Once I opened them again, everything remained, only slowly beginning to dissolve as a fire crept into the edges of my vision. All-encompassing darkness followed, swallowing the world of remembrance whole until nothing remained.

My eyes shot open, and the faded ceiling welcomed me. The dim glow of a flashlight and the ominous flick of fire barely illuminated it, reminding me of the onslaught we were in the middle of. A harsh cough escaped my lungs, echoing through the desolate space and overpowering the crackling of flames nearby. I immediately pressed my hands against the cold ceramic tiles, grounding myself in the realization that I was somehow still alive. My gaze traveled forward as I pushed myself up, locking onto Onyx who knelt in front of me.

His usual black henley clung to his muscular frame, emphasizing the strength that had shielded me from the initial attack. His dark hair appeared disheveled, strands clinging together with the styling help from a mixture of soot and sweat. Black ash smudged his face, accentuating the scar that marred his features. Concern flickered in his haunting blue eyes, barely visible in the shadows threatening to consume us.

He was the one calling my name.

"I hate to interfere, but now isn't the best time to be napping," he replied roughly yet playfully.

I followed his glower to the wall, where he'd pinned Gael. Two long hunting knives were embedded in his shoulders, anchoring him to the sheetrock. Blood trickled from his wounds, and a bruise had already begun to darken. His expression twisted in pain and ire, the fresh cut marring his lip accentuating their notability.

"I need an update, Oakes!" Radley's call echoed from a distance, drawing my attention away from Gael.

I didn't know how long I had been unconscious, but it was clear that numerous things had transpired while I was. Onyx and Gael had clashed, and Radley had likely taken down Briar and Lyons to ensure Imelda remained protected. The fire, which had started in the living room, spread rapidly, the timber floors feeding its ravenous hunger. The flames had not reached us, but their heat was palpable, thickening the air with a dense cloud of smoke.

"Astrid is fine." Onyx turned to face the fire, the command coming from him with ease. "The flames cut off all viable exit routes. Take Imelda out one of the back windows and grab what you can. We will meet you outside."

"Alright," Radley responded, a slight hesitation prevalent. I understood his hesitation, but there wasn't time to contemplate trust or intention. "If you don't bring Astrid with you, I'll gut you alive."

Onyx rolled his eyes, dismissing Radley's threat with a look of exasperation before turning back to me. He extended his hand, pulling me to my feet. "We've got to move. This place will belong to the infernal depths of hell if we wait much longer, and I'd prefer not to go out being burned alive."

I nodded, dusting myself off one time over. My eyes drifted to Gael, who struggled against the knives anchoring him to the wall. His life force smeared the tiles, the scent of it intermixing with the smoke.

"If you think either of you are getting out of here," Gael hissed, ripping one blade from his shoulder, blood spraying across the tile. "You're gravely mistaken."

Onyx kept his back to Gael, glancing over his shoulder with disdain. The firelight reflected in his eyes, making them bloom with a dangerous intensity. "The irony in that statement is that you're the one pinned to the wall with two downed, completely useless counterparts." Hardened contempt laced his words. "You're going to die here like the worthless bastard you are."

Before Gael could respond, the window to our right shattered, glass exploding inward as an unseen force ripped away the boards that once shielded it. The cool night air rushed in starkly contrasted with the searing internal heat.

"Let's go," Onyx said, motioning for me to climb out first. His eyes never left Gael, the unspoken threat hanging in the air.

As I obliged and pushed myself into the windowsill, Gael's reply came from behind me, laced with desperation. "You're going to leave me here? What happened to the confidence you spat about killing me yourself?"

His scream stirred something deep within me, and my gaze wandered back to spot a single bottle of whiskey on the countertop—something I hadn't noticed before I fell unconscious.

"You don't deserve a quick death, especially when I can bask in your screams while your skin sears and bubbles at the mercy of the fire you started." Onyx chuckled darkly. "It's funny how things come full circle, isn't it?"

There was no remorse, not an ounce of sympathy—just a monotone voice laced with pure wrath. It was what cloaked his darkness.

"You bastard!" Gael bellowed as I swung my other leg over the frame.

My bare feet hit the tall, dried grass, the foliage pressing against my soles. The iciness of the earth leveled me amid the havoc, the mud squelching between my toes as I took a few steps forward. I peered over my shoulder, watching the flames consume the bunker, the fire's smolder vibrant against the dark sky.

"Let this be a learning opportunity," Onyx's sneer carried through the window as he grabbed the bottle of whiskey, spinning the cap off and taking a long swig before he spoke again. "Once you step into the Wilds, without your bullshit protection and bird-caged society, you better come prepared to face your demons. Every single one of them."

"Fuck you!" The walls of the burning building muffled Gael's roar.

"How many minutes do you think you can last? Do you want to give me a number?" His query held an indifference that hinted at a deeper, untold story.

Gael's silence was all the confirmation Onyx needed.

"Full circle, remember?" Onyx sneered, a condescending hum escaping him. "The fact that I have to waste delicious whiskey on you is a godsdamn disgrace." He glanced at the bottle before raising it once more. "I'll catch you in hell, Adler."

Gael's last name came from Onyx's lips with a poisonous bite as he tightened his grip on the bottle before hurling it at the fire's base. The flames roared to life, doubling, spiraling into the space where the two stood. The fire consumed the last standing section of the bunker in seconds, signifying its path of carnage that Gael was in the way of.

"I will kill you, Onyx! Mark my words!" Gael's scream echoed through the night as he struggled against the final knife restraining him.

Onyx shrugged as he pushed himself through the window, looking back at him one last time. "Yeah? Just like you've tried to in the past? It's time you accept your fate. Death is easier that way."

The footsteps approaching from the distance caused my stomach to drop. My mind assumed the worst, pondering the likelihood of other Venturers' presence to partake in the fight we'd thought we won. I spun toward their source, spotting Radley and Imelda approaching. Radley smirked, raising a hand to wave, a few bruises on his face confirming his opposition.

He dropped our gear, boots, and socks before stepping closer and pulling me into a tight hug. "Shit, Astrid. I thought you died back there."

I hugged him tightly, a sigh escaping me. Fear and relief mixed into a torrent of emotions, the weight of the night's events pressing down on me. I clung to him, fearful that if I let go, something else would happen and potentially rob him from me like everything else I'd lost. Death had been seconds away from coaxing me into the afterlife, Onyx's unexpected intervention the only thing that saved me.

"Bury it." Onyx's sudden proximity startled me.

I pulled away from Radley, noticing a deep laceration that marred Onyx's henley, blood visible through the torn fabric and marking a deep shoulder injury. He seemed unbothered by it, his hands buried in his pockets as he commanded the young woman I knew would do anything for him.

Imelda nodded once, her eyes shifting from deep brown to fiery red and orange. The flames consuming the bunker seemed to grow as she focused on it, reaching skyward in an irrevocable act of destruction. The heat intensified, shooting sparks into the sky and making home nothing more than a burning pyre.

"I believe an explanation is necessary at this point, " Onyx said calmly, though barely restrained.

Their haven was destroyed in mere minutes, exposing them to the elements, Runners, and the potential threat of other Rebels. I attempted to understand how Venturers and likely other government officials successfully tracked us down.

We were the reason behind it all.

He wanted answers.

"Look, we never—" I began, but a knife unsheathing cut me off. Before I could react, the blade's tip pressed against my throat.

"You think I give a damn about intentions right now?" Onyx rasped, his eyes boring into mine as he held the weapon steady. "I want to know where these tracking devices are so we can destroy them. Before I destroy both of you."

"If you could stop being an asshole for five seconds, you'd realize she was about to tell you we don't know." Radley snarled sharply, his glare locked on Onyx. "Are you that dense to think we'd lure them here and then help you kill them?"

Onyx scoffed, shifting his scowl from me to Radley. "How about, for once, you open your godsdamn ears and listen so I don't have to repeat myself?" The tension between them became more suffocating than the smoke clogging the starry sky. "I asked where the devices were so we could destroy them and prevent this from happening again. Does your singular brain cell understand now?"

Before I could intervene, Radley lunged at Onyx, tackling him to the ground. The two of them hit the earth hard, simultaneous grunts escaping them. Radley's fist connected with Onyx's nose in a swift, brutal motion. Crimson red spattered onto the grass as Onyx quickly countered, trapping Radley's leg and throwing him onto his back just as he'd done to me on the rooftops.

Onyx straddled Radley, blood dripping from his nose. "I do not have the damn energy to deal with this," he growled, his hand wrapping around Radley's throat and tightening like a vice. "You want to survive out here on your own? Be my guest. But remember, you're in my territory, hated by many, and now fugitives from the Walls. Your survival without us is slim to none. So, perhaps consider that before you decide to lay your hands on me again."

Radley kicked his legs uselessly, and I cut in before he could speak, unsure of what he might retaliate with. "We understand and appreciate your willingness to house and work alongside us." I exhaled deeply as I continued, including an underlying warning to the man beneath him. "We know the risks you're taking and the size of the target that resides on your back because of your decision to align with us, and we don't want to make things harder than they already are."

I wasn't just repeating Onyx's words to appease him—I meant every word.

We were labeled enemies of the government, the Walls, and every Venturer out there. Without Onyx's protection, our chances of survival were slim to none.

His grip on Radley's throat eased slightly, but their strife remained.

There remained no other choice but to rely on him, and I only hoped Radley could understand the gravity of our situation.

We were in uncharted territory, with enemies on all sides. The Wilds were unforgiving, and we were unprepared to face them alone.

But with Onyx, there was a chance—if we could survive each other first.

Onyx glanced over his shoulder, his eyes momentarily locking with mine. "You're mistaken. As a Venturer, those in power have wanted me for years. Your betrayal and minuscule worth don't change that." He raised an eyebrow before turning back to Radley. "But you ought to learn a few things from her because, for hell's sake, you've got a long road ahead."

With that, he released his grip and pushed himself off the ground, deliberately slamming his boot into Radley's side as he stepped over him.

Radley gasped for air, groaning in the aftermath of the elected assault. I clenched my jaw, trying to hold back what I desired to say, but it became useless, the question snapping from me. "Was that necessary?"

Onyx shrugged, a soft chuckle escaping his lips. He wiped the blood from his nose with his sleeve before refocusing on me to respond verbally, leveraging my comments of desiring more than a single reply. "The little shit did nearly break my nose."

I bit the inside of my cheek, biting back a retort. Before I could say anything else, Radley's hand wrapped around mine, and I turned to help him off the ground. Once upright, his eyes immediately fell on Onyx, a scoff escaping him.

"You got something you'd like to say?" Onyx's haunting blue eyes shifted from me to Radley, a brow cocked expectantly. "Admittance, perhaps?"

Radley held his tongue, shaking his head. It became clear he wasn't about to push our luck any further.

Onyx's patience ran thin, and we both knew he wouldn't hesitate to unleash his wrath if provoked again.

Despite his calloused exterior, I began to see him more clearly. He was patient, but his patience had limits. Once someone tested those limits to the brink, he exploded with a force that could level anything in his path. His protective nature was instinctual and deeply embedded, especially with those he cared about, like Imelda. Yet, despite all his power, parts of him remained a mystery.

Why had he chosen to help Radley and me? Why were we spared out of all the Venturers he had encountered and presumably killed?

Every story had painted him as a ruthless monster, but his truth was far more convoluted.

"Good," Onyx finally said, exhaling deeply. He turned to Imelda, a recognizable shift in his demeanor. "I hate to be the one that requires saving, but—"

"That's not how I see it." Imelda rolled her eyes, smiling softly as she interrupted him.

She stepped forward, placing herself in front of him and examining the gash in his shoulder. I had nearly forgotten that Gael had injured him during their fight. The blood loss, subsequent events, and heightened adrenaline had kept him on his feet, but the aftermath and its toll started to become apparent.

"You need to stop putting yourself in near-death situations, you know? This isn't something we collect trophies for," Imelda teased, kneeling beside him.

"Yeah, well. If only that were possible in the current state of the world, then I would gladly obey your command," Onyx replied, slowly lowering himself to the ground.

He looked at her, the softness in his eyes returning as he allowed himself a rare moment of vulnerability.

"Imagine me having all the power in the world to command you on what to do," Imelda joked, giggling as she cocked her head. "At this moment, I will reign, and we will start with my rulership. You'll have to remove your shirt so I can assess the wound effectively, Sir."

Onyx rolled his eyes before tugging his shirt free from his pants and stripping it off. He winced as the fabric grazed the laceration, his brows furrowing together as he bit down an irrefutable groan of agony. I watched intently, the fire's glow illuminating his muscular, broad-shouldered physique, revealing a body marked by countless scars. Each one seemed to tell a story, a testament to the hell he'd been through.

"This makes it..." Imelda held her hands a few inches apart as she counted. "Twenty—"

"Twenty-three," Onyx sighed heavily. "This is the twenty-third time you've had to heal me, and it stings a little extra every time you remind me."

The number startled me, revealing how many close calls Onyx had survived and speaking to the capability of his opponents. Yet there were far more than twenty-three scars that marred his porcelain skin, pointing to events that transpired before he'd met Imelda—perhaps even before the Fall.

Imelda focused on her hands, inhaling as she closed her eyes. Her shoulders relaxed as she channeled her energy, the whitish-orange hue of her healing ability igniting in her palms. The radiance mirrored the fire in the distance but with a far more benevolent purpose.

She leaned forward, placing her hands over Onyx's shoulder, her fingers gently wrapping around the muscle. Onyx exhaled sharply, clenching his jaw as the hiss of searing flesh filled the air—a sensation I hadn't experienced when she worked on me. In his case, her touch cauterized and sealed the wound within seconds—her power a testament to their bond.

"Good as new," she said with a grin, watching him closely.

"Per usual. Thank you." Onyx nodded, pulling his shirt back over his head as he got to his feet.

"Now that's taken care of," he continued, grabbing his backpack from Imelda. "We're going to visit an old friend of mine. He has a sanctuary for Rebels about six hundred miles from here in Great Falls."

Radley nodded slowly, his expression shifting. "A community of Rebels?"

"Yeah, you could call it that. It's a sanctuary where Rebels can find support and safety. It's nothing like the Walls, but it is a haven for those in the Wilds. The community is close-knit, a family of sorts. But even with sanctuaries, the Wilds are a battleground, not just against the Runners but between ideologies and past allegiances." Onyx replied as he holstered his pistol. "Among us, there's another group known as Scavengers. They're former military personnel, some with abilities, others without. Their skills make them formidable, but their past ties to the government make them untrustworthy in the eyes of the Rebellion."

Radley leaned forward, puzzled. "But why would the Rebellion despise? Aren't they just survivors like the rest of you?"

"It's not that simple," Onyx replied, crossing his arms. "The Scavengers have a dark history. Even before the Fall, they were involved in covert operations, missions designed to suppress dissent and maintain control. When the government began experimenting on soldiers, some Scavengers were directly involved or benefited from those experiments, gaining abilities that made them more dangerous. They were complicit in the systems we now battle, but they eventually turned against the government once they released how deep the corruption ran."

"So, they were trying to dismantle it from the inside?" I asked.

Onyx nodded grimly. "The Scavengers saw the Fall as an opportunity to continue their mission of tearing down what remained of society. They believe in a world where only the strong survive and chaos and violence are the natural order. The Rebellion, which aims to create a new society, is everything they hate. They see our efforts as fruitless, a refusal to accept the world's harsh realities."

"Hell," Radley muttered. "So, they don't want to rebuild because they never believed in it in the first place?"

"They see society as a weakness, a structure that coddled the weak and allowed corruption to thrive." Onyx clarified, his eyes glinting with buried knowledge. "To them, the Fall was just a catalyst, a chance to speed up the collapse of a world they despised.

The Rebellion, with its goal of rebuilding, is an obstacle to be eliminated."

"The scars of the past run too deep. The Scavengers can't let go of their hatred, and we can't let go of their questionable intentions." Imelda whispered, her words carrying a weight of sadness.

"So, we're stuck in this cycle of distrust," I said, the enormity of the situation sinking in.

Onyx dipped his chin, his reply hardening. "That's the harsh reality of the Wilds. It's a fractured world where everyone tries to carve out their place. The Scavengers have chosen their path, and we have chosen ours. There's no middle ground and no room for compromise. It's a fight for survival, and only the strong—or the lucky—make it out alive."

It all made sense, but a part of me questioned if there was something more significant than a surface-level explanation—something even the Rebellion didn't know.

"There's one thing we need to establish before we head to Great Falls," Onyx said, his tone becoming more orderly. "Everyone in the Wilds despises Venturers, whether part of the Rebellion or Scavengers. If anyone in that community finds out you're from within the Walls and served as Venturers, they will kill you without hesitation. No questions asked."

I swallowed, turning to Radley, who nodded though his jaw tightened with realization.

Onyx's warning wasn't a threat—it was a grim reminder of the reality we faced. In a world where survival was the only rule, trust was a luxury no one could afford.

TEN

The metal gate loomed before us. Its towering structure guarded the heart of the city, repurposing it into a fortress. Its protective barrier shielded those within from prying eyes, offering safety to the hidden and the hunted. Two guard towers flanked the gate, their presence a stark reminder that trust was hard to earn in our desolate world. Trees surrounded the perimeter, their canopies blending with the man-made defenses, camouflaging the entrance into what was once a bustling urban center.

A bold painting of the Rebellion's emblem adorned the gate, a testament to the community's resilience against all that opposed it. The vivid hues and sharp lines made the symbol impossible to miss, serving not only defiance but also a warning to potential intruders.

We'd landed about a mile away from the community after teleporting, a precaution Onyx insisted on. Within the neighborhood we'd found ourselves in, we spent time scavenging, searching for anything of use, and, more importantly, changing out of our Venturer uniforms. They were a glaring sign of where we came from and who we were. In their place, we found clothes that helped us blend in—black jeans, worn jackets, and scuffed boots. It wasn't much, but it was a start. Once we'd removed the identifiers of our ex-government affiliation, Onyx meticulously checked them for tracking devices. He ordered Imelda to disintegrate them once he found them so no trace of our past was left behind before he allowed us to continue.

The walk to the sanctuary was quiet, providing a much-needed reprieve from the night before. The surrounding area remained eerily still, likely cleared by the Rebellion to ensure no Runners, Venturers, or Scavengers lurked nearby. The higher-ups in Region Three had always warned about the dangers beyond the one-hundred-mile radius of any city's center. They told us these sections were wastelands, teeming with Runners and other threats.

They'd all lied.

We stood in a fully functioning city, hidden away in what we had been told was a fallout zone. My stomach dropped with fleeting recognition of how much they'd kept from us, the entanglements of their darkness never ceasing to find an end.

A sharp click broke the silence as we neared the gate, followed by the unmistakable sound of rifles being racked. Two barrels appeared from the guard tower to our left as a voice called, "Stop right there."

Onyx raised his hands, his movements deliberate. I followed suit, glancing to the side to see figures emerging from the trees, their weapons trained on us.

We were surrounded.

"State your business," came a brisk order from behind us—a woman's voice, authoritative and unwavering.

"Oh, just the usual," Onyx replied casually, though a sharpened edge laced his words and suggested that he was well-acquainted with this routine.

It struck me that they might not recognize him from this distance, or perhaps this was how they greeted anyone who approached, familiar or not. Either way, I knew we were walking a fine line.

"Onyx Oakes," a gruff voice called out from the gate, drawing our attention.

"Jasper," Onyx nearly hummed, something entirely different from what we'd heard. "Long time no see."

The newly named male stepped into the light, his appearance becoming clear as he moved out of the shadows. His hair, a fiery orange, fell to his chest. Its shorter sides blended into a light beard. He was built like Onyx, tall and muscular, with stormy gray eyes that seemed to pierce through the morning fog. Analyzing the similarities, their closeness in age became more apparent, though Jasper appeared to hold a couple of years over Onyx. He looked us over, his gaze lingering on Radley and me, suspicion etched into his features.

"And you've brought guests?" Caution laced Jasper's query. "You know how we feel about outsiders."

"They're harmless," Onyx said, the words stinging my pride but likely necessary to keep our cover intact.

Jasper stepped closer, his glower narrowing as he studied us with an expression that indicated he was far from convinced. "Strange thing is, I've never seen either of them in the Wilds. And we both know the amount of sway I have out here and the number of individuals I'm familiar with or have connections to."

His gaze drifted to the men beside us, followed by a slight head gesture. The reverberation of boots on concrete came again as the gap between us and those in the shadows closed abruptly. One individual stood beside me, unidentifiable due to the military-style neck gaiter they wore, the barrel of their gun inches away from the side of my head. Exhaling deeply, I moved my line of sight to Onyx to spot a male behind him, the barrel of his rifle pressed tightly to the back of Onyx's skull.

Onyx loosened a sigh, clearly agitated. "This isn't how you treat an old friend, Jasper. Especially one you haven't seen in months." He shook his head and added, "They're not from around here. Imelda and I spent time on the East Coast, checking for other Rebel communities. We picked them up along the way."

If it was a complete lie, he delivered it flawlessly.

Jasper raised his hand as the surrounding guns lowered. "You visited the east? Where?"

Imelda nodded, backing up Onyx's bluff, making me question its validity. "New Jersey. It's as bad as they say, maybe worse."

"Essentially, it's a fallout zone from nuclear detonation and other bombings." Onyx took over, holding the community leader's attention. "As for the areas that remained miraculously untouched by warfare, they are now crawling with Runners and other mutations that we haven't experienced on this side of the country. If I had to guess, it's a mix between the virus and living within the radioactive contamination zone during the Fall."

Mutations?

"Further mutated Runners?" Jasper's question reflected my thoughts, "I guess it shouldn't be surprising, considering that governmental operations have always contained too many secrets and confusing complexities."

Jasper's suggestion made me wonder if he'd worked alongside those in power before the Fall, and considering the length of time he and Onyx seemed to know one another, it made me question the latter's past as well. Imagining Onyx as a government soldier seemed impractical. Still, if my assumptions were accurate, it would make more sense why the target to take him down was so large.

Onyx shrugged, looking at his friend. "I wanted to discuss a few things with you regarding experiences in Jersey and Scavenger encroachment, as well as the technological advancements we have encountered with Venturers."

"I've got to say, you always come prepared." Jasper stepped forward, resting a hand on Onyx's shoulder as he smiled. "It's great to have you back. We have gravely missed your presence."

"And it's great to be back." Onyx returned the notion with a smirk as he nodded his head.

With that, I watched as Jasper looked at those who were surrounding us with the conspicuous intent to kill. He raised a hand before brushing it to the side, commanding without a spoken word. They shifted, holstering their weapons or placing the slings of their rifles over their shoulders before dispersing. Some of them vanished into the foliage they came from, while others walked toward the gates, returning to the sanctuary.

I glanced at Radley, his eyes reflecting the same unease that gnawed at me.

The uncertainty of our welcome hung in the air. We were stepping into their world where trust was fragile, and any misstep could lead to our demise. Onyx and Imelda had vouched for us, but their words alone couldn't erase the suspicion etched in the glares of the surrounding Rebels.

Before we could consider potentially turning back, the gates creaked open to reveal the bustling community within. Our presence was a gamble—one that could cost us everything.

OUR PROGRESSION through the overgrown streets of the community remained ominous, the first light of morning barely kissing the horizon. The various individuals who greeted us at the gate returned to their posts, the rest of the inhabitants likely asleep due to the early hours, leaving the streets nearly empty. Vegetation reclaimed most of the area. Plants sprouted between the cracks in the asphalt, the foliage extending to the sidewalks. Boards secured the various buildings that once housed bustling businesses, with their former functionality barely notable beneath the apocalyptic wear.

Various fruits and vegetables thrived in the garden beds that lined the storefronts. The blend served as a reminder of how humanity adapted to the wild and cultivated a new world. Sun rays filtered through the trees, casting warmth over the structures and adding a tinge of beauty to a place crafted for survival.

Jasper led the way to a building on the street corner. Its brick remained intact but weathered, a symbol of the haven's resilience. As we approached the door, my eyes snagged on the faded lettering above that read 'Pharmacy.' The distraction became secondary as the familiar jingle of a bell echoed beneath Jasper's movement into the threshold. The four of us followed tightly behind him.

The shelves once stocked with medicine held various weapons, from handguns to bows, and more ammunition than I'd seen since being inside the Walls—transforming the interior from a drugstore into a war room. Maps and charts covered the walls, with colored strings marking varying areas. In the center of the room, there sat a large oak table. Another map sprawled over the top of it, acting as a makeshift tablecloth with notes scribbled in its margins. It became clear the space was the keystone for the operations in their ongoing fight for survival.

Jasper moved toward the table, and we followed, the air dense with unspoken tension. Suddenly, Jasper pivoted, his hand flashing to his thigh holster. I barely had time to react before he leveled a pistol at Radley, his expression remorseless.

"Alright, I will give you one last chance to explain what the hell is going on," he spoke through gritted teeth, moving his glare to Onyx. "And how *dare* you lie to my face with no hesitation. Did you truly think I was that naïve? I would also love to know why he—"

"You had us surrounded, Jasper. What else did you expect me to do?" Onyx exhaled in indignation. "I needed to get you alone so we could talk without a firing squad aiming at our heads. If I'd tried to explain everything, we'd all be dead by now."

"So, what you're saying is that there is a valid reason for us to kill all of you?" A wave of pique rolled through his words as he raised a brow, releasing the safety. "Do you recognize the level of threat that you've brought here, Onyx?"

Tension built as the two stood across from one another, cold-ness billowing off them. Despite the gun raised at my counterpart,

Onyx shifted from his position to my right and side-stepped, placing himself in front of me.

"Will you let me explain, or do you plan to shoot first and ask questions later? We don't have time for stubbornness and emotion to reign over logic."

Jasper's grip on the gun tightened, his knuckles whitening. "I will not ask you again."

"Onyx..." Radley clenched his jaw, the feathering hinting toward unspoken words he wished to utter.

"Do you want the full truth or half-truth?" Onyx questioned, standing with his hands at his sides, unphased by the threat his friend posed.

"I want an explanation as to why you brought them here, and if you lie to me one more godsdamn time, I will kill them both." Jasper hissed, his annoyance palpable.

"I mean, theoretically speaking, that would make my life a hell of a lot easier." Onyx stepped forward, wrapping his hands around the gun barrel before lowering it. "For starters, don't make me make you lower your weapon."

Jasper rolled his eyes as he stepped away, the gun staying at his side as he flipped the safety back on. "Speak."

"They're Venturers, Jasper. Ex-Venturers."

Without hesitation, he disclosed the secrets he warned us to keep private—at least those I'd elected to share.

Immediately, the gun safety flipped off as Jasper raised it to Onyx's chest.

"I already knew they were government pigs," the octaves of anger in Jasper's tone increased. His eyes jutted in Radley's direction and remained there for an extended period. "Why you haven't killed them is beyond me, especially—"

"They *were* government pigs. That's no longer the case. The various higher-ups banished them from the Walls and revoked their privileges. Three Venturers hunted them down with tracking equipment, which I destroyed before you had an aneurysm about it." He wrapped his hand around the gun barrel again, pushing it back toward its position at Jasper's side. "May I also add that Gael was with those who ambushed us?"

His mention suggested that Jasper knew of him, further complicating the story.

Onyx remained before me as he spoke, not shifting from his position. "Many things have happened since we last saw one another that have shifted perspectives. And dare I say it..."

He looked over his shoulder at me, our eyes locking before he turned back to Jasper.

"I trust them."

I trust her.

Jasper glanced down at his boots and chuckled, shaking his head. "You've got to be out of your godsdamn mind, Onyx. Regardless of whether they are or aren't with them any longer, government pigs are beside the point. They allied with those responsible for both our exile from the Walls and the deaths of our people. Just as one of them—"

Onyx was quick to cut him off. "Yeah, just as we are at fault for the deaths of theirs. How many Venturers have you killed, Jasper? We both know that neither of us is innocent in this equation, regardless of who lost their lives. We've all killed people. Every single one of us. Just because one is from within the Walls doesn't make them more or less innocent than you or me."

Jasper's eyes remained low as his jaw tightened at Onyx's words.

We had all taken lives, each accumulating our kill counts, regardless of whether those numbers belonged to Venturers, Rebels, or Scavengers. No person living in our dystopian society remained innocent, no matter which region they inhabited. Even though we all wished that was far from the case.

Jasper slowly raised his head before glancing at Onyx, the tension present on his face. "How do you expect me to explain this to those inhabiting the sanctuary? Do you think everyone here will willingly accept Venturers with open arms after all that? You've got to be—"

"You don't tell them anything." Onyx interrupted Jasper again, "There's no point in disclosing the information when neither poses a threat. They said they would shed their titles as soon as they entered your community. If anything, telling your people will cause further division than what already exists in the Wilds and create further panic. As a leader, do you truly want that?"

Jasper's expression contorted with Onyx's opposition, his eyes tracing between Radley and me. I watched as his fingers constricted around the gun grip once more, his knuckles seeming to glow in protest. "I can't believe you are putting me in this situation."

"I'm surprised you would expect any less from me." Onyx shrugged as he stepped away, pivoting to lean against the table. The simplicity of the movement clarified that he no longer viewed the situation as a threat. "So, what'll it be, Jasper?"

"I'm only going to say this once." Jasper looked at him before shifting his attention to the two of us. "If anyone else finds out that you two were once Venturers, I will pretend we never had this conversation and execute both of you in front of them."

It was a clear sign to protect what was his—something we were all doing in one way or another.

"As for you," he turned back to Onyx before continuing. "If that happens, we will banish you from this community, which means we will terminate your protections from our agreement. Once your stated alliance ceases, the likelihood of you becoming targets, not just for Ventures and Scavengers but also for my people, will increase exponentially."

Onyx nodded. "That's a rational expectation, and I wouldn't anticipate any less from you."

"We will address the *obvious* issue later," Jasper scoffed, expressing his disappointment at receiving a straight agreement instead of some level of negotiation. "They are your responsibility. So, if they act out in any manner that poses a threat—"

"I'll kill them instantly." Onyx's words were bitter as he

continued, "I already planned to do so. They are nothing but numbers to me and bodies to use if necessary."

Once aimed in our direction, the gun slid back into the holster on Jasper's thigh as another deep exhalation of annoyance left him, evidence that Onyx's last words were convincing enough—at least temporarily.

He clenched his jaw as he turned back to Radley and me. "Why did you join the Rebellion after siding with those in power for so long?"

Radley promptly responded before any further questions could be posed. "We had little choice."

"Answer of the century." Imelda finally commented from the corner of the room, lifting her hands and laughing slightly.

Onyx cocked a brow, shaking his head in warning to stay out of the conversation and not test her luck. All things considered, I presumed it was a good call on his end.

Jasper snorted. "Desperation makes strange bedfellows, doesn't it?"

"It's not desperation. It's survival," I interjected, my voice steady. "There's no reason for us to go back when there were many things that drew us away—events yielding discomfort, and it all happened to come to a halt with a recent engagement just before our latest venture."

"What events occurred within the Walls created sudden unease after years of obedience?" Jasper folded his arms over his chest, his sudden prodding surprising me.

"If they detected any level of disobedience, those in applicable positions would detain the opposing person until they set a date for a public execution. Infected or Uninfected, it never mattered." Radley chimed in, his response earning a look of mixed intention from the coppery-haired male.

I watched Onyx clench his jaw, dissenting with the government's actions.

Radley continued, "When dealing with Rebels, there was a transfer of responsibility between officials to relocate them to high-security zones. Venturers, myself and Astrid included, generally lacked entrance authorization, yet there were regular conversations among Venturers about their theories on what transpires there."

"Likely for some level of testing. At least, that would be my guess." Jasper glanced at Onyx. "Based on what we heard during our time serving."

And just like that, I gained an answer.

"You two were soldiers?" I asked, anticipating the answer to my perceived assumptions.

"Regretfully." Onyx raised his eyes to meet mine, still leaning against the oak table with his arms folded tightly over his chest. "We were both Command Officers."

"Commanding Officer." Jasper corrected with a pointed finger in the raven-haired male's direction. "Onyx was the Captain of our unit."

"Not only with the government but high-ranking," I exhaled slightly, thrown off by Radley's sudden silence. "I'd imagine the two of you have a lot of information then."

"Oh, unimaginably. Our positions and what we learned during our service are only one of the many reasons they are hunting me down." Onyx shook his head, pushing himself up from the propped position he was in seconds before. "The outbreak wasn't coincidental."

"Far from," Jasper jumped in, exhaling deeply. "The original aim was population control. The virus was supposed to kill people to secure infrastructure, not turn them into monsters, nor result in the development of supernatural abilities."

Disgust and horror assaulted me, which I presumed was the reason behind Radley's silence. "Wait, they manufactured a virus in-house intending to thin out the population?"

Onyx nodded. "That was the original plan, but it all fell apart once they released it to the general population. It mutated quicker than in the test subjects and became uncontrollable, resulting in all the greatness we experience now."

This was all news to me.

Neither of us had any clue that the government tried to end the lives of hundreds of thousands of people. We all held opinions around the conspiracies we discussed, but nothing quite reached that level.

"The situation you spoke about," Jasper interrupted my thought. "What happened before you headed out to complete your assigned duties?"

"There was an execution scheduled the morning they called us to the outpost building for a mission assignment. As we made our way there, we watched people rush to the courtyard to watch the execution take place." I shook my head to clear the memory from my mind. "Radley and I have never agreed with the government's abrupt willingness to execute people simply for venturing outside the Walls out of curiosity."

"Some people just desire to know more," Radley finally commented beside me.

"Full means to control." Jasper rubbed his hand over his beard, his fingers twisting the hair between them. "They are doing it to keep people leashed in. No one will dare to go against that if everyone knows that questioning or expanding beyond their ideals or what they deem correct is frowned upon and can cost them their lives."

Onyx followed him, "These are the same people who watched the Fall unfold. They saw how easily people get thrown out of their communities without a second thought. No matter if they once worked with the government—were teachers, medical professionals, you name it—nothing kept anyone safe. The government banished or executed them as soon as they perceived them as a direct threat. And after experiencing that firsthand fear, they now believe that compliance is the only thing to ensure their safety and survival."

"So the government keeps up with the story," I looked between them. "They execute to insinuate fear and to spread the message that only those who obey them can continue to live."

I watched as Jasper and Onyx nodded, their expressions revealing a deep unease. The room fell quiet as we all looked at one another, our thoughts mirrored—the corruption stemmed far deeper and darker than we'd imagined.

"What about Gael?" I quickly interjected. "The two of you spoke about him as if you knew him. I wasn't sure if that familiarity was just because of encounters in the Wilds or—"

"He was a Command Officer too, but he worked directly with the President." Jasper sighed heavily. "His involvement leading up to the Fall and afterward was no secret, though he once used to not be bound by the ideals of higher-ups."

My thoughts slipped back to the burning bunker where Gael was left inside, bile building in the back of my throat with the repetitive images. Onyx had intended to end his life without a second thought, even though they shared similar titles at one point.

He meant it when he said he would kill the two of us without batting an eye. Not only that, but he proved himself capable of doing so many times.

Gael, not having been the first.

Our safety was becoming a foreign concept. No matter where we went or who we were with, it seemed nearly impossible to grasp.

I raised my eyes to glance at Onyx, his dark, henley shirt pulled taut against his biceps. The length of his fingers rested on them as the width of his forearms covered the entirety of his chest. His powder-blue eyes remained emotionless regardless of the conversation, although flickering upward to the auburn-haired male beside him in some level of warning as if he desired him not to delve further into their past.

"Speaking of him." He spoke, cutting into the conversation. "I left him pinned to the wall of our burning bunker."

Jasper pivoted, looking over at his friend as surprise spread through his words. "Dead?"

Onyx traced his bottom lip with his tongue before responding. "Who knows? That bastard is slippery as hell. He could have easily escaped. We didn't hang around to find out."

"Good. He had it coming. I'm grateful you got to him before I did because I can't promise I wouldn't have had my way with him before you could." Jasper shifted. "While I hope he is dead, for all that he did, that will put an even greater target on your back because of his importance to McKinley."

"The target is already there." Onyx shrugged as he continued, "His death will not change its size."

"Onyx, I don't think you realize—"

He cut Jasper off. "Realize the consequences of my actions? Jasper, we're both aware that my abilities surpass those of others. We know what I can do, even though I despise most of it."

The ability to stop a bullet mid-air and combust a window by a mere thought.

Teleportation.

Mind reading.

Refined defense and combat skills.

The reality of whom we were walking alongside sunk in, and I couldn't help but feel a confusing mix of anticipation and unease slither through my veins.

Onyx continued, "You and I both know the government's wishes. We have since the beginning. Between our investigation, the countless warnings we received, and what we experienced first-hand—it's no longer a secret. They desire and have desired to use my abilities to end the Rebellion against the Walls and questions within them. If they could get ahold of me, their fear of losing control would become a distant memory." Onyx's iced gaze locked with Jasper's, "And not to be an ass, but the existing target can't get any larger than it already is. Regardless of my actions or the people I kill, they will always want to get their hands on me, and that will not change until they capture me."

A level of distress and concern remained in Jasper's eyes as they raised to look at Onyx. "I hate that I know you are right."

ELEVEN

I knelt beside one of the garden beds, dirt clinging to my fingernails as I harvested vegetables. Radley worked across from me, his light hair catching the early afternoon sun, turning it almost silver against the white of his T-shirt. His usually sharp and focused cerulean eyes seemed dull with exhaustion.

I glanced at the horizon, my fingers still buried in the soil. The sun's golden rays cast a warm glow over the surrounding vegetation, and the remnants of morning dew clung to the leaves, a subtle reminder of the day's early hours.

It had been a few days since our tense encounter with Jasper and the agreement to keep our identities hidden while we stayed within his community. During that time, Jasper wasted no opportunity to put us to work. Gardening and harvesting had become our regular duties, along with taking turns on security patrols along the perimeter. The night before, they'd added guard tower watch to our responsibilities, leaving us running on fumes and limited sleep.

Jasper had made it clear that if we wanted to stay, we had to contribute and prove our worth to the sanctuary.

Onyx had been in and out over the past few days, likely

assigned duties as punishment for bringing us along. It seemed he, too, had to prove himself to Jasper.

With our new routines, our interactions with Onyx became severed. Radley called it a blessing in disguise, but that wasn't how I'd felt. Something about Onyx's presence intrigued me, though I hadn't yet figured out what it was.

Then there was Imelda.

"You almost had me!" Her laughter echoed through the hazy morning air as she darted away from another kid her age. They vanished as quickly as they appeared, her dark hair still visible in the distance.

Radley exhaled in annoyance, pulling my focus from the momentary simplicity that seemed to exist.

"Something wrong?" I asked, using a spade to loosen the soil around a carrot's head.

He yanked a radish from the earth, frustration etched on his face. "Oh, you know. Living the dream."

In the years I'd known him, he thrived on sleep. Considering Jasper's strict expectations, he had gotten little of it, making him a bomb awaiting detonation.

"Wake up on the wrong side of the bed?" I teased, pulling my carrot from the soil and dropping it into the bin beside me.

"More like I didn't sleep long enough to wake up on either side." He tossed the freed radish into the bin with more force than necessary. "Never thought I'd become a farmer by day and a slave by night."

"Yeah, I hear you. I'm running on two hours of sleep and the pure thrill of getting down and dirty with the earthworms." Sarcasm laced my words, and a small smile tugged at the corners of Radley's lips.

He shook his head, chuckling softly as the sound of roots tearing from the earth filled the quiet. I was about to offer another joke when I spotted Onyx exiting a building across the street. For the first time, I noticed a tattoo on his left arm, partially hidden by his usual long sleeves. Its pattern seemed intricate and intentional, encasing a story woven across his skin that seemed far more heart-felt than the scars I'd noticed. He wore his typical outfit—a dark henley, military-style cargo pants, and combat boots. The deep color of his shirt blended with his raven hair, which he'd tied back into a messy bun at the base of his skull.

He shut the door behind him, his usual utility bag missing from his back. Was he free of duty for the day?

His attention landed on Radley and me, his piercing eyes glowing despite the sun's luminous cast. He pivoted and began crossing the street towards us, intention laced in each footstep.

"Heads up. Company," I muttered, glancing at Radley, whose back remained pointed at the approaching male.

"Great. Probably another—" Onyx's sudden appearance cut Radley's complaint short.

"Morning." His voice wrapped with its usual rasp, giving no indication if he'd just woken up or been up as long as we had.

I nodded. "Morning."

"Wow, risen from the dead, huh?" Radley turned slightly, glancing over his shoulder. "I thought your sudden disappearance was a blessing. It seems I spoke too soon."

"It seems we're equally disappointed by our anticipations," Onyx replied dryly. He looked me over, his sharp gaze taking in my disheveled appearance. "You both look like shit, by the way."

His comment, though accurate, was uncalled for.

"Okay, asshole," Radley muttered, standing up and blocking the rising sun from my view.

While Onyx had him beat in muscle, Radley held a couple of inches over him. With their obvious differences, both were intimidating in their own right, even more so when they targeted one another with a murderous intent that would have deemed them enemies under any watchful eye.

Onyx raised an eyebrow. "Problem?"

"*You*. You're the problem." Radley's annoyance flared as he stepped closer to Onyx.

Onyx chuckled before lowering his tone. "Last I checked,

you're alive because of *me*. You have protection and a safe place to stay. Again, because of *me*. I had the option to abandon you in the city, something I should have done given the secrets you possess. Considering it was your fault the bunker was destroyed, I could have stranded you back there as well. But here we stand. You have a roof over your head, food to eat, and clothes to wear. You are free from Runners, other Rebels, and the government you fled."

Radley clenched his jaw, muscles feathering as his fist closed at his side. His knuckles whitened, holding back the desire to unleash on the raven-haired male in front of him in broad daylight. I tensed, ready to step in if needed, as Onyx leaned forward, his face inches from Radley's.

"I kill without remorse, so watch your tone. I am far from the problem here, and you know that." Onyx's bitterness added to my list of questions, burning through the air with warned potency. "If you want, I can quickly become far more than a thorn in your side. It would take seconds to out your truth to everyone, so consider your standing a privilege."

The two men locked in a silent standoff for what felt like minutes, neither refusing to move nor back down. I bit my cheek, contemplating the benefit of my interference as my anxiety spiked with Onyx's retaliation.

Radley finally sighed, shaking his head. "Fine. Have it your way. I'm too tired to argue with someone who's the epitome of crass."

"That says a lot coming from you," Onyx shot back, continuing without allotting enough time for him to be interrupted. "You're off gardening duty for the rest of the day. Jasper wants to speak to us about a few things."

Finally, some good news.

"Did he say what about?" I dusted my clothes off and grabbed the bin.

"Not directly." Onyx didn't move from his spot in front of Radley. "But, if I had to guess, it's probably mission-related. He's still focused on our trip east."

"Is this about those mutated Runners you mentioned?"

Radley, running on fumes and frustration, was a dangerous mix that I knew needed a moment. My pointed queries aimed to keep the Most Wanted user busy before he could prod to the point of eruption.

"Further exploration, yeah." Onyx nodded, finally stepping back. "The Runners out there are different, but I couldn't give Jasper much more insight than that statement. It wouldn't surprise me if he ordered us there to gather more information."

"A scouting mission, then," I said, glancing at Radley, who stood with his arms crossed, still bristling. "Where did he want to meet?"

"The mission debrief room," Onyx replied dryly.

The same place where Jasper nearly killed us days prior.

Lovely.

I nodded. "We'll clean up and head over. We will try not to keep you and Jasper waiting too long."

Onyx looked at me, a slight smirk playing on his lips before he turned to leave. He stepped from the curb, crossing the street and making his way back toward where he'd come from. The breadth of his shoulders spoke minimally of the strength he held, each encounter with him painting an inch more of his truth—a truth I wished to uncover more of.

"Hey, Onyx," Radley called after him, a mischievous glint in his eyes.

Oh gods.

Onyx glanced back, unamused. The minimal grin he'd cast was gone.

"I thought I'd give you my seal of approval. The man bun suits you, considering you're a walking, breathing douchebag."

Onyx smiled, his tongue clicking against his teeth. "It's a title I wear with pride. It's much better than yours—a two-faced government puppet. But we don't have time to delve into those weeds, do we?"

With that, he walked away, leaving Radley speechless and me pondering the deeper meaning behind his words.

I PUSHED OPEN the door to the mission debriefing room, the jingle of the bell announcing our presence. Onyx and Jasper sat at the large oak table, and a map spread out before them with a few new circles marking significant areas. It was clear they had started without us.

Jasper turned his head, his gray eyes narrowing as he examined us. "You finally made it."

"We had some cleaning up to do after our morning shift," I interjected before Radley could speak. "Sorry if we kept you waiting."

We'd snagged a couple of muffins on our way over, which appeased one of Radley's irritations, but the lack of sleep remained and made him unpredictable.

Jasper nodded, accepting the excuse. "We have a lot to discuss. Take a seat."

I crossed the room, pulling out a chair. The cracked leather back rubbed roughly against my hands as I settled in. Onyx sat to my left, and I'd intentionally elected to leave a couple of chairs between us.

Radley dropped into the chair beside me with a heavy sigh. Jasper's gaze bore into us, waiting for us to settle before he began.

"I'm unsure if you recall much of our conversation upon your arrival," Jasper began, a brief pause filling the room. "But Onyx provided some information about a venture he and Imelda took out east."

"We recall," Radley responded sharply, his tone edged with irritation.

Onyx turned his head toward us, giving Radley a pointed look —a firm warning and likely the only one he'd give.

Jasper leaned forward, his fingers interlacing as he rested his elbows on the table. "Good. That saves me from recapping." He kept his tone clipped, a light jab at Radley's agitation.

I exhaled, leaning back in my chair, nudging Radley with my elbow. He returned the gesture with a glare.

"Essentially," Jasper continued, "we need more information on the Runners within this area." He pointed to a marked portion of the map, highlighting a stretch of what once was New Jersey down to North Carolina—Region One. "If Onyx's description is accurate, they may have breached the Walls of Region One. The spread of a mutated infection could outpace the original virus, potentially wiping out the entire infrastructure there."

"So you want us to go into Region One to determine if it's still standing?" I asked, my eyes lifting from the map and finding his gray irises.

"And to gather intel," Radley added, his reply tinged with skepticism. "Haven't Onyx's findings been enough?"

"It would appear your recollection isn't as clear as you stated," Onyx replied evenly, not taking the bait from Radley's tone. "We didn't have enough time to get a full assessment of the Runners out there."

"Why does it even matter when we're across the continent?" Radley's words sharpened. "Life on the East Coast doesn't apply to our survival, so why the hell does it matter what's going on over there?"

Onyx closed his eyes, exhaling deeply to contain his frustration.

"It's a fair question," Jasper responded calmly. "As a Rebellion leader, I need to know the functionality of surrounding walled cities. My people deserve to know what's out there and could potentially threaten their survival. Not only that, but providing that valuable intel to our contacts along the East Coast could strengthen our alliances. It's an opportunity to establish and secure our communities."

"Why not send your men then?" Radley questioned, a hint of consideration notable.

"Because it's time we prove ourselves," Onyx answered before Jasper could. "We've been living within Jasper's walls, benefiting from his hospitality. Now, it's our turn to gather intel and support his community."

There was something in Onyx's tone—a mix of valor and duty that showed he felt he still owed Jasper for all he had given us and his people. I pondered his sacrifices, including secretly housing two individuals with prior alliances against those he had worked so hard to protect.

It was time we proved ourselves.

The room stood silent for a few moments before I decided to speak. "I think it's a fair trade. I'll go to New Jersey."

Jasper nodded, his stern expression softening in appreciation. It was a side of him I'd have yet to see—a glimpse of the man behind the hard exterior of an ex-soldier.

Radley exhaled deeply. "Wherever she goes, I go."

Onyx smirked. "An obedient pup. I expected nothing less."

Anger flared in Radley, his body tensing, his frustration evident.

Before he could respond, Onyx continued, "I was about to say Astrid and I would've been fine without you chaperoning, but it seems you're desperate to tag along. We leave tomorrow morning. Please, for all our sakes, get some rest tonight, *Princess*. The last thing we need to be dealing with is you moping about lack of sleep."

I cleared my throat to keep Radley from going after him, but it was useless. "Truly, your comments have become tiresome. Don't you have anything better to say?"

Glancing at Jasper, I hoped for some interference as they squared off for the second time of the day. Instead of annoyance, a mirrored smirk traced Jasper's lips.

He was enjoying this.

Onyx shrugged, looking down at the map before raising his glower back to Radley. His brows descended to hood his icy glare, its intensity hinting at a deeper story I had yet to uncover.

"I'll keep reminding you of your inadequacies," Onyx said, his reply a deadly promise, "because, as we both know, I have my eyes on far more valuable things."

Radley chuckled, leaning forward. "It's flattering that you're so fixated on me, but you value yourself too highly."

Onyx laughed coldly, happy to continue engaging. "I know my worth, and that's why you see me as a threat. Perhaps we should explore that?"

Silence stretched between them. I waited for Radley to retaliate, but he didn't. The tension grew, seconds turning into minutes.

I cleared my throat again, pushing myself up from the table. "Alright, well, I think that's enough—"

Radley interrupted, barking as he stood. "Do you care to explain why you look at Astrid how you do?"

As soon as the question left him, my cheeks flushed. The conversation took an unexpected turn, traversing a route I never expected. I wasn't sure whether he'd unleashed the snarled interrogation to bite the mention of sharing what they'd discussed in the clearing.

I glanced at Jasper, who remained unfazed, stroking his beard as if he had expected the retaliation.

Onyx raised his brows, amused. "Oh? Did my comment about being a threat get under your skin?"

Radley snarled, "Are you going to keep beating around the question, bastard? Or will you answer a question when it's given to you? Considering your history, I thought you'd know how to respond properly."

"You want to get on my case about being a military dog?" Onyx's retort came through gritted teeth, Radley's prodding hitting a nerve.

A flash of light into his past—a part he preferred to keep buried—an invasion of privacy.

Radley went to speak, but Onyx's anger erupted, his voice rising. The windows rattled as his power surged, bowing to his beckoning wrath.

"That's bold, coming from someone who's been targeting people outside the Walls since the Fall. You've taken orders without question and ridden the laps of anyone who would give you a mission, hoping it'd make you feel something." Onyx glanced at me, adding me into the mix of mindlessness and government affiliation before he turned back to Radley. "It's ironic coming from someone who has put bullets between innocent people's eyes for quite some time. Even more hilarious that you want to sit here with deemed accusations, considering you've blindly obeyed for years regardless of the blood that stains your hands."

"Onyx, I—" I tried to intervene, but my words fell flat.

The floor rumbled as his agitation built. The windows began to strain against their frames, the glass seconds away from shattering as he loosened his hold on his abilities.

"Remember what you did before you crossed me," Onyx continued sternly. "Before you label me, think about your prior missions, the orders you followed, and who you served."

I swallowed hard, his pushback heavy with indignation.

"At least I held the logical decency to question things and consider the inhumanity weaved into the surrounding operations. With empathy, a trait you lack, I took a step back and observed the bigger picture of the unfolding shit show. I took the time to sympathize with those around me, suffering at the hands of those they figured were there to protect them—those they trusted to keep them safe. I stepped away from all that on my own, regardless of what it cost me—making the conscious decision to do so *myself.* Not simply because my counterpart started looking into the depth of the buried corruption. Not simply because the girl I desperately desired to stick my dick into went against protocol."

"Onyx." Jasper's interference served as a warning.

My breath caught in my chest as the color drained from my face.

"How dare you—" Radley tried to speak, but Onyx wasn't done.

"How dare I what? Call you out for how desperate you are for Astrid to bat an attracted eye your way? I can spot a hopeless man from a mile away. The desire you have to—"

"Enough." Jasper snapped, glancing between the two of them. "Onyx, you're twenty-seven years old. Act like it. Walk a damn lap to cool off. This level of disrespect is frowned upon within my community regardless of previous standing, and you know that."

Onyx muttered a curse under his breath as he turned on his heel. The vibration of the build in pressure put on the surrounding windows stopped suddenly. His broad frame headed for the door, shoving it open before stepping outside. The morning sun consumed him in white light as he vanished from our view.

Jasper turned to look at Radley, shadows highlighting his face even though he remained beside me.

"I suggest you learn how and when to control your anger," Jasper said, his tone a blend of disappointment and warning. "People's pasts aren't weapons to be wielded. You should understand that well enough, Radley."

Fumbling through the references to Radley's past, I began to speculate the possibility of something existing that dove beyond the surface—something even I didn't know about and dismissed as mere coincidence.

I contemplated what had triggered Onyx's outburst—whether it was a blind reference to a military dog or even the mention of answering questions obediently when given. Whatever yanked the cord had triggered a darkness, and I couldn't help but wonder what the shadows contained.

Jasper sighed, his gaze sweeping over us before continuing.

"Some things are best left buried. Unless you are ready to deal with the monster unleashed when disturbed and awakened."

146

TWELVE

Tomorrow.

We were leaving tomorrow.

I exhaled deeply, my boots connecting with the asphalt beneath me as I executed my tenth lap through the community streets. I wasn't sure if I was walking aimlessly to distract myself from what had happened or simply trying to clear my head.

After the explosive argument in the mission debrief room, Radley had opted to return to our shared space for some much-needed rest. I hadn't hesitated to suggest he do exactly that, not just for his sake but for everyone else's.

As for Onyx, I hadn't spotted him during my rounds, which wasn't surprising considering the heated exchange between him and Radley.

I offered a gentle smile to the men who passed me, their rifles slung over their shoulders—a clear indication they had just returned from patrol.

"Afternoon, Astrid," one greeted, dipping his chin in acknowledgment.

"Afternoon," I replied.

The others mirrored his expression, returning the pleasantries I extended. Their boots progressed, moving past me without any further engagement. They were eager to rest after a day of courageous protection, walking alongside Jasper's leadership without question—the same commitment that shifted my frame of mind day by day.

I glanced in the direction they had come from to find another group of men making their way to fill the vacancies. Among them was the very person who had been occupying my thoughts.

Onyx extended an arm, patting one of them on the shoulder as the conversation progressed. Expressions of admiration and adoration on each of their faces as they listened to whatever he had to say. Onyx spoke the words evenly as the corner of his mouth cast skyward. Considering that a line of disinterest was frequently drawn there, the sight alone was one for the history books.

A Captain.

That's what he had been before the Fall—a continuation of the mannerisms painted before me.

They nodded in agreement or acknowledgment before shifting toward their designated area. One of them extended a hand to Onyx, and a brief shake was provided before pulling away and progressing with the others.

Onyx watched momentarily as if the send-off had created some unease before he turned toward me. The snide grin vanished the instant his gaze connected with mine.

Lovely.

He strolled toward me, hands burrowed into his pockets. His hair had come loose from the bun, cascading in subtle waves to his shoulders.

"You have a thing for spying on me, it would seem," he remarked, his tone laced with a hint of challenge.

"To be frank, I was walking around aimlessly and happened to land where you were out of pure luck."

Suppose we wanted to call it that.

"And *chose* to stick around." He raised an eyebrow, not letting me off easily.

There was no winning with him.

"I'll give it to you," he continued, smirking. "For electing to stick around instead of hunkering in your room out of utter avoidance—unlike some."

"He *chose* to take a breather," I said, defending Radley, though I knew it was a losing battle.

Onyx's grin turned devious. "Right."

"What is your issue, anyway?" I demanded, my patience wearing thin. "One moment, you're perfectly civil, and the next, you're unbearable, as if there's been no progress toward decency between us."

"Decency?" He mocked, the snarkiness in his question impossible to miss. "Don't mistake tolerance for propriety."

"How eloquent of you to use such tasteful vocabulary while continuing to be a prick," I retorted, glaring down my nose at him despite our difference in size.

"Is that a compliment I'm sensing?"

"Don't flatter yourself."

"Oh, Astrid," he murmured, his voice dropping an octave. "Flattery is my area of expertise."

I cleared my throat, my cheeks warming at his sudden shift in demeanor. Or, at least, the transition that he seemed to extend.

He leaned forward, his lips brushing against my ear. "If you think I directed that at you, you're drastically mistaken."

I stepped back, my face flushing from embarrassment to irritation in a split second. I swallowed the frustration, my glare locking with his icy blue eyes that glinted in amusement.

"Aw, don't look so disappointed."

"What is there to be disappointed in when nothing was appealing about you in the first place?" I hissed, my jaw tightening at the end of the query.

"Except for my eloquent language?" He chuckled, and his lips curled further. "Right, we can play pretend."

"Pretend that you're enticing?" I laughed, low and bitter. "You're so egotistical that you don't acknowledge that both demeanor and personality matter. Given how vile you are, it's no wonder you lack any semblance of intimacy. Being around you is miserable enough. I can't imagine anyone wanting to be with you."

The words flew out of my mouth before I could stop them, the bite behind them not fully registering until they had landed.

His tongue trailed over his lips, his chin dipping as he looked down before returning his glower to mine. His smile faltered momentarily, something dark and pained flashing in his eyes before he quickly masked it.

He chuckled, the sound gravelly and low. "Do you suck with that bite?"

I clenched my fists at my sides, fury building inside me. "Do you treat every woman this way? Like a mindless, prick-driven asshole?"

He lifted a brow, his smirk returning. "Assuming my sexuality now, are we?"

"Oh right, you are what you eat, so it would make sense that you swing both ways," I shot back, not missing a beat.

Another demeaning chuckle.

Another glint beneath his eyes.

Our engagement was merely an enjoyable game to him.

"You know, considering our conversation back at the bunker about being able to pick better insults, I would *almost* say I'm proud of you for your retaliations. I knew your logic and mouth were rather useful—"

My knuckles connected with the side of his face before he could utter another word. The feeling of his flesh colliding with them pulled me back to reality. Adrenaline covered the pain that sprawled across my hand, my vision returning to normal from the tunneled rage that had encapsulated it moments before.

The same realization I had when I slapped him during our verbal clash returned.

Except this time, it had been a closed fist.

"Hey!" Jasper hollered, rushing toward us.

Onyx staggered slightly, bringing a hand to his mouth to wipe away the blood that now stained his teeth. I braced myself for the retaliation, expecting a deadly glare or worse, but instead, he grinned—wild and almost unhinged.

"I'll give it to you," he began, spitting blood onto the asphalt. "You know how to punch."

"My hell," Jasper groaned, his gaze bouncing between us as he approached. "What the hell is going on?"

I opened my mouth to explain, but the words wouldn't come. I was still reeling from what I'd done and the shock of landing a punch on the strongest, Most Wanted power wielder alive.

"Harmless bickering," Onyx said smoothly, filling in for me as I struggled to find my voice.

"Harmless? Is that what we're calling it now?" Jasper echoed, his gray eyes narrowing in disbelief. "That's why she rocked your shit, right?"

I bit down on the laugh that threatened to escape.

Onyx spat another mouthful of blood onto the ground, the dark red nearly blending into the asphalt. "Oh, if you could, for one second, stop mother-henning."

Jasper rolled his eyes. "I'm just surprised, considering I can't remember the last time someone landed a hit on you."

"I'm sorry," I finally said, my voice quieter than intended.

Onyx raised an eyebrow. "Apologizing now?"

"Onyx," Jasper warned, his tone sharp.

"By gods, let me finish," Onyx hissed at the copper-haired male before turning back to me. "An apology isn't necessary. If anything, I deserved it."

"He definitely did," Jasper added, drawing a reluctant smile from me.

Onyx punched his shoulder, forcing Jasper to sway slightly. "Ass."

"Don't you have somewhere to be?" Jasper asked, glancing pointedly at Onyx.

"Yeah, I do," Onyx replied, his eyes resting on me for a moment longer. "I guess I got a little distracted."

Before I could say anything else, he turned, heading in the direction Jasper had come from. There was no parting retort or biting comment—just a lingering glance that left me feeling guilty about our interaction.

I watched him go, the words I wanted to say stuck in my throat. *I'm sorry that I spewed blind hatred at you. My unfiltered retaliation wasn't an accurate portrayal of how I see you. I don't believe any of the accusations they've made about you.*

As if sensing my implicit thoughts and open mind, Onyx glanced over his shoulder. He smirked, dropping his chin—a look of knowing and understanding—before he continued forward.

An implied interaction.

Jasper exhaled, rubbing his eyes with his thumb and pointer finger. "Let's take a stroll."

SILENCE FELL between us as we walked the outskirts of the community. Varying smells clung to the air, the most prominent belonging to pine and earth. Their combination provided a freshness that served as a nostalgia for much simpler times. The crisp air filled my lungs, and I savored the rare moment of peace from the turbulence that defined our survival.

My gaze wandered to the trees surrounding the sanctuary's perimeter. Their leaves rustled in the timid breeze, their overarching presence mirroring sentinels responsible for providing protection. The dense barrier of the canopy provided a reclaimed sense of security in a timeless and unwavering world, almost as if Mother Nature disagreed with all that happened and worked to shield those standing in opposition.

Jasper released a breath, breaking the silence between us. "For starters, I believe I owe you an apology."

I turned to face him, my braid sliding down my back. The sun's rays highlighted the copper tones of his hair, giving him a near-ethereal glow. "What do you mean?"

"For how reactive I was when you first arrived," he clarified, stepping closer. "Even if I don't always portray correctly, my defensiveness is rooted in good intention."

I shook my head. "You don't need to apologize for protecting your people—for protecting yourself."

"I do, though." His retort was immediate, his eyes softening. "You didn't deserve my reactivity, regardless of the vigilance behind it."

"Well, thank you," I replied, offering a sympathetic smile. "I appreciate the concern, but I want you to know that I understand where you're coming from—at least as much as I can."

I swallowed after the words left, knowing the reaction they brewed within Onyx when I had spoken to him similarly. The attempt resulted in emotional shutdown and corresponding hostility, even though it had been a mere effort to stick out a hand for a man who seemed to be drowning.

"So, no, you don't fully get it. Not yet."

There was depth to Onyx—a complexity mirrored in how he interacted with his men, protected Imelda, and led his community with unwavering commitment. Despite the continuous avoidance and heated exchanges, a part of me wished to understand him better and see the layers beneath his hardened exterior.

Jasper interrupted my thoughts, the sun catching his hair. "I hope you know that how you see others doesn't go unrecognized."

"I don't know," I admitted, sighing deeply. "Sometimes, I feel like I struggle to see people for who they are instead of who I'd like them to be."

"Onyx?" Jasper chuckled reassuringly.

My shoulders dropped as I looked at him. "Is it that obvious?"

He grinned, the gray in his eyes glinting with unspoken stories. "He's complicated."

"You don't say?"

Another chuckle. "I've known him for years, and there have still been far too many occasions where I've wanted to either pummel him or put my hands around his throat."

"I'm not sure if that's a good or a bad thing," I laughed, embracing the warmth he brought.

It became clear why the people here stood by him, unmoved amid desolation. He wasn't just a leader to those who followed him; he was a friend and someone they knew they could trust and confide in.

"Onyx is..." Jasper shook his head, his grin growing infectiously. "He can be infuriating, but he's also incredibly loving and deserving of far more than he's received, even though he doesn't believe it. His life has been far from decent, but that isn't my story to share. The most I can offer is a base-level explanation of why he is the way he is—why he operates with that perfectly curated, hardened asshole exterior. There are reasons he's closed himself off so effectively—honestly, so godsdamn efficiently that it's a headache to get him to lower the walls he's built."

I pondered countless instances where we had clashed, and I regretted my words almost as soon as they left my mouth. Each time, I sensed his attempts to avoid connection, to hide who he truly was.

"Loss," I said, the breeze catching the loosened strands from my braid. "He's fearful of it."

Jasper's throat bobbed as he averted his gaze. "Incredibly."

"I believe it would be a lie to say we all aren't afraid of it, at least in some capacity."

"It would." His admittance was soft, as if some of him had struggled to vocalize it.

"He closes himself off to avoid attachment, so when he loses someone, it doesn't hurt as much." I sighed, understanding the logic behind it. "I get it."

"There were many questionable things we did during our time serving—decisions he had to make as a leader. And I know those actions still haunt him. Not only that but our experiences leading up to the Fall..." Jasper's voice trailed off as if weaving together a story of inferred words. "Monsters continue to lurk in the shadows, and Onyx does his best to keep them concealed for the betterment of others—but more so, for himself and his sanity."

The weight of his words was palpable, filling the silence that followed. Onyx had been no exception to the trauma that haunted those who'd survived the Fall. Yet, he carried it with an unwavering resolve that both fascinated and frustrated me.

"His valiancy, amidst it all, is what I admire most." Jasper's voice cut through the stillness. "The government's portrayal of him has crafted a false expectation of who he is—a villainized version of a man who has done nothing but fight for those who can't fight for themselves. They've demonized and demoralized him to justify their actions and keep people in line."

The higher-ups endlessly reminded every Venturer and living person in the Walls that Onyx was a ruthless enemy and danger to society. But the more I saw him, the more I realized how much of that was a fabrication—a story crafted to serve the government's agenda.

"So yes," Jasper continued. "He is nearly impenetrable emotionally and a labyrinth of complexity, but I can promise he is worth exploring. The male you will find underneath it all is someone you will never have the grace of experiencing."

"How you speak about him is beautiful."

"Even doing so, I don't feel it's an accurate portrayal of my feelings for him." His lips shifted in a tight line as if he were holding something back. "Onyx doesn't view himself this way, but he is a beacon for hundreds, if not thousands, of people. His impact is indescribable, and the government's obsession with him stems from fear. Fear of his power, his influence, and what he represents—a force of change and a challenge to their control. They know he's the symbol of resistance for the Rebellion, and that terrifies them."

Those in power became expert manipulators to counteract Onyx's influence, currating their definition of opposition to enforce falsified beliefs. While executions took place for those who traveled outside of the mapped expectation, others had learned and were conditioned not to question the slaughter and to even advocate for punishment. Venturers who believed they protected the last remnants of our world failed to acknowledge imprisonment and hand-offs of power wielders, regardless of their shared humanity.

All attempts to leverage Onyx's abilities had been to instill fear and obedience inside the Walls and fill the holes in their fabrication. Those responsible for safeguarding protection stripped away the concept of humanity, and government ideology and policy enforcement remained, even in the aftermath of destruction. And while the assumption remained that control lay in their hands, it had been far from the truth.

The government's relentless obsession with the man who had stood in opposition from the beginning led to overlooking their grand scheme.

Onyx had strung the delusion of security remaining within the Walls, a fortified personification of their attempts to keep their lies and secrets contained. While those within them yielded to the belief, he persisted in the Wilds as the most significant obstacle, unwavering in conflict with opposition from what he freed himself from and all they attempted to deceive.

His story and impact were of heightened degree, complexity, and entanglement, interlacing it all; those in power knew that. Yet, he shifted into the monster they drafted him to solidify the standing they assumed they had, which he could effortlessly destroy.

The ghost of a memory surged, and I pushed it down, breaking the encompassing stillness, "Considering the complexities and the time you have known him, what do you suppose is the best way to navigate the labyrinth, that is, Onyx Oakes?"

"Honestly," Jasper dipped his head, the sunlight dancing across his near-blonde lashes. "Give him a chance. That's all he needs."

THIRTEEN

The moon reached its apex in the sky, casting a silver glow over the community as night came to a close. The sounds of day faded into a quiet hum; the distant rustle of leaves and the occasional call of settling birds were all that remained to signify life.

Gazing into the darkness, I stood at the edge of the community, my thoughts a mixed bag of emotions and uncertainties, opposing one another like the shade of black that clung to the night regardless of the moon's presence.

My thoughts settled on the mission to New Jersey, its weight on my mind as dense as lead. A part of me hoped that night would provide ease, but the shrouded seclusion merely amplified every potential outcome I seemed to fixate on.

Radley approached, the grass muting his footsteps. "Can't sleep?"

I shook my head, staring skyward. "There's far too much on my mind."

He nodded, opting to give me space and not push the conversation further. Silence clung between us for a while, the night embracing with open arms. Even though we didn't speak, him staying comforted me—though something inside me knew there was more to it than mere simplicity, and it'd become a nagging feeling I couldn't quite place.

"Tomorrow is going to be difficult for numerous reasons," he said, breaking the silence. "And even with Onyx's continuous ability to grate my nerves, I know we will get through it. We always do."

I turned toward him, the moonlight highlighting half of his face. A level of sincerity remained in his gaze, but there was a flick of something hidden—something he refused to tell me—and I couldn't help but feel betrayed by his secrecy. Which, ultimately, made me the world's greatest hypocrite.

"I've been meaning to ask you something." I started, derailing his reassurance while biting back my hesitation. "Back in the mission debrief room, when Onyx and you were arguing, what did he mean by 'who you served under'?"

His expression tightened, the easy camaraderie of the moment vanishing. "You know my past isn't something I like to discuss."

"I know," I whispered. "I guess I just wanted to ask if there was something you needed to tell me before we left tomorrow."

Radley sighed, his shoulders sagging under the strain of secrecy, all while mine held their own weight. "We both served— you and I—as well as him. I took orders like I'm sure he did, but it was never about loyalty. I did it to survive and protect myself and those I cared about—who I care about—*you*."

"But what about now?" I pressed, walking a thinning line.

"There isn't a now, Astrid. Not when it comes to government affiliation." He looked away, his jaw clenched. "I made choices I regret, but they were necessary. For hell's sake, we all have, but I need you to trust me."

In our world, the most minute misstep could shatter trust to the point of no repair. It became our currency, something we traded selectively with others, deeming those deserving of it while revoking it from others.

I trusted no one.

"I do," I replied, swallowing everything else I wanted to say.

"But I need you to trust me, too, and that comes with sharing our pasts. We have made mistakes and done things we wished we didn't have to. For as long as we've known one another, I hope you'd be comfortable informing me of your truths and anything that might put us at risk."

He nodded, his eyes meeting mine. "I am, and I will. I promise."

I tried to allow his vow to sink in and provide the reassurance I desperately needed. We both knew trust was delicate and rarely earned. And while I did trust him, something felt different. The risks were higher, and the end goals seemed elusive as the shadows of our past began overlapping with the present.

I wanted to know his reasoning for refusing to confide in me, and I couldn't help but find myself questioning where I'd faltered in our relationship. Even in my uncertainties, I understood far too well why he'd elected not to—there were things neither of us shared with anyone—not even each other. His past, his decisions, and the orders he had followed created a void that felt impossible to bridge. Whereas my past, the secrets I held, and the motives beneath the surface became near-impenetrable.

Neither of us could cross the barrier we'd created with each other without risking everything we'd built.

Radley broke the silence again, drawing me from my internal dilemma. "Do you ever find yourself imagining the alternate paths our lives might have taken if the world hadn't collapsed?"

I exhaled slowly, his question holding more weight than I wanted to address. "Sometimes, but it feels redundant to do so when our reality is too far from the peacefulness I wish for. It's becoming increasingly difficult to remember how things were before the Fall, so framing a fantasy around the idea seems impossible to grasp."

He nodded, a shadow of contemplation passing over his face. "Yeah, I've found my recollections becoming blurry as the years pass. I suppose envisioning something that isn't this takes away from all we lost. The lives, the people, the relationships—the humanity."

"Every loss haunts me," I admitted, my eyes burning with unshed tears. "Even before the Fall, when I lost my brother, and after when I lost connections that meant the world to me. It all torments me. But I know if I let the regret consume me, it blinds me to what we fight for."

Radley sighed, the melancholy in his eyes deepening. "I know you're right, but I'd be lying if I said there are never nights when the ghosts of my decisions keep me awake."

"We all bear the scars of regret," I offered, attempting to reassure myself of all I was. "But our pasts are unchangeable and interwoven tapestries. Our only choice is to move forward and retaliate for all those we've lost and everything we've sacrificed."

The cerulean hue of his irises shimmered as he pondered the honesty behind my words, stillness looming between us. The kindling of resolve faded, and a level of questioning appeared.

"Is something on your mind?" I asked, my brows furrowing.

"I didn't envision our night turning into an interrogation, so I won't ask but tell you instead." Radley's jaw tightened, his chest rising with a deep inhale as he turned toward me. "Neither of us is obligated to share our demons, especially if they are areas we are ashamed of. But I want to let you know that, just as you offered to me, you can confide in me if you need. Always."

His sincerity caught me off guard as he extended a moment of vulnerability—one that exposed the layers of our friendship and the trust we'd worked to establish.

Words caught in my throat, and I hesitated. There was an array of things I wished to tell him, and so much I needed to say but couldn't. The secrets I held were a crushing weight that threatened to suffocate me and reminded me of the thin line I walked. In our world, alliances shifted, and our loyalties were constantly tested, leaving established relationships one of the only things to rely on. And yet, even in that regard, there remained too much uncertainty of the potential of catastrophic consequences —some I was far too familiar with.

"I'm working through something on my own," I sputtered, part of me wondering if admitting it would do more harm than good. "I just need you to trust that it'll be okay."

His eyes searched mine, a mixture of concern and frustration flickering in their depths. "I get it. I do. Just promise me you'll be careful through whatever turbulence you're navigating, and if it comes down to it, you'll ask for my help if needed."

"I will," I whispered, hoping the two words would provide enough reassurance.

The tension eased slightly, but doubt remained on both ends. We stood there, silence enveloping us again, and I couldn't help but find my thoughts wandering to Onyx. He was an enigma, something I couldn't piece together, and that was the most frustrating component of it all.

His figure appeared at the edge of the clearing as if on cue. He moved quietly, eyes scanning the darkness as if searching for something. When his gaze found us, he paused, a flicker of unspoken words radiating from his eyes.

"Couldn't sleep?" he asked, his voice carrying across the distance.

"Seems to be a common problem tonight," Radley replied unbothered.

"I planned on giving the pep talk tomorrow, but I suppose I can offer it tonight." Onyx's stare clung to me for a moment longer before he turned to Radley. "We need to be prepared for tomorrow. Believe me when I tell you, any misstep will become immediately consequential."

"We know," I said, though he'd aimed his words at the man beside me. "We've weighed the potential outcomes and understand the pertinence of preparation far more than you're giving us credit for."

His eyes searched mine, looking for answers. Their depth held a complexity that intrigued and unsettled me. It was as if he could see straight to the core of who I was.

Of who I was afraid of him knowing.

"We need to work together," he breathed through the warning. "All of us. Regardless of disagreement or prior opposition."

I nodded, feeling the weight and seriousness of his words and using them as a play on mine. "Believe me when I tell you we'll make it work."

Onyx's expression softened slightly, a hint of a smile playing at the corners of his mouth. "Oh, I believe you."

FOURTEEN

I stood in the center of what looked to be an old park, the fragments of Jersey City looming beyond. Jasper's words from the day before consumed my thoughts.

The buildings before us once stood tall and proud, defining function and prosperity. Now, they were ghosts of a world long gone. I could almost hear the echo of car horns and the rush of footsteps from a morning commute, but the ominous slosh of water against the land we stood on replaced the city's once-thunderous livelihood. The rising sun cast a spotlight on the city, painting the slight cloud cover in purplish pink and orange hues —a scene reminiscent of a painter's canvas.

Some skyscrapers that once housed thriving businesses now lay toppled, their jagged edges and twisted metal the only remnants. Those that remained amidst destruction cast long, taunting shadows onto the surroundings, their exteriors riddled with holes and missing sections. The contrast between the warm hues of the sky and the harsh lines of the buildings created an unnatural divide as if the city warned us to stay away.

"Welcome to the home of one of the first attacks," Onyx said beside me.

I glanced at Radley on my other side, the backpack he bore,

hugging him tightly. Before teleporting into desolation, we had equipped ourselves for the dangers we might face—mutated Runners and other threats. While Radley and I gathered weapons, Onyx argued with Imelda about staying behind at the camp. He insisted it wasn't up for debate and that she would answer to Jasper until we returned. Disappointment had been evident in her voice; she had wanted to leave the Rebellion's walls just as much as we did. But her concern for Onyx, I knew, ran deeper than just wanting to stretch her legs.

"Looks lovely," Radley remarked sarcastically.

I returned my gaze to the skyline. "It seems mercy was an incomprehensible thought to those who deemed these attacks necessary."

"They dropped twelve consecutive bombs on this portion alone," Onyx stated, his tone unrevealing emotion. "They figured if they hit the city hard enough, there wouldn't be anything left for opposition to cling to."

"And they were mistaken."

As if in response, a snarled shriek echoed from the canopied structures, reminding us of the unknown threats that awaited our arrival.

Onyx nodded silently before stepping forward, heading toward the crumbling walkway into the city. He didn't offer any explanation for the inhuman noise, and neither Radley nor I bothered to prod. I exchanged glances with Radley, who smiled softly before we followed Onyx.

The pathway was mostly intact, enough that we had a clear route, though some sections had tumbled into the harbor below. We carefully navigated the gaps, using the remnants of cement blocks to continue our journey. The destruction became more pronounced the closer we got to the heart of the city. The pathway became far more treacherous, speaking to the President's goals for the more populated areas—pure and utter annihilation.

With each step, the tension between us grew. The silence was thick, laden with our implied fears and expectations. Each distant sound added to the sense of impending danger, but Onyx moved with determined grace, his eyes scanning our surroundings with perfected vigilance.

Before we left the community, he clarified that he would conserve his energy, anticipating the likelihood of hordes. He had briefed us on the variances in the Runners due to how their body responded to the virus. Where some were what we'd typically expect, others had adapted to creatures far more disturbing than anything we'd dealt with, which was exactly why they'd observed from a safe distance. He'd been clear to elaborate that their once-human features had turned monstrous, with speed and strength far beyond the ordinary and more on par with a wielder.

He had also warned us about the possibility of encountering Scavengers on this side of the continent, those who were once Rebellion members but separated due to opposition in beliefs and were willing to kill anyone who opposed them—two very different but equally deadly threats. With the varied risks, Onyx demanded we stay on high alert, emphasizing that our mission would only last until sunset—not a second longer.

Jasper had been adamant about that, just as those responsible for designated Venturer missions had been. It became apparent that, even in the Wilds, surviving past sunset in a city crawling with Runners—especially those who were further mutated— didn't pose any livable outcome.

"The attacks over there were even worse," Onyx interrupted, pointing to the skyline of New York City beyond the water. "They wanted to destroy every route between the two cities. It worked, which is good considering what we've seen here. I can only begin to imagine what lurks over there."

"You haven't had the balls to find out?" Radley's sarcasm dripped from his query, the strife between the two still palpable.

"When you see what's in this city, you'll understand why." Onyx's response came clipped, unwilling to argue further. "Once we approach the city's opening, I want both of you armed. Safety's off."

I nodded, recognizing the sharpness in his voice as the voice of experience. It'd come from the pieces of him that'd witnessed the Runners on this side of the continent firsthand and someone who'd been in operative missions in the past—a well-knowledge-able soldier.

As if echoing my thoughts, Onyx continued gravely, "Imelda and I observed without engaging, and that was far enough. With us stepping into the innards of the city, there won't be time for bantering. If we want to survive, we have to drop all of the bull-shit and result in reliance."

I glanced over my shoulder at Radley, raising an eyebrow. He sighed, nodding in reluctant agreement with Onyx's assessment.

"Got it," he muttered.

I turned my attention back to Onyx, his broad shoulders pulling at the fabric of the forest green henley he had swapped for the usual black. Compared to us, he stood practically unarmed. While Radley and I were with an array of weapons—crossbow, assault rifle, handguns, and machete—Onyx carried only a handgun on his thigh and a hunting knife on his hip.

Considering the threat we faced, he seemed underprepared. Then again, did he need weapons when his abilities were more powerful than any arsenal?

We stayed buried in our thoughts for the rest of the walk, contemplating the dangers that awaited us. Instead of analyzing the inevitable further, I recalled Onyx's conversation with Jasper before we'd left.

"If we don't make it back, please take care of her for me."

Onyx's boots were the first to cross the threshold between the pathway and the city, a silent declaration that there was no turning back. With our weapons drawn and safeties off, we followed him into the heart of the city's ruins.

The air grew colder, and the shadows became more oppressive as the skyscrapers loomed above us. It was a labyrinth of decay and restfulness, where the past haunted and the future remained uncertain. The morning sun struggled to make an appearance through the dense cloud cover. The wind ripped through empty streets, carrying the faint echoes of a reality that no longer existed.

Onyx led us, his movements nearly indecipherable as his eyes scanned every shadow and dark alleyway. Radley and I mirrored his caution, our weapons readied for use.

The silence magnified every noise, no matter how small, as the city seemed to hold its breath in anticipation. My ears perked as rusted metal groaned against itself, a clatter of debris following to disturb the deafening stillness that suffocated us.

Onyx stopped suddenly, raising a hand and halting us in our tracks.

Stopping.

Listening.

Observing.

The quiet stretched on, unnatural and oppressive. Something was wrong.

"Don't drop your guard," Onyx muttered, barely audible. "We'll start sweeping the buildings. The likelihood of a run-in increases exponentially once we're inside."

We both nodded, acknowledging his command.

He progressed toward one of the last remaining skyscrapers, its structure still largely intact despite the destruction surrounding it. Shards of glass clung to each frame, leaving the ground-floor windows shattered. Creeping vines covered the sides of buildings, weaving through the cracks in the weathered bricks.

Onyx slipped inside with a practiced ease. I followed, carefully placing my hand on the frame to avoid the remaining glass. As I swung my leg over, Onyx reached out to help, his calloused hand wrapping around mine. There was a momentary warmth in his touch, my body surging with newfound energy. As soon as I'd embraced it, it vanished, proving to be a fleeting connection between us that couldn't be fully savored. Once inside, he released me, the moment of gentleness replaced by his usual guarded demeanor.

Radley grumbled as he climbed through the window, his tall frame making the maneuver look effortless. The three of us had barely taken a step forward when a shriek pierced the silence, echoing through the building from the floors above. Onyx's jaw tightened, his body rigid as another screech sounded from a different direction. With each echo, another followed, creating a sinister orchestra that seemed to signify a communication method and an alert of our presence.

I opened my mouth to speak, but a voice cut through my thoughts—Onyx's, clear and firm, though his lips hadn't moved.

"Don't."

It took a moment for the realization to sink in.

He infiltrated my thoughts.

I glanced at Radley, who looked equally bewildered, but I had no time to process it. Onyx's words echoed in our minds again, far more urgently.

"We move quietly. Neither of you speak. I'll give instructions telepathically. We can't afford to draw attention. Watch your steps, control your breathing, and move in silence."

We nodded, the gravity of his words sinking in. It was no longer just about survival but about outsmarting the Runners that awaited us.

The reception area resembled a graveyard of forgotten lives, the remnants of office furniture and personal belongings strewn in chaotic disarray. Dust-covered desks lay overturned, their surfaces littered with yellowed papers and broken computer monitors. Scars of violence marked the walls—bullet holes and burn marks—telling the story of the madness that had unfolded here. The once-busy elevators were twisted wrecks; their cables snapped, and doors hung off their hinges.

We rounded a corner and came to a stairwell. Onyx paused, glancing over his shoulder, electing to speak verbally. "It seems clear. Let's move to the next level."

As I stepped onto the landing of the second floor, a gun cocked, echoing through the stairwell.

"Don't move another step." The command was sharp, female, and interlaced with venom.

We froze, weapons at the ready, as Onyx slowly turned to face the source of the threat. Radley and I followed suit, our eyes locking onto the woman who had appeared behind us.

She was striking—fire-red hair braided loosely over one shoulder, her face framed by dark brows that sharpened her glare. Her deep brown eyes were filled with a familiar mix of anger and betrayal as she leveled a handgun at Radley. The uniform she wore was unmistakable—she was a Venturer. The material clung tightly to her body, highlighting every curve of her figure. Each of her forearms had guards for further protection in case she was to be attacked by a Runner. A belt of knives surrounded her hips, an electric baton on her opposing side, and a katana poked out from behind her shoulder, speaking to her well-versed capabilities.

Before either Onyx or I could speak, Radley beat us to it. "Adira?"

The familiarity of her name on his tongue brought forth a wave of shock. Instead of lowering her gun in recognition, she held her position. Her glower was deep and extended through Radley, training it on the raven-haired male who'd led the charge.

"Why're you with *him*?"

Him.

"Adira, listen." Radley calmly pleaded, memories surging with the sympathy in his voice and creating a yearning for the side of him I'd been used to before we'd joined the Rebellion.

"I don't give a damn about anything else you tell me, Radley. I asked one question, and I want it answered. Why are you with him?"

Onyx intervened before Radley could follow, "Do you care to explain where your counterparts are?"

Onyx struck a nerve with his question, the taunt behind his words igniting a fire as he held mirrored her sneer. I knew how she felt, being stared down by the male deemed the most significant threat to the Walls.

I looked at her, speaking with composure and an aim to soothe the situation: "I suggest you lower your weapon before putting yourself in a situation you don't want to be in. We aren't here to cause issues."

"Adira, stop and think for a moment." Radley positioned his hands near his shoulders, his palms open to display the truth behind my negotiation. "We are in a stairwell of a building likely infested with Runners. Yeah, you could shoot one of us right now. Hell, maybe even all three of us. But think about what would happen to you, even if you were successful in doing so."

She shifted in her stance, a flash of consideration rolling through her eyes. But as quickly as it had been there, it was gone.

She clenched her jaw, her brows narrowing even further. "Radley, I want an answer. Why are you with *him?*"

Onyx chuckled, his gaze assaulting her. "Him? Now, is that the proper way to address someone? The least you could do is ask for my name, considering I now know yours, Adira." He articulated the vowels of her name sharply. "Respectfully, wouldn't you enjoy getting to know the man responsible for the deaths of those you're allied with? As well as the one who is about to be responsible for yours?"

I knew it was a mirage, but my stomach still plummeted. Based on how Radley's body flinched, his concern became decipherable.

"Adira, I am begging you to put the weapon down," Radley advised, trying to talk her off the ledge she stood on.

Knowing Onyx wouldn't mindlessly kill her, I also knew he wouldn't hesitate if she went to pull the trigger and put all of us in a walking line of danger.

"I think you should listen to your friend," Onyx replied carelessly, wearing the mask he'd become known for. "Don't get me wrong; I'm more than happy to end your life here and now. But I assume you have someone to go home to. And all of us know, you included, that if you fire that weapon, you would awaken things in this building that you couldn't fend off alone."

He paused momentarily, continuing to prod and challenge her with his gaze. Even through apparent loathing, his ice-blue eyes remained hauntingly beautiful and contained so much depth —the same eyes that had once glared at me with the same hatred.

"If you don't get her to stand down, I have no choice. She is putting all of us at risk, including herself." His words slithered through my subconscious, serving as an extension of one final warning. *"She can walk away from this. But if she keeps pushing, I can't guarantee her life any more than she can guarantee ours."*

"Adira, put your weapon down," Radley urged. "This is far from the engagement we need to be having with one another, and believe me when I tell you, it isn't one you want to be partaking in either."

The dissension climbed to a breaking point, one wrong move seconds away from sending us into a deadly spiral.

"Adira, I can sympathize with your anger," I added, steadying my voice. "But this isn't the solution to your hatred, at least not one you will survive. You know Radley—you trust him. He wouldn't be here if he didn't stand behind what we are doing."

Disgust filled her expression, her gaze never leaving the man I attempted to leverage for our betterment. "You keep avoiding the question. Why can't you answer me honestly if you're so trustworthy?"

"I will explain once you put your weapon down."

Her lips curled in response, a near-snarl on the horizon.

"I ought to give you the willingness to keep testing the waters." The raspy reply rolled through the stairwell, reverberating off the walls in a near-coax.

Adira spoke, disregarding what Onyx said to her, and instead aimed her response at Radley. "Answer my question if you don't want me to blow your head clean off your body."

"It's complicated," Radley shook his head, providing a surface-level retort.

"Complicated? That's your excuse?" She laughed as her glower narrowed. "Heroux, please clarify the intricacies of willingly sleeping with the gravest threat to humanity."

"I'd rather slit my throat with a rusty blade than bed Radley. He isn't exactly my type." Onyx snapped sarcastically, striving to draw us away from the plummet we were seconds away from making.

Once Onyx finished his sentence, Radley's glare became decipherable through the back of his skull. Instead of giving him time to compose a planned response, I intervened and allowed the words to spill from me.

"There are a lot of questionable things happening, Adira. Things that the higher-ups aren't disclosing to even the upper ten percent of their Venturers."

"Yeah? Did he tell you that?" The two challenges came through gritted teeth. "How do you know he's not stringing you along and using your ignorance to his advantage?"

"Lying?" Onyx scoffed, an annoyed chuckle coming from his chest. "And what would I have to lose by telling the truth when the entire world opposes me?"

Another wave of rumination rolled through her eyes, and she paused, contemplating the various pleas and logical arguments we'd posed.

They'd banished him outside of the Walls. They'd placed a mass bounty on his head. Amidst it all, he had to fend for himself while protecting the ones he loved. He had nothing to lose by disclosing the truth of the operations and his once-standing position amid them, and she knew that.

"Adira, the weapon." Radley moved forward, reaching for the gun she had pointed at him.

Her hand seemed to loosen around the grip. Recognition

crossed her expression that what we had spoken had been truth-ful, with no intention of deceiving. Radley took another step forward as his fingers deliberately wrapped around the gun barrel, working to pull it from her hands before she could change her mind. Once the realization of what she was doing coated her expression, her hand tightened around the weapon again, her finger sliding back to its place on the trigger.

Radley remained in the line of fire, and no level of remorse crossed her expression.

Time slowed to milliseconds as the chaos unfolded, each tick more unbearable than the last, and with careless ease, she pulled the trigger.

N
E
S

FIFTEEN

My heart pounded as I braced for the sound of agony to escape Radley—any sign the bullet had ripped through flesh and organs.

Nothing.

Adira's eyes widened, fixed on the space between her and the one she'd fired at. She'd expected to see blood, a lifeless body. Instead, her face betrayed the impossible truth as the abilities of the male behind me became known.

The bullet hung in mid-air, spinning from the velocity released upon firing. Its deadly intent halted inches from Radley's skull. Relief surged through me, nearly overwhelming in its intensity.

Onyx's groan broke the silence, filled with irritation rather than relief. "I didn't want it to have to come to this. I expected better judgment from you, but I was apparently wrong."

"What the in the f—" Adira's whisper was a mix of horror and awe as she stared at the suspended bullet.

I went to confront her for acting so carelessly regardless of our warnings, but before I could, an ear-piercing shriek came from the level we had just exited.

Radley pivoted, looking over his shoulder as the color drained from his face.

The sound snaked from just around the doorway we had passed through moments before. We'd swept and deemed the first level clear, but it became immediately clear that it'd been a mistake, and my heart sank with the thought. Part of me contemplated what we could have overlooked, but I knew Runners would seemingly manifest out of thin air if something prompted their presence.

"Move!" Onyx barked, his grip on my shirt ironclad as he ripped me up the stairs.

The sudden shift barely gave me enough time to turn around to steady myself, watching as he rushed toward the next flight. We were running away from one threat and potentially into the arms of another, but at this point, we didn't have a choice other than to go up.

While Onyx and Radley held an advantage in stride length, the adrenaline pulsating through my ears and forcing my heartbeat to match the pummeling of my feet allowed me to keep pace with them.

I glanced over the railing ledge as the now four of us ascended, the shrieks below multiplying into a twisted symphony. Two figures emerged from the doorway, their eyes locking onto us.

Onyx hadn't lied—monstrous evolution erased their humanity, replacing it with something far more sinister.

The first one still wore the expected attire of a once-business professional: a loose-fitted vest and pair of brown pants. But its clothing was all that remained of its human features. Its face had morphed into something resembling an insect, with paired jaws extending grotesquely from its mouth. Its mandibles snapped in response to our panicked footsteps. Two additional sets of eyes sat unnervingly on its forehead, providing an undeniable visual advantage. Jagged pieces of bone protruded along its arms while sharp, long talons extended from its fingertips. It moved inhumanely, a perverse blend of human agility and mutated ferocity, its progression up the stairwell directed straight at the four of us.

The second's grotesque structure resembled a Venus flytrap. Instead of eyes, tentacles protruded from the folds between its parted ribcage, scurrying to determine the source of the sounds echoing through the stairwell. Sharp teeth lined the edges of its parted skin, and ribs jutted out, joining its unnatural maw. Two additional arms extended from its back, and I pondered their use until it shifted quickly and turned around. Watching in horror, it bent backward onto all fours before beginning its rapid ascent toward us.

"What are those things?!" Radley's questioned sharply, fear lacing his query as we trudged upward.

"Now you understand why I didn't bother with New York City, don't you?!" Onyx snapped, taking a sharp turn onto the next flight of stairs.

We'd cleared five levels when the two creatures infiltrated the cement box that seemed to imprison us all. Adira's mindless decision to pull the trigger sent us scrambling for our lives.

We rounded the corner of another landing, passing the number eight painted on the sign to the right of the door. A crack sliced down the center, separating the perfectly stacked circles in half. Onyx's fingers wrapped around my arm as we traversed the next flight.

Using his abilities, the door to the ninth floor sprung open, and he yanked me with him, the two of us passing the threshold. Radley followed, squeezing through the remaining crack to join us on the level Onyx elected safe enough for consideration. Without mercy, the door slammed shut with the force of Onyx's mind, leaving Adira in the stairwell to fend for herself.

"You can't just leave her—" Radley began, but a loud bang from the other side cut him off.

My thoughts temporarily fixed on the Runners outside the door and the seconds that separated us from them. My stomach churned with the realization that while some continued to chase Adira up the stairwell, others remained far more interested in us.

"She's armed," Onyx growled, dragging me behind him. "At least enough to fend for herself until she can find somewhere to hide. If she's a real Venturer, she'll figure it out. We can't afford another body to protect, nor do I have the energy to defend her. I'll gladly feed her to that horde after the stunt she pulled. Frankly, it's her fault we are in this shit show to begin with."

Radley swallowed, recognizing the grim truth in Onyx's defensiveness.

We were moving again before I could respond to either of them or even inspect our surroundings. We quickly worked our way to the other end of the skyscraper, the paired building beside it visible through the windows. The taunting drop to the cement below became a beckoning call of desire to return to where we had been moments ago.

Before, numerous mutated runners trapped us on the ninth floor of a building.

Before, we were running out of options for escape.

They had cornered us with what seemed to be no way out—at least any viable one that wouldn't lead to the three of us running into more of them. The images of the mutated Runners crossed my mind again, and my blood turned ice cold with a nearing inevitable outcome.

"Why do they look like that?" I whispered, realizing how divulged I'd become by my thoughts.

Onyx exhaled, his eyes studying the disarray that littered the floor. "We don't know for sure. My guess is the bombings in the larger cities spread radiation that mixed with the virus, creating what you saw in that stairwell."

Radley, walking beside me, glanced at Onyx. "Those things are far from human. One of them looked—"

"Like an insect," I finished, the memory of its snapping mandibles fresh in my mind.

"And the other, a plant," Onyx confirmed with a brief nod.

"They all look different. Their bodies somehow adapted a disturbingly different uniqueness that seems to have the potential of surpassing power wielders. While I would love to sit and have a science lesson about it to dissect our questions, we don't have the time. We need to work through this floor and figure out how to get the hell out of here."

Without spoken word, we'd reached an agreement and immediately began scouring the space. We knew our survival depended on our ability to quickly and efficiently search for anything to aid our escape, marking every second as increasingly important.

The ninth floor was a chaotic reflection of the devastation we'd seen before—overturned desks, shattered furniture, and debris that made every step a calculated risk. Once adorned with motivational posters and company logos, the walls were cracked and peeled, the paint flaking in large chunks. Radley strategically navigated the area, Onyx following but keeping a short distance as if waiting for something to appear in a shadowed corner that Radley had missed.

While they focused on the open floor plan, I began a silent sweep through the halls, gridded throughout the floor. The layout was a notably complex maze of intersecting corridors, each turn potentially hiding danger or a path to salvation, but I continued scouring for an exit sign or some hidden route out.

Another bang, more brutal than before, reverberated from the door we had used as a temporary shield. Seemingly summoned by the sound, Onyx rounded the corner of the stairwell, coming back into view behind one of the still-standing cubicles. His brows furrowed as the threat outside loomed, apprehension apparent in his hardened stare.

"The stairwell is clear. We can—" his sudden reply cut short, a shriek echoing from the hall I hadn't ventured down.

Radley shifted to look over his shoulder to examine the open office space separating us, and a level of uncertainty flashed through his gaze. Until his expression shifted, I hadn't paid much attention to the space between us and remained more focused on the task at hand.

Another screech, this time closer but singular, resulted in another bang against the door we had entered.

Onyx's gaze locked with mine, and a flash of protection circled his irises. His jaw tightened, and the backlight of the window that shielded us from the outside world glinted against the tension. It was a beckoning call, its frame butting up against the stairwell Onyx had claimed to be clear—our way out, our escape.

"Quiet. This one is blind. Be mindful of your movements." His warning came telepathically, Radley nodding in agreement.

I steadied my breathing so as not to cue the mutated Runner to my location. Once leveled, I pivoted, spotting her stumble into the fork of the hallway.

Once professional attire, now tattered and stained, was the only remnant of her humanity. A torn white button-down clung to her chest, and shredded black dress pants covered her lower half. Barefoot, she staggered toward us, her clouded, milky white eyes confirming Onyx's observation. Her jaw hung loose, swinging unnaturally as if unhinged. Once free, her arms had fused to her sides and nearly melted to conjoin with her hip bones. Elongated, gnarled fingers ended in sharp claws that clicked against the floor with each step, using them like a walking cane to track her surroundings.

Then, arms emerged from behind her.

At first, I thought it was just a second pair, similar to what we had seen in the stairwell. Instead, they fanned out, protruding from different body parts. My eyes widened as ten surrounded her, each twisting and cracking in protest of the movement. Some appeared almost childlike, others outstretched further than usual, with the bones jutting out under the thin, mottled skin at odd angles.

Each hand bore a hole in its palm, mimicking ears. Dark, fleshy membranes lined the edges, pulsing and quivering as she strained to gather information. Through each orifice, she sensed her surroundings, an abhorrent adaptation that, leveraged alongside her nails, allowed her to hunt despite her blindness.

"Don't panic," Onyx commanded sternly. *"Remember. She can't see. Watch where you're going, make your way to me, and keep your steps soft. We're taking the east stairwell down and getting the hell out of here."*

I appreciated his command more than I cared to admit, finding a rare comfort in it. We'd seen enough for one day and gathered the intel we needed, securing the need to leave before any other unwanted surprises graced us.

Jasper would be enthralled to know the Runners were nothing like what we were used to and not worth the risk of studying or understanding further. I quickly vowed never to return to the continent's eastern side, no matter the temptation.

She shrieked again, hunting for any sound that could betray us. Another bang rolled through the metallic door, rattling its hinges. She screeched in response, all ten hands turning toward the entrance as she rushed to investigate—distracted by her own kind.

Onyx motioned for us to move, leveraging the diversion. I didn't hesitate, clearing the space as quickly as possible. Radley followed suit, his movements tactical, ensuring we escaped without further incident. We closed the gap just as the door to the stairwell gave way, releasing the horde onto our level.

Onyx's eyes widened as the mash of Runners rushed toward us, their screeches and shrieks nipping at my heels. Directed by Onyx, I ran past him and through the doorway of the stairwell. Radley followed behind me, but Onyx held his place, unmoved from the window that acted as our beacon as we navigated through the space and to him.

He refused to close our trail even with the stairwell mere feet away from him and the two of us in it.

The horde closed in, the gap between them and Onyx shrinking to nothing. My horrified gaze lifted to meet Onyx's smirk—a devious glint in his eyes, an undisclosed plan hidden within that look.

Before I could process it, the window behind him shattered, and he stepped back into the void. His hands raised in a shrug of indifference, and serenity washed over his features. Gravity took hold, and in that instant, I realized his decision was a mix of selfishness and selflessness. His face showed recognition of his choice —to ensure our survival and possibly give Adira a chance to escape. But he'd made the decision knowing it would shatter the two people he held closest.

His request to Jasper echoed as I watched him plummet past our line of sight.

"If we don't make it back, please take care of her for me."

I went to scream, but Radley's hand clamped over my mouth, muffling it. The horde poured out of the window after him, one after another, until I lost count. They crawled over each other, desperate to be the first to reach Onyx's flesh.

The snarls and shrieks died off one by one as they hit the concrete below. In no particular order, flesh smacked the ground and pursued the eerie silence that lingered for a few seconds before impact.

My breath caught as the disarray concluded, and Radley slowly removed his hand from my mouth. I waited tensely before daring to speak.

"He just..." I looked at Radley, shock tightening my throat.

Onyx's decision tore through the part of me that understood him, the part Jasper had confided in about the man he loved. My heart ached with a yearning, a hidden wish that I could have extended before he made his sacrificial fall.

Radley sighed, disbelief etched on his face. I moved back to the shattered window, grabbing the frame to steady myself before looking down at the slaughter below.

Bodies coated the asphalt. The collision of bodies against the unforgiving surface attracted the attention of other Runners, who swarmed the pile, feasting on the remains. A crimson ring expanded around the stack, blood trickling from the corpses.

I pushed myself away from the window, my stomach sinking at the thought of delivering this news to Jasper.

To Imelda.

Radley's hand brushed my back, his brows pulling together in sympathy. "I never thought he'd throw himself out a window—"

"For us?" The question escaped before I could stop it.

"Yeah," Radley replied, something undecipherable lacing his reply. "There isn't anything we can do now besides going back to inform Jasper about what happened. And breaking the news to—"

"News?" A raspy voice cut him off, both of us pausing.

My heart stalled, the tension dissipating as the all-too-familiar tone registered. Gravelly and strained from what I presumed to be screaming—another portion of a story untold—and yet unmistakably laced with the sarcasm we knew too well.

I turned to find Onyx standing behind us, hands in his pockets, looking none the worse for wear. His forest green henley clung to his chest, highlighting his raven hair as it brushed against the fabric. He lifted his powder blue eyes to meet mine and smirked.

"How touching. I never imagined you'd hold a funeral for me."

"I think it was more depressing to consider you'd toss yourself into that mix of hamburger meat below," I replied, playfulness lacing my words.

Onyx raised his brows, stepping closer to glance out the window at the pile of corpses. "What a mess."

"I'm assuming you teleported back then?" Radley asked.

"As soon as I stepped out of the window." He shrugged indifferently as if his decision couldn't have been detrimental. "I planned to return immediately, but I took a few minutes to hunt down our fellow stairwell interferer."

Adira.

"Is she dead?" Radley asked, though his tone suggested he almost didn't want to know.

"No." Onyx's response shocked us both, earning stares of disbelief.

"She's alive?" I asked, astonishment clear in my voice.

"Alive and well," Onyx said, stepping away from the window. His fingers brushed mine briefly as if checking I was okay before he turned away.

"But how is that possible?" Radley demanded, needing to know the details of Onyx's engagement to satisfy his analytical nature. "She got chased up the higher floors. I thought—"

"She appears to be a valuable Venturer," Onyx interrupted, his tongue trailing across his teeth. "She had what she needed to fend for herself. And she was smart enough to do just that."

"And you just left her?" I questioned again. "You didn't kill her?"

Onyx smiled softly, "No, as shocking as it is, I didn't kill her."

"Then what were you doing before coming back here?" Radley pressed, demanding answers to solidify proof. "You said you went to hunt her down. That sounds like you intended to kill her."

"I never said I didn't want to kill her. I just didn't act on that desire," Onyx replied, his gaze shifting to the level we had fled. "Besides, why kill someone willing to give me all the information we needed?"

"Information?" I stepped closer, meeting his powdered-blue stare. "You mean she willingly told you about operations?"

He chuckled, brushing a thumb across my cheek. "Don't mistake me for a man who takes things from women without informing them. Though I suppose in this case, I had to make an exception to my morals."

His eyes drilled into mine, my cheeks flushing as he grazed his thumb across them again before pulling back. My breath halted as Onyx brought his thumb to his lips, running it across them as his tongue followed.

"So, you gathered intel? In what form?" Radley asked, his curiosity piqued.

"I rule over the mental domain. It's easy to get information when it exists in someone's thoughts." His eyes narrowed with mischief. "She gave me everything I needed without me even asking."

Radley's eyes widened. "You mean you—"

"Yes," Onyx confirmed with an all-knowing smirk. "I took what I needed. Her mind was an open book, and I didn't even have to flip through the pages."

SIXTEEN

My gaze lingered on Onyx after he spoke, my heartbeat quickening. A tingle spread from the base of my skull down my spine, chills following its snake-like path. My breath caught as I swept my eyes over his features—his hauntingly beautiful eyes framed by dark brows, the imperfectly perfect scar etched across his skin, and his now glistening lips.

It felt like we were the only two people in the room.

"What did you find out?" Radley's question abruptly interrupted my thoughts.

"So eager." Onyx chuckled, stepping away from me, leaving a sudden emptiness where warmth had been moments before.

Radley glanced at me, his expression questioning my silence. "Well, we came here to see if the Walls were still intact, so I am intrigued by what you uncovered."

Before I could insert myself, Onyx responded. "The Runners from this side of the continent breached the Walls of Region One. There's no standing community anymore, and those who lived there have dispersed. It's been that way for three months. From what I gathered, they found many bodies, including former government officials, Venturers, and others. There's not much left here in terms of survival. Runners and Scavengers intercepted those trying to reach Region Two. Adira was part of that group and survived, but leaving this side of the continent has proven futile."

"So Jasper's assumptions were true," I said, focusing on Radley, whose eyes were wide with shock.

Onyx nodded.

Radley exhaled softly. "Well, with that information, have we gathered all we needed?"

We had encountered enough of the mutated Runners to take a detailed report back to Jasper. The nightmarish creatures assaulted my mind—how their bodies moved unnaturally, their humanity wholly erased. They were entirely different from the Runners we were familiar with, who still retained some traits of humanity. Between their attributes and desire to feed, an explanation formulated in the back of my mind to ensure Jasper kept himself and his people the hell away from here.

There was nothing left and no reason to entertain another field day to the east.

"Almost," Onyx said, his response catching us off guard. "We'll head down to the streets below. I want to inspect the Runners we encountered in the stairwell before we leave."

"For what good reason?" Radley nearly plowed over Onyx's decision. "Those things nearly killed all three of us. We have what we need. Why the hell aren't we leaving?"

"I'm with him." I shifted my gaze from Radley to Onyx. "We have all the information Jasper requested. I can describe those... things in detail. Going down there risks another encounter, whether with more Runners or Scavengers."

"Not to mention Adira," Radley added, his eyes locked on Onyx. "We don't know if she's communicating with other Venturers or the government, which exacerbates the threat."

Onyx stood before us, his hands tucked into his pockets. When he spoke, his tone was reminiscent of our first encounter with him. "While I appreciate the concern, let me remind you—I'm the one who brought us here."

Radley clenched his fists, the tension in the room thickening with each word. We both knew what was coming next.

"And I'll be the one to take us back, so when I decide to leave is when we will leave."

"You're just going to let your selfishness keep us here, disregarding our safety?" Radley's words came through gritted teeth as he stepped toward Onyx.

Onyx's posture remained unchanged with Radley's attempt to provoke him. He met Radley's challenge with icy eyes—unmoving and unbothered.

"You view us as disposable because we're not *her*, is that it?" The blind rage in Radley's voice only added to the tension. "If Imelda were here, you would've turned back when those mutated Runners crossed that doorway."

The gap between them had shrunk with each word Radley hurled at Onyx.

I hastily moved forward, anxiety building with the mention of Imelda and the fire it ignited in Onyx. As soon as her name left Radley's lips, his eyes blazed with a heated rage, Jasper's warning echoing in my mind as the situation escalated.

"Some things are best left buried. Unless you are ready to deal with the monster unleashed when disturbed and awakened."

"Radley, back off." I tried to steady my command, but it was useless.

Radley turned to me in disbelief, his features contorting with billowing aggravation. "What the hell is wrong with you? You're just going to sit here—"

Before I could react, Onyx grabbed his shirt, ripping him backward and slamming him into a structural pillar. Radley grunted as his body collided with the stone, the force reverberating between us.

"Never speak to her like that again," Onyx snarled, malice filling his tone.

I stared between them, dismayed at how quickly things had escalated. The man who'd stood by my side for years was now at the mercy of the one I'd feared weeks ago. Yet, the latter defended me when Radley's aggression turned my way.

I didn't need defending—I could handle myself, but no one knew that.

Radley raised a hand to Onyx's forearm, wrapping his fingers around it. "I'm going to say this once. Let go of me."

Onyx leaned in closer, his power radiating off him in waves of rising animosity. "If I ever catch you speaking to her disrespectfully again, I promise I will splatter your brains across the floor. Got it?"

Before Radley could respond, Onyx released his grip and ripped Radley forward, practically tossing him to the side. Radley staggered, barely catching himself before he tripped over his own feet.

Onyx turned to me, a flicker of concern in his eyes, before shifting his glare back to Radley. "I'm leaving with or without you. By all means, set up camp here. I don't give a damn."

I glanced at Radley, who only looked at me out of the corner of his eye before stepping forward to follow Onyx. I sighed and trailed behind them, closing the line as we made our way from the ninth floor toward the stairwell leading to the city streets below.

The descent was silent. The only sound belonged to our boots striking the cement stairs. Though I wanted to break the stillness, I knew they needed time to cool down.

Radley had never been one to snap at me, not in all the years we'd worked together and been friends. I knew Onyx got under his skin, but that provided no excuse.

I counted our footfalls as we reached the ground floor, passing the reception area and the visibly broken elevator to arrive at the window we'd crawled through before everything went sideways. For the second time today, I grabbed the windowsill, avoiding the shards of glass, and pushed myself out behind Radley. My two larger companions easily crossed the threshold, exposing themselves to the outside world first.

Radley kept his back to us as Onyx walked past him, their shoulders grazing. Onyx glanced at me, extending a hand to help me through the window as I awkwardly straddled it.

"Thank you." I accepted his help, noting the surge his touch sent throughout my body for the second time. My heart soared until my feet met the unforgiving asphalt, our reality slipping back into place.

He nodded before continuing down the city streets, heading toward where the Runners had plunged to the ground. From the overhead view, the pile of bodies and the fresh blood pooling beneath them had been unforgettable. The repeated slap of flesh hitting concrete was a rude reminder of the lives we never agreed to live.

Lost in thought, I didn't notice Radley slowing his pace until he spoke beside me. "I'm sorry for how I spoke to you. It was incredibly uncalled for."

I peered at him before returning my gaze to Onyx's back. "Yeah, it was. And I didn't appreciate it."

He sighed, dragging his attention forward again. "I figured. I don't know, Astrid...with everything that happened in that stairwell, I was so focused on our safety that I—"

"Lashed out to provide protection," I finished for him. "I know. But directing your anger at me was uncalled for."

Stillness fell between us before he spoke again. "I know, and I'm sorry."

I nodded in acknowledgment, not verbally addressing it further. We rounded the corner of the building, stepping into the sunlight that cast a warm, comforting glow over the city. For a moment, it almost felt normal, but then I remembered.

The Runners.

Onyx stopped abruptly, exhaling sharply in incredulity. "Exactly what I was worried about."

I moved around his large frame to see what had caused his concern. Where we expected to find a pile of corpses, there was nothing—no sign of the creatures that had charged Onyx with bloodlust. Aside from a singular pool of blood glowing tauntingly under the sun, the streets were empty.

"Where the hell did they go?" Radley asked breathlessly.

I immediately scanned the area, searching for any sign of where they might have gone and listening for any cue.

Nothing. The silence remained eerie, and the lack of visual remnants was unsettling.

"None of it makes sense," Onyx muttered, clenching his jaw as he glanced between the bloodstain and the broken window. "A fall from that height would kill anything."

He was right—a free fall from a hundred feet would end any life instantly. We'd heard the bodies hit the asphalt, the snap of bones as they plummeted. Runners from our territory wouldn't have survived that plummet.

These were unexplainably and horrifyingly different.

"They just got up and walked away?" Radley questioned doubtfully. "How the hell is that possible?"

"It isn't," I said, shaking my head. "Or at least, it shouldn't be."

Onyx spoke without turning to us. "The fact they did speaks volumes about this mutation's influence on this side of the country. The Runners here seem nearly indestructible to the point I am wondering if we can even kill them—if *anything* can."

"Are you suggesting that even a headshot wouldn't suffice?" Radley asked, uncertainty lacing his tone.

"I can't confidently answer that." Onyx exhaled as he turned to face the two of us and dragged his foot along the asphalt. "My goal was to kill them in one swoop with a death fall, but that proved insufficient."

I nodded, staring at the bloodstain on the ground. "I'd be lying if I said it didn't make me uneasy."

"I don't disagree." Onyx ran a hand through his hair. "I knew they were different when Imelda and I observed them—their visible traits, enhanced speed, and strength. But surviving a fall from a ninth-story window was beyond what I anticipated as possible."

"Nothing about them—" A guttural snarl from the alleyway cut off Radley's reply.

A limping gait followed, mixed with the unsettling crack of dislocated bones. As footsteps approached the clearing, another growl echoed from the shadows cast by the surrounding buildings.

I reached back slowly, gripping the crossbow strapped to my back while my left hand curled around an arrow. Onyx stepped forward, placing himself in front of us just as the click of Radley's safety released. I loaded my weapon and raised it, aiming into the dark alley, bracing myself for whatever was coming.

The Runner emerged from the shadows, stretching upward— its form unlike anything we'd encountered in the skyscraper. Its body was a sickly grayish-pink, covered in growths, and its eyes glowed with a sickening yellow hue. Its shin bones had snapped and twisted outward, jutting grotesquely from its calves. A once-intact spinal column protruded from its stomach, coated in an inky crimson blood. Despite injuries that should have incapacitated any ordinary Runner, this one moved as if they were irrelevant.

It opened its mouth, snarling at us, its jaw hanging in two fractured pieces. Jagged teeth lined the loose flaps of skin, which drooped to its collarbones. The open throat visible to its mid-chest rasped with every breath as its lengthy tongue lashed from its mouth, tasting the air with a disturbing eagerness.

Its eerie yellow eyes tracked our movements with unsettling intelligence as if studying and calculating our next move with mindful anticipation.

I inhaled deeply, my finger sliding along the trigger of my crossbow. I fired, the arrow slicing through the air before planting itself between the Runner's eyes.

It staggered backward, its eyes closing briefly before it shook its head. Once they opened again, it gazed up from the ground, acknowledging what had just happened and working to gather its bearings. It straightened to full height, and we watched in horror as it reached up and ripped the arrow from its skull.

"It's intelligent," Onyx muttered, his speechlessness echoing our collective shock as the Runner examined the arrow before tossing it aside.

Radley fired his rifle, a shot aimed parallel to where my arrow had been. The Runner stumbled back again, its eyes closing as blood spewed from the back of its head, splattering brain matter on the sidewalk. Its body shook off the impact, its head snapping slightly to the side before it opened its glowing eyes again, fixing on us with renewed determination.

It released a jarring screech, then broke into a sprint toward us. I reached for another arrow, but before I could react, it closed the distance, tackling Radley to the ground.

"Shit!" Radley hit the asphalt hard as the Runner slammed into him, his gun firing another shot through its body, but it didn't flinch.

I grabbed the hunting knife from my thigh, hoping that if headshots didn't work, decapitation might. As I moved, the Runner's clawed hand closed around Radley's throat, lifting him off the ground. It was more than just intelligent—it was deliberate.

Radley kicked desperately, struggling against its grip and battling to gather oxygen. The Runner hurled him through the air before we could predict its next move. Radley's body slammed into the edge of the brick alleyway, the impact loosening some of the structure before he crumpled to the ground.

Gripping my knife tightly, I rushed forward. The Runner's focus pinned on Radley, shrieking as it loomed over him. I took advantage of the distraction, sprinting closer and swinging my blade at the base of its skull. The moment of contact sent a shock-wave through my arms, like hitting metal with a baseball bat.

My attack spoke true, but the knife merely bit into its skin but went no further as blood spurted across my face. With its skin proving to be resistant, I ripped the knife out and swung again. The Runner anticipated the attack and pivoted to dodge, my strike missing. I stumbled, the force of my missed swing throwing me off balance.

"Astrid!" Onyx's voice rang out, apprehension definable in my name.

I adjusted my stance but proved too slow as the Runner moved with alarming speed. Its arm slammed into my stomach, lifting me off my feet and sending me crashing to the ground.

The memory of my encounter with Gael in the bunker flashed through my mind as I hit the concrete, an internal part of me screaming in reminiscence. Pain shot through my forearms, which had taken the brunt of the fall and saved my head from the impact. I struggled to breathe, rolling onto my side to look at Onyx, the last of us still standing.

Onyx clenched his jaw as the Runner shifted its attention to him, a deep snarl emanating from its open airway. His eyes glowed, contrasting sharply with his dark hair. He slipped a hand into his pocket, glancing down at the gun on his thigh before returning his gaze to the Runner.

At that moment, it charged.

The Runner raised its arm, swinging at Onyx, who quickly sidestepped the attack. Another attack followed, but Onyx pivoted on his heels, effortlessly avoiding the claws of the mutated creature. The scene was a disturbing dance—one fighter overly eager, the other seemingly indifferent.

The Runner let out another ear-piercing screech, but Onyx remained unfazed. The attacks quickened, as did Onyx's movements, dodging each one almost casually. He treated the creature that had thrown Radley ten feet across the road and knocked me flat on my back as if it were nothing more than a minor nuisance.

It attempted a horizontal slash across Onyx's torso, but he stepped back, its talons grazing his shirt. Onyx raised his free hand as it prepared for another strike, pointing it directly at the Runner's head.

"You're one ugly bastard," he muttered, his blue eyes glowing with undeniable indignation. "And I think playtime is over."

Before the Runner could react, a blast of energy erupted from Onyx's hand, blowing its head clean off its body. The display of power was a stark reminder that we had yet to uncover the full extent of his abilities, stirring up something far more complex than apprehension within me.

The creature's arms flailed, reaching for the space where its head had been before it stumbled back and collapsed to the ground. The sound of its body hitting the concrete was a wake-up call to Radley, who stirred slightly from the heap he had become.

I turned to find Onyx beside me; his hand extended to help me off the ground. I gladly took it, his grip firm as he pulled me to my feet.

"That was one hell of a hit you took," he said, his eyes scanning me from head to toe before meeting mine again. "Are you alright?"

I nodded, bending down to retrieve my hunting knife that had clattered to the ground. Once I had fastened it back into place, I made my way to Radley while Onyx focused on the decapitated enemy.

Radley struggled to sit up, groaning in pain.

Kneeling beside him, I looked at him with concern that became apparent when he opened his mouth to speak.

"I'm alright."

I shook my head. "You're not alright. That thing tossed you through the air and into a damn brick wall."

He inhaled sharply, finally sitting upright. "I said I was fine."

I rolled my eyes, knowing it was an argument I wouldn't win. "Can you stand?"

He pushed himself up, wincing, his movements slowed. I stood beside him, watching for any signs of injury.

"He'll survive," Onyx retorted sarcastically, his back to us as he studied the fallen Runner. "The impact was hard, but miraculously, it didn't break any bones."

Radley cut in before I could clarify his level of certainty. "It knew we were attacking and pulled the arrow from its head. How is that even possible?"

"Highly functioning and intelligent," Onyx dipped his chin, his hands remaining in his pockets. "Another piece you're overlooking—it could have secured a meal, but instead, it used you as bait against her."

"Why would it do that?" I asked, glancing between them as he jerked his thumb in my direction.

"To put you in a vulnerable position and effectively harm you both. Which is exactly what happened," Onyx replied, running a hand down his face in contemplation. "But how it knew to direct its attacks and think that far ahead is beyond me."

"How it knew to leverage me is something I can't comprehend," Radley added, walking over to Onyx as I followed, his eyes fixed on the mutated creature sprawled on the blacktop.

The early afternoon sun highlighted the boils along its body, the ivory bones protruding through its skin. While its head was missing, the lower portion of its mouth remained, jagged teeth still visible along the flaps of skin that melted into its collarbones. The exposed muscles of its chest and neck were all that remained of its upper torso. An unknown force had shattered the bones in its forearms, forcing them through its elbows to form sharp and jagged points.

"This one wasn't in the group that fell out of the window," I murmured, continuing to study it. "Why does it look like this? The fractures, the misformed bones—what happened to it?"

"Maybe there's a bigger enemy," Onyx suggested, looking over his shoulder as he exhaled deeply. "The complexities of the Runners here are beyond what I imagined. This one displayed intelligence, which makes me wonder if more are out here, surviving within the city."

Radley kicked its limp arm, the body reacting to the force.

"You think there's another group of Runners that are more mutated and intelligent than the others?"

"Is it far-fetched?" Onyx raised an eyebrow. "We saw how this one reacted. It displayed a recognition I've never seen before."

"Maybe it was the only one?" I asked, staring down at the grotesque remains.

"That's a hopeful outlook," Onyx chuckled, shaking his head. "For two people who worked with the government, you'd think you'd be more realistic about the state of things."

"Whether it's the only one or not, we shouldn't stick around to find out," Radley said, tugging on the straps of his backpack—likely the thing that had saved him from severe injury. "Let's get the hell out of here before we test our luck beyond its limits."

Onyx nodded silently, his eyes fixed on the Runner as if trying to piece together the puzzle of its existence. The mutation was a known factor on this side of the continent, but this level of variation—intelligent, responsive—made little sense.

"Earth to Onyx," Radley chimed in, irritated. "Are you just going to ignore what I said? Let's get out of here before something else—"

"Holy shit," Onyx breathed, his voice barely audible as he stared down at the Runner, his eyes widening with realization.

"What?" My question lapped with concern as he locked eyes with me.

"It was..." He hesitated, scanning the body once more to confirm what he saw was real. "It was one of us."

"What?" Radley and I inquired in unison.

"Fucking hell, our assumptions were wrong." The words he mumbled seemed to be more of a demeaning comment toward himself, and before we could clarify, he continued. "The mutated Runner—it was once part of the Rebellion. A power wielder." Onyx pointed down and my eyes followed, watching as its skin worked to overlap and weave itself back together. "It's not just the radiation that created the mutation, it's their altered genetic code from the Fall mixed with the effect of the bombings."

"What the hell?" Horror laced every syllable of my question as I watched the sluggish process, the intricacies of its work near useless as it neared its finality.

"It's the manifestation of everything we questioned. The access restrictions they gave to specific Venturers, the conversations behind closed doors, and the clearance into the laboratory bays all make sense now." Radley closed his eyes and sighed, the realization dawning on him.

"Testing facilities within the Walls." Onyx clenched his jaw, the revulsion evident in his voice. "Jasper and I have been suspicious about the possibility for a while with the shifts we've seen in the Infected population. My guess is that they're capturing Rebels for experimentation to decipher the full extent of their abilities. We've discussed the possibility of them pushing power users beyond their brink, which could ultimately result it," he glanced at the Runner before resuming. "They're altering the Infected even further to aid in serving their twisted purpose to destroy anyone who stands against in their way."

I swallowed the lump building in my throat. "I knew there was corruption but didn't realize it went this deep."

"That's why it attacked instead of feasting. It didn't care nor desire to waste time with either of you," Onyx said, his powdered blue eyes greeting mine with a newfound understanding. "It was interested in me."

Before we could respond, a sharp crack came from the mutated Runner at our feet. I looked down to where its spine protruded from its stomach and watched as its chest cavity began to split open. Its ribs forced themselves through the skin, and the body caved in on itself, turning inside out.

I stepped back, nearly tripping over my feet. "We need to get the hell out of here now. There's no way that thing is still alive."

Onyx mirrored my shift, shoving Radley back while keeping his gaze locked on the Runner. Its body thrashed violently on the ground, bones snapping backward at the joint. It fell limp momentarily before it jolted into a contorted crab-like stance, its palms splaying to support its frame. Onyx extended his hand toward us, but the Runner lashed out before Radley or I could grab hold. Its tongue looped around Onyx's arm, yanking him away and hurling him through the wall of the building across the street.

The structure briefly withstood the force of Onyx's impact until its bricks finally cracked, his body crashing through it. Debris scattered, the audible clash reverberating through the eerie silence clinging to the city streets.

Tearing my gaze away from the building and back to the Runner, my body surged with the need to act.

"Shit!" Radley peered at the hole in the wall, then back. "Go for its limbs! We need to slow it down!"

I nodded, gripping my hunting knife as the Runner scuttled across the ground, heading for the gap in the brick it had sent Onyx through. Radley unsheathed a blade from his utility belt, responding promptly with my implicit plan.

The Runner shrieked as it moved, its spider-like limbs propelling it toward the building. I positioned myself in its path, waiting until it was inches from me before sidestepping and pivoting around it just as I'd seen Onyx do. I swung my knife at its back leg, slicing clean through it. Blood splattered across the asphalt, the crimson hue stark against the inky black that inter-mixed it.

Its severed limb rolled toward Radley as the Runner released a sharp screech. Radley didn't hesitate, moving swiftly to drive his blade into its remaining leg and temporarily pin it to the ground.

"You're mine, you persistent fuck," Radley growled, yanking the blade toward him as his forearms tensed.

The Runner snarled, its attention shifting from Radley to me despite its lack of eyes. Its elongated tongue shot out with terri-fying precision. Before I could react, it coiled around my throat, trapping the wrist on the hand that held the weapon beside my neck. I struggled against the suffocating grip, but the more I did, the tighter it constricted. Panic clawed at my chest as my airway closed, the air thinning with each passing second.

With a sickening lurch, the Runner lifted me off the ground, my feet dangling helplessly. My free hand hopelessly clawed at its tongue as the sensation in my fingers dissipated, and the knife slipped from my grasp and clattered uselessly to the ground.

"Astrid!" Radley glanced up at me, then back at the knife buried in the Runner's limb.

If he let go, the Runner would be free and continue to attack Onyx with me in its grasp.

My vision faded quickly, the mutated creature's grip tightening to the point my wrist cracked under its hold. A cry of agony tried to escape my lips, but only a muted whimper emerged. I clenched my jaw, fumbling for another knife on my utility belt. My fingers found a hilt, and I quickly freed it, struggling to keep it in my grasp as darkness lurked closer. With the last of my strength, I drove the knife up through the tongue wrapped around my neck, sawing through the thick muscle. The Runner howled, its tongue flailing in response, but it refused to let go.

Gasping for oxygen, I twisted the serrated edge deeper, eliciting another screech, but still not my release. My gaze drifted toward the building where the Runner threw Onyx, and I saw him in the dimming light of my vision.

He stood before the gap his body had created, his dark hair disheveled in a way I'd never seen before. His brows furrowed, hooding his powder-blue eyes with pure mania. Blood coated his forehead and the side of his face, contrasting with his glower. His lips were a taut line, an expression I'd seen on him a handful of times, but something darker joined it. A large cut trailed across his green henley, the slit resembling a fresh wound, with crimson staining the edges.

He wiped his thumb between his brows, examining the life force that coated it before peering up at me, and something within him erupted.

The monster that Jasper warned us about.

The building behind him collapsed in on itself like an accordion. The structural framing that had kept it standing through years of apocalypse shattered into microscopic pieces. Steel beams crumbled under the pure force, bricks disintegrated into dust, and windows exploded, spraying glass across the sidewalk. Yet Onyx remained untouched, as if destruction bowed to him.

He stepped onto the asphalt as the Runner shifted its attention to him, tightening its grip on my neck. I couldn't tell if it was trying to inflict more pain or if it feared what was coming as it scurried backward, trying to escape. Radley held the position, unmoving, regardless of his desire to help me, ensuring the Runner wouldn't get away no matter how desperately it tried.

My vision had almost faded, the blackness encroaching as I teetered on the edge of unconsciousness. Before the darkness could consume me, Onyx lifted his hand toward the Runner, his eyes narrowing as they shone with a bright, whitish-blue light.

"I'm done playing nice," he growled through gritted teeth, barely moving a finger on his outstretched hand.

In an instant, the Runner went from being a tangible threat to vanishing entirely, wiped from existence in milliseconds. Ash drifted upward from where the creature's tongue had held me nearly ten feet in the air, the only remnant of what had once been. The wave of destruction surged toward me, and I feared it might take me with it, but then the pressure around my neck dissipated, and oxygen rushed back into my lungs, burning my throat with its intensity. I was no longer held hostage by the Runner, which now existed only as a faint memory, and its elimination served as another pure display of Onyx's immense power.

I plummeted toward the asphalt below, bracing for the impact. But instead of hitting the ground, strong arms wrapped around me, cradling me with the protective comfort I hadn't felt in years.

I slowly opened my eyes and looked up at Onyx. His rage was still apparent, but I could see relief beginning to clear it. He held me close as if letting go was the last thing he wanted to do. The pressure of his forearms and biceps around me conveyed a deep fear of loss. But for me? It didn't seem applicable.

He exhaled, clenching his jaw before electing to lower me to the earth. "I can't believe I'm asking you this for the second time today, but here we are. Are you alright?"

Radley had moved to stand beside Onyx, his expression of disquiet as he cut into the conversation. "I'm sorry I couldn't have—"

"It's fine," I interrupted, shaking my head as I looked at him. "Truly. I knew what you could and couldn't do given the circumstances."

Onyx huffed in slight annoyance, glancing at Radley from the corner of his eye. "Dodging my question has me thinking you're far from alright."

A sharp pain shot down my throat as I swallowed. "I promise I'll be okay."

Onyx kept his eyes on me briefly, blood trickling down his face before meeting the concrete.

"You, on the other hand, have seen better days."

Radley chimed in with a playful edge. "As you once said, you look like shit."

"I don't know if either of you recalls, but I did get thrown through the side of a building," Onyx chuckled softly, though I noticed his jaw clenched in anguish.

He was hurting despite his attempts to hide it. The adrenaline from his rage must have masked the pain initially, but now that it had subsided, he was feeling the full impact of the collision.

A part of me wanted to help him, to ease his pain, but I wasn't sure how. Our eyes locked again, and I knew he could see it—my desire to help, my guilt for not preventing his injury, and for being unable to stop the Runner before it attacked him, attacked any of us.

Onyx shifted, his head tilting slightly, his eyes speaking volumes. But he didn't think the gesture was enough. *You did enough. Believe me when I say that.*

His words came to me mentally, and an accompanying smile tugged at the corners of his lips. One I couldn't help but return.

Radley cleared his throat, looking between us for a second time. "So, is there any chance we can get out of here now? Before we have to deal with any more bullshit?"

Onyx nodded without turning toward him, keeping his stare pinned on me. "Let's go home."

SEVENTEEN

I pushed myself out of the cot that had become mine since joining the Rebellion. As I stood, I stretched, groaning with the protest my muscles wrought with another restless night. Golden rays of sunlight pierced through the curtains, brightening the small room. The beams danced joyfully, creating rainbow patterns on the worn wooden floor to celebrate a new day.

Pulling the blanket up to cover the cot, I straightened the pillows, smoothing the creases with care. Though simple, it provided me with much-needed rest amidst the chaos and a sense of control—a small sanctuary in our tumultuous world.

I approached the mirror on the opposite wall, a piece salvaged from a house nearby. Even with slightly cracked edges, it became a silent witness to my daily routine. I hadn't looked at myself much during our time here. The mundane tasks consumed my days, and my reflection was often just a fleeting blur as I rushed from one duty to the next.

But things had changed since our harrowing trip to the East Coast. Jasper had given us a few days to recover, recognizing the toll the journey had taken. None of us immediately spoke to him about the trip—all it took was one look from him, and we were ordered to divulge in the allotted time to heal before discussing anything.

Onyx needed time to recover from the injuries he sustained at the tail end of our trip. Imelda had cussed him out when we returned, inspecting him amid her lecture. Then she worked to heal him, clarifying that it would take more than one session to mend the damage completely. He had returned four times for her to continue her work after his collision with the brick wall. According to Imelda, he was lucky to be alive as one of his broken ribs had punctured a vital organ, and if we had waited any longer to return, he would have bled out internally.

That thought alone kept me tossing and turning our first night back.

Imelda did all she could with her abilities, leaving his body to take care of the rest. With her admittance to being unable to assist further, Jasper didn't hesitate to list Onyx out of commission. He remained highly wary about ability use and exertion, forbidding Onyx from engaging with any threat until further notice, regardless of the circumstance.

I exhaled as I approached the mirror, bracing myself for the reflection that awaited me. The memories of what we had faced were still fresh, vivid images etched in my mind. Standing in front of it, my struggles and unspoken secrets materialized.

Once bright with enthusiasm, my hazel eyes held a depth of experience and resilience—the only remnants of their former brightness were the golden rings that refused to bid farewell to my irises. Dark circles resided beneath them, a testament to sleepless nights and constant vigilance. My hair, usually tied back in a braid, had come loose, cascading around my shoulders in deep brown waves. The scar on my eyebrow, a souvenir from an encounter long past, seemed more pronounced in the morning light.

But despite everything, I saw my mother looking back at me.

I allowed myself a moment to truly see the woman in the reflection—the one most underestimated and didn't truly know.

It was a rare pause in the relentless pace of our lives, a chance to acknowledge the subtle and significant changes that had occurred over a few weeks. I differed from the woman I was when I started my journey, though my goal remained unchanged.

Sighing, I reached for my shirt draped over the chair. As I continued to examine myself, the bruise around my neck from the mutated Runner's attack became more pronounced. While it had finally faded, it remained a more muted brownish tint, replacing a once patchy greenish-purple. Its presence served as a reminder of the encounter—a week separating us from our return.

Our alliance with the Most Wanted user alive had begun three weeks ago.

I tugged the shirt over my head before pulling the hair tie off my wrist. Wrapping my thick hair around my fingers, I worked it into a messy braid, fastening it at the end before slipping into my chosen pants. They fit perfectly, and the gray-military style cut highlighted my frame better than any others I had worn. I tucked in my shirt, secured it with a belt, and grabbed a pair of socks from the clothes box brought by Hayzen, a kind woman with beautiful orange hair.

Onyx had ensured that Jasper provided us with some wardrobe upon our return, understanding Jasper's seriousness about his temporary restriction from missions due to his injuries. Jasper, more concerned about our well-being than a few pairs of pants and T-shirts, was happy to oblige.

I tugged the socks over my feet and put on my boots, fastening them before standing. I peered at myself one last time and caught a minor glimpse of my brother through my hazel gaze and freckled cheeks—a man I'd looked up to growing up and who had once served our country, but in an entirely different light. A gentle sigh escaped me as I clung to the semblance we shared, memories of his death stirring within me.

Part of me was grateful he lost his life before the Fall and didn't have to witness the horrors that came with it, but another piece ached for all he had once been. Yet, his resemblance remained a part of me and reminded me of all I had fought for.

Pulling myself together, I wrapped my hand around the door handle and tugged it open to cross the open floor plan Jasper provided.

We occupied what had once been a pet store, now stripped of its former purpose. The shelves that once held pet food and supplies were long gone, leaving a vast, empty space behind. The walls, still adorned with faded murals of pets, bore witness to a time before the Fall when this place had been a bustling hub for animal lovers. Now, it stood as a hollow shell, repurposed for our survival.

The building held a living space and two rooms, a fortunate feature that suited our needs. The front area, where customers once browsed for their determined needs, served as a shared space. It remained barren except for a few scavenged chairs and a makeshift table crafted from an old door balanced on cinder blocks. Scuffed and worn, the linoleum floor echoed with the ghosts of footsteps long gone. The large windows at the front, now covered with plywood and faded newspaper, provided a semblance of security while allowing just enough light to filter through during the day.

It was a place where we could sleep soundly, knowing that, for the time being, we were safe from outside threats.

Reaching Radley's door, I knew the likelihood of him still being asleep was high—he had never been a morning person.

The cascade of the sunlight greeted me first, cascading throughout his room similarly to mine. It projected various colors of reflections along the walls, yet its brightness wasn't enough to wake him.

His clothes laid over the chair in the corner of the room, his boots neatly placed beside it. His weapons leaned against the wall, displayed like trophies and defining his meticulous mannerisms earned through years of service. My eyes continued to scan the room, landing where I knew he would be.

He lay on his side, the golden rays highlighting his light blondish-white hair. His lips were parted, each breath barely notable with a slight rise and fall of his chest. The intrusion of the outside world made the lighter lines on his skin stand out, defining the scars from past battles that sat against the pale backdrop.

He was gone to the world.

I recalled the restless nights we often experienced, even within the Walls of Region Three. There wasn't an instant when we weren't on edge. Our inability to relax was controlled by those in power and our consistent anticipation of something happening.

But it was different here.

Something was different.

Something for which I could never thank Jasper enough.

I took a soft step forward, walking toward him to gingerly touch his arm. His skin was warm, a testament to the comfortable cocoon he had found in sleep.

"Radley," I whispered, a gentle attempt to wake him.

He stirred, a soft groan escaping as his eyes fluttered beneath his lids. Despite my assumptions, his rest remained surface-level. Years of survival taught us that deep sleep was a luxury we couldn't afford—not when more significant threats loomed.

"Radley," I repeated, my fingers brushing down his tricep. "Come on, it's time to get up."

He huffed, raising his arm to his forehead as he rolled onto his back. Slowly, he opened an eye to look at me, a soft smile tugging at his lips. The morning light made his vibrant blue eyes appear more gray than usual.

"Already?" He groaned, his voice gravelly from disuse. His forearm brushed down his forehead to cover his eyes. "Come on, can't I have just a little while longer?"

"As much as we would both enjoy more sleep, we're on our third day since returning, and our scheduled meeting to debrief Jasper about what happened has arrived."

Memories of our venture to New Jersey flooded back—Adira,

the horde, the mutated Runner, and witnessing the full extent of Onyx's power.

Or at least some of it.

Radley groaned, throwing off the blanket to reveal his lithe upper body.

My eyes traced the contours of his abdomen, noting the movement of the muscles as he pushed himself upright. Scars traversed his torso, each telling a story I had yet to learn and many he insistently refused to tell me.

"Are you just going to sit there and stare at me, or?" Radley chuckled, his query pulling me from my thoughts.

My cheeks burned as I shook my head. "No, I just never realized the extent of your scars."

He smiled, trailing his fingers over some lighter patches of skin while avoiding others. "You were there when the medics cleaned me up after a mission outside the Walls, so I find it hard to believe you have forgotten about them. Especially considering how upset you were."

I licked my lips, swallowing the lump in my throat. "To be fair, I know some, but not all. And besides, I didn't forget, I just—"

"I hope you realize I don't mind." Radley leaned back, propping himself up with his elbows, stretching his long frame across the bed. The sunlight cast shadows along his body as it waltzed through the room, further highlighting the contours of his form.

"What do you mean?" I played dumb, though it was becoming increasingly difficult.

I had known about Radley's interest in me for a while but avoided entertaining his advances because of our positions as Venturers. I deeply valued our friendship and didn't want to jeopardize our bond and all that came with it.

He raised an eyebrow, a mischievous grin playing on his lips. "Oh, nothing, I suppose."

He moved forward, pushing his towering frame off the bed to

stand before me. His height devoured me as I looked up, catching the moment he gently touched the braid over my right shoulder.

His fingers wrapped around it softly before setting it back down. "One of my favorite hairstyles of yours."

A deep warmth spread through me, the softness of his words laced with something deeper. My cheeks heated further as I gazed up at him, admiring the deep lines in his cheeks that twinned his smirk. He stroked his hand to my cheek, mirroring the motion Onyx extended in Jersey City, and I struggled to bat the thought of him from my mind.

Radley's eyes remained fixed on mine, glinting with something unreadable. His tongue trailed over his bottom lip, slowly grazing across his teeth.

"Are you going to tell me—"

Before I could finish, his lips met mine. The connection seemed natural, like a missing puzzle piece snapping into place. My eyes closed instinctively as he consumed my mind, making me crave his taste. A build of desire surged through me, pushing me deeper into him. I obliged without needing to control, my hand resting on his abdomen as our lips moved in perfect synchrony.

I returned sway with fervor, each movement expressing my painted yearning. His steady heartbeat reverberated through my fingers, a testament to his anticipation. His hand moved to the back of my neck, gently cupping the base of my skull as his fingers wove through my hair.

My lips parted briefly, only to press against his again, but far more intensely. He stepped forward, his other hand finding my waist. His fingers traced a soothing rhythm along my back before beginning a tantalizing journey toward the waistband of my pants.

In response, I moved my hand down from his chest, trailing it toward the start of his sweatpants—a silent invitation for him to continue. My breath quickened, and my core ached with his temptation. I matched his pull with a push, my tongue brushing his teeth, and a deep growl elicited from him. I pulled away momentarily, gaining control of the dance we engaged in, before leaning in once more to press my lips into his.

A throat clearing came from the doorway, shattering the moment and pulling us back to reality.

Onyx stood there, his expression cold. His hair was loosely tied back, a few strands framing his clenched jaw. My eyes traced over his attire—a form-fitting black T-shirt that hugged every curve of his frame. His biceps straining against the sleeves as he folded them across his chest. His tattoo, intricate and more visible without the usual henley, wound across his skin.

His icy gaze flicked between Radley and me, tangled together in the middle of Radley's bedroom.

"You could've knocked," Radley snapped, his finger still hooked under my belt.

"Why bother knocking when the door is wide open? Redundant, don't you think?" A harshness laced Onyx's questions. "Maybe next time you're about to get your dick wet and you desire privacy, have some decency to shut the damn door."

My face flushed as I remained beside Radley, the heat of the moment snuffing out.

"Unless," Onyx added, his gaze shifting to me, a dangerous glint in his eyes, "privacy isn't what she wants, and the thought of being taken in broad daylight excites her."

"I don't recall anyone asking your opinion," Radley hissed, his aggravation building to match Onyx's.

"And I didn't say I was giving it, but don't let me interfere," Onyx replied, pivoting to leave. "I sure hope you know how to satisfy a woman. It would be a shame if you left her disappointed and craving something better after all the pathetic desperation you've displayed."

Before Radley could respond, I placed a hand on his bare chest to stop him, allowing Onyx to leave without another spoken word—and Radley and my planned excursion unfinished.

THE BELL above the pharmacy door clanged as I pushed it open, Radley close behind. I could sense his lingering annoyance over the abrupt end to our planned adventure, thanks to Onyx's unexpected intrusion. The mood had entirely shifted after he left, and neither of us felt inclined to continue. Though, if I were honest, part of me shared Radley's frustration.

My eyes swept over the space, which had remained primarily unchanged since our last visit—except for a few more black circles added to the map draped over the large oak table. I still had to figure out what each color meant, but I knew it would likely take years of establishing trust before Jasper would enlighten me. A few more weapons scattered along the shelves suggested a successful supply run during our recovery, and the community's daily flow remained unchanged.

Jasper sat at the head of the table, wearing a deep green flannel that made his bright auburn hair stand out even more. He sipped from a coffee mug before glancing up, his eyes lighting up at our presence—a stark contrast to our initial encounter with him.

He set his mug down gently, the clatter reverberating through the space. "Morning."

"Morning," Radley and I muttered in unison as we progressed toward our usual positions.

Onyx sat across from us and to Jasper's left. His eyes moved over me, the glint from our earlier engagement still present, but his gaze shifted away from me the instant we made eye contact.

Radley offered me a chair, and Onyx expressed his irritation with an audible huff, shifting before kicking his legs on the table. Jasper grinned, knowing Onyx's actions carried more weight than we understood. His expression turned to a playful smirk, and he held back a laugh once Onyx raised his glower. Pure annoyance radiated from him as he shook his head—a clear warning.

"Well," Jasper began, clearing his throat and forcing down the chuckle that was seconds away from spilling. "Lovely to see the three of you together again."

"Nowhere else I'd rather be," Onyx responded dryly, keeping his eyes off us.

"I'd second that," Radley said, targeting his words at the raven-haired male across from us.

Jasper studied them before turning to me with a smug smile. "I won't force anyone to speak first, so I'll present a question to the group. Whoever desires to answer may. What happened in New Jersey?"

I glanced between Radley and Onyx, neither offering an answer. As they exchanged glares filled with animosity, I broke the silence.

"Where do we even begin?"

"Likely from the beginning, right? Doesn't that seem like the logical thing to do?" Onyx snapped, still avoidant over providing any notable attention.

Radley inhaled sharply, about to retort, but I spoke up.

"Alright, listen. I refuse to continue this conversation without addressing the glaring issue." I fixed my stare on Onyx, indifferent to whether he met it. "If you have a problem, Onyx, express it openly. I won't tolerate sitting in a room with two grown men who continue to cast their frustrations on everyone else with passive-aggressive jabs. We're here to discuss our findings from the excursion, not to engage in petty banter until someone erupts. I hold an expectation to be treated with respect; you didn't accept disrespect from Radley, so stop being a hypocrite against your own standards."

I bit my tongue, preventing myself from divulging further.

Jasper raised his brows, nodding in approval before shifting to his friend. "Got to give her props for standing up to you, considering it's a rarity."

"Well, he brought it upon himself," Radley muttered beside

me, earning an elbow jab from me, which immediately resulted in a low cuss.

Onyx scowled at me, ire billowing as he flashed a fake smile. "My bad, *equal.* Feel free to continue."

I ignored his undermining tone and refocused on Jasper. "Apologies for the two temperamental children who, unfortunately, decided to join us."

Jasper smiled, dipping his head slightly. "No worries. Such is life. Please, continue."

I felt their resulting glares but remained unfazed. "The inner workings of the city were intact," I began, tracing my finger along the circle marking our trek. Most structures seemed functional, but the streets were silent—there had been no signs of activity for months, maybe years. Onyx led us into one of the only functioning skyscrapers, where we planned to scavenge and gather intel and explore more of the area once we cleared the first building."

"Did you manage to do that?" Jasper asked.

"No." I shook my head. "Everything was going smoothly until a Venturer from Region One confronted us."

"Adira," Radley interjected, peering at Jasper.

"You knew her?" Jasper's brow arched.

"I met her during a supply run to the East Coast. She was my contact, but beyond that, I know little," Radley shrugged.

Jasper stroked his beard, then looked at me, a cue to continue.

"Adira pulled a gun on Radley and trapped us in the stairwell before we could reach the second floor. We tried to explain why we, as two Venturers, were with Onyx." I recounted, glancing at the man I referenced, who seemed wholly detached from the conversation. "She refused to listen. When she fired, Onyx had to intervene."

"Did you kill her?" Jasper directed the question at the raven-haired male.

"I love how everyone assumes I kill on sight," Onyx replied, his voice edged with vexation. "If I wanted, I could wipe the entire human race off the face of this planet." He paused, letting the weight of his words sink in. "No, I didn't kill her. She was too valuable as a source of information."

Before Jasper could press further, I continued. "The gunshot woke whatever was sleeping in that skyscraper. We saw two mutated Runners before we had to run up the stairs to escape."

I paused, expecting questions about the Runners' appearance, but none came. Remembering their grotesque forms was unsettling enough.

"We cleared multiple floors as they chased us before we found a way to dive through one to escape. Onyx made sure Adira couldn't follow, closing the door just in time to keep the horde at bay," I finished as I glanced at Onyx, his disinterest gnawing at me.

Sensing my distraction, Radley took over. "We cleared that floor and were about to descend the other stairwell when we encountered another creature. Like the others, she was mutated, which we concluded was an outcome of the bombings. Fortunately, she was blind and couldn't locate us, but even with that on our side, the horde breached the door."

Jasper ran a distressed hand through his hair, clearly grasping the gravity of our situation.

Onyx interrupted, "I led them out a ninth-story window. These two," he gestured between us, "assumed I'd sacrificed myself."

He licked his lips, preparing to say something else but refrained. Dragging his boots off the table, he straightened in his chair. "While these two held the most pathetic funeral, I gathered intel on Region One."

Jasper's head snapped up toward his friend.

"The Walls were breached. The community hasn't existed for months. They tried to reach Region Two, but most died. The survivors are scattered throughout the city, and I wouldn't be surprised if some of them are attempting to move elsewhere."

Jasper rubbed his temples. "Do we know how many survived?"

Radley responded, "We can estimate. Reports showed over 10,000 survivors after the Fall, with about 3,000 to 3,500 in each community."

Jasper nodded at Onyx. "And with the conclusion of what you gather, what would you say the remnants would come out to be?"

Onyx exhaled deeply. "Between the mutated Runners, Rebels, and Scavengers—maybe twenty percent, if they were lucky."

Radley raised his brows at the defined loss; the infiltration and eradication of at least 2,400 lives proved to be unsettling.

"Good to know," Jasper nodded, refocusing on us. "Continue."

I swallowed, replaying the details. "Onyx decided it would be best for us to investigate the Runners he'd led out the window, but once we got down there, nothing was left."

Jasper frowned. "You're telling me over ten Runners vanished after falling from the ninth story?"

"Yep," Onyx replied, leaning back in his chair. "Where their bodies collided with the concrete was vacated as soon as we got down there."

I clenched my jaw, remembering what came next.

"Then shit went sideways," Onyx said, unfolding his arms. "There was a Runner out there that was nearly impossible to kill, requiring me to dive further into my reserves to wipe it out entirely."

Jasper's shock was evident. Onyx's use of the abilities he briefly mentioned seemed rare. I understood why he rarely used them, needing to control a level of power that seemed out of the question.

"Impossible to kill how?" Jasper asked.

"It was intelligent," I said.

"Intelligent?"

"It pulled an arrow from its head, acknowledged it, and tossed it aside. Even after a headshot, it recognized the weapon used against it. It also tried to pit us against each other to cause injury,"

Onyx explained, though every syllable seemed laced with utter indifference.

"How is that possible?" Jasper looked at us for insight.

Onyx spoke up, sharing the conclusion he'd come to while we were out there. "It was once a power wielder, like you and me."

"Are you suggesting—"

"I'm not suggesting. I know," Onyx interrupted, his jaw feathering with too many untold stories.

"It aligns with what we discussed but is far more convoluted than we expected." He ran a hand through his hair, his expression darkening. "We have the information we need. I'll relay it to the other Rebellion communities and spread the word quickly."

"That's probably the best call. It has become apparent that the higher-ups are desperate to maintain control at any cost," Radley added, mental exhaustion present in his voice.

Onyx gave Radley a brief, assessing glance before turning away, his thoughts returning to where they'd been before he chose to contribute.

"Is there anything else you need from us?" I asked Jasper, desperate to get out of the room that was a ticking time bomb.

He met my gaze, the storminess in his gray eyes betraying the turmoil our report had stirred. "For now, no. I appreciate your willingness to take on that mission and uncover what you did. It put you in grave danger, and your sacrifice speaks volumes. This information could be the key to uniting the Rebellion communities and finally dismantling what's been happening."

"It's about damn time," Onyx muttered, anticipation and hatred mingling with his raspy reply.

Jasper's expression softened slightly. "Until then, I believe the three of you deserve a moment of celebration for your bravery and contribution to the community."

EIGHTEEN

I offered to help with the preparations for the celebration Jasper had mentioned, but he immediately turned me down. He insisted that our participation would undermine the community's gesture of appreciation. Despite my protests, he remained firm, instructing us to find something to occupy our time and excusing our duties for the rest of the day.

I found a quiet spot on the grass near the courtyard, settling under the shade of a fir tree with a copy of *The Sun Also Rises*—a book I had stumbled upon in a guard tower during a shift. Opportunities to read had been scarce, always overshadowed by more pressing matters. Even within the Walls, interruptions were constant. Now, with a few hours to spare, I could finally lose myself in one of my favorite pastimes.

Once nestled against the tree, I took a moment to appreciate my surroundings. The early evening sun filtered through the leaves, casting intricate patterns of light and shadow on my skin. A soft breeze rustled the branches, offering a silent comfort. Birds chirped in the distance, their songs a cheerful accompaniment to the tranquil scene.

Then I heard a joyous sound—Imelda's laughter. It was bright and warm, as infectious as the sunlight kissing her golden-brown skin. Innocence and unfiltered joy filled it, reminding me of much simpler times.

Setting my book aside, I watched as she soared into the air on a swing. The breeze from her ascent blew back her dark brown curls, which bounced with each movement. Her smile was wide, her teeth flashing as she let out another peal of laughter, a giggled screech woven into it.

"You're going to spin me around the pole!" she exclaimed to the person responsible for her building height in the sky.

Onyx stood behind her, partially obscured, as she swung up and down. He still wore his black t-shirt, the fabric clinging to his muscular frame. One arm pushed her while the other hand rested casually in the pocket of his black military-style pants. Loose strands of hair swept across his face, casting a shadow along his defined jawline.

As an unfamiliar sound reached my ears, surprise greeted me —Onyx was laughing.

A genuine, heartfelt laugh that transformed his usually stoic features. A broad smile lit up his face, and I realized I would have captured the scene in a painting if I were an artist. His laughter, deep and resonant, was as breathtaking as the expansive night sky that I'd found myself frequently admiring here. His eyes closed to near slits as the sound rolled from him, his shoulders moving in its wake. The pure joy of the moment softened the usual raspiness in his voice. It was a rare glimpse into his softer, more compassionate side.

The two of them enjoyed each other's company without a care in the world—no fear of loss, no worry about survival. They simply existed together, creating a fleeting but beautiful memory in which Imelda could be a child again, and Onyx could be himself.

"You better hold on then," Onyx said, his voice uncharacteristically light, devoid of its usual edge.

Imelda squealed, kicking her legs as he pushed her higher. Her laughter echoed through the park, filling the emptiness inside me with warmth.

"Stop!" she giggled, the lines in her cheeks deepening.

"Stop what?" Onyx chuckled, pushing her again.

The chains of the swing clanked as she reached the apex, the sound echoing before the tension snapped back into place. Her laughter grew louder, pure joy radiating from her small frame.

"Stop what?" he asked again, catching her as she swung back, wrapping his large hands around her.

He playfully squeezed her sides, and she folded in on herself with laughter. A deep belly laugh followed her squeal, a slight snort escaping her, and I couldn't help but smile.

She slid off the swing, panting between giggles. As she looked back for him, he had already moved. Before she could turn entirely, he appeared behind her and lifted her off the ground, tossing her into the air. She shrieked with delight, and as she fell back toward him, he caught her effortlessly, cradling her close. His broad frame enveloped her as one arm swung under her legs, the other resting on the back of her head. She wrapped her arms around his neck, tucking her head under his chin.

They stayed like that for a moment—a silent exchange of comfort and protection.

But then Onyx's happiness faded, replaced by a shadow of worry and sadness. The harsh reality they lived in eclipsed their brief joy. His jaw tightened as he held her, the weight of their situation pressing down. He lifted his chin slightly, pressing a kiss to the crown of her head, whispering something softly. She nodded in response before he set her down.

I knew then that he would have held her forever if time allowed.

The grass rustled beside me, and I looked up to find Radley towering over me, his arm resting against the tree. He wore a light blue, loose-fitting T-shirt and gray sweatpants that hung low on his hips. He took a sip from the glass of amber liquid in his hand before smirking at me.

"I was wondering where you'd gone. I should have known you'd be out here reading."

"I've been meaning to open this book for a while now, and well," I glanced back at Onyx and Imelda, watching as he ruffled her hair playfully, "I guess I got a little distracted."

Radley followed my gaze, a soft smile growing as he listened to Imelda's continued laughter. "A valid distraction."

We watched as Onyx and Imelda approached the gathering crowd, exchanging playful shoves. Onyx engaged with a few men I recognized from perimeter shifts while Imelda weaved through those setting up tables and bringing out an array of food selections.

"I can't imagine what she's witnessed," I muttered.

"Neither of us can," Radley replied, taking another drink. "She's seen this apocalypse unfold from the beginning. Being with someone who isn't family tells me she's faced unimaginable loss."

I shook my head, pulling my knees to my chest and rubbing my eyes. "It's unfair, you know? All of this."

Radley sighed, glancing at Onyx as he interacted with the Rebels, a soft grin crossing his features. More people gathered, smiling and sharing stories with one another. Food was piled on the tables as those responsible for the setup worked to finish, scattering bottles of alcohol amongst the selection. The park's center bustled as a few community members stacked firewood in a large pit, each clatter of wood reminding us of how we'd gotten here and all we'd overcome.

"The whole thing is unfair," Radley uttered, breaking the silence. "And sadly, there was nothing we could have done to stop it, even if we'd wanted to. But now, we can try to help those displaced and misunderstood. We can work to dismantle what's inhumane. It won't undo the damage, the lives lost, or the trauma, but it's a step. And that's something."

I beamed, nodding in response.

"No words, huh?" He chuckled, raising the glass to his lips again.

"When you're not temperamental, you speak from an admirable place. How you articulate your thoughts—it's inspiring. You're a leader, Radley."

He rolled his eyes slightly before smiling back. "Well, in true leadership fashion, how about I help you up, we grab a drink, and start enjoying our evening? It's been a while since either of us could relax. And might I add, this celebration is for all three of us, so hiding under this tree with a book is out of the question."

I gave in and extended my hand, which he grasped firmly, pulling me to my feet. I dusted off my pants and glanced at the book under the tree, its pages untouched and the cover glinting against the sun now edging closer to the horizon.

Radley chuckled softly. "It'll be safe there."

He gently tugged my hand, guiding me toward the gathering. I looked back again at the tall grass cradling the book; every unspoken meaning behind its pages seemed to stare at me as the distance grew.

I SAT BY THE FIRE, my knees tucked into my chest. Night had fallen after we finished the dinner prepared for us. The contrast between the darkness and the fire's light created dancing shadows, casting flickering shapes of those who moved in and out of the pit's glow. Conversations continued around me, a harmonious murmur that blended with the crackling wood and the fire's nightly serenade.

Radley had left my side a few minutes earlier, drawn away by a sudden need to speak with Jasper. Part of me didn't mind. I relished the silence, the sight of those around me finding comfort in each other's company. The community was a mosaic of people —elderly, young children, those close to my age—all united by shared loss and a longing for something more.

A sense of family, of belonging.

A community. A found family.

All things that Jasper had so selflessly given them.

I watched a couple embrace near the fire, sharing a glass of alcohol. They huddled close, exchanging a few kisses before slipping into the shadows. I wondered if they had survived the Fall together or met within the Rebellion and fallen in love. Either way, the thought ripped at something I'd come too comfortable with harboring deep within myself.

Before I could dwell on it, I heard a deep exhale beside me. Someone lowered themselves to the grass, and I turned to see Onyx holding two glasses, his gaze flicking toward me. The firelight intensified his eyes; his dark raven hair accentuated their depth.

"A peace offering," he raspily stated, extending one glass to me.

I took it, eyeing the contents. "What is it? Poison?"

He chuckled, shaking his head before taking a sip of his own. The glow of the fire highlighted the sharp lines of his jaw. "How messed up would it be if I poisoned you on the night we're supposed to be celebrating our success and survival?"

"Heartless," I teased, taking a drink and quickly recognizing its dry and floral taste.

White wine. He had been paying attention.

"Kind of on brand, though," I added, shrugging before hugging my knees again.

At my retort, he nearly choked. I watched him from the corner of my eye as he set his glass down and stretched his legs, planting his hands behind him to stay upright. Despite the darkness, the firelight highlighted the sleeves of his T-shirt, which clung tightly to his arms, their breadth undeniable.

He cleared his throat, glancing up at the stars. "I wanted to apologize."

I raised a brow, looking at him as he stared upward. "For what, exactly?"

"All of it." He lowered his head, his striking features softening as he met my gaze. "For how I've treated you—from the beginning until today with Jasper. It was uncalled for, and you didn't deserve it."

I took another mouthful from my glass, feeling the warmth of the alcohol spread through me and providing a bit of courage. "Oh, you mean you're apologizing for demeaning me? Is that it?"

"Yes, I apologize for being a demeaning asshole," he said, crossing one leg over the other, his posture unexpectedly open. "You didn't deserve my wrath. You're a good person. I hope you know that."

I almost coughed on the wine, not expecting the conversation to take this turn. "And this is coming from where?"

"Does a compliment need a reason?" He quirked a brow before leaning back on his forearms. "I'm just stating facts, and I feel it's something you don't hear often."

A dig in an unexpected place.

"Tell me," he continued, leaning closer, "do you get told that often?"

"Is this an interrogation now?"

He shrugged, smirking before looking away. "If you want to see it that way, sure."

I exhaled, lifting the glass to my lips for more added courage. It wasn't a topic I expected to discuss, especially with him. Once I finished my drawn-out drink, I lowered the cup, tracing its rim with my finger and lowering my eyes.

"To answer your question, no."

"I already knew that, but thanks for being honest." His cocky tone forced my head back toward him. "I feel you forget what I'm capable of. And before you accuse me, no, I didn't read your mind without your consent."

He knew where my thoughts had gone.

"I can pick up on things. How people carry themselves often speaks louder than words. You're no exception," he continued. "I could tell exactly what kind of person you were when I landed on that rooftop."

"What kind of person are you referring to?" I found my eyes wandering over him, tracing the length of his muscular legs to his torso and finally meeting the scar etched along the expanse of his face.

If only he knew my entire truth.

He already had his eyes pinned on me. "The kind who would do anything for the people they love, yet rarely receives gratitude. Someone others take advantage of because of an unwavering kindness. One who often prioritizes others over themselves."

I bit my lip, exhaling as I dropped my eyes from his.

"Reading you to filth, huh?" Onyx shifted his weight, finished his drink, and set the glass aside.

"Something like that," I replied, taking another sip and hugging myself tighter.

"There's a reason I can read you so easily," he admitted, even though it was something I already knew and was far too familiar with.

"Because you're superior and know things on a whim?" I joked, trying to distract myself from the rising tension and prods into areas that were far too personal and could give away too much if crossed.

"I'll take that backhanded compliment," he smiled, "but no, it's because you and I are undeniably similar."

My breath caught in my throat, an unexpected curiosity and concern stirring within me.

"An avid people-pleaser, too, huh?" I asked, forcing my unease beneath the surface.

He cocked his head, answering with a gesture. "I would sacrifice myself for those I love without hesitation. But sometimes, I care too much in the wrong situations with the wrong people, which has landed me in questionable circumstances."

I unfolded my legs, no longer needing to close myself off. "And that's led you to shut people out the moment you meet them, hasn't it?"

"Now it's my turn, huh?" he glanced at me with a soft smile.

I returned the look. "It's only fair we both get read to filth. It's an equal trade."

"Right, an equal trade from *my equal*." He winked.

I elbowed his shoulder, making him laugh—the sound similar to what I'd heard with Imelda earlier.

"Okay, fine." He looked at me, shifting until he was lying on his side, propping himself up and placing a fist under his cheek. "Hit me." I raised my arm again, and he shook his head. "Not like that, smartass."

I chuckled softly and turned to face him, folding my legs and setting my cup between them. "You put up a tough exterior to guard yourself from emotional pain, likely because of something you went through in the past. Ever since, you've preferred to appear a heartless prick to avoid attachment, protecting yourself from heartache. You choose to be misunderstood rather than seen, sacrificing yourself for those you care about to avoid it."

He nodded and pursed his lips, making his scar more prominent. "Ouch. That was nearly too perfect."

I shrugged, wrapping my hands around the glass and taking another sip.

He watched me, his eyes softening as his lips began to softly tug upward. His expression mixed with admiration and appreciation, though I doubted I was reading it correctly.

"You are," he announced as quickly as the thought crossed my mind.

My cheeks heated instantly. "You said you don't read minds without consent."

"Occasionally. It depends on the situation," he grinned. "I should've been more specific, huh?"

"You're a bastard. You know that, right?"

He raised a finger. "And I'd be lying if I said your insult was incorrect."

I laughed, shaking my head, and looked down before returning my gaze to him. I found him still watching me with the same unreadable expression.

"Do you have something you'd like to say, *bastard?*"

"Is that a new term of endearment from *my equal?*" The playful snarkiness in his voice almost made me smile.

I narrowed my eyes, his grin infectious over a joke he found far more amusing than I did.

Our eyes locked, the flickering firelight casting shadows that danced across Onyx's face. I pondered his willingness to open up, starkly contrasting to the man who had greeted me on the rooftops. Onyx had always seemed unapproachable, shrouded in a protective shell that deflected any attempts at deeper connection. Yet tonight, there was a softness to him, a vulnerability that caught me off guard. It was as if the hardened exterior he so carefully maintained had cracked, allowing glimpses of a more complex, perhaps even tormented, inner world.

The air between us felt charged with implied words and untold stories, making me question the layers of his persona and the shadows lurking within my own.

I finished my drink and set the glass beside me, shifting my attention to the night sky. The stars twinkled against the dark canvas, a few shining brighter than the others. Despite the sun having set, the air remained warm. I wasn't sure if the fire provided it or if I needed to extend gratitude to the alcohol coursing through my veins.

I considered Onyx's interactions with others, particularly his protective nature toward Imelda. He had a soft spot for her, a part of his heart that remained unguarded.

"Is that why you are the way you are with Imelda?" The question slipped out, fueled by my wine, and I reminded myself to remain guarded.

"What do you mean?" Onyx lay on his back with his arms tucked behind his head and his eyes fixated on the stars.

"Your desire to shield yourself from attachment failed with her. Is that why you're so protective?"

"That's a fair question," he stated into the darkness as if speaking with himself. "I found Imelda when she was twelve. She didn't tell me what happened to her family, but she allowed me to tap into her memories after a few months of our survival together. I won't share what I saw, but it was something no child should witness. I vowed to protect her with my life, no matter the cost."

I clenched my jaw, recalling her earlier happiness, the purity that somehow survived. I could only imagine the horrors she had shown Onyx.

"The innocence, the lives, the families taken by the government's decisions are inexcusable. It fuels my rage," he continued. "The secrecy and planning behind it needed to be stopped when I was in the ranks, but I failed. We knew their secrets, their lies, the extent of their betrayal. It started with a desire for control, which turned into an intent to wipe out all who opposed them. I can't accept living with the horror of knowing those I care for are at constant risk."

"I understand your desire to protect those you love. I feel the same way," I whispered.

He glanced at me from the corner of his eye before returning to the sky. "I can't imagine what I'd do if something happened to her. It would forfeit my promise to keep her safe, let her see the world, and teach her. It would unleash a part of me I might not control."

I nodded, understanding his fear all too well and recalling the extent of his abilities he'd unleashed in Jersey City.

It was just the surface.

"Enjoying yourselves?" Jasper questioned, and I turned to find him accompanied by Radley.

Jasper smiled, the glint in his eyes providing a load of questions to his best friend. Radley, on the other hand, narrowed his gaze with what seemed to be a mix of aggravation and jealousy over Onyx and my closeness.

"We were just conversing," Onyx stated, glancing at Radley with a glint of something I couldn't quite place—bitterness, perhaps.

Jasper nodded, but Radley remained unphased, keeping his arms crossed and his lips drawn in a tight line.

"Hopefully, you've learned Onyx isn't as big of a prick as he seems," Jasper said, breaking the tension with a grin.

"Not *as* big of one, I suppose," I smirked, standing up. "Though, I did read him to filth."

"Must've been rough for you, then." He chuckled, glancing at Onyx, who loomed over me as he came to stand.

"I survived. That should say enough, shouldn't it?" Onyx replied with a smile.

Radley's eyes shifted between us, assessing every word. I flashed him a reassuring look, but it only seemed to provide minimal reassurance.

"Well," Jasper sighed, the lightness in his tone vanishing, "I hate to ruin the evening, but we need to talk. Now."

Onyx's demeanor changed instantly. The relaxed, easygoing man from moments ago was gone, his hardened exterior making its usual appearance. His eyes locked onto Jasper, the powder blue in his gaze shifting to a near-white as he moved into the discussion.

"What happened?"

Jasper pinched the bridge of his nose before speaking. "While Radley and I were catching up, we went to the mission debrief room to lock up for the night. With the celebrations and kids around, I didn't want to risk anything."

Onyx's jaw tightened at the mention of youth, but Jasper raised a hand. "If you're worried about Imelda, don't be. She's safe."

"Okay, then, what's the issue?"

"The map detailing our community's layout is missing," Jasper muttered, not wanting to alarm the others.

Onyx's face drained of color, the fire casting an eerie glow on his now pale skin. "You mean the map with all locators on it?"

Jasper's sympathetic look was enough of an answer.

It was.

"Damn it, Jasper," Onyx hissed. "Do you know what this means?"

Radley and I exchanged confused glances, unsure of the map's importance.

"I'm sorry if this is a stupid question," I nearly whispered, "but what exactly is the significance of this map?"

"Go ahead," Onyx prompted Jasper, his agitation growing. "Tell her."

"The map contains a detailed layout of the entire camp. It shows the storage locations of our weapons caches, which buildings house what, and where each person stays," Jasper explained, sighing heavily. "I think you get the point."

Someone had access to the community's most intricate details —a map that could be deadly in the wrong hands.

Radley shook his head, distressed. "Who would take it, and how would they even know about it?"

"Only those closest to me in rank know of its existence," Jasper explained, looking at Onyx. "I trust them with my life."

"So, someone close to you had to be the one to take it?" Radley suggested.

"That seems likely, but logically, it makes no sense," Jasper clenched his jaw. "I trust them completely."

Onyx raised an eyebrow. "You're sure none of them would cross you if it benefited them?"

"No," Jasper answered confidently. "They wouldn't cross me."

"Not even with government incentives?" Onyx prodded, glancing at Radley before returning his gaze to Jasper.

The two friends exchanged looks, a silent understanding

passing between them. Jasper's expression held a mix of caution and something close to a warning.

I sighed, stepping in before accusations flew. "Is it possible someone misplaced it?"

"No," Jasper responded immediately. "That map is highly valuable and has never been moved."

Onyx's temper flared. "If you trust everyone with access to the map, and it wasn't moved, how did it seemingly vanish?"

Jasper ignored most of what he had said. "Since I have permitted you the same access, are you suggesting *you* would cross me, Onyx?"

The tension thickened, Onyx's rage palpable. "You want to question me right now?"

"You suggested I question those who know its location, and you're one of them," Jasper inferred, his anger building to match Onyx's.

"After everything I've done for you, you think I'd take it? And for what?" Onyx's voice was lethal.

"I didn't suggest that. I'm stating you brought up the idea of questioning my trusted people, and you're one of them," Jasper stated nonchalantly.

I quickly cut through the tension. "Whoever took the map likely wanted this. They knew it would cause strain between you two."

"I agree," Radley joined in, attempting to prevent the two from going at one another. "If they knew your relationship and Onyx's reaction, it seems tactical to create a wedge."

Onyx shifted his gaze between Radley and me, scrutinizing Radley closely as his pulsating gaze swept over his frame a handful of times. Jasper rubbed his eyes, sighing. "You're right. Leverage like this could cause a fallout, opening us to weakness, which is exactly what an enemy would want."

Onyx's harshness softened slightly. "Okay, if only a few people knew the map's location, it's a process of elimination, right?"

Jasper nodded in agreement.

I spoke next. "How do you confront them without making them feel untrusted? Sensitive topics like this could cause even more issues."

"As we just saw," Radley added, "this needs to be handled strategically. If a mole is leveraging the Rebels, they might have others interested in causing a split."

Jasper turned to Onyx, his trusted friend, who he relied on most. "Onyx?"

Onyx nodded, understanding the unspoken question in Jasper's tone. "Yes, we're on the same page. I'll do what's necessary for your community, even if it goes against my principles."

Jasper exhaled deeply, tucking his hands into his pockets as he nodded in gratitude—the weight of his ask weighing heavily on his shoulders.

"We have to keep you out of the line of fire somehow," Onyx stated calmly, squeezing Jasper's shoulder. "If that requires a sacrifice on my part, I will gladly oblige time and time again."

FOR THE REST of the night, Onyx immersed himself in the task Jasper had entrusted him with. He moved through the crowd, conversing with those privy to the map's location and subtly probing their subconscious minds. The dialogue often seemed random, almost inconsequential, giving him the cover he needed to delve deeper without raising suspicion. Despite the casual tone of these exchanges, each person left the conversation with a sense of gratitude, thanking Onyx for his unwavering commitment to the community.

He was a pillar of strength and a protector, offering his abilities while expecting nothing in return. The community recognized his sacrifices, respecting and admiring the quiet resilience that defined him.

As the night wore on, Onyx approached us, his expression grave. His face, usually composed and inscrutable, now reflected the weight of his findings—or the lack thereof. He explained that his efforts had yielded nothing suspicious. No one had shown any interest in the map, let alone the intent to steal it.

Despite his thorough and diligent efforts, the perpetrator remained elusive, hidden in the shadows. The threat lingered, undisclosed and unknown, leaving a palpable tension in the air as we grappled with the mystery and the potential danger it posed to our fragile sense of security.

NINETEEN

adley and I strolled down the quiet streets of the Rebellion community. The night deepened, and most of those who had joined the celebration had returned to their quarters. Onyx and Jasper were among those who had excused themselves, but their reasons went beyond fatigue. They needed to discuss the pressing issue of the missing map and strategize after coming up empty-handed, even after Onyx had used his abilities to probe the minds of those involved.

Six individuals, including Onyx, knew the location of the map. Onyx carefully curated each conversation, subtly probing for any signs of betrayal, yet each person proved their loyalty to the community. While it was a relief to know that none of Jasper's trusted confidants were involved, one unsettling question remained—who had taken it?

The answer eluded us, and the map remained in the hands of an unknown individual with potentially dangerous intentions.

Radley's near-white hair seemed to glow under the moonlight as he walked beside me, his hands buried in the pockets of his sweatpants. He kicked a rock, sending it skittering along the barren street, which triggered the memory of us walking the city streets just outside Region Three—before everything changed.

He sighed deeply and turned to me; concern etched his eyes alongside an emotion I couldn't quite decipher, one that had lingered since we agreed to stand beside Onyx and the Rebellion.

"Are you okay?" he asked softly.

My eyes wandered to the inky black sky above. The stars had grown brighter as the night wore on, outshining any I'd witnessed before our escape. The air had turned brisk, and I wrapped my arms around myself, tracing the goosebumps on my skin. Despite the cold, I wasn't ready to return to our quarters. My mind was too full.

"I'm worried," I confessed, exhaling deeply as I pulled my gaze from the sky.

"I'd be lying if I said I wasn't," Radley sighed.

"It makes me wonder who in this community could harbor such malice," I said, shaking my head while walking a fine line. "To put innocent lives at risk after all we've been through—it's beyond insensitive. It makes them no better than those responsible for the Fall."

Silence enveloped us, the tranquility of the night stark against the backdrop of our uneasy thoughts. The distant murmur of conversations floated through the air as the last remnants of people retreated to their homes, locking the doors behind them to settle in for the evening.

Home.

This community was a sanctuary for its residents—where they felt protected and surrounded by people who shared their desires.

To survive.

To live.

To be free from the government's grip.

To escape the constant chase from Venturers, Runners, and Scavengers.

They longed for a place to belong after enduring exile and loss.

Radley's statement aligned with my thoughts. "It's hard to believe someone would betray this sense of family, this unity."

His words stirred a string of emotions—anger, frustration, and sadness for all those who attempted to rebuild and hold on to fragile peace that could shatter at any moment—something I knew too well and was forced to embrace.

"It reminds me of the beginning. When everything fell apart." I said, bitterness lacing my words. "How those we trusted turned their backs on us, treating every life as expendable. And for what?"

Radley shook his head. "I don't know."

"I'll never understand why some still oppose each other after witnessing the devastation firsthand," I continued, rubbing my arms as a chill of unease passed through me. "We stepped away from the government once we learned the truth. We refused to perpetuate the damage. But those who remain aligned with their ideals continue to cling to control and corruption."

"Like Gael," Radley said, his voice heavy with disdain.

The mere mention of the name made my stomach churn.

I nodded, feeling the weight of past associations. Speaking out against them wouldn't change anything—it wouldn't bring back the lost lives or erase the trauma endured by millions. It wouldn't restore innocence or heal the extensive damage done.

It took back nothing.

We continued walking, our boots thudding quietly against the concrete, the only signs of the remaining human presence in the enveloping night. I wasn't sure of the time, but I knew we were moving into a new day—a chance to start fresh.

The cold set in, and I rubbed my arms again, shifting slightly. "I say we head back and get some rest before tomorrow. I'm sure—"

Before I could finish, a deafening blast shattered the night's silence. My body jolted, and I turned to see a building on the main street, where the celebration had been, engulfed in roaring flames. The orangish-yellow hue contrasted sharply against the dark sky, signifying the chaos that had erupted.

"What the hell..." Radley whispered as another explosion followed, sending more fire into the sky.

We froze, the peaceful night quickly molding into unimaginable destruction. I grabbed Radley's hand, pulling him forward as we sprinted toward the source.

Toward the imminent threat.

We cleared the street we had walked down moments before as people poured out of the homes they'd just entered, confusion and fear coating their faces. Many were half-asleep, jolted awake by the detonation and its implications.

Radley shouted warnings and words of caution to those emerging from their thresholds, urging them away from the destruction.

"Get everyone you know outside!"

"The community is under attack!"

His words barely registered as my mind focused singularly on reaching the site of the explosions. I needed an answer for the attack that clashed with delivered promises while clinging to my need to find the others. My feet moved with an urgency fueled by adrenaline as we rounded a corner, bringing the burning buildings into full view.

Under the intense heat, the structures on the main street crumbled, no longer able to withstand the fire's ferocity. The building beside the mission debrief room, where they stored most of the weapons, was reduced to smoldering rubble.

Nearby, another building was ablaze, its wooden beams groaning under the heat of the flames. Its structure was familiar—responsible for housing several community members, Onyx included. The windows had shattered from the heat, sending a cascade of broken glass across the sidewalk. Flames licked at the wooden frame, the intense heat warping the metal fixtures and reducing the interior to remnants of what once was. As the roof collapsed, fiery debris fell into the flames below, adding to the growing pile of destruction.

The targeted nature of the attacks was evident. They aimed to dismantle the defenses and cause maximum damage. Whoever had taken the map knew precisely where to strike, intending to hit us at our most vulnerable points.

Radley and I moved closer, the searing heat penetrating our clothing, a relentless reminder of the onslaught ravaging a community that sheltered innocent lives. Smoke and the acrid stench of burning wood and metal clung to the air, making it difficult to breathe.

Suddenly, Radley slammed into me, pushing us both to the ground just as another explosion rocked the area. A flash of light came first, the only warning before the detonation followed. The blast sent glass and debris shooting in all directions, the intense heat singeing my arm hairs and filling the one-peaceful night sky with smoke.

"Shit!" I pushed myself off the ground, ash coating my cheeks as I scanned the destruction. Fires raged in all directions, illuminating the night with their deadly glow. People fled their homes and rushed toward the open field, trying to make sense of the chaos.

Desperately, I searched the crowd but couldn't spot any familiar faces.

I had to do something.

Tearing away from Radley, I sprinted toward the building where Onyx slept, hoping he had foreseen the attack or escaped in time. My name echoed behind me as Radley shouted in concern, unable to snag me before I broke away.

The heat intensified as I neared the building, which was teetering on the brink of collapse. As I reached the threshold, my progress halted, and my body collided with another's.

I looked up to see Onyx, his eyes glowing with rage and concern over the unfolding situation. Ash and a deep crimson stained his white T-shirt and military-style cargo pants.

Blood.

I attempted to address it, but he shook his head.

"It's not mine," he confirmed, his voice monotone but simmering with fury.

"Whose?" I asked, part of me dreading the potential answers.

"Another community member. They didn't make it." He clenched his jaw and extended a hand to help me up. "I don't know who the hell is attacking, but we need to find the others."

Radley joined us, scanning for injuries before speaking. "They're attacking from the inside, which means—"

"There's a fucking mole," Onyx growled, anger billowing from him, highlighting his eagerness to unleash on whoever was responsible.

He moved toward the park where people gathered, approaching the crowd, and we followed. Everyone who had fled quieted as soon as Onyx came into view, a wave of relief washing over them at the sight of one of the Rebellion's pillars of strength.

Yet Jasper and Imelda remained unaccounted for.

Onyx's voice, though urgent, carried a calming force, cutting through the chaos. He was not just a leader but a Captain—someone they deeply trusted.

"Listen up. I'll only give orders once. I need someone to perform a head count. Protect each other and stay vigilant. Got it?"

A chorus of agreement rose from the crowd, their faces reflecting a mix of fear and conviction.

"We're still trying to identify the threat. There's a traitor among us, but I promise they will be dealt with accordingly. Stay away from the buildings—they're being targeted. Anyone with medical knowledge tends to the injured. I'll gather more supplies. Take charge, use your abilities, and don't back down."

The members nodded, some embracing each other for comfort and drawing strength from their shared bond. This was more than a community—it was a family.

Before I could speak to Onyx, he vanished, only to reappear moments later with his arms full of medical supplies. Another explosion engulfed the building he had just exited. Based on the timing, the perpetrator seemed close enough to follow Onyx's movements, leading me to scan our surroundings for anyone who seemed suspicious. I came up empty-handed, my gaze locked on the fire consuming the structure from all sides, highlighting the enemy's strategic intent.

The image of the ignited bunker and how Imelda obliterated it flashed through my mind. The pattern of demolition was disturbingly similar but far more sinister.

Radley grabbed my arm, pulling my attention back to the park where the medical team sorted supplies, taking inventory of what Onyx had scavenged. The raven-haired man vanished again, reappearing seconds later, tossing weapons to a few trusted members—likely from a hidden stash.

Those he handed them to were the same faces Onyx had spoken with earlier—Jasper's trusted five.

He tossed weapons to us with a stern order. "Equip yourselves accordingly. You're part of this community now; defend it at all costs."

We nodded, grabbing the rifles and checking the clips before slinging them over our shoulders. While fully loaded, I knew we had to make every shot count. Radley and I exchanged a look—mine held determination to protect the community while his carried something else entirely.

"Niel and Patrick cover the park's south end. Hansen, Brooks, and Lennox search the buildings for survivors. The medical team will assist the injured," Onyx commanded. "Defend each other with everything you have. That's an order."

"Yes, Sir," they replied in unison, moving to their assigned tasks.

Onyx turned to us. "You two are with me. Let's move."

Without waiting, he strode past us, prepared to do whatever was necessary to protect his home—the community—and the innocence that remained.

TWENTY

We advanced toward the gates, the memory of our initial confrontation with Jasper looming on the community's perimeter. The rifles once trained on us by his command felt distant now, dulled by the disarray of the present.

The guard towers loomed ominously above the closed entrance, their dark silhouettes stark against the fiery glow from the main street. Despite the locked gates, which should have signaled security, an unsettling dissonance permeated the atmosphere. It was as if the walls whispered secrets of unseen horrors, concealed yet ever-present.

As we pressed forward, my gaze swept the tree line, searching for any hint of movement. Every step felt monitored and watched by unseen eyes. Silence clung to the air even with the destruction, creating an oppressive stillness.

Everything felt off.

Our boots transitioned from cold concrete to softer grass. Damp with dew, it brushed against our calves and provided a slight chill, contrasting the heat from the fires that nearly scorched our skin.

As we neared the guard towers, more details became apparent.

The left tower housed a still figure, slumped in a position that suggested something far more final than sleep. A dark, slick line trailed down the side of the structure, fresh blood gleaming in the dim light. Despite appearing vacant, the right tower radiated something ominous that made my heart sink.

"Maddox," Onyx called out, his raspy voice cutting through the silence as he glanced up at the visible figure in the left tower.

The name hung unanswered, amplifying the knot of concern twisting in my stomach.

He called again, but no answer came.

Death had beaten us here.

"Shit," Onyx muttered, stepping forward with a desire to help and avenge those fallen.

Even with the desire to provide aid, we had no choice but to move forward and leave the men behind. Their fates were a grim reminder of the price of vigilance.

The grass grew denser with each step, its blades whispering warnings against my legs. The air grew cooler in tandem, and the scent of damp earth mingled with the lingering smoke that shrouded the community. I raised my weapon, placing my finger on the trigger, ready to face whoever had unleashed the attack.

A figure emerged from the depths of the tree line, and the three of us raised our guns in sync, moving like a finely tuned military unit ready to strike.

I froze as my finger brushed the trigger, recognizing the bright copper hair that seemed to glow against the fiery backdrop. Jasper stumbled into view, clutching his side as blood seeped through his fingers.

His shirt was torn, and his pants were dirty, likely from maneuvering through debris when the attack began. His breaths came in ragged gasps, getting more shallow with each inhale. Relief momentarily flickered in his gray eyes before an undercurrent of dread replaced it as he looked us over.

"Jasper," Onyx called out, urgency lacing his voice as he rushed to his side. "What the hell happened?"

Jasper wheezed as Onyx looped an arm under his, helping him stay upright. The hand covering Jasper's side slipped, revealing a deep gash visible through the cut in his shirt. It wasn't deep enough to be lethal, but it, alongside the blood loss, had created enough of an impact.

His response was barely more than a whisper. "They're here."

"Who?" I pressed, my voice tight with tension.

Radley's gaze shifted toward the gates, and I followed his line of sight. Two small metallic objects soured through the air, highlighted by the moonlight as if on cue. A split second later, they detonated with a deafening roar.

The shockwave hit me like a physical blow, and my knees buckled in response. A high-pitched whine sounded from it, drowning out everything else. Instinctively, I covered my ears, trying to block out the intensity of the blast.

Smoke billowed from the explosion, thick and suffocating, quickly swallowing the area we stood in. The world around us dissolved into a white haze, visibility reduced to mere inches. Disoriented, I struggled to my feet, fighting to control my breathing while avoiding inhaling too much of the unknown gas. Raising an arm, I covered my mouth and nose and began a blind search through the dense smoke, hoping to find the others.

Reaching out, my fingers brushed against a chest, but the relief that followed quickly turned to dread as I realized the rough, familiar fabric belonged to a Venturer uniform.

Panic surged through me as a hand clamped around my throat, lifting me off the ground with familiar strength. I kicked my legs, struggling desperately to gather air as the male ripped me from the haze.

As the smoke cleared, my vision adjusted to the figure holding me. First, I saw a mix of mahogany and black hair, then emerald eyes gleaming with amusement and satisfaction. His lips curled into an unnatural and inhumane smile, delight coating every inch of his expression.

Gael.

"Hello, Astrid," he greeted, his voice low and mocking. "You weren't expecting me, were you?"

I gripped his forearm, trying to loosen his hold. "How...how are you..." I choked, the words cut off as his grip tightened.

"Alive?" He raised a brow, contempt glinting beneath his glower.

He lifted his free hand, revealing scars that marred his skin—burns from our last encounter. The damage didn't stop at his hand but tracked up the left side of his neck, disappearing beneath the collar of his uniform.

Radley called out from within the smoke, and my eyes shifted in concern.

Gael sneered, slamming me against a tree with enough force to send pain radiating down my spine. I bit back a cry, the agony sharp but fueling my anger.

"Some unfortunate, disgusting power wielders within the Walls healed me." Gael continued, his voice laced with malice. "They thought they'd save themselves by extending the graciousness of their services, but I sent them off for experimentation." He chuckled, the sound dark and twisted. "There's something so satisfying about telling someone I'll spare them if they comply, only to break that promise when they oblige."

"You sick bastard," I spat, fury igniting within me as I held his bright emerald gaze. "You should be dead."

His smile widened, a sinister expression darkening his features. "Should be, but I'm not. And now, I'm here to finish what I started—what I *promised.*"

I thrashed against his grip, desperate for leverage. My foot scraped for purchase, but he sensed the attempt and countered, wrenching me away with a brutal yank. He tossed me to the ground, and I landed hard, the impact driving the air from my lungs. For a moment, I could only gasp, savoring the fleeting relief of oxygen filling my chest as the crushing pressure lifted.

I struggled to push myself onto my hands and knees, pain

radiating through my body. Through blurred vision, I caught sight of the thick cloud beginning to dissipate.

Gael's voice cut through the chaos, "Still baffled about how we found you?"

His words were a taunt, a reminder of our failed defenses. Before I could muster a response, his boot slammed into my stomach, a vicious blow that stole my breath. I choked on a cry, the sound strangled by the agony that surged through me. My body curled inward, instinctively trying to shield itself from further harm. I fought to roll onto my side, my gaze searching through the smoky veil until I caught sight of Onyx.

He trembled, his hand moving to his arm, tearing away an electric cord. His dark brows furrowed over his eyes, rage burning within them the storm that brewed beneath the surface. The crimson stain on his shirt had spread, the once-white fabric now a canvas of blood, blurring the line between ally and enemy.

Gael met Onyx's rage with a sardonic grin, stepping away from me to face him directly. "Pleasure seeing you again."

"Who sent you?" Onyx snarled, each word laced with barely restrained violence. His body trembled, not just from the aftershocks of the electric assault but from the sheer force of his hatred —the only thing keeping Gael from being obliterated were the prongs buried in his skin.

Gael raised an eyebrow, meeting Onyx's fiery gaze with a detached demeanor. "Sent? I think you mean guided."

Onyx's jaw tightened, every muscle in his body straining with the desire for annihilation. His eyes flicked to me for a moment, the anger in them shifting into a fierce need to protect not only me but the community as a whole.

"You know, for her having been a government puppet post-Fall, I figured a man like you would've killed her immediately." His tongue clicked against the roof of his mouth, the words seeming almost conversational. "Such a shame."

Onyx didn't flinch. "And for the longest time, I assumed that standing alongside the President made you capable. Seems we were both wrong."

I couldn't help but smile at Onyx's defiance, watching as annoyance flickered across Gael's face.

The two locked eyes and the air between them remained thick with implied threats. I kept my gaze on Onyx, analyzing his intentions and searching for any sign of his next move. As the remaining smog cleared, the gruesome scene unfolded before us. Jasper came into view first, slumped against a tree, one hand clutching his side and concealing his gash. Remarkably, he seemed untouched by the surrounding carnage—a testament to Onyx's brutal efficiency in dispatching the soldiers who had dared to challenge him.

The bodies of Gael's guards lay strewn across the ground, dismembered and lifeless. Blood soaked the grass, contrasting against the lush greenery and serving as a morbid display of Onyx's wrath.

The message to Gael was clear—the same fate awaited him.

My hand crept toward the pistol strapped to my side, my rifle lost in the chaos. But before I could reach it, Gael's boot slammed into my back, pinning me to the ground. Agony radiated from my spine as he pressed down harder, forcing a pained grunt from my lips.

"You sure know how to make a mess, don't you?" Gael taunted, his voice dripping with disdain.

Onyx's expression transitioned to a murderous glare. "Says the one responsible for the fires in our community."

"Your community?" Gael sneered, grinding his heel between my shoulder blades. "Ironic, coming from the black sheep."

"It is *his* community," Jasper scolded, each syllable harsher than the last. "Bold of you to speak on matters you know nothing about, but then again, that's always been your strength—bullshitting your way through a make-believe world, blinded by the assumption you hold any sway or importance."

The pressure of Gael's boot intensified, confirming his aggravation. "I would think a community leader could stand his ground, yet Onyx continues to clean up after you like the worthless piece of shit you are."

Onyx's snarl came as a low and dangerous warning, his patience wearing thin. "You're here for a reason, Gael. What do you want?"

"Want? I came for revenge, for leaving me in that godsdamn bunker to burn alive."

Onyx's eyes narrowed, his voice harsh. "Burn alive in the fire you started? It seems you keep picking battles with your own kryptonite. Maybe it's time you found a new element."

He shifted slightly, the movement almost imperceptible, but I knew it was deliberate. He was biding his time, waiting for his abilities to return, using the banter to mask his growing power.

As their verbal sparring continued, I shifted my focus beyond the battlefield. The smoke had cleared, revealing the carnage left in its wake. My eyes scanned the area, searching for any sign of Radley—his light blonde hair, his tall frame—anything to confirm he was still alive.

Nothing.

My throat tightened as panic surged through me. A rustle from the nearby vegetation interrupted Gael mid-sentence, drawing his attention. I turned toward the sound, my heart pounding. Emerging from the shadows, Radley stepped into view, a wave of relief washing over me despite the blood trickling down his forehead. His eyes locked onto Gael as he raised his pistol; the glint beneath them I'd caught throughout our duration in the community remained.

"Get your foot off her," Radley commanded, venom lacing his words.

"Oh, if it isn't the hero," Gael sneered, digging his heel further into my back. Pain exploded in my chest, stealing my breath once more. "I ought to give you props. For being such a coward, I'm surprised you're standing here trying to defend her."

Radley's jaw tightened, his finger poised on the trigger. "I'm the coward?" he retorted, a sharp edge in his voice. "That's bold, coming from the one who targets a community in the dead of night when no one can react."

"I believe we call that strategy." Gael shrugged nonchalantly. "I enjoy catching people off guard. It's far more enjoyable."

"Yeah, it sure is." The soft voice came from the trees behind Radley.

Imelda stepped forward, her tawny brown hair catching the glow of the distant flames. Her eyes blazed with the same fiery determination as Onyx's, a mirror of his rage and resolve.

Gael's lips curled into a snarl. "There's the little—"

Before he could finish, Radley squeezed the trigger. The gunshot echoed through the darkness, violently interrupting the tension. In the split second that followed, a gasp of pain escaped Gael's lips, a guttural sound that unnerved me.

The bullet struck him with a sickening thud, burying itself in flesh. His body jolted, his legs giving way as the force of the impact wrenched him back. The pressure on my back suddenly lifted, and I seized the opportunity, pushing myself up despite the lingering pain in my chest. I scrambled away, desperate to put distance between us as I caught my breath. My gaze darted around, searching for my allies in the chaotic aftermath.

Onyx stood tense, his eyes locked on Gael.

Jasper clutched his side, an expression of relief mixed with uncertainty.

Finally, my eyes landed on Radley and Imelda. Radley lowered his weapon, his expression unreadable, while Imelda's eyes were wide with fear and relief.

I turned to look over my shoulder at Gael. A dark red stain blossomed across his Venturer uniform, spreading into a blooming circle. He staggered, his knees hitting the ground as another wheeze of pain escaped him. He raised a trembling hand toward Radley, disbelief and shock etching his features. The realization of his vulnerability flickered in his eyes before they rolled back, and he collapsed in a lifeless heap.

Onyx wasted no time, striding over to me with purposeful steps. He reached down, his strong hands pulling me to my feet. His touch was a grounding force, steadying me amidst the chaos. He pulled me close, shielding me from the sight of Gael's crumpled form.

"Are you okay?"

I nodded, struggling to steady my breathing. He looked at the tree line, his expression softening as Imelda rushed toward us. She flung herself into his arms, a sob escaping her lips.

"It's okay. I've got you," Onyx murmured, holding her close as he brushed a coaxing hand through her curls.

Radley stood nearby, his eyes scanning Gael's motionless form before he turned to me. He pulled me into a tight embrace, my voice choking with emotion.

"I thought I had—" I couldn't finish.

"No, you didn't. It's okay." He hugged me tightly, reassuring me of his presence. "It's going to be okay."

I wrapped my arms around him, continually reminding myself he was alive, aside from the potential head injury I noticed as soon as I spotted him. I pulled away and glanced up at him, a soft smile crossing his lips as he wiped a fallen tear from my cheek.

We lingered until Onyx's spoke. "I have to give you props. That was a nice shot." He stood beside Imelda, a hint of a smile playing on his lips.

Radley chuckled, glancing back at them. "Yeah, I suppose we can say that I'm decent with weapons," he joked, quickly changing the conversation. "I found Imelda in the woods after breaking away from the soldiers. She heard the commotion and came running. I'm glad I could intercept her before anything happened to her."

Onyx nodded, gratitude apparent in his gaze. "Thank you."

Jasper's voice carried from the tree line. "You should take me up on the offer I posed earlier."

Radley grinned, shaking his head. "I suppose I should. Though I'm just glad I could help."

Onyx's eyes roamed over me, a silent sigh of relief escaping him. He placed a gentle hand on Imelda's shoulder, his eyes softening as they met mine. The chaos seemed to settle, the air thick with unspoken gratitude and shared relief.

But then, as Radley turned back toward Gael's prone form, a sense of foreboding gripped me. He paused, staring down at the body, his back to us. "I didn't know if I would make it in time."

I stepped in front of him, placing a hand on his shoulder. "But you did, and that's—"

A sudden, sharp pain seared through my abdomen, cutting off my words. My breath caught in my throat as I gasped, the agony radiating outward with a deep pulsation. I looked down, and a cold, sinking sensation gripped me. Horror dawned as my eyes fixed on the hilt of a knife embedded in my stomach. Radley's hand, steady and deliberate, clutched the handle, his knuckles white with the force of his grip.

He grinned, his smile twisting into something I'd never seen before. "Oops."

TWENTY-ONE

Shock and betrayal flooded my veins.

The world tilted as my breath caught in my throat, tears beginning to blur my vision. Radley—my friend, my protector—stood before me as my assailant. Our bond and promises had been nothing but a façade to mask his deception.

He was the traitor. He had stolen the map and conspired with Gael. The realization struck as painfully as the knife lodged in my stomach.

It was all a lie.

Gael's low groan pulled me back, a somber reminder of the depth of our situation—of *my* situation. With a smirk, he pulled out a blood bag hidden beneath his uniform, tossing it aside with a casual flick. My heart sank with the realization, the agony in my abdomen becoming an afterthought as my thoughts assaulted me.

"Next time, aim higher. That knocked the wind out of me."

Radley's chuckle echoed, devoid of the warmth I once knew. It was the only thing I heard as blood surged to my ears, his wrist digging the knife further into my flesh. The agony shot through me like lightning, tearing a scream from my throat.

Through the fog of anguish, I heard Onyx. His shout was a lifeline and a tether to reality as my world blurred at the edges. His anguish mirrored my own, a shared torment that connected us far deeper than anyone realized.

"Astrid!"

My name.

I had a name. This was real.

Real.

Radley's smile broadened. "I don't think you realize how long I've waited for this moment."

Onyx took a step forward, anger racking his body. The air became dense with hostility, a metallic tang of blood, and something darker. His eyes darkened, the familiar blue fading further until an eerie, spectral white took its place. A feral snarl escaped his lips as his power surged within him, rippling outward with a ferocity that made it nearly tangible.

Suddenly, the sound of footsteps crunching on the underbrush halted his advance. I forced my gaze upward, focusing on the tree line as shadowy figures emerged. Soldiers, clad in dark uniforms, moved with precision. One placed a gun against Jasper's temple, while others trained their weapons on Onyx. But Onyx didn't pay any mind to those surrounding him and instead fixated on the one threatening his best friend's life.

Before he could react, the soldiers around him fired. Electric wires and nets shot out, wrapping around him with a violent snap. He dropped to his knees, a guttural cry tearing from his throat as the prongs embedded in his skin. The electricity coursed through him, a cruel mockery of his power that immediately turned against him, bowing to the unrelenting current.

Panic surged as Gael pushed himself off the ground, a triumphant grin splitting his face. My instincts screamed to protect Imelda, to do anything to stop him, but Radley's grip and the knife in my abdomen kept me pinned.

I struggled against him, forcing out a plea through labored breaths. "Leave...her alone..."

Gael cocked a brow, amused by my defiance. "And what will either of you do about it?"

His emerald eyes flicked to the knife in my stomach and the blood staining my clothes as his sneer grew further. I pulled my gaze from him and looked at Onyx, who remained helpless on the ground, his eyes burning with fury and desperation as he ripped at the prongs embedded in his skin.

"Gael, I swear I will murder you," Onyx hissed, freeing one wire.

Gael laughed mockingly. "Adorable, considering you can't even move. What a familiar set of circumstances, isn't it, Oakes?"

Imelda stood frozen, her eyes wide with terror. Her breaths came in shallow gasps, each one beginning to transition into a sob that shook her shoulders. She glanced between Onyx and me, tears streaming down her cheeks. The fear in her eyes was palpable, an emotion I'd rarely seen her show.

"Onyx..." His name came from her in a broken whisper.

Onyx struggled against the wires, a pained plea escaping him. "Imelda...you need to get out of here."

"I can't!" She screamed, her voice cracking under the weight of her emotions. Tears fell freely as she looked at Onyx, who now lay powerless before her while she remained unable to save him. "Onyx, I can't leave you here. Tell me what to do!"

Despair clawed at me, driving me to break free from Radley's hold. My muscles tensed, straining against the pain that radiated from my wound. Each attempt sent another wave of searing agony through my body, my breath hitching as my vision blurred, further clarifying the battle against my rising tide of helplessness.

Radley's bitterness cut through my struggle. "Uh-uh. I'd be careful doing that. Forcefully yanking this out will cause far more damage than the insertion did. I would hate for you to knick an artery."

His words were a twisted attempt to assert dominance over me in my weakened state. There was no trace of the friend I once knew, only a brutal stranger.

I trembled, speaking through clenched teeth. "I trusted you.

Despite everything, I *trusted* you, and you betrayed me. Remember that as you rot in hell, you bastard."

"I don't know why you're so surprised. It's been this way since day one, Astrid." His devious smile faded slightly, replaced by a look of mock sympathy. "Is it because I stole your heart, even though you refused to admit it?"

His words stung, ridiculing the trust we once shared. I clenched my jaw, steeling myself against the rising tide of emotion.

I wouldn't give him that power. Not anymore and never again.

"You've been plotting this since day one? I didn't think you were smart enough to do something that complex," I spat, the taste of iron filling my throat.

"Your attempted insults are pathetic." He twisted the knife, drawing another sharp gasp from me. "It shows me you were far more misled than I ever imagined."

I bit my lip, refusing to let him see the full extent of my suffering and swallowing everything I wished to unleash.

He sneered as he continued, "You never took the time to consider some of the red flags that presented themselves while working together?"

"What are you talking about?" The question came from me far more strained than I wanted it to.

"I always dropped hints, Astrid. *Always*." His tone was condescending, as if explaining something to a child. "I, being the only Venturer without high clearance in the room with Quinn and the other government bodies. That never led to any level of pondering?"

He had been there to gather information for the enemy while pretending to stand by my side, wearing the mask of an ally, all while basking in deceit.

"You never questioned how Gael tracked us down without issue?"

"There were tracking devices. We destroyed them," Onyx

seethed, unaware of the complexities that dove beneath the surface.

Radley's eyes glinted with satisfaction. "There were no tracking devices, just lights that I had tacked onto our uniforms before we went out that day. We had to make it believable, right?"

I recalled the sudden 'request' to send in our uniforms for inspection before we ventured beyond the Walls. It hadn't struck me as suspicious then because we frequently sent them in for patchwork and other adjustments, but even without the immediate warning siren, I'd known something was off.

He continued casually as if recounting mundane events. "Then there was the fact that Imelda and I escaped the bunker untouched by Gael's counterparts, who are still alive and well if you cared to know."

His eyes flicked to Imelda, who stared back in shock, her face reflecting the dawning realization of his manipulation. He shrugged nonchalantly. "And, of course, Adira knew we were in that skyscraper. She intercepted us before we could even reach the second floor." He smirked, enjoying the wrath that filled Onyx's expression. "Which, by the way, was where she stationed her team."

"You bastard," Jasper spat from the tree line, disgust thickening his voice. "You knew you were putting her in danger? Onyx could have killed her."

Radley rolled his eyes, dismissing Jasper's outrage with a wave. "Meh. Just another necessary sacrifice. Something you two know all too well, don't you? Especially you, Onyx."

"Your brother..." I breathed, struggling to process the treachery. "This was all supposed to be for him."

"Funny," Radley's voice cut through the haze of agony. "Never had one."

The tail end of his reply became a muted roar in my ears. The story he'd crafted and the lies he'd spun were all a game. There was no remorse, no hesitation—just a chilling detachment and a lever of similarity he used against me.

"You're disgusting." The words felt insufficient, barely ample in reflecting my revulsion.

He responded with a sadistic grin, twisting the knife still embedded in my abdomen. The searing pain made my knees buckle, but I fought to stay upright.

"I wasn't done," he snapped coldly, his grip on the blade tightening. "Don't think you get to interrupt."

Staying conscious felt like a battle in itself, each breath a struggle against the affliction that threatened to consume me.

"And last but certainly not least, the map," Radley continued, his grin widening pridefully. "I snagged it one night while the others were too busy playing cards to notice. Perhaps you ought to thin the herd, Jasper. You've got some useless and lazy men in your ranks."

"I'll kill you," Jasper growled, his glower drilling into Radley with burning intensity.

"Last I checked, your community is the one under attack while you sit here helpless. That vulnerability is painfully familiar, isn't it, Bandell?" Radley's smirk deepened, malice glinting beneath his cerulean scowl. "Everything you've built and hidden is under the line of fire, and that will never change."

Onyx, still on the ground, snarled in response. "If you think you'll survive the long game, you're pathetically naïve."

Without a word, Gael stepped forward, closing the distance between him and Onyx. He raised his booted foot and drove it into Onyx's stomach with enough force to send him a few feet across the field. Onyx gasped raggedly, oxygen robbed from his lungs faster than he could gather it. His body convulsed as he struggled to collect himself, the electric shocks amplifying his pain and leaving him at Gael's mercy.

But the President's right-hand man was far from finished.

The assaults continued, each blow more intense than the last. In finality, Gael drove his foot into Onyx's face, forcing his head to snap back violently. Blood trickled from his nose and mouth as he gaped in agony, the spread of his life force a motivating factor for the male who stood over him.

Imelda's distraught cry broke through the brutality. "Stop! Leave Onyx alone!"

Gael's voice lowered as he addressed her, every syllable of his question heavy with implication. "What would you do to save him?"

Her love for him was evident, and Gael knew he could break her with the ultimatum.

Imelda stepped back, tears streaming down her cheeks as she looked at the man who'd rescued her. A quiver rocked her bottom lip, and the desire to help save him as he saved her drove her refusal to leave.

But little did she know, she had already rescued him endlessly.

Onyx struggled to drag himself across the ground, his eyes locked onto hers, filled with tears. "Imelda, I need you to run..."

She struggled to step back further, horror coating her expression and words escaping her.

"Imelda!" Jasper shouted, frantically struggling against the guards that held him.

One drove his foot into the gash on Jasper's side in response to his opposition, the tread digging into raw flesh. Jasper screamed, the anguish in his cry enough to make my stomach churn. The second soldier silenced him with a brutal punch, crimson coating his hand as Jasper's head snapped back. He raised his bloodied knuckles for another blow, delivering it followed by a handful of others until Jasper slumped forward, blood dripping from his nose.

Recklessness fueled my following action.

I yanked back against Radley, the strain nearly unbearable. A sadistic glint flickered in his eyes as he released the hilt of the knife, sending me crashing to the ground. The impact triggered a fresh wave of agony that blurred my vision, but through the haze of pain, one thought remained clear.

I had to get to her.

I had to stop this.

I had to intervene before my mistakes haunted me for the rest of my life.

Imelda took another step back and lost her footing, stumbling over a dismembered limb from one of the fallen soldiers. Her petite frame hit the ground with a thud, a panicked gasp escaping her lips in her attempt to scramble away. Gael stepped closer, his controlled expression twisting with satisfaction.

"Do you remember what you did to me?" he snarled, anger radiating from him. He planted his foot firmly on top of hers, pinning her in place and preventing any means of escape.

She looked up at him, distress consuming her coffee-brown eyes. "I'm sorry... I can heal you. I'll fix it... Please."

Gael clicked his tongue disapprovingly. "I think it's a little too late for apologies, don't you?"

"Gael, get away from her!" I tried to crawl with the blade embedded in my abdomen, every agonizing inch a battle against the darkness threatening to overtake me.

Gael pivoted, glancing over his shoulder with a look of contemplation before it shifted back into a hate-filled sneer. "I told Onyx I would rob him of the light that freed him from his internal hell, and that's what's going to happen. It's about time you all accept the inevitable."

His hand shot out, his fingers tangling roughly in her dark curls. He yanked her off the ground with ruthless force, her limbs flailing in a desperate attempt to escape.

Imelda's scream pierced the night as he dragged her towards Onyx. Her feet barely touched the ground, sneakers scraping against the dirt as he forced her forward.

Onyx's voice was raw and strained, each word a struggle. "You can take me..." Though clouded with pain, his eyes hardened with a willingness to sacrifice himself for Imelda's safety. "Take me back to the Walls, claim the reward for my bounty... Throw me in a cell again... Torture me like before... Whatever you want, but please, leave her alone..."

My heart shattered under the weight of all I had and hadn't done. His plea consisted of heartfelt grief and a readiness to endure unimaginable suffering to spare the youthful innocence he devoted his life to protecting.

Gael paused, his expression unreadable as he stared down at Onyx. Imelda's breath hitched, her eyes darting between the two men, her fate hanging in the balance. Onyx's eyes never wavered, even as his body trembled from the effort it took to speak.

Gael finally flung Imelda to the ground beside Onyx, a smirk playing on his lips. "You know, that honestly wouldn't be a terrible idea."

Jasper's voice, filled with anguish, followed. "Have you lost your mind, Onyx?! They nearly killed you in those cells! They tainted every part of you and will do it all over again!"

Onyx had fought so hard to keep her safe, to give her a chance at life beyond the horrors of their world. His eagerness to sacrifice himself was evident, a painful testament to his love for her. No matter the cost, he would save her.

"I'll go willingly..." Onyx's words hit me like a physical blow—an offering I was far too acquainted with.

Jasper's repeated pleas echoed from the tree line, his voice cracking with emotion. The thought of losing Onyx again threatened to shatter his entire world.

Imelda shook her head in denial, her voice choked with tears. "No, you can't. You can't leave me. You promised me you wouldn't!"

The lump in my throat grew, suffocating me as I lay helpless. Radley stepped over me, his tall frame advancing toward them. My attempts to follow were futile, my body betraying me with every movement. The distance between us felt insurmountable, mere feet stretching into what felt like unforgiving miles.

"There are various options," Radley stated, pondering the consideration with the male who craved revenge. "His bounty is large and has only grown. There's the continuation of testing, which is extremely painful given his capabilities. Or chaining him in a cell and bringing out his preferred methods of torment—tempting, isn't it?"

Gael's eyes flickered between Onyx and Imelda, weighing his choices with a minor mirror of hesitance.

Onyx, the man with the highest bounty, could bring untold rewards and the sick satisfaction of continued torture. Or Imelda, the innocent girl clinging to hope for a better life—a life he was eager to extinguish.

I dragged myself forward, the pain intensifying with each inch. My vision darkened, the edges closing in as blood seeped from the wound in my abdomen. The knife's serrated edge dug deeper with every movement, sending sharp bursts of agony through my limbs.

"Onyx!" Jasper screamed from the tree line, his voice raw with desperation as he elected to fight against the men restraining him, regardless of the consequences. "Get the hell off of me!"

A smile spread across Gael's lips as his hand moved toward the holster on his thigh. My heart raced, panic surging through me as I realized the implications of what was about to happen. But before I could warn, Gael had already drawn his gun.

The next moments played out in a mocking slowness that spoke to our inability to save her.

Gael flicked the safety off, his expression darkening with malicious intent. And then he fired.

A deafening crack echoed through the night as the bullet tore through Imelda's chest. She jolted back, the metal that pierced her flesh mixed with her whimpered cry, creating a heartbreakingly grotesque symphony of loss.

Imelda's eyes widened, struggling to process the violent intrusion into her body. Her hands met her chest to try to staunch the blood that slipped between her fingers, her very life force draining before her eyes.

A single tear escaped from the corner of her eye, gliding down her cheek in silent acknowledgment. Her eyes drifted to the starry night sky, fluttering once before she collapsed. The vast darkness enveloped her as the universe sought solace in her last moments.

Onyx's scream tore from his throat—a sound of pure, unfiltered agony. Tears streamed down his face, intermixing with the blood that coated his skin. He reached for her, the movement frantic, but the distance remained between them.

Those who inflicted such devastating damage began to shift and turn away, their movements unhurried and almost casual. It was as if the life teetering on the brink of death at their feet was nothing more than a fleeting inconvenience and another tally to reach their goal of control. They fled in a moment of immense vulnerability, not out of guilt but from the awareness of the wrath building within the man they left broken and grieving.

"Cowards!" The scream ripped through my sobs as I struggled to reach Onyx and Imelda. "I will fucking kill you all!"

Their footsteps continued, ignoring me—a calculated decision to avoid the inevitable confrontation with a man on edge. They left the destruction behind, their hearts devoid of empathy as they abandoned the lives they'd affected beyond the point of return. Yet, in their departure, there was a tacit acknowledgment of the power they'd awoken. They had lit the fuse of a volatile bomb and now stepped back to watch it detonate from a safe distance.

Their silhouettes faded into the darkness, indigestible laughter trailing behind them. Bile surged in the back of my throat, and the roar in my ears drowned out the whimpers in the distance until the shuttered breaths replaced them.

Imelda.

I needed to comfort them.

I needed to help.

Jasper struggled to grasp the horror before him, disassociation swarming his senses and acting as a defensive mechanism against the overwhelming grief. The surrounding guards dispersed as quickly as they had come, leaving him alone in the aftermath. Silent tears streamed down his cheeks as he swallowed, fumbling to provide comfort or the right words to the man who was falling apart at the seams before us.

Onyx, driven by a surge of strength that defied the pain wracking his body, closed the distance and gathered Imelda into his arms. Another wail tore from his throat, reverberating through the community and marking the night with anguish. The sound was raw and unfiltered, a visceral expression of the unbearable sorrow coursing through him. It was a cry for the imminent loss of someone so young and full of promise—a life that had once been a beacon of hope in his dark world.

He cradled her small, fragile frame against his own, their contrasting figures coming together in a final, heartbreaking embrace.

"I've got you... it's okay." Onyx sobbed. "It's going to be okay."

He held her close as he pressed trembling hands to her chest for any flicker of hope. But all that resulted was a broken whimper.

His body continued to convulse, a cruel reminder of his help-lessness. The electric wires—the singular barrier that prevented him from saving her—solidified his failure.

"O...Onyx..." Her voice came in ragged breaths, tears slipping down her cheeks.

"It's okay. I promise I'll fix it. I'll fix this," Onyx pleaded, his hand on her chest now stained with her blood.

A sob escaped him as he faintly rocked her, trying to comfort her through the inevitable. Her light brown complexion rapidly paled, the warmth draining from her body with each passing second. Yet, he continued to cling to her, unwilling to accept the impending doom that encroached.

"Onyx... it's..." she wheezed, weakly raising her fingers to his cheek.

Her touch was soft, a final gesture of love and comfort, even as she faced her end. The realization yielded devastating clarity as her words sunk in, and any semblance of the composure he had shattered.

"Somebody help!" he screamed, the two words fracturing.

It was a cry for a miracle.

He shook his head in denial, refusing to accept the nearing truth. Imelda's bright, beautiful life was being torn away from him, and there was nothing more he could do to prevent it. It was a loss for him and everyone who had known and loved her.

Jasper limped from the tree line; the sight of Onyx crumbling under the weight of his grief was a devastating blow. As I pulled myself toward them, my pain felt like a distant echo compared to the overwhelming grief that enveloped us all.

Approaching Onyx, Jasper's face etched with sorrow and understanding. He placed a soothing hand on Onyx's shoulder in a silent offering filled with a depth of emotions that words would never convey.

As I tenderly brushed a few loose curls from Imelda's face, her eyes met mine. Her gaze held a deep understanding far beyond her years, an acceptance of the grim reality before her.

She knew.

She knew she was dying, and there was no escape from the cold inevitability of it.

She would never see the world as Onyx had promised her and never experience the life she had dreamed of. This was her last goodbye, and the knowledge of it weighed heavily in her once-bright eyes.

Her small hand reached out again, trembling as it gently stroked Onyx's cheek—a tender, continued gesture to console him even as her life slipped away. Her eyes filled with tears of acceptance, her voice barely a whisper. "Please stop trying... It's too late..."

Her words carried quiet resignation, a soft plea for peace in her final moments. The exuberance of youth in her voice was now frail, tinged with the sorrow of what could never be.

Onyx's eyes widened, his cheeks wet with tears. His bottom lip trembled as he shook his head. "I promised you... I can't..." He choked, his sobs halting his ability to speak, each word a painful admission of his powerlessness.

Her eyes fluttered, signaling the end. "You did...so much... You showed me...so much love...and for that...I am grateful..." She looked between me and Jasper, her gaze filled with serene acceptance. "Please...keep him safe... Don't let him...lose himself... Let him show you the side of him...that I got to know... Love him...love him for me... He deserves so much..."

Jasper clenched his jaw, a tear slipping down his cheek. "We will uphold your request, Imelda. I promise with all that I am and ever will be."

I looked at Onyx. An overwhelming sorrow dulled his usually vibrant blue eyes. The moment Gael pulled the trigger, a part of Onyx died with her—his will to fight and live.

I laced my fingers through his hair and pulled his head toward me. As I rested my forehead against his, and his pain became detectable through every ounce of my being, I whispered, "We've got you..."

Imelda released a gentle breath, her hand slowly slipping from Onyx's face. It was the final relinquishment of the life she had clung to so fiercely. Onyx pulled away from me, tears streaming down his cheeks as he laced his fingers with hers and brought their hands down to rest on top of the one covered in her life force.

She looked at us with a soft smile, her expression serene despite the pain. "Thank you... For being here...with me... For staying...with me..." Her voice was faint, each word a precious gift as she slowly sank deeper into Onyx's embrace. "You have been...more than enough... I love you, Onyx..."

As she drew her final breath, her body stilled, and a profound silence enveloped us. Onyx stared down at her, his shoulders shaking with the weight of his grief.

There was nothing he could do to bring her back, no power in the world to reverse fate's cruel hand.

His lips quivered, and a heart-wrenching sob escaped him. "I love you, Imelda, and I always will."

The words were simple, yet they carried the full depth of his affection and the tragedy of their untimely separation.

Onyx curled into her, cradling her lifeless body as guttural screams of agony and rage erupted from him. His world had crumbled, and the foundation of his existence shattered beyond repair. In holding her, he clung to the last remnants of their shared life—a life now reduced to memories.

As I looked up at the sky, my silent tears flowed freely. Each precious moment with her—every smile, every laugh—was now a fading echo of a life stolen too soon.

One star among the countless others shone brighter than the rest, offering a last goodbye and silently promising she'd never be forgotten. It was as if the universe mourned her passing, offering a glimmer of light in the overwhelming darkness.

Medics from the community arrived, carrying supplies in a fruitless attempt to help. Sorrow etched their expressions, knowing their efforts would be in vain. Jasper directed them with a voice heavy with grief, each instruction laced with the painful knowledge that nothing could undo what had happened.

The medics respected the sanctity of the moment, understanding the profound significance of Onyx and Imelda's final embrace. They stood back, acknowledging the space around them —a wordless recognition of a love that transcended the physical, a bond that those in power brutally severed.

Once warm and full of life, Imelda's hand now lay cold against Onyx's touch; once a source of comfort and warmth, it was now a farewell—a gesture of love and sorrow that would resonate long after this night.

The girl who had brought so much light and joy was now gone, her life extinguished by the cruelty of a world we never asked for.

TWENTY-TWO

Remorse clung heavily to the air as the community began the formidable task of cleaning up after the attack. The physical damage was severe, but the emotional toll clung to the destruction.

Even though buildings remained, their walls bore the scars of battle, a hole ripped through the heart of the community. The structures that had been focal points during the initial onslaught lay in ruins, reduced to smoldering rubble. Fires that once raged within them had finally died down, leaving behind charred skeletons and smoke that twisted into the night sky. Moonlight bathed the scene in an eerie glow, casting shadows over the lives lost on the grass—once a place of laughter becoming a graveyard.

As the five trusted members scoured the perimeter and searched through the debris, they found the bodies of those caught in the crossfire. They treated each with care, covering them with cloths as a temporary burial. The infiltration resulted in the death of fifteen people, Imelda tragically included in the count, her loss snuffing out the liveliness that once existed. Onyx refused to let any of the others touch her, desperate to lay her to rest himself before he'd contemplate help from the medics. Even once he draped the cloth over her face, sobs rocked his body, letting her go becoming a reality he couldn't accept.

The weight of the loss pressed down on the survivors, yet amidst the grief, there was also a gnawing uncertainty surrounding five members who remained unaccounted for.

Rendered helpless because of my injuries, I found myself seated with Jasper as medics worked quickly to tend to our wounds. Their hands moved with practiced efficiency, aware that time was of the essence. Onyx sat beside us, silent and distant, as another medic carefully removed the embedded electrical prods from his skin. Despite the medics' continuous apologies, his expression was vacant and devoid of reaction to the physical discomfort. Instead, his face was a canvas of agony, further laced with a palpable hatred.

The depth of his grief was evident in every fiber of his being as he teetered on the brink. In losing the one person who brought immense meaning into his life, his heart shattered into a million unfixable pieces. My chest ached with the rage lingering beneath the surface that became decipherable in his gaze. It was a desperation that radiated sorrow and an overarching need to channel his mourning into something he could control.

It became clear—there remained nothing more for him to lose.

He was free—or perhaps condemned—to be reactive and vindictive. War was on the horizon, and for Onyx, it no longer mattered whether or not the Rebellion stood with him.

The medic tended to Onyx and finished, nodding at him to signal that the procedure was complete. Onyx shifted slightly, turning his body away from my concerned gaze, trying to shield himself from scrutiny.

I winced as the medic attending to me inserted a needle into my abdomen, momentarily pulling my focus away from the raven-haired male who worked to close himself off.

"I'm sorry," he murmured, glancing up at me. "I used most of my healing abilities to address the internal damage, so an external stitch is necessary."

"It's okay," I managed a small smile, hoping my gratitude was present despite the pain. "You've been taking care of everyone all night. Thank you."

A flicker of shock crossed his face before he smiled back, appreciating the acknowledgment. He returned to his work, stitching with care to inflict as little discomfort as possible.

Jasper sighed heavily as he lowered his shirt. The medic attending to him finally finished. His eyes traveled over me before settling on Onyx, who sat with his back to us. Jasper's jaw tightened as he studied his best friend's demeanor, noting the abrupt and unsettling shift in Onyx's behavior—a shutdown and burial of emotions. Jasper placed a gentle hand on the crown of my head, his eyes locking with mine in a sympathetic gaze.

At that moment, everything crashed over me. The loss, the betrayal, the image of Radley's smirk as he plunged the blade into my stomach, all the secrets I hadn't shared, and their influence resurfaced, bringing with it a wave of nausea. I shook my head, trying to stave off the tears that threatened to spill. My vision blurred, and I struggled to keep myself composed, shame threatening to consume me for taking away from Onyx's grief.

"You're wrong. Your feelings have a place in the aftermath."

The words broke the silence, spoken in a voice that carried a hidden undercurrent of sadness. Onyx's back remained turned, but the resonance of his statement was unmistakable, and it took a moment for me to realize he was responding to my thoughts.

Even in his agony, he reached out to validate my pain—a minor act of empathy, regardless of the depth of his suffering. He constantly gave to others no matter the cost, and I couldn't help but empathize with his sacrifices.

Jasper sighed heavily, breaking the silence. "There was substantial loss tonight. Every emotion and feeling is justified and valid for everyone who experienced it."

His words broke the dam I had been holding back, and hot

and relentless tears instantly streamed down my cheeks. The medic working on me glanced up, his brows knitting together in sympathy. He reached over and placed a gentle hand on my thigh—a silent gesture of comfort.

My shoulders shook with each sob as the waves of sorrow drowned me, every ounce of my being breaking for my influence and inability to prevent what I'd promised myself I would. An invisible weight clung to my chest, laboring my breathing as the panic set in, my heart breaking alongside it.

"I'm so sorry." My voice cracked, barely a whisper over my internal dialogue. "It's all my fault."

At that, Onyx's head snapped in my direction. His icy-blue eyes, usually so clear and intense, swirled with a storm of emotions—rage and sadness blending. But beneath that desire for violence, there was something else.

Sympathy.

Concern.

A softness that cut through the anger, a silent understanding of the burden I was carrying.

"Don't for one second blame yourself for what happened tonight." He stated firmly in a command that left no room for argument.

The medic finished his stitching and quietly packed his kit, moving away to give us space. Jasper offered him a slight nod, a pat on the shoulder, and a silent thank you for his work.

"If we hadn't come here... If we had never returned with the two of you, then" I pulled my knees to my chest, my voice trembling with the weight of my secrets. "...then..."

Onyx exhaled deeply, moving from his seated position to kneel before me. Our gazes locked, his unwavering. "Then yeah, she may still be alive, but it's more complicated than that." His eyes flickered as if weighing whether to reveal more. "If there had been a planned attack on the community, this outcome could have been just as likely. What happened isn't, in any magnitude, your fault. You didn't know he would side with them and turn against you. You did not have control over the situation, nor did you cause it."

Jasper, who had been quietly listening, turned his attention to me. "None of what happened tonight reflects anything different."

Dropping my head to my knees, heavy sobs continued to wrack my body. Even in the open space of the field, the world around me seemed to close in, the air suddenly suffocating. With each stuttered breath, my chest ached, sadness pouring from me and into the wounded night.

I was losing control.

Radley had filled the void left by the loss of my family and risked his life for me. We shared secrets, dreams, and even a kiss—an intimate moment that was now a cruel mockery. The one man I trusted who stood by me through countless trials turned his back on me. The bitter taste of faithlessness tainted all the memories of our time together, the moments of shared laughter.

The grass rustled, and I looked up to find Onyx sitting beside me. He moved one hand to my face, his touch soft and reassuring. His thumb brushed away a tear, and my stomach fluttered with the gentle intimacy of the gesture. "Listen to me when I tell you this, and know I mean every word."

He waited until I nodded, a silent promise that I would hear what he had to say.

"I understand how you feel right now, and while I have my own grieving to do, it doesn't mean that you don't. Or that your pain is less valid than mine. The person you thought you could trust, who made promises and went against everything they had ever told you, turned a blind eye. And now, you have to force the thought of him out of your mind. You have to learn to live without him and forget him while still knowing he's alive. Betrayal is a near replica of death. It is a pain that I do not wish upon anyone, and it enrages me he willingly did that to you."

Onyx's voice softened but remained firm as he held my gaze. The blues of his irises sparked compassion and suffering, conveying a deep understanding of my anguish. His words resonated with a painful truth, acknowledging the torment of losing someone not to death but to disloyalty.

He continued, tender yet unwavering, "And while I can't change what he said or his actions, I promise I will never put you through something like that. You are not alone, Astrid, and you never have to be again. From this day forward, I will face the world with you through hardship and turbulence. I will stand by your side through it all. And as painful as this may be, we will make it through—together." His voice hitched, and his bottom lip trembled, hinting at an openness he hadn't offered in years.

Throughout his life, he bore many titles, but with them came the burden of enduring unimaginable hardship and setting aside his sorrow and guilt to comfort others. It was a trained habit he quickly sunk into after years of refinement. It also provided a testament to his character. The sole fact was that, even as he battled his loss, he reached out to assure others they weren't alone.

A saddened smile tugged at the corner of his mouth, holding a promise of solidarity, a vow to stand by my side no matter what. Warmth swarmed my chest at the thought, and the broken part of me did not expect to feel so emotional over the promises he made.

A single tear rolled down his cheek, mingling with those who had already ventured. The depth of his commitment remained in his reddened eyes.

I swallowed, moved by the sincerity in his gaze as I slowly raised my hand to touch his face. "And I can promise you the same."

In one fluid movement, he wrapped his arms around me and pulled me into his chest. The embrace was warm and protective against the realization of Radley's betrayal that continued to haunt me, comforting me in the darkness of my thoughts.

He ran his fingers through my hair, bringing forth memories that I forced myself to bury and the helplessness that clung to them. There were too many things to remember and moments to recall, instances that could never be reversed. I'd made too many mistakes, most of them out of my own greed, with irreversible consequences that still hadn't come.

It was all for a greater purpose—to continue moving forward despite the damage. As he comforted me, the hours blended, and my throat became raw from sobbing. His presence was an unwavering tether in the darkness, reminding me of the reason behind all I battled for.

THE LIGHT from the morning sun flooded through the park, heralding the end of the terror-filled night. My eyes fluttered open, struggling against the harsh glare, and I realized I had dozed off in Onyx's presence. As my senses returned, I noticed the fabric of his shirt balled tightly in my fist, desperate for the security he made me feel. Even though I had drifted off for who knows how long, Onyx hadn't let go. He hadn't turned away or left—as he had promised.

I nuzzled deeper into his embrace, unwilling to surrender the warmth. His thumb traced a gentle path across my temple in silent reassurance. I felt him shift, not away from me, but with me —he was walking.

"Are you taking her back to her room?" Jasper's voice came from beside us, breaking the silence.

Onyx paused, his chin brushing lightly against the top of my head. "That building is likely the last place she wants to be."

He was right.

After everything that happened, the thought of returning to that space filled me with dread. The last thing I wanted was to be surrounded by the memories of him.

Jasper yawned. "That's fair. I can clear a room in South Plaza. There'll be vacancies now that..." His voice trailed off, the weight of loss pressing down.

"That'll work," Onyx interrupted to save him from his divulgence. "But for now, she can have the bed in the space you've elected as mine. I don't want her waking up to more unfamiliarity, especially after tonight."

Jasper's silence was agreement enough. The two men walked on, the sound of their boots shifting from soft grass to hard concrete. The rhythmic echo of their steps lulled me back toward sleep as exhaustion finally caught up.

Onyx paused before it could claim me, shifting slightly as his hand reached forward. The soft click of a door followed, its hinges squealing in protest as it opened.

"Jasper," Onyx's voice cut through the stillness, carrying a quiet urgency.

There was a brief silence before I sensed Jasper turning to face him. Onyx spoke again, his words filled with a deep, heartfelt conviction. "Just as you told her, none of this is your fault. It doesn't define your leadership or your friendship. You did what you could for your people, and that is enough. You are enough."

As footsteps approached, I felt Jasper's presence close. He wrapped his arms around Onyx, pressing into him—and me. "Thank you," Jasper's voice broke with a raw and vulnerable sob.

I wished I could offer comfort, but I knew this moment was best shared between them. Onyx shifted, holding me securely with one arm while hugging Jasper tightly. The sound of his calloused hand rubbing circles on Jasper's back was a soothing gesture, small but significant.

"Get some rest," Onyx urged tenderly.

Jasper pulled away slightly, his hand resting on my head gently and reassuringly. "You don't need to bury your sorrow just because we're experiencing loss. You deserve to mourn, too, Onyx. Don't forget that. You aren't alone, and you never will be." He paused briefly before adding, "Give her the chance to be there for you."

Onyx swallowed hard, his voice thick with remorse. "Thank you for everything, Jasper."

It was a deflection, a subtle way to avoid the depth offered to him.

Jasper's hand slipped from my head. "Thank you. For all that you are and continue to be."

With that, he pulled away, his footsteps fading in rhythmic progression as he retreated down the street. Onyx moved forward, gently closing the door behind us. His boots on wooden floors echoed softly in the quiet space. We continued down a seemingly endless hallway, the occasional creak of old wood underfoot. Reaching a stairwell, the change from wood to metal was apparent, each step ringing out as he climbed.

The journey felt endless, each step a reminder of the distance we were putting between ourselves and the night's events. The reappearing groan of wood beneath his feet transitioned to another hallway. His boots thudded against the floor, a metronome that pulled me back toward sleep.

His exhale pulled me from it, the length of it harboring everything burdening him. He nudged a door open, shifting slightly to maneuver through it. The muted click of a latch followed, sealing us in a sanctuary.

Before I could gather anything further, he lowered me onto a bed. My back sank into the mattress, and exhaustion washed over me, pulling me deeper into sleep. Onyx carefully pried my fingers from his shirt tenderly. I looked up at him, my eyes heavy with sleep.

"Hey. It's alright," he whispered, his voice a soothing murmur.

"Where are we?" I mumbled, my words slurred with fatigue.

"You're in my room for the night. Well, the new room, considering the old building..." He shook his head, a shadow passing over his expression. "I'm going to take your boots off, okay?"

I nodded weakly, my eyes already fluttering closed. I felt him move to my feet, unlacing them with the same care and gentleness he had shown me throughout the night—a softness I didn't deserve.

Drifting in and out of consciousness, I vaguely realized his hand brushed a stray hair from my face.

"Would you like a blanket?" he whispered so as not to disturb me.

Keeping my eyes closed, I responded with a brief nod.

He lifted my body and pulled the comforter beneath me back just enough to lay me beneath it. Its warmth enveloped me, and I rolled onto my back, savoring the safety that came with it. His hand lingered momentarily as he adjusted the blanket to ensure it covered me entirely.

The floorboard creaked beneath him, indicating his shifting position from beside the bed. I instinctively reached out and grabbed his arm. "Where are you going?"

"The couch," he replied with a gentle smile. "You can have my bed for the night."

I looked up at him through half-lidded eyes, sighing. "Would it be stupid if I..." my words trailed off as exhaustion nipped at me.

Onyx looked down at me, amusement twinkling in his eyes. "I'm not sure if you'll be able to finish your sentence."

I struggled to stay awake and utter the words I wished to speak, but the fatigue was unbearable. Involuntarily, my eyes closed briefly before my body jolted awake again—embarrassment overriding everything.

Onyx remained patient, watching me with a look of gentle affection.

"Join me?" I whispered, my voice barely audible.

He hesitated, glancing at the space beside me before meeting my eyes again. "Are you sure?"

I nodded, my grip on his arm loosening.

Onyx lowered himself beside me, the bed dipping under his weight as the springs creaked softly. Listening to the gentle rustle of fabric, I deciphered each movement of his fingers as he unlaced his boots. As each shoe hit the floor, a soft thud followed as he slipped toward a newfound level of comfort with me.

The mattress shifted as he slid under the covers, a quiet sigh full of exhaustion escaping him. The warmth of his body seeped into the sheets. Each of his moves was deliberate, as he worked to position himself beside me in a manner that I wouldn't view as intrusive. I was relieved by his consideration of my comfort but couldn't help burn yearn for him to close that distance.

To be *with* me, wholly and entirely.

"Thank you," I whispered, breaking the silence between us.

Shifting, I wrapped my arms around him, positioning my head near his shoulder to show him the same respect he offered me. Part of me expected him to pull away and create distance between us, but he stayed close, keeping me nuzzled beside him.

Onyx's hand found its way to my face, his touch soothing as he traced gentle lines along the side of my jaw. The tenderness of his fingers urged me to the oblivion I had been battling against while also taking me back to a time far simpler than the world we lived in.

But I knew my path was far from simple—a shadowed intent that even Onyx, with his perceptive nature, might never fully grasp.

TWENTY-THREE

The sterile, icy walls pressed inward, trapping me inside. A faint scent of antiseptic burned my nose and seared my lungs as the air buzzed with an unnatural hum. The lights flickered overhead, and the shadows cast were far less sinister than reality.

Disoriented, I struggled to push myself up from where I lay, the metallic table beneath me impossible to navigate with the drugs coursing through my system. My eyes fixated on a corner of the room, a figure hovering on the edge of my vision. Their form was nearly indistinct, encapsulating a blur of restricted movement and equal confinement. The only detail that cut through the haze was eyes—light green and piercing, filled with a plea.

Suddenly, the room's door swung open, bringing with it the impending sensation of doom. The figure turned toward the door, struggling against those who held them while I battled against the invisible force that held me back. My fingers reached out, the distance between us seeming to grow as the shadow of dread encroached on the space, and an earth-shattering scream tore from my throat.

I jolted awake, tearing myself from the suffocating grip of the blankets. My lungs burned with each frantic gasp, the air feeling like fire in my chest.

Another nightmare—too vivid, too real.

Raking a trembling hand through my sweat-soaked hair, I tried to shake off the lingering dread, but reality settled in far heavier than any dream could be.

They attacked the community.

Without mercy, *they* destroyed buildings and snuffed out lives. Imelda.

Her name forced a surge of bile to the back of my throat.

Stumbling from the bed, I rushed to the bathroom, my knees crashing to the cold tile floor with just enough time to spare. The violent heaving wracked my body, tears blurring my vision, a sob tearing free as I pressed my forehead to my arm.

This wasn't just a nightmare. It was real.

I wiped my mouth with my hand, forcing myself to my feet. The rough wall bit into my back, its chill keeping me from falling apart. I squeezed my eyes shut, willing my breath to slow to silence the spiraling thoughts that threatened to consume me.

This was real, which meant that Onyx—

My eyes snapped open. The unfamiliar surroundings jarred me. I was in Onyx's space—his bathroom.

Oh gods.

The weight of where I was and what had happened crashed over me. The stitches in my stomach screamed as I pushed off the wall, the pain a sharp reminder of my failure. I rounded the corner, peering into the empty bedroom beyond.

Empty.

Relief and anxiety twisted in my chest, his absence both a reprieve and a puzzle. It spared me payne the shame of vomiting in his presence, but it also left me questioning where he'd gone. Last night's shared vulnerability—his kindness—felt distant now and overshadowed by the space between us.

Any hope I had dared to harbor was just that—a fleeting wish that was quickly snuffed out.

"Oh, stop pouting." I shook my head, chastising myself.

Onyx and Jasper had suffered immense losses, yet they had set aside their grief to acknowledge mine. They hadn't wallowed or let sorrow consume them. And here I was, in Onyx's room, allowing self-pity to cloud my judgment.

There was work to be done—damage to assess, lives to mourn, and people to console.

I took a deep breath, the cold air snapping me back to reality. I couldn't change what had happened, but I could control what came next, and the nightmare was a reminder—a warning.

It wasn't just about surviving; it was about fulfilling the promises I made and the agreements that led me here.

My footsteps echoed down the hallway of the makeshift clinic, where the bustling activity around me starkly contrasted the silent devastation outside. Each community member worked tirelessly, and their unity was palpable despite the carnage and loss. Even in hardship, resilience and a collective determination to push through the aftermath remained.

Earlier, as I moved through the city streets, I offered my aid, driven by a need to contribute. But they gently declined my offers, meeting me with grateful smiles. They reassured me that it wasn't that they didn't want it, but that it wasn't essential. Despite their adamance, I felt helpless in all I wished to do—help and heal.

Lost in thought, I rounded a corner and collided with a large frame. I stumbled back, looking up to find the very man I had been searching for.

Jasper stood before me, his presence commanding yet unexpectedly gentle. The strands of his copper hair wound in tight braids along the side of his head and secured with a band at the base of his skull. Clinging to his muscular body, the dark T-shirt emphasized the strength he concealed, both physically and emotionally. It was a striking reminder of the immense power he held, not only in terms of physical strength but also character.

"Good morning," Jasper greeted, a purplish bruise marring his cheekbone.

I winced, too distracted to note his generous demeanor. "My hell, that bruise looks awful."

The corner of his lip lifted, a faint light coming to his expression. "I appreciate the compliment, truly."

"It wasn't a dig," I retorted, playfully nudging his shoulder. "Just an observation."

"Whatever you say," he chuckled, his gaze dropping to the wound he knew I carried. "Let's find a medic to see if they can help heal you any further."

"And if I say no?"

"It wasn't a question," he replied, grabbing my arm and pulling me further into the building.

The previous clinic had been one of the many casualties of the attack, its structural remains consumed by fire. A small repurposed school served as an updated medical location and was the only part of the community's medical infrastructure that remained standing.

Jasper and I navigated the hallways that branched from the heart of the clinic. Each led to a room equipped with cots and chairs for those under care. Though busy with medics and volunteers, the hallways carried a subdued energy—an undercurrent of determination and hope.

Jasper ushered me into one of these rooms, ignoring my protests. His insistence was polite but unmoving, a quiet authority that brooked no argument.

We entered a modestly furnished room, with a cot pushed against one wall and a couple of chairs placed nearby. The space's simplicity belied its purpose.

Jasper ushered me to sit as I debated with him the concept of wasting the medical team's time when there were far more pertinent things they needed to focus on. Yet, his presence remained constant, even if minutely pestering.

"I'm fine," I insisted as I sat in the chair.

He leaned against the doorway, a smirk playing on his lips. "Fine, isn't good enough. Let's take care of that, yeah?" he said, waving over a passing medic.

"Jasper," I groaned.

"Good morning," a soft, gentle voice greeted us.

"Good morning, Elowen," Jasper hummed, glancing down at her.

He'd slipped on his unshakeable demeanor, concealing internal wounds to continue engaging with those who looked up to him.

"I have a quick favor if you don't mind," Jasper continued.

"Of course not. How can I help?" Elowen queried, an audible beam present in her voice.

Jasper gestured into the room toward me. "She suffered a deep stab wound last night. The focus was on healing the internal damage, so stitches were necessary."

Elowen stepped into full view, and my breath halted.

Her midnight black hair cascaded to her hips in loose curls, each strand gleaming with an ethereal sheen. She elegantly secured part of it away from her face, adding to her mesmerizing presence. Her oceanic blue eyes locked onto mine, her gaze both piercing and soothing. They were deep and expressive, reminiscent of a tranquil sea that could calm and conceal unfathomable depths. Her warm and welcoming smile softened the intensity of her gaze.

"Astrid, lovely to meet you, officially," she clarified with a wink.

"Officially?"

"People have spoken of you," she glanced at Jasper, a playful smile tugging at her lips. "Positively, of course."

I raised an eyebrow at the copper-haired male, who chuckled warmly. Her eyes lingered on him with a warmth that made my heart ache.

"May I?" Elowen asked, gesturing toward my wound as if sensing its location.

I nodded, offering her a tentative smile in return.

She knelt before me, her movements careful and eluding a quiet confidence that spoke of her experience. With a practiced hand, she gently lifted the hem of my shirt, revealing the fresh gauze covering my wound.

As the cool air hit my exposed skin and her warm fingers contrasted against it, a sudden memory of Onyx's thumb brushing my cheek returned. I swallowed, shoving back the fluster it awakened and praying Jasper hadn't noticed.

Elowen grazed the edge of the patterned stitch, sending a jolt of pain through my body. Her touch was gentle, but I winched at the sudden and sharp sensation.

"The examination is always the worst part," she whispered, her words laced with apology. "I'm going to have to lift your shirt a little further to get a full look at your wound."

"Away," I muttered, gesturing with a pointed finger toward Jasper.

He laughed and turned, lifting his hands in mock surrender, suddenly finding the crevices of the door jam incredibly interesting.

Elowen continued her examination, her touch methodical. I couldn't help but feel a sense of vulnerability, both physical and emotional. Being cared for became foreign to me once my brother had passed, only extending myself to others after he was gone. The realization was enough to stir up the uncertainties I'd worked tirelessly to forget about, specifically when connecting with others.

"Everything looks okay," Elowen finally declared, lowering my shirt. "I'm going to remove the stitches and seal the wound, which will require a few tools. I'll be right back."

An apology was uttered as she brushed past Jasper and out the door, her midnight hair following her like a dark-swept night. Her footsteps continued steadily, becoming less audible the further she moved.

I lifted a brow once the recognizable pattern dissipated. "She looks at you in a way that leads me to believe she's interested."

He pivoted, reaching to grab the top of the doorframe. "Is that so?"

"Glaringly obvious."

"I'll applaud you," he smirked, "for being so observant."

My eyes rolled, but a smirk followed closely behind.

"Since we are on the topic," he added, "why don't we discuss other *interests*?"

I tossed a vulgar gesture in his direction, already knowing where his mind was heading. "In a similar but more important topic of conversation, have you seen Onyx?"

"No, but I presume that since you're asking me, you woke up, and he was gone," Jasper sighed, running a hand through his hair.

I nodded.

"Isolated," he explained, a deep exhale accompanying the word. "Onyx detaches when dealing with things. He believes it's better to face his emotions alone rather than burdening others."

The sudden recollection of him clinging to Imelda's lifeless body flashed through my mind, guilt tightening its hold. Yet, beneath it, there remained a web of conflict.

"He's been this way since I met him during our time as Command Officers," Jasper continued, his voice carrying a weight of deep familiarity. "Even back then, Onyx had this natural inclination to take on the burdens of others, and that presumed obligation continues to rest on his shoulder. The Rebellion sees him as a symbol of resilience and more than just a leader, but a beacon of hope. But it isn't just them; it's the government, too. He bears the weight of having never wanted to be a hero or a martyr, all while being forced into it—being seen as both a threat and a leader by two wildly conflicting sides."

"He doesn't talk to anyone?" I asked, my voice barely above a whisper.

"Sometimes," Jasper admitted, "but getting him to is like pulling teeth."

"It sounds like he shuts down out of fear of dealing with things or because of the familiarity of facing everything alone for so long."

He nodded. "As I told you, Onyx is complicated on various levels."

A vulnerability with Onyx mirrored my own, a shared understanding and connection between us that ran deeper than words, and I couldn't help but lean into the pull I felt with him.

Jasper interrupted my thoughts, a firmness accompanying his comfort. "His choice to isolate isn't your fault, nor is it because of you. Like the rest of us, he needs time to process what happened. Imelda was his entire world for years, and there were vows made that he now sees as failures—likely things he will never forgive himself for."

Jasper's words held quiet wisdom and a deep understanding of the complexities at play. Part of me recognized the truth; the actions and responses of others were beyond my control. Yet another part couldn't help but fixate on the magnitude of loss apparent in Onyx's gaze.

"Is there anything we can do for him?"

Jasper smiled sadly. "We honor him for who he is and respect the process he takes to heal. We give him space and time, support him if he's ready to open up."

I nodded, understanding Jasper's experience with him. His advice came from a place of deep care and respect.

"As of right now, he needs time." Jasper bit his cheek. "I contemplated sitting him down to discuss what happened, nearly backing him into a corner so he wouldn't self-isolate, but doing so would do more damage than good. Onyx needs space to breathe and to evaluate his responses to what occurred, and the greatest thing we can do is allow him that."

"I'm worried about him."

Jasper loosened a pained sound. "I am, too. I worry about him immensely and all the damn time."

The melodic drum of footsteps became audible again, building in intensity as Elowen approached. Jasper offered a gentle smile to ease my feelings before he pulled his hand from the doorframe and stepped aside to allow her to re-enter.

Elowen slipped past him with a tray of supplies. "I apologize for keeping you waiting. I couldn't seem to find what I needed as efficiently as I would have liked."

"No worries," we chimed in unison, and Jasper shot a wink in my direction.

"If you could lie down on the cot," she suggested, lowering the tray to a table in the corner. "It would likely be far more comfortable for both of us."

I inclined, pushing myself from the chair and moving to the suggested position. The cot's stiff sheets felt sterile against my skin, nipping at my back with a cold bite and an aggravation of knowing all the secrets I held. As I lay there, the clinking of metal instruments filled the room, amplifying my nerves about everything.

Her siren eyes swept downward, focusing on the task at hand. "To summarize the process, I will cut and remove the stitching as quickly as possible. Then, I'll use my abilities to heal and seal the wound. There shouldn't be any issues because the medic who helped you treated the wound effectively, but it will be painful because of the tenderness of the area."

Dipping my chin with acceptance, I braced for the discomfort.

Sensing my unease, Jasper approached, his presence an anchor. His large hand reached out, and I grasped it, feeling the reassuring roughness of his skin. His implied promise of support offered a small measure of comfort.

Elowen's movements were systematic, each action deliberate. Her warm hand brushed my skin, contrasting with the briskness that coaxed my exposed abdomen.

"Would you like a countdown before I begin, or for me to just go for it?"

"Just go for it." I breathed.

The frigid metal of the scissors met my skin before I could back out of my decision. Swiftly, she cut through the threaded overlaps, the wound separating with a sharp and searing pain. I bit my lip, stifling the cry that crawled up the back of my throat.

"Step one, check," Elowen announced as she discarded the scissors and quickly reached for the tweezers. "You're doing great."

Jasper's hand tightened around mine as his thumb brushed against my knuckles, silently celebrating the minor victory. His stormy gray eyes flickered with encouragement, holding my gaze to distract me.

The tweezers connected with the first thread as she worked it from my skin, the sensation akin to barbed wire being removed. Hissing between clenched teeth, I closed my eyes to manage the relentless tugging. Each subsequent pull heightened the sensitivity, and my grip around Jasper's hand tightened out of reflex.

With the repetitive motion of the unwinding sutures, pain roared across my abdomen and back. I battled to keep my breathing steady, focusing on the texture of Jasper's hand instead of the memories of Radley that threatened to consume my mind.

"Wow, you're one tough cookie," Elowen commented as she worked on the third thread. The compliment, however small, was a brief distraction from the pain, a reminder of my strength.

The third was by far the worst. My shoulder blades dug into the cot as I worked to brace myself with composure, the confines of my control slipping with the building agony.

"One more," Jasper murmured, his grasp tightening slightly. "You're almost done."

When I forced my eyes open, I saw Jasper's stare through my teary eyes. Elowen clasped the tweezers around the last thread, pulling on it swiftly and gently. The searing sensation reached its peak, and a shuttered whimper escaped my lips. My head slammed back against the cot, and my teeth bit down hard enough on my lip to draw blood. The metallic tang was immediately detectable.

"All done," Elowen declared, moving quickly and depositing the tweezers on the tray before returning to my side.

I slowly raised my head, watching her hands glow with a soft, ethereal blue light. The hue matched her eyes, a calming color that radiated warmth and healing. The vibrancy intensified as she hovered her hands over my wound, a gentle warmth working through my abdomen.

Observing the light from her hands, I couldn't help but feel a deep ache in my heart. The sight was too reminiscent of Imelda; her delicate touch and the soft glow of her abilities were uncannily similar. The memory of her healing powers in the bunker was too fresh in my mind.

"Your hands are blue," I murmured, blinking back tears.

Elowen hummed in acknowledgment. "They are."

Her response carried a weight of unspoken meaning, one that Jasper picked up on. "Users whose abilities center solely around healing emit a blue, green, or purple hue when channeling them. If one wields power outside of the art of healing, the color is often a direct reflection of their base-level ability."

So, since Imelda was a fire wielder, orange was the color that manifested once she learned to heal. He seemed to add without speaking.

"Is it common?" I asked, struggling to keep my voice steady. "For users outside of the domain of healing to learn how?"

"No," Elowen replied, a hint of sorrow in her voice. "Imelda was the only one we encountered who could wield abilities outside our expertise and within the domain of healing as well."

That's why they targeted her.

Not only because of her attachment to Onyx and the void her death would leave but also because of the rarity of her unique ability as a dual wielder.

Elowen pulled away, the glow dissipating from her hands. "You're all good to go. Just take it easy for the rest of the day. The area will probably remain sensitive for the next couple of days, so monitor it and come visit if there are any issues."

Jasper helped me sit up, his hand lingering on my shoulder as I adjusted my shirt. "Thank you."

"Don't mention it," Elowen replied with a sincere smile. "We are always happy to help whenever we can."

The last three words resonated with deep regret.

Whenever.

They had done all they could for me, but their inability to save Imelda hung heavy in the air. Her presence had left an indelible mark on everyone, and her kindness and innocence were a beacon that had touched many lives.

We needed it to heal, mourn, and come to terms with losses, but time seemed to be both an ally and an enemy—a currency we were no longer granted.

TWENTY-FOUR

The following months were a tapestry woven with threads of grief, healing, and adaptation. Each person in the community grappled with their own sorrow, facing the aftermath of that fateful night in deeply personal ways.

For me, it was betrayal-tinged mourning. I grieved the version of Radley I had believed in, the person I thought I knew, and the illusions he curated. The disloyalty cut deep, forcing me to confront a harsh reality. It wasn't just about mourning him; it was about bereaving a part of myself that had been too naïve and trusting.

Jasper's grief was a heavy burden, anchored in the loss of those he had vowed to protect. The weight of leadership bore down on him as he struggled to reconcile his sense of duty with the harshness of reality, trying to balance between comforting those who'd lost while also comforting himself. He mourned the people who had looked to him for safety and security, spending hours at the elected burial site to pay his respects for an attack that fell beyond his control.

Onyx's bereavement was perhaps the most visible, the loss of Imelda leaving a gaping hole in his life. He'd avoided community meals, skipped out on any missions that involved others, and avoided engaging with those who looked up to him as much as he could. Every conversation with him had been short, barely a handful of words, and the light in his eyes had dimmed. He'd become a shell of the man he once was, avoiding attachment to any others out of the fear of someone else being taken from him.

The community members, too, faced their own forms of suffering. They had to adapt to a world that felt less predictable and far more dangerous, adjusting to the aftershocks of the violence that had touched their lives. In leveraging each other's abilities, they'd worked to rebuild all that had been destroyed. In the hours they spent with one another nurturing the community they loved, their connection and bond strengthened even as a collective vulnerability remained.

It felt like the attack had reset everything, leaving the community to start from the beginning and rebuild. The fresh start was far from clean; it was scarred and broken, filled with the echoes of loss. Yet amidst the rubble of their previous lives, there was a faint glimmer of perseverance. They'd continued to band together, each person bringing their own strengths and sorrows to the collective effort of rebuilding.

Onyx had become more guarded, putting on a mask of casualness whenever prompted with the idea of mourning. Navigating him became a complex task that created an undeniable level of tension between him and anyone who attempted to extend a helping hand. Even in brushing off his struggles and plastering a faked smile to make others happy, there had been moments where his feelings of powerlessness seeped through the cracks—nights when I'd heard him cry into the silence that enveloped the community.

It no longer became about fixing or saving him but acknowledging the multifaceted layers of grief and appreciating the complexity of his character. His pain reminded me of my own, the two of us drowning in similar but vastly different ways that linked us together on the path toward healing.

It was Imelda who said, *"Let him show you the side of him that I got to know."*

And I would continue to do just that.

Onyx groaned from across the table as he glanced at Jasper, pulling my attention from the thoughts that consumed my mind. "If you tell me to weed one more godsdamn garden bed, I am going to lose my mind."

I looked at Jasper, who sat in his usual spot at the head of the table with a coffee mug to his lips, wearing a snide grin. He had cut his hair since that night, and the shorter style suited him better—having freshly trimmed his beard with whatever he could get his hands on.

"Oh, come on, you don't get satisfaction from ripping roots out of the ground?" He chuckled with the query.

Onyx shot him a look that transitioned the chuckling to cackling.

"You two are worse than children, I swear." I rolled my eyes and glanced down at the map sprawled before us that continued to act as a tablecloth.

Per Jasper's request, we gathered to converse, although we were unsure what it would entail. Since that night, Jasper paused missions to allow people time to recuperate and mourn their losses. Both Onyx and I received orders to allow ourselves the proper time. And as a leader, Jasper was sure to take his.

The summer months passed quickly, and just as our lives changed drastically, our surroundings also transitioned. Leaves turned a golden brownish-orange with some hints of red and yellow as the air crispened. The foliage that coated the streets was another task handed off and passed around by community members. Luckily for us, most of the gardening had ceased, but per Jasper, it also became the perfect time to focus on upkeep and stocking while the community rebuilt itself from the inside out.

After progressing for a couple of months, it was time to return to normalcy, which I presumed was why Jasper called the meeting.

Jasper took a sip from his mug before continuing, "I apologize for assigning you two the mundane tasks of self-care and community upkeep."

"I don't think an ounce of sorrow is flowing through your veins right now." Onyx cocked a brow, kicking his legs up onto the table.

"I mean," Jasper's eyes flickered between us. "You two seemed to enjoy each other's company often during that time."

"Jasper." Now, it was my turn to cut in.

He wasn't wrong. Every chance I got to spend time with Onyx was one I took. Whether it was locking ourselves in the space we shared to avoid exerting energy that came with engagement or sharing a drink together at the bar, I'd been happy to join him when he'd provided the offer.

Even in the accuracy of the statement, it wasn't a comment I had prepared to step into. Nor was it about to be a conversation that the three of us would dive into at this point. On top of that, I remained unsure where Onyx and I sat with one another, which was something that I'd prepared to go without knowing for quite some time.

It was a hot topic when the time came to take up residency in the South Plaza, I politely declined. This drew Jasper's attention, yielding questions about what was going on behind the closed door of the space Onyx and I shared. According to him, he had known that the two of us had had an eye on each other for quite some time, and his suspicions were high as he awaited some level of disclosure from his best friend.

And per Jasper's disappointment or jealousy—I wasn't sure— nothing had been deemed share-worthy.

Onyx and I functioned like fraternity roommates and nothing more. The space we shared was merely that—*a space* —especially considering I did what I could to allow him the time and room he needed to heal, as Jasper had suggested months prior. It was vital for him to have the freedom to process his grief without interference, and I respected that boundary while holding onto my reasonings for staying close.

"While you're not wrong, I think we came here to discuss other things," Onyx spoke from beside me as he leveled his icy eyes at his best friend. "Why did you call this meeting?"

Jasper exhaled as he set his cup down on the table. "I heard from the communities along the East Coast following the information we provided involving your excursion."

"And?" the question came from both of us simultaneously. We exchanged a simple glance before looking back at him.

He raised his gaze at Onyx. "For starters. Cromwell is alive."

Onyx's expression shifted as he looked bewilderingly across the table at Jasper. Relief coated his features, but a stinging presence of utter shock followed an array of flooding emotions.

He shook his head, his reply filtering through a stuttered breath. "That's impossible."

"Is it?" Jasper cocked a brow as he folded his arms over his chest. "Because he was the one who responded to my message. He is the newly appointed head of the Rebellion community based in the outskirts of Region One—alive and well."

Onyx rubbed his eyes with the palms of his hands as he exhaled deeply. "After everything that happened, that seems highly improbable. When everything heightened, and we were forced to make a split-second decision—"

"He told us to go," Jasper finished his sentence and nodded. "Trust me. I remember that moment all too clearly."

Silence clung in the air momentarily as I shifted my gaze between them. "So, is there any possibility that I can know who this Cromwell person is?'

"His name is Rayne," Onyx said from beside me as he raised his head from his hands. "He was a Command Officer who served with Jasper and me and was another dear friend of ours."

"Just over a year before the Fall happened, we still held stationed at one of the government facilities within the Capital." Jasper looked over at me, picking up for Onyx on a conversation that seemed far too taxing. "After a specific mission, we learned of the manufacturing of the virus and the government's plans to unleash it on the surrounding cities. We planned, the night of our escape, to work our way out of there and take that information to whoever we could give it to—journalists, news stations, and the like. But there was a mole that we weren't aware of."

"Gael." His name felt like near-poison on my lips.

Jasper nodded. "The President ordered him to tail our initial research because of higher-ups' suspicions of our opposition. Through him, they learned about our plans to leave and intercepted us."

Onyx swallowed before speaking. "The three of us did what we could to get out alive and together, but we were unsuccessful."

Memories surged of the executions that took place in the Walls, bodies dropping while those they loved battled against the soldiers to try and prevent the inevitable, even if it cost their lives. I knew they were no different, agreeing to protect each other before officially planning anything. Yet, there were always risks and the possibility that someone would end up left behind— something I was far too familiar with.

"Instead of joining us in our attempt to flee, Rayne offered himself up to those in power and gave us the leeway for a successful escape." Jasper clenched his jaw, his throat bobbing as he swallowed the surge of emotions memory seemed to stir.

Onyx sighed, drawing the attention away from their pasts and back to the present. "How can you confidently say it's him? It could just be some other government prick playing their pawn, luring us out to the Capital to capture us as soon as we get there."

Jasper's brow furrowed, his expression thoughtful. "I understand your skepticism, but the message contained specific details only Rayne would know. He mentioned things that happened during missions that only we shared with one another."

Onyx's eyes lit slightly at Jasper's words, a beam of hope shining through but dampened by questioning. It was as if allowing himself to dream of the possibility of encountering his friend alive again was too much for him to stomach. He needed factual proof to yield his belief that it was Rayne and not another betrayal sitting on the horizon.

Jasper continued, understanding Onyx's needs. "He answered every question I posed accurately."

Onyx shook his head as a breathy chuckle of disbelief fell from him. "There's no way."

"Needless to say, we've got another ally—one ready to pave the path of warfare further than we started," Jasper smirked, his gray eyes softening as he held his friend's gaze.

"He agreed to infiltrate?" I asked, working my way back into the conversation.

"If there's one thing you should know about Rayne, it's that he is far more reckless than even Onyx is." Jasper chuckled as Onyx rolled his eyes. "He has been waiting for the perfect time to breach the Walls for years."

"A hateful, snide, and prideful bastard." Onyx smiled softly, positive memories coaxing his uncertainty. "I never imagined he would grace us with his presence again."

"You and I both," Jasper exhaled in relief before running a hand down his beard. "Rayne has established alliances with the Rebellion sanctuaries along the East Coast. And everyone within them is equally ready for blood as our people here."

Onyx's grin only seemed to grow at the mention of others just as revenge-hungry as he was, every ounce of him desiring to retaliate for all they'd robbed him of.

"I think that speaks to everyone in this room as well." I lifted my eyes to look at Jasper, and he nodded in agreement.

The months that passed after the attack were full of sorrow and grief, but there was also an underlying drive.

Hatred.

Revenge.

Everyone had lost something the night Gael and his men breached the community—all equally tired of constantly being on the defense. They'd continually worried that the President would unleash an attack on the communities they'd spent so much time building and fostering. That consistent paranoia acted as the tipping scale they'd officially breached.

For the longest time, they played nice.

For the longest time, they refused to breach the Walls for the sake of the innocent lives within them.

But the games were over.

"Does he have abilities?" I asked, prodding further, just as I had when trying to decipher Jasper's abilities.

During my interrogation, Onyx informed me that Jasper would enlighten me once he was ready and that I should keep my nose where it belonged if I desired to keep breathing. Part of me couldn't help but overanalyze his statement, wondering if Jasper could manipulate the very air we breathed. Without an answer from the man himself, I continued to remain just as clueless and curious.

"Yes, he does." Jasper stood up and pushed himself from the table, walking to one of the shelves within the space and grabbing a folder before returning to us. "He mentioned it the first time we spoke to one another. He's a mimic."

"Of course he is." Onyx dropped his boots from the table before leaning forward, placing his forearms against the oak.

"A mimic?"

Jasper looked at Onyx as he tossed the manilla folder onto the table. Gliding across the table with the force of his throw, it landed directly in front of Onyx. "You want to enlighten her on our terminology out here?"

"In simplistic terms, he's a shapeshifter." Onyx looked at me before turning his attention to the folder, pulling it toward him, and flipping it open.

"That's likely how he survived then, right?" I looked up to Jasper, knowing I had officially lost Onyx's attention.

To my surprise, Onyx responded, even as he buried his face in the documents. "Likely. As I mentioned, he's a snide bastard."

Jasper cut in, providing more clarity on Rayne's survival up to this point. "He informed me he laid low for nearly a year after the Fall and then made his escape. He gathered a few Rebels within the city, and then from there, they began building the sanctuary near the Capital."

"You said that he recently became head of the Capital Rebellion." I paused as I glanced over at Jasper. "If he was the one to gather the bodies for it, why didn't he take the place of leadership?"

"He holds a deep hatred for authority because of his family's past ties with the government." Onyx shut the folder and pushed it back across the table to Jasper. "Plus, he's always been reactive, and he likely knew that a personality trait like that wouldn't be the best for one in a leadership position."

"He is smart enough to realize where his faults lie. He passed off the title to someone else within the community." Jasper grabbed the folder and dropped it in front of where he had been sitting before lowering himself back into his seat. "There was a breach within their walls recently, and that attack resulted in their leader's execution, which is a large reason his people are so vengeful. It would seem that the government didn't just come for us; they have also been making their way to other Rebellion sanctuaries."

"As a statement," Onyx put a hand on his chin.

My mind scoured the conversations I had heard amongst other Venturers during my time within the Walls, and there was never a discussion of those in power making any level of statement to prove their control to the masses by implementing attacks on communities. Then again, most of those who held my prior position had been just as misled as I was.

"But what of?" The question came from me as I looked between them.

Neither responded and instead, Onyx slid the file in my direction.

A sign of trust.

I swallowed as I flipped it open, and Jasper spoke again. "The folder contains the intel Rayne provided during our discussion with one another."

My heart sank as my fingers skimmed through the papers. The recollection of the power-wielders Radley and I had been responsible for capturing slipped to the forefront, including those without abilities who escaped the Walls out of curiosity—the lives I brought back and handed off without thinking twice.

Nausea turned my stomach, memories I'd buried haunting my mind as remorse surged throughout my entire body.

"Rayne took the opportunity when he offered himself up to those in power to prod and learn more about their motives. It seems the discussions Onyx and I had about the intention behind the handoffs you mentioned match our assumptions about them testing on power wielders." His voice sharpened as he continued, "But it's even more twisted than expected, though we shouldn't be surprised."

As he continued speaking, my eyes scanned the words in the documents, and my brain stopped registering what he said.

Responsible for a basic handoff resulting in experimentation or the Eradication Rites.

I closed the folder, pondering everything I thought I knew and all I'd tried to prevent. My mind raced with implications, uncertainty pressing down on my chest and threatening to suffocate me. Every part of me curled inward, realizing how far I'd dropped the ball, and the guilt of those I had been unsuccessful in saving nearly consumed me.

Yet Radley had known all along.

He was aware of the handoffs and the horrific consequences that followed, but he still participated despite knowing about the experiments and these newly discovered Eradication Rites.

I forced the words out, my throat dry. "What does that even mean?"

"You stopped reading," Onyx said, rubbing his temples. "It seems the government's corruption and vile methods still thrive in their underground operations."

Jasper nodded, pushing his mug away, clearly as sickened as I felt. "These handoffs result in torturing power wielders to the brink. They aim to break them in every way—physically, mentally, emotionally. The goal is to find where they begin to shatter and then push beyond that boundary."

Onyx cursed under his breath, his body flinching instinctively. The reaction spoke volumes of the horrors he'd endured, his eyes glazing over as if he'd been entrapped by a haunting memory at the mention. Each twitch and subtle wince told a story of suffering that went far beyond physical torture. The government's cruelty had left a lasting imprint on him mentally, physically, and emotionally.

Jasper continued, understanding Onyx's resistance to the conversation. "Some power wielders survive the torture, while others either die or mutate into Runners. There isn't a known explanation for it, at least not that we've been able to uncover. It seems that with the more intense mutation, the Runners become weapons that inevitably get unleashed into the cities as the government's 'watchdogs.'"

Images of the faces we'd encountered during our missions flashed through my mind. I ran my fingers across my eyes, trying to process it all. "What about those that survive without changing?"

"The Eradication Rites," Onyx answered through clenched teeth. "They pit the surviving users against one another in a brutal tournament, making participants eliminate one another. By orchestrating it, they maintain a semblance of detachment, as if the power wielders' fates were merely the result of their own actions rather than the President's schemed cruelty."

Jasper folded his arms, adding, "Not all captured end up experimented on—some are just thrown into the Eradication Rites. It's a spectacle and warning to those who oppose the government or leave their communities. A statement that they are in control, no matter what. That even the strongest," he briefly glanced at Onyx, "can't escape their reach."

"So, it's a show of dominance," I murmured, looking at Onyx, who nodded in agreement. "They'll pit us against each other whenever they can."

Onyx shook his head, disgust evident in his expression. "They think our lives are some type of game and show that by their willingness to have attendees who watch as the banished tear each other apart."

The executions within the Walls, which turned into public events with refreshments, highlighted the capabilities of those in power, showcasing the corruption they siphoned both within and outside the Walls. Even though I had no choice in the matter, the faces of those I had been complicit in taking flashed before my eyes as I realized the depth of my involvement and the impact my secrecy would undeniably have.

"If you're blaming yourself, Astrid, it's not your fault," Jasper said gently, attempting to comfort me. "You didn't know what these handoffs would lead to."

"None of us did," Onyx added, his thumb soothingly rubbing my shoulder. "And to avoid delving into it any further for the time being, let's change the subject before we all sink into the what-ifs and what-could-have-beens."

Jasper pulled the folder away, sensing my discomfort.

"Rayne," Onyx said, keeping his hand on my shoulder. "When do we meet with him to discuss the next steps?"

Jasper nodded, a lazy smile marking his expression. "Spoken like a genuine leader. Though, I can't say I'm surprised. We need a solid plan before executing."

Onyx's comforting gesture stopped as he caught the hint of sarcasm in Jasper's tone. "What are you plotting?"

Jasper raised an amused brow. "You think I have some grand scheme?"

"Don't you always?" Onyx retorted, referencing the risky mission he had sent us on. "You knew the risks of sending us to the East Coast and still elected to do just that."

Jasper shrugged, unbothered. "You hid the truth, and you agreed to go. I suppose that makes us all responsible."

Onyx rolled his eyes. "Like we had a choice."

"You always have *somewhat* of a choice," Jasper smirked, receiving a glare in return.

"When do we leave for the Capital?" I interjected, cutting through their banter.

"We don't," Jasper said, looking at me as Onyx's attention snapped back to him.

"What do you mean we don't? We need to join forces and plan accordingly if we want to be successful," Onyx demanded, removing his hand from my shoulder.

"Yes, you're correct," Jasper replied, his tone undermining something else entirely.

Onyx groaned, pushing further as his patience slipped. "Okay, Jasper, cut the mysterious ploy. What is going on?"

Jasper merely raised his eyes to the doorway behind Onyx and me. Before I could turn to see what had caught his attention, the bell rang.

TWENTY-FIVE

The man was striking, radiating a quiet confidence that commanded attention. He removed his black trench coat, revealing a fitted black long sleeve beneath that accentuated his build. His physique mirrored Onyx's and Jasper's in size and definition, the sharp edges of muscles becoming apparent even with the most minor movements. The coat, now draped over his forearm, added a casual yet commanding element to his appearance.

He pivoted, the light catching a couple of necklaces resting against his chest, one of which was a dog tag. His hair, a rich tapestry of brown shades, fell just past the back of his neck, with a few strands draping over his forehead. Its tousled style framed his sharp features—high cheekbones, a defined jawline, and expressive eyebrows that added to his intense gaze. His eyes, a piercing midwinter sky-blue, scanned the room with a calm yet assessing look, taking in his surroundings with a practiced ease. Once he spotted his friends, a cheeky grin spread across his face, emphasizing a pair of dimples that sank into his cheeks, softening his presence.

"Long time no see," he stated playfully, the joyfulness behind the four words beyond palpable.

His voice was deep and smooth but carried the weight of unspoken history; his statements rich with reminiscence and contentment.

Onyx sprang from his seat, his movement a blur of urgency and awe. He crossed the room in a heartbeat, closing the distance between them faster than Jasper or I could react. Unspoken sentiments charged the air as Onyx enveloped his old friend in a tight embrace. Rayne responded in kind, wrapping his muscular arms around Onyx's broad shoulders. The embrace was firm and reassuring, a physical manifestation of their bond and the time they'd lost with each other.

"It's great to see you," Rayne spoke, his voice softening.

Onyx's shoulders trembled slightly, betraying a rare moment of vulnerability that Rayne held without judgment.

Jasper watched them, a soft smile playing on his lips. The admiration that flashed through his stormy gaze gave way to his understanding of the reunion being more than just a meeting but a lifeline for Onyx.

The moment stood as a beacon of hope and reminded us that not all was lost. Onyx, who carried the weight of his burdens with resilience, allowed his guard to fall, even if only momentarily, sitting with his feelings in the safe embrace of a long-lost friend. Rayne held him, offering silent support and understanding the pertinence of their embrace.

"It's been quite some time, hasn't it?" Rayne remarked, his eyes shifting to Jasper and then to me. His gaze was scrutinizing, filled with curiosity and a protective edge—a silent warning that was clear to anyone paying attention.

"Indeed, it has," Jasper said, standing and crossing the room to join them in what seemed to be an attempt to break Rayne's fixation on me.

"Over four years," Onyx finally spoke, pulling back slightly to look at Rayne. He placed his hands on his shoulders to reassure himself that his friend was real and not a figment of his imagination.

Rayne extended a hand to Jasper, which quickly turned into another embrace.

"It's good to see you, Rayne," Jasper said, relief and warmth present in the words.

"Likewise. I'm glad to see you both alive and well." Rayne's gaze slid back to me. "And there's someone new, I see."

Jasper nodded, subtly gesturing toward me as a means of introduction. "Astrid, this is Rayne. And Rayne, this is Astrid."

Rayne raised an eyebrow, a hint of intrigue in his expression. "Ah, the ex-Venturer," he said, the term carrying a weight. "Jasper spoke of you when we last talked."

"I hope it was all good," I replied, rising from the table to face him.

He nodded. "Yes, good things. Aside from your counterpart, who left quite a mark on this community."

The mention of Radley hit like a punch to the gut, and I struggled to maintain my composure under the weight of his words. Onyx's expression tightened, a flash of concern crossing his face.

"Her piece of shit counterpart who misled her for years," Onyx clarified with his exclamation, anger sharpening his words.

He didn't direct the venom at Rayne but at the whole situation that had brought us all to this mess.

Rayne's eyes lingered on me, trying to decipher the truth of my character. The air surged with energy that seemed to prod at my edges in search of my truth and anything I'd worked to keep hidden—an intrusion into my depths that I found easily detectable.

He took a deep breath before returning to Onyx, the divulgence into my being vanishing. "They hit the Capital Rebellion hard as well."

"I heard," Onyx replied, nodding towards Jasper as Rayne continued. "How many did you lose?"

"Over fifty people," Rayne said, the gravity of the situation apparent in his voice.

Jasper's eyes widened. "For hell's sake. How many did your community have beforehand?"

"Close to a hundred. We're down to about thirty-five now." Rayne sighed heavily, his sorrow as a leader matching all that I'd witnessed with Jasper.

Onyx exhaled, his brows knitting together. The room fell silent, the reality of our world sinking in, further solidifying all the ways we'd been incapable of preventing the inevitable. With the undisclosed vows I made to myself, a moral dilemma remained. Far too much still needed to be done, especially after I'd witnessed the impact of the infiltration and reflected on my powerlessness in preventing it from happening.

"Luckily for us, the dent wasn't that bad here," Jasper finally stated, his words striking a nerve in the raven-haired man beside him.

I could see the tension ripple through Onyx's body, his jaw tightening. In his eyes, Imelda was worth over fifty lives. He inhaled, suppressing whatever words threatened to escape him, knowing Jasper hadn't meant to belittle his pain.

"An attack is an attack. Damage is damage," Rayne intervened, his voice steady as he looked between them. "I got word this morning before I arrived that Augusta got hit as well."

Jasper's exhalation was deep, and frustration and resignation became notable in the sigh. "Any word about the extent of the damage there?"

"Close to fifty lost as well," Rayne responded grimly. "Though I'm uncertain what their original numbers were."

"For hell's sake," Onyx muttered, shaking his head. "The back-to-back infiltrations threaten to dismantle the Rebellion even further than the damage they've already caused. We already stand in opposition to the Scavengers, and the attacks only seem to prompt uncertainty surrounding the community members' safety and protection on our part."

"Over fifty lost," I spoke up, my train of thought mirroring

Onyx's consideration. "Does that mean dead, or includes those left unaccounted for?"

Rayne turned to face me, a flicker of annoyance highlighting his features before intrigue replaced it.

"Total," he replied curtly.

I glanced between Jasper and Onyx, my thoughts churning to uncover the coordinated intention. "I wonder if there is some type of pattern across the communities that link the attacks together."

I held Rayne's gaze, challenging his suspicion with a steady, unflinching stare. His wariness was understandable—my association with Radley, the traitor who had betrayed Jasper's people, marked immediate question on my loyalty. But I wasn't here to seek his approval or prove myself to anyone. Not when there was far too much to lose.

My reasons for aligning with the Rebellion went beyond mere loyalty or revenge.

"She may be onto something," Onyx acknowledged, glancing at me with a hint of surprise before turning back to Jasper. "We lost fifteen people, and five others remain unaccounted for."

Rayne's eyes widened slightly, his expression thoughtful as he calculated. "A thirty-three percent ratio," he murmured, stepping closer to the table and glancing at the map that served as a tablecloth.

"How many people were left unaccounted for in your community?" I asked, feeling the continued weight of his scrutiny regardless of whether he realized my intrusion had a purpose.

"Fourteen unaccounted for, forty-three dead," he answered steadily, his gaze marking his mind's racing thoughts.

"Close to thirty-three percent as well," Onyx noted, realization coating his powder blue eyes.

Jasper's eyes widened, the number seemingly having far more meaning than a simple percentage. "It's their beginning goal."

"Beginning goal?" I echoed, turning to the others for clarification.

Rayne moved forward to trace a line on the map, revealing a deep scar that ran up his left pointer finger before disappearing beneath his shirtsleeve. "The original aim was population control. As I'm sure you're aware, the government was losing its grip—resources were dwindling, and the infrastructure collapsed. Panic began setting in, even within the inner ranks and those walking alongside those in power. They manufactured the virus with an aim to reduce the population by thirty-three percent—which seems to match the ratio between the deceased and those deemed missing."

"So now they're selectively breaching communities, targeting a specific ratio of casualties and captures to fulfill their original plan? Why wouldn't they shift the narrative?" I asked, watching Rayne intently.

He shrugged, his eyes cold. "It's their measurable standard of success. No need to recalibrate when they had a pre-determined target."

"It's easier to continue with an old plan than come up with a new one," Jasper added, every syllable further laced with frustration. "While battling the Rebellion and opposition, there isn't time to re-evaluate, so they stick to what's comfortable."

"Exactly." Rayne nodded, glancing at Jasper. "They failed the first time, so now they're committed to seeing it through by any means necessary—to prove a point."

"Experimentation or Eradication Rites," I muttered, horror settling in my chest at the realization that those missing likely got forced into both. I aimed my next question at the man who'd continued to prod me with his gaze, "Do you know anything about the Eradication Rites beyond what you shared with Jasper?"

The question slipped out before I could stop it, instantly drawing Rayne's attention. His gaze snapped to mine as he leaned forward, the air around him growing bitter.

"What do I know about the Eradication Rites?" he repeated dangerously, the answer easily detectable even as it sat laced in his tone. "Quite a lot, considering they threw me into them, and I barely survived."

The shock of his revelation stole my breath. I hadn't expected this level of personal connection to the horrors we were discussing.

"You were a participant?" Onyx's whispered, his eyes widening with disbelief.

Rayne shrugged as if recounting something merely mundane. "Yeah, I was. Maverick, the former leader of the Captial Rebellion, sent me on a mission to Silver Spring after receiving a distress signal about potential Rebels. As his right-hand man, I took the lead on the rescue mission. But it was a trap. Men ambushed us and nearly killed everyone with me. Government soldiers recognized me, captured me, and then threw me into the Rite. As I told Jasper, they revel in tormenting those who oppose them, especially those who once served them."

Onyx's face twisted, the reality of Rayne's ordeal and the possible fate he narrowly escaped becoming near suffocating.

Jasper broke the silence. "Did you get any insight into where they hold these Rites?"

Rayne sighed, folding his arms over his chest, the fabric of his shirt straining against his arms. "I can't give you an exact location. But based on the military presence and the high-ranking officials I saw, it can't be far from the Capital."

"I apologize for interrupting again," I began, looking at Rayne. "Are you saying there's an operational military base near the Capital?"

"Yes," they all responded in unison, puzzled by my apparent lack of knowledge.

"Did you not know that?" Jasper asked, his focus landing entirely on me.

I shook my head, "No, I didn't. The only three bases ever disclosed to us as Venturers were Regions One, Two, and Three. There was never a mention of a Fourth or any potential militant presence in the Capital."

"It's a coverup for the Eradication Rites," Onyx inserted, my admittance solving a piece of the puzzle. "Which further clarifies their location."

Rayne nodded in agreement. "So it would seem. They're avoiding handing out information that would make them vulnerable. Only a select few within each of the walled communities likely know about those operations to keep themselves guarded. They store a lot of valuable intel within that base, so it makes sense why they wouldn't want many to know about it."

It was all beginning to connect, one piece at a time.

"It comprises all of their dark secrets." My stare locked with Onyx's before trailing to the others. "They withheld it because they knew it would leave them wide open to attack if someone opposed them or switched sides. Not only is it an incredibly valuable location, but it becomes even more vulnerable with insight."

"Now you're getting it," Rayne mumbled, his tone carrying a subtle edge. There was a hint of backhandedness, as if he was testing the depth of my understanding or perhaps hinting at a level of knowledge beyond what I'd shared with the others.

Jasper's eyes narrowed slightly, focusing on him without delving into his suggestive implications. "Well, considering that you brought your top men to discuss attack strategies, shall we get started?"

CHAPTER
TWENTY-SIX

Four individuals from Rayne's community joined us shortly after Jasper requested their presence.

As the eight of us gathered around the table, I tried to place names with their unfamiliar faces.

The first to enter forced bile to burn the back of my throat, my heart drumming against my chest with heightened anxiety. He bore an uncanny resemblance to Radley, with a similar height and build that was almost manageable to overlook. However, the short, whitish-blonde hair and piercing blue eyes made my stomach churn, and I had to swallow the bile rising in my throat. My fingers curled around the table's edge, struggling to keep me grounded.

There were only two things that pulled me back.

The first was the deep scar trailing from behind his left ear down his neck, disappearing under the collar of his shirt—a distinguishable feature that Radley didn't have. The second was Onyx's reassuring hand on my thigh under the table, gently squeezing it to remind me he was there.

The next person was eye-catching in his own right, with deep chestnut skin that seemed to glow even in the dim autumn light. He wore a maroon turtleneck, an intricate dragon tattoo peeking over the neckline. His green eyes contrasted his dark black curls, some of which fell over his forehead. A lighter scar crossed his right brow and eye, and unlike Onyx, he hadn't been fortunate enough to keep his sight.

The third was a tall, muscular male with dirty blonde hair styled shorter on the sides with a longer top. Most of it fell over the left side of his face, not to shield him but perhaps a preference for displaying his personality. His caramel-brown eyes darted between Onyx and Jasper, showing a mix of unease and admiration that would likely become clearer with interaction. A five o'clock shadow framed his sharp jawline, accentuating the contours of his face against the room's shadows.

The fourth individual shocked me, though I couldn't quite pinpoint why. I found my eyes drawn to her as soon as she crossed the threshold. She wore her blonde hair in a bun atop her head, with a few loose strands framing her round yet sharp face. The sides of her shaven head bore tattoos that snaked beneath the remaining hair. Though slim, her frame hinted at underlying strength, clear even through her long-sleeve shirt. Two scars marked her face—one beneath her left eye, slashing horizontally across her cheek, and another through her right brow. Her hazel eyes met mine, a flicker of surprise and a soft smile curling her lips.

"Lovely to meet each of you," Jasper said, glancing between them.

They nodded in acknowledgment.

Rayne chuckled, his smug smile teasing. "Care to provide them with your names, or would you all prefer to remain mysterious?"

The woman spoke first, her voice soft but tinged with untamed energy. "I'm Raven."

"Riggs," the deep-chested man introduced himself as he raised his hand, the depth of his voice nearly knocking me over.

The third man, who had been eyeing Onyx and Jasper, spoke next. "Mykel."

"And last but certainly not least," Rayne gestured to the Radley look-alike, folding his arms.

"Everett," he said with a smile that didn't quite reach his eyes.

Jasper's face lit up as he looked between them. "It's lovely to put names to faces. I'm sure Rayne had much to say about Onyx and me."

Onyx raised his free hand in a casual wave, acknowledging them.

Everett's indifferent tone cut through the room as he jutted a thumb at Onyx. "We knew a lot about him before Rayne spoke about his past with you two. The Most Wanted Rebel around. It's an honor to meet you in person, Onyx."

"The pleasure is mine," Onyx replied, a fleeting smile crossing his lips before his expression returned to its usual guarded calm.

Mykel turned to me, his head slightly bowed. "And you are?"

"Astrid," I replied with a smile, which he quickly returned.

Everett raised an eyebrow at me. "The ex-Venturer turned Rebel. I can appreciate that. Suppose we should extend an official welcome to you as well."

His acknowledgment was profoundly validating despite my differences from them. It was a rare feeling I hadn't experienced in a long time—being seen and valued for who someone believed me to be rather than what they thought I could do. I swallowed the lump in my throat, the sense of belonging making me far more emotional than anticipated.

Jasper hesitated before querying, "Is it too much to ask about abilities? I don't want to pry or make anyone uncomfortable."

Rayne rolled his eyes, smirking. "Since when did you become so soft, Jasper?"

Onyx stifled a laugh while the rest of the group chuckled at the joke.

Rayne's leadership style was different, more relaxed, and less rigid than Jasper's. Yet, they shared mutual respect and recognized the skill and strength required to lead in such turbulent times. Their camaraderie was evident, even with the jest.

Jasper glanced playfully at Rayne. "Gods forbid I have a level of respect and decency."

"Meh," Rayne shrugged dismissively, waving a hand.

As I watched their exchange, a smile tugged on my lips. Onyx nudged me, and I turned to find him smiling, his hand gently squeezing my leg. The gesture was a silent affirmation, a reminder that we still had moments of light despite the chaos.

Riggs gestured to Raven. "Ladies first."

"I'm a cross-user," Raven explained, leaning back in her chair.

"The golden child," Everett teased, earning Raven's glare and the group's chuckle.

"Ignore the thick-skulled idiot over there," she said, focusing back on us. "Invisibility and healing are my domains."

"And she loves scaring the shit out of Rayne whenever she can," Mykel added, laughing as Rayne rolled his eyes.

The lighthearted dynamic Rayne showed with Onyx and Jasper that continued with his group was refreshing, starkly contrasting the tension and distrust I felt and making me feel safe in their presence. It was a side of him I had suspected existed but hadn't witnessed with anyone other than those he'd known for years. Despite the weight of leadership, he was a man who could still laugh and joke with his people, balancing authority and companionship.

"You wanna go next, dipshit?" Raven teased, glancing over at Everett with a playful smile growing on her lips.

"It would be an honor, my lady," Everett replied, his blue eyes glinting with mischief. "As Raven's defined scoundrel, since I'm not blessed with her double-wielding talents, I'll simply state that I am an ice user, though it has its perks."

Raven threw a vulgar gesture his way, which he gladly returned, the two of them grinning at each other. Their friendship was evident, a shared bond of mutual respect and playfulness.

"That will be incredibly handy," Jasper noted, nodding in appreciation for Everett's willingness to share.

"The four of them love to spite me, needless to say," Rayne remarked, cocking a brow at Everett, which drew a genuine laugh from the group.

"And what about you two?" I asked, glancing between Riggs and Mykel, curious to learn more about them.

To my surprise, Everett chimed in, "Riggs is special, too."

A throaty chuckle escaped Rayne, and Raven covered her growing grin with her hand.

Riggs glanced at his friends before speaking. "I'm a cross-user as well, and it's clear that this pansy is just jealous because he isn't blessed like Raven and I."

Raven huffed, "Oh hell, could you imagine Everett with multiple abilities?"

"Gods help us all," Rayne muttered, shaking his head. "Thankfully, we were graced on the manner."

Everett smiled, tracing his tongue across his bottom lip. "I would make all of your lives a living hell if that were the case."

"You already do," the group chorused back at him, their laughter ringing through the room as Everett's eyes sparked with pure amusement.

Riggs turned his attention back to us. "I can leverage both teleportation and telekinetic abilities."

"Oh, so like Onyx," I noted, glancing at the raven-haired man beside me before looking back at him.

He shook his head modestly. "I'm nowhere near what Onyx is capable of. We share some similarities, but the extent of his abilities has always amazed me."

"Are you all going to kiss his ass?" Rayne groaned before looking at Onyx with a soft smile, recognition prevalent in his gaze.

"You're just mad because you have to mimic those you admire," Everett shot back, a teasing edge in his voice.

Rayne waved him off with a laugh. "Yeah, yeah, yeah. Are you going to come up with any new insults or keep recycling the old ones?"

Onyx chuckled, the sound warm and rich. It made me smile as he watched the interactions between someone he held dear and those he led. A flash of pride crossed his expression, but it was so subtle that one would've had to pay close attention to his mannerisms to have caught it.

Shit.

I caught Jasper looking at me, a knowing smirk on his lips. He cocked a brow, recognizing where I focused my attention. I shook my head, silently warning him not to dig further. He shrugged in response, the promise of teasing withheld—for now.

"And what about you, Mykel?" Onyx asked, his hand still resting on my thigh to continue to serve as a soothing and grounding presence.

"Gravity manipulation," Mykel answered.

"Holy shit," Jasper exclaimed, his focus shifting entirely to the male.

"A scarce ability," Onyx nodded approvingly. "Impressive."

"I told you he'd be the one to get the praise," Riggs said, glancing over his shoulder at Everett, who grinned. "You owe me."

"This is bullshit," Everett retorted, holding Riggs' gaze.

"A bet is a bet, Z," Riggs shrugged, his hearty laugh filling the room.

The sound was warm and inviting, gently comforting a broken and raw part of me, providing a sense of home I hadn't had in years.

The love they shared was undeniable. Their bond, forged through playful banter and genuine interactions, became undeniable. Despite the world's chaos, they cherished each other in a connection that transcended simplicity.

They were more than just a group of survivors—they were a family.

TWENTY-SEVEN

Onyx stood a few feet from me, his hair tied back in a loose bun. A few strands escaped to frame his face, giving him a harsh yet composed appearance. The autumn breeze played with the fallen pieces, adding its own touch of softness.

He had rolled the sleeves of his henley, revealing the defined muscles of his forearms, which were further accentuated as they crossed over his chest. The sunlight highlighted the dark hues of his hair, creating a stark contrast with the paler skin of his arms. He looked at the oak tree, now serving as our makeshift target. An arrow sat embedded in the center of a hand-drawn bullseye.

"I've got to give you credit. You're one hell of a shot," he remarked, nodding toward it.

I lowered the compound bow to my side. "I've known how to shoot a bow long before my time as a Venturer. My dad taught me as a kid, and my brother made sure I practiced regularly to keep up with him."

"That's clear." Onyx glanced back at me, a subtle shift in the conversation. "Speaking of your prior title, what did they teach you during your training?"

The question took me back to the early years when I used our training as an outing for the anger of losing my brother. I brushed off the memories of nearly killing another woman in a blind rage, focusing on something more neutral than the things that crept in the shadows.

"Decently advanced weapons and combat training."

"So, you're confident going up against a high-ranking, ex-Command Officer in hand-to-hand combat?" Onyx asked, a playful grin crossing his scarred lips. It was a sight I was beginning to see more often, my heartstrings surging with longing every time it greeted me.

"I never said—"

"I'd love to see her kick your ass." Rayne's voice cut through the crisp afternoon air.

I glanced over my shoulder to spot him striding across the field with a confident, easy gait. His hands casually tucked into the pockets of his trench coat, its long hem flaring out slightly with each step. The coat, now an extension of his persona, commanded attention, swaying with a life of its own.

"Shouldn't you be discussing infiltration plans?" Onyx challenged, not bothering to turn toward Rayne.

"My portion of the discussion is over. Riggs is best with delegation, so I left him and the others with Jasper to finalize things." Rayne looked at the tree, raising his eyebrows slightly before returning his gaze to us. "Plus, you know how Jasper is—the master analyst."

The comment forced Onyx to acknowledge him as he finally glanced over his shoulder. "That's one hell of a leadership decision."

Rayne shrugged, closing the gap between us. "You know authority has never been my thing. I stepped up because I helped establish the Capital Rebellion, and when we lost our leader during the breach, our people needed someone they could trust. My team and I were the best suited for the responsibility."

I flicked the taut string of the bow. "So, you'd prefer not to be a leader?"

"Oh, hell no. There are far more enjoyable things to life than ordering people around. That's why I delegate duties to those better equipped," Rayne said, squinting against the sun as he glanced at Onyx. "Training, I presume?"

Onyx nodded. "I've seen Astrid in action a few times, but it's essential to test her skills with weapons and hand-to-hand combat before the infiltration. We all need to be prepared for the worst-case scenario, and a solid foundation is crucial in ensuring that."

The upcoming mission loomed in my consciousness. We all knew it was high-risk, but the guilt that gnawed at the essence of my being spoke to all I'd elected to keep from them, things that would inevitably have an influence even though I tried to run from them for as long as possible.

Rayne grinned. "Well, you're in luck, Astrid."

Hearing my name from his lips caught me off guard, jolting me back from the whirlwind of thoughts and anxieties clouding my mind.

Rayne continued, "You're training with the individual praised for his hand-to-hand combat skills. Close-quarters combat is Onyx's specialty."

My cheeks flushed as Onyx shifted closer to me. "I'm rusty," he murmured.

"Rusty, my ass," Rayne laughed. "We all know you don't get physical too often as a mental user, but those of us who've seen you in action know damn well what you're capable of."

"This is news to me," I replied, trying to hide my curiosity.

"Oh?" Rayne looked between Onyx and me. "You haven't bragged about it at all? That's shocking."

Onyx chuckled deeply. "Unlike you, Rayne, I know when to keep my pride to myself."

Rayne smirked, shaking his head. "You've gotten more stone-faced over the years, but I'm unsurprised."

"What about you?" I asked, steering the conversation. "What were your specialties before everything went to hell?"

"Getting as many women into his bed as he could," Onyx quipped, a smirk playing on his lips.

Rayne shrugged, unfazed. "Not my fault the ladies adored me. But, to answer your question, I balanced my skills—I was proficient in long-range attacks and close-quarter combat."

"Thanks to me," Onyx interjected.

"Yes, thanks to Onyx's training, I became well-rounded," Rayne acknowledged with a wink. He then gestured to the arrow in the tree. "I see you're a great shot with a bow."

I nodded. "I've been shooting since I was seven."

"Impressive. How are you with other weapons?" Rayne asked, genuinely curious.

"I'd say equally skilled," I replied confidently.

Onyx smiled, nodding in approval. "The confidence speaks again."

Rayne slid his hands back into his pockets. "How about we strike a deal? Being the best with hand-to-hand combat, Onyx can ensure that you are efficiently equipped in that capacity. And I'll take on the privilege of weapons training."

"Don't you have a community to get back to?" Onyx teased.

"You can swing by and pick me up when the time comes, or I can have Riggs bring me over," Rayne grinned. "Don't worry, I'm not here to be competitive."

I swallowed my building nerves while Onyx remained composed. His demeanor was unflinching, his face revealing no sign of the inner dialogue that plagued me.

"If you want to train her with weapons, go ahead," Onyx shrugged, his furrowed brows and straightened lips giving away the freighted indifference.

I looked at Rayne and nodded. "I'd be honored to learn from you if you're willing to teach me."

"Then it's settled," Rayne said, smiling genuinely for the first time.

I returned it before turning toward Onyx, who was already looking at me.

His intense eyes held a piercing quality that seemed to see through me. In the mid-afternoon sun, they appeared even more vibrant. The familiar scar that cut across his face caught the light, adding a rugged charm to his otherwise detached expression. He held my gaze with a comforting and disarming softness, a momentary connection that felt like an eternity. It was as if the world paused around us, leaving only the silent understanding between our locked eyes. Then, with a slight nod, he turned back to Rayne, the moment dissipating as quickly as it had formed.

"When do you head out?" Onyx asked.

"As soon as—" Rayne began, but Everett's voice interrupted.

"You ready?" Everett asked, approaching with the others.

"I guess that answers it," Onyx remarked, a hint of something unspoken in his tone, perhaps a touch of worry that this goodbye might be their last.

Rayne seemed to sense it, offering a reassuring smile and a subtle shake of his head. Onyx clenched his jaw and nodded in return, a gesture of gratitude and understanding.

Rayne turned to the others, a whine leaving him. "That time already, huh?"

"You're worse than a five-year-old at a birthday party," Raven teased, rolling her eyes with a smirk.

Riggs chimed in, "The discussions are over for today, but we'll be back. We need to complete our plans and ensure everyone is ready for what's ahead."

Riggs' formal tone resembled Jasper's, which made me realize why he was such a testament to Rayne's trust in his team—he was a near-replica of the man he'd put his faith in for years in the ranks.

Rayne turned to us. 'This isn't the last you'll see of us."

"How lovely," Onyx replied, raising his eyebrows. "Can't wait to see your ugly mug again."

"Likewise," Rayne grinned before addressing his team. "Alright, let's head back so I can continue to play leader."

Jasper's voice called out from behind them, "Do us all a favor, and don't burn down the Capital Rebellion."

Rayne's smile widened at the playful request.

Raven groaned, rubbing her temple. "Don't worry, we'll keep him in check."

Everett chuckled, "Because without us—"

"I don't know where I'd be." Rayne finished his sentence as Riggs placed a reassuring hand on his shoulder. The momentary softness that swept over Rayne's face was palpable, a seemingly rare vulnerability that underscored the depth of their bond. He held my gaze briefly, offering a nod. "I'll see you around, Astrid."

With that, the five vanished as swiftly as they had appeared, slipping out through the community walls like shadows. Their sudden absence left a quiet emptiness in their wake. Onyx exhaled deeply, his shoulders relaxing slightly. The shift in his posture exposed the concern he tried to mask, a lingering worry that seemed to persist despite Rayne's reassurances.

Onyx's gaze lingered on the arrow lodged in the tree before he turned back to me. "You heard him. He'll cover weapons, and I'll cover hand-to-hand. Let's get started."

I glanced down at the bow, and, in an instant, a cold blade pressed against my throat. My breath hitched as I looked up, finding Onyx standing before me, a sneer playing on his lips. His hand gripped the hilt of the knife firmly, the steel resting lightly against my skin.

"Rule number one," he breathed, his voice low and controlled. "There is never time for distraction."

TWENTY-EIGHT

Onyx reached for me for what I counted as the twentieth time. His calloused hand wrapped around mine, pulling me up from the ground to stand beside him.

After the last takedown, I had stripped off my jacket, leaving me in a black tank top smeared with dirt from our makeshift sparring ring in the open field. Sweat dripped down my forehead, starkly contrasting Onyx's composed demeanor. Despite the exertion, he remained unphased, his rolled-up henley clinging to his muscular frame without a hint of sweat.

"You're ruthless," I huffed, wiping sweat from my brow with the back of my hand.

"You know what you're doing and how to fight. Your weakness is in your form. Until you correct it, I will continue to kick your ass," he replied, shrugging nonchalantly. "You're bound to learn your lesson at some point."

I groaned, moving a few feet away from him before I turned and slid my right foot behind me. Finding the balance between the balls of my stance, I stacked the weight evenly between my feet before raising my hands in front of my face.

"Please elaborate on what exactly I am doing wrong." I

pressed, narrowing my gaze at him through the gap between my fists.

He chuckled softly, "Honestly, that's the best your stance has looked all day."

"Okay, asshole," I replied, rolling my eyes as he walked toward me.

Placing himself beside me, his eyes swept my body from head to toe. I exhaled, clenching my hands into fists and savoring the feeling of my bare feet pressing into the cold earth beneath us.

Onyx had insisted I train without shoes to better connect with the ground and understand the edges of my center of gravity. Complying with his instructions, I had tossed my boots and socks aside at the beginning of our session, which now felt like hours ago.

"Your feet are the roots that keep your body in place. Once you have a solid and well-balanced stance," he said, nudging my left foot forward with his boot. "It will be far harder to knock you over."

I inhaled deeply, adjusting to the sudden shift.

"You want to rotate your leg just enough so that your toes and knee both point toward your opponent." He moved around to face me, waiting for me to adjust.

I shifted slightly before looking up at him and lifting a snarky brow. "Good?"

"Lovely," he smirked, circling me again. "The gap in your stance looks good, roughly shoulder-width apart."

"So, I am doing something right."

"I never said you were doing *everything* wrong," he replied, a playful grin evident in his voice. "Now, rotate your dominant leg so that your toes and knee point away from your opponent. Angle them slightly from the direction of your front foot to aid in your stability."

I moved my right toes and knee outward, feeling an immediate improvement.

"Beautiful," he murmured before continuing, his questioning coming off as a surprise. "May I touch you?"

I worked to keep my tone level even though everything inside me screamed. "Yeah, that's fine."

He stepped closer, his hands finding my hips. The warmth of his touch seeped through the thin material of my tank top. "Moving along, the torso is next."

His fingers pressed into my hip bones as he adjusted my stance. The movement brought the small of my back into brief contact with his body, a touch that was as much about correction as it was about connection. It was a taste of intimacy in an unmistakable moment overshadowed by the formalities of training.

"You could've just told me to bend slightly," I quipped, trying to mask the flurry of thoughts and sensations his proximity stirred.

"Where's the fun in that?" he retorted sarcastically. "Hands-on is more my style, anyway."

I threw an elbow back at him, but he caught it easily, his grip firm yet gentle. His breath brushed the back of my neck as he whispered, "You almost had me," before he guided my arm back into position and stepped around me.

"I feel like a lab rat," I muttered, peering back up at him between my hands.

"That's how you should've felt during your first training," he suggested candidly. "The fact you didn't speaks volumes about the quality of your training and why your form is so...*poor*." He raised a brow, the corner of his mouth lifting slightly.

"You wanted to say pathetic," I challenged.

"Are you the mind reader now?" He folded his arms over his chest, continuing with instructions before I could respond to his jeer. "A slight bend in the hips and curling your shoulders inward gives your opponent a smaller target to attack. Combining the two allows your fists to sit along your cheekbones while your elbows guard your ribs. Though this won't save you in every fight, a solid foundation is crucial, but you have to be able to protect yourself and anticipate attacks for it to matter."

Before I could respond to his advice, Onyx moved with startling speed, positioning himself directly in front of me. His palm struck my abdomen with a controlled but forceful blow. Instinctively, I flexed to brace for the impact, but it wasn't enough to absorb the full force. Gasping as the air rushed from my lungs, I cursed heavily. Yet, to my surprise, my stance held firm.

I lifted my head to glare at him, and he returned my look with a smirk. "Look at that, stability. But next time, keep your core engaged and your back straight. It will help negate the impact of blows, and considering that was only about twenty percent of my strength, I think you'd prefer to spare your internal organs next time."

"Prick," I spat as he circled me again, ignoring my insult.

His fingers traced down my shoulders and triceps before gently positioning my elbows. "As I mentioned, your elbows are pertinent. Your arms are your first line of defense and protection."

I groaned. "Oh, so I had this wrong, too?"

"No," he corrected, pushing my elbows in slightly. "You were just a bit too open. I want you to tuck them tighter against your body to where mere inches separate your elbows from your waistline. The tighter you are here," his fingers grazed over my hips and to my stomach, "the more you'll discourage your opponent from targeting you as I did. Trust me when I tell you that side shots are far from enjoyable and can do far more than knock the wind out of you."

I was in awe of the depth of Onyx's knowledge of self-defense and the intricacies of body positioning for shielding and protection. What Rayne had said about him wasn't an exaggeration in the slightest. Onyx's experience and expertise spoke for themselves; he delivered each movement and instruction with the confidence of someone who had mastered these techniques and tested them in real-world scenarios. His understanding of the human body and how to use it offensively and defensively was far beyond the basics I had learned during my training as a Venturer. Though I held knowledge that dove further than I'd ever let on, things that came before the Fall.

As an experienced Venturer, I prided myself on my proficiency in combat and survival skills, but the training we received focused more heavily on ranged weapon attacks to prepare us for run-ins with Runners or the Rebellion. The instructors taught us to consider hand-to-hand combat as a last resort and to use it solely when all other options proved forfeit. Because of this, understanding of close quarters remained heavily superficial.

During my training sessions with Onyx, it became glaringly obvious how much I had overlooked the importance of foundational self-defense techniques. Onyx's approach was meticulous; he drilled the significance of stance, balance, and core engagement. His teachings went beyond simple punches and kicks; they were about understanding leverage, reading an opponent's movements, and maintaining composure under pressure. It became apparent how many mistakes I could have made in the past because of the gaps in our training that could have led to disastrous outcomes. One poorly executed stance, a singly misjudged block, or even a momentary lack of focus could have been the difference between survival and death.

Onyx stepped back, a few strands of his raven-black hair caught in the wind. He nodded in approval as he looked me over for the millionth time after making all deemed adjustments.

"Satisfied?" I challenged, meeting his gaze.

"We're getting there." he conceded, stepping forward again.

He reached between my hands, his thumb brushing against my chin while his fingers gently cupped my jaw. The contact was unexpected, causing my breath to hitch and a surge to rock my frame. In that moment, everything else faded away. The world seemed to narrow, concentrating on the subtle guidance of his touch as he adjusted my head position, guiding my chin down towards my collarbones. His eyes, catching the glint of the afternoon sun, held an implicit depth. There was something unvoiced in his gaze, a thought or feeling hovering just beyond expression.

"Defense placement for your head is vital," he explained, his voice steady though his stare contained something far beyond the surface of what he offered. "There are many delicate bones around your eyes and nose. Being hit in the face isn't pleasant and can put you on the ground before you can even contemplate you were standing."

My mind flashed back to the day I had punched him, the memory of his flesh against my knuckles feeling distant yet vivid and a reminder of the opposite positions we held in the world. His hand left my face, drawing me back to the present.

"Not only do we want to avoid going to the ground and fighting from there, but a blow to the temple will knock you unconscious. Keep yourself guarded at all times, no matter how tired you may be," he finished, his tone carrying a weight of caution.

I nodded, making the final alterations to my stance and gazing at him beneath my eyelashes. "Is that better?"

"In my eyes and by my standards?" He looked me over once more. "Yes, you look far more prepared to face an opponent."

"So, does that mean—" I started, but Onyx had already slipped into his stance, raising a brow in challenge.

"That we test what you've learned?" he asked, a chuckle escaping his lips as he nodded.

A slight wave of nervousness washed over me as I prepared for the next phase of my training. Memories of the last handful of spars flashed through my mind—moments when his unpredictability and skill had left me on the ground, breathless and defeated. He had no clear preference for any specific combat style, seamlessly transitioning between stances and techniques. When you assumed you'd figured out his southpaw methodology, he'd seamlessly flip to orthodox to keep the fight going and ensure you remained on your toes, making it impossible to decipher which side his dominance stemmed from.

Onyx abruptly interrupted my dissection of his movements by slamming his leg into my right arm. The rudeness of the impact jarred me, barely granting me enough time to react and drop my elbow to absorb the blow. I staggered, my balance wavering as I battled to regain my footing.

"Get out of your head, Astrid!" he taunted, a devious grin spreading across his face as he recoiled his leg.

Inhaling between clenched teeth, I cussed under my breath. Resetting my stance quickly, I pulled myself into the position he drilled into my mind. "Choosing to attack me when I wasn't paying attention seems to be a bit of a low blow, even for you."

Onyx circled me, and I mirrored his movement, shifting on the balls of my feet. "Didn't I say something about there not being time for distraction?"

I was about to retort when I saw his front leg lift, signaling an imminent kick from his back leg. I braced myself, tightened my core, and watched his footwork intently. Analyzing his movements had paid off; I was beginning to predict his patterns.

Just as fast as I thought I figured him out, an open hand connected with the right side of my head. The unexpectedness of the slap sent a jolt of agony through my skull, accompanied by a high-pitched ringing. Its sting was momentarily disorienting, but the mere shock blinded me far more. Shaking my head, I attempted to clear the fog it created and refocus, but the ringing remained—a harsh reminder of how quickly someone could lose the upper hand in a fight.

"You let your guard down because you focused too intently on your core," Onyx chastised. "You're lucky that wasn't a punch, or it would've ended our session."

I snarled, shaking off the lingering pain. "I'm thinking you enjoy this more than you should."

He laughed, a rich sound that warmed the chilly autumn air. "While you're not wrong, there are things I would enjoy far more."

My cheeks flushed, the implication behind his words unmistakable. His smile widened, and the playful glint in his eyes only deepened my embarrassment.

"Something on your—" he began, but I didn't let him finish. I spun on my left leg, raising my right foot to aim a kick at his chest with all the force I could muster.

As I launched a kick towards him, my heel connected with his body. Onyx's elbow swept forward just in time, deflecting the attack with a practiced ease. The contact was minimal, my foot barely grazing him before his counteraction. A devious grin spread across his face, a silent acknowledgment of the narrow escape. His expression was infuriating and exhilarating, a challenge that spurred me to push harder.

"Beat his ass, Astrid!" Jasper's voice rang out, and my eyes flickered to him.

The brief distraction was the opening Onyx needed. He charged forward, closing the distance between us with alarming speed. But as I had learned from him—*there was never time for distraction*. I baited him with my apparent vulnerability, and now, with an audience watching, I had things to prove even as I continued to bear the mask of vulnerability.

As Onyx closed in, I pivoted on my heel, lowering my body and moving fluidly through the grass. The cool, damp blades brushed against my skin as I spun under his left arm, aiming a punch at the vulnerable spot between his third and fourth ribs. My movements were swift and calculated, the culmination of his teachings and my own instincts.

I had him—a clean shot.

But Onyx anticipated my move. His left elbow dropped just in time, trapping my arm against his side. In one fluid motion, he yanked me towards him, forcing me to stand upright. His left arm looped around my elbow, drawing me in until my chest pressed against his.

The sudden closeness was electrifying. His body's warmth and the scent of his skin enveloped me—a husky mix of eucalyptus and sandalwood.

"That was a close one," he murmured, his voice rough yet carrying an undercurrent of softness.

I swallowed, steadying my breath. "I figured you'd take the bait, considering you've harped on me about paying attention."

I waited for him to release my elbow and step away, but he didn't. Instead, he kept me close, his forehead resting against mine.

"You leveraged your presumed weaknesses to your advantage." His finger traced lightly along the backside of my arm as he continued, his voice low. "You realize you're as equally quick on your feet as you are with your mind, don't you?"

I shrugged indifferently. "I figured it'd be a decently easy way to lure you in."

His hand moved abruptly, shifting from my elbow to the back of my neck as he pulled me closer. The swift transition brought us to a far more intimate proximity, leaving little room for anything other than heightened attention to his presence. My heart pounded as his body pressed against mine, his warmth intoxicating. The thin barrier our clothing provided felt nearly intrusive as if it were the only thing that prevented us from fully connecting.

His breath brushed against my ear. "If your goal has been luring me in, then you'd be pleased to know you've baited me for a while now."

I swallowed the whimper that threatened to fall from my throat, my place in the grandness of everything far too over-whelming. The burn that singed my cheeks rivaled with the intensity of his gaze. Struggling to maintain my composure, I grasped for the reins of some semblance of control. Yet the words I wished to utter eluded me, caught in a complex tangle of emotions that threatened to rise.

The gesture felt insignificant, but I nodded anyway. The movement was slight, barely perceptible, yet it resonated with a silent admission. His grip on the back of my neck tightened just enough to affirm the connection, and his fingers warmed against my skin.

"You know, I thought you'd have figured me out by now," he whispered, the breathiness of his words almost coaxing the whimper from me.

I fought to keep myself contained, my voice barely a whisper. "Says the one who acts indifferent. You've always seemed more interested in everything else."

He chuckled, the sound low and intimate, making my toes curl into the moist ground. "You really have learned nothing from being around me, have you?"

I bit my bottom lip, hidden from his view, feeling the weight of his question. "You like to play hard to get. Is that what you're getting at?"

"Perhaps," he replied teasingly. "Or maybe, unlike other men you've dealt with, I have a little respect. Would it surprise you that I've been dropping hints, waiting for you to pick up on them?"

A glimmer of hope sparked within me. If I pushed just enough, maybe I could tip the scale. "So you're admitting you don't make the first move?"

Another deep, husky laugh escaped him. "Is that what you think, Astrid? That I'm afraid to go after what I *want?*"

I clenched my jaw, shoving down the memories of someone else that threatened to emerge. "I mean, you're the one who said you drop hints. Why not just act instead of beating around the bush?"

His response was immediate, his voice dropping an octave. "Do you want me to do something about it? Is that what you're implying?"

The words hung in the air, thick with tension. Part of me wanted to beg him to bridge the gap between us that had existed for so long. The allure of his presence was undeniable, a magnetic force pulling me closer that anyone else wouldn't have questioned. I inhaled, fixating on the flicker of something else deep within me—a calculated decision and a need to keep him within reach.

In an instant, before I could let another thought cross my

mind or another word escape my lips, Onyx shifted. I looked up at him, and he leaned forward before I could analyze his expression.

My heartbeat intensified, and the tightness in my core became a desperate ache. The anticipation building between us reached a crescendo as his lips finally met mine. They were softer than I had imagined, far more delicate than any man's lips I'd kissed before, as if crafted perfectly to match mine. The way he tilted his head felt like we were two pieces of a puzzle fitting together, a position that felt natural and right. As our lips collided, his grip on the back of my neck loosened, his fingers gently sliding up to rest at the base of my skull. Simultaneously, his other hand traveled up my leg, settling gently on my hip bone, tethering me to him.

We broke apart briefly, gasping for air before coming together again more intensely. The kiss was like a wave crashing against a rocky shoreline, powerful and unyielding yet caressing the complexities of the moment with tender admiration. I lifted my arms, placing my hands on either side of his face. His jawline fit perfectly in my palms, and I pulled him closer, feeling the warmth of his skin under my fingers. His grip on my hip tightened, drawing me even nearer. Slightly tilting my head to the side, I deepened the kiss, my breathing intensifying as our bodies pressed against one another.

Desire surged through me as I inhaled his scent—an intoxicating aroma of sandalwood and musk mixed with something darker and more elusive. I noticed each inch that our bodies conjoined by the undeniable evidence of his arousal pressing against me and the surge roaring through the back of my skull. As our lips met for a third and final time, I poured everything I had into the kiss, savoring every second. His hand explored my body as his soft lips trailed mine, etching a connection into my mind. Each touch and each breath were moments I wished to remember, even if only temporarily.

I pulled away reluctantly, needing to collect my thoughts. Inhaling, my eyes slowly fluttered open to meet his gaze. He peered down at me, his eyes clouded with intoxication. His tongue trailed across his lips as I admired the sight of him—disheveled and panting.

His voice was rough. "So, was that *move* up to your level of satisfaction?"

The kiss had surpassed my expectations, leaving me craving more than just his physical closeness.

"Yes," I answered simply, the word barely escaping my lips. The corners of his mouth lifted in response, a knowing smile spreading across his face.

Onyx leaned in slightly, releasing me from his grasp. "If you had dirty thoughts about me or things you wanted to execute, you could've just asked, *Sweetness.*"

The returned endearment hit me like a sledgehammer, forcing my knees to nearly buckle. I swallowed hard, trying to quell the rising heat. His words only heightened the tumult of thoughts racing through my mind. From his smile, he knew his effect on me.

Taking a deep breath, I stepped aside, my eyes landing on Jasper. He stood where he had been, arms folded across his chest, a wide grin plastered on his face.

"Go ahead," Onyx said, gesturing toward Jasper, already having mapped out his reaction.

"It's about *damn* time," Jasper laughed, glancing between the two of us as something else glinted in his stormy gaze. "I thought the tension between you two was going to be the death of us all."

I let out a soft laugh, finally allowing myself to release the tension that had been building. The impact Onyx had on me was undeniable; the chemistry between us was something that had been undeniable, but there was something I didn't want either of them to know about the depth of its impact. Although I suspected Onyx had already figured as much.

Onyx raised a brow teasingly. "Just think about the tension we will release once we sleep together."

My cheeks burned with a blaring red, a heat that spread rapidly across my cheeks and neck. Jasper's laughter broke through the gaze, drawing my attention. He grinned from ear to ear as he looked at Onyx with an expression of newfound happiness, as if he had waited for this moment for years.

I gathered myself, managing a playful retort that concluded our evening of training as we returned to the community's innards. "He wishes."

TWENTY-NINE

A faintly sweet aroma lingered in the dining hall's air, mixing with the soft sounds of utensils clattering and shuffling from the adjacent kitchen. These noises were a comforting reminder of the busy activity within as community members diligently prepared meals for everyone.

Once a bustling café, the space retained a cozy charm despite the passing years. Crammed tables in the room hinted at a former life—a place once alive with conversation and daily work commutes. Once Jasper took over the area, he worked to restore the tables and revamp the interior, transforming it into a communal space where his people could gather, share meals, and attempt to find a level of normalcy and connection in our fractured world.

As Jasper led the way, he acknowledged the seated groups with a nod, a gesture of respect and camaraderie. The community members returned the gesture with warm smiles, and I followed Jasper's lead, offering one of my own as we passed. This exchange of silent greetings felt natural, a ritual that reinforced the bonds of their shared experience and dedication to life. The atmosphere was undeniably warm, infused with a deep sense of community and shared history. It was as if the walls themselves held the stories of those who had found refuge here, each meal a small testament to their resilience and unity.

"When did he leave?" I asked, pulling out a wooden chair from underneath Jasper's chosen table.

"I'd say probably twenty minutes ago," he replied, sitting across from me. "They should be back soon."

When I woke up that morning, the space Onyx and I shared was empty, and his abrupt absence immediately stirred concern. When I found Jasper, he informed me that Onyx had gone to retrieve Rayne for my training session, as we'd agreed upon. I shared my frustration about the lack of communication, and Jasper met me with a playful joke, stating that I should've been able to detect Onyx's presence, considering how bonded we'd become. Before I could react, a slender brunette approached our table.

"Good morning," she greeted us softly, glancing between Jasper and me.

"Good morning, Lila," Jasper responded with a smile. "If I could get a black coffee to start, that would be great. We're waiting for a couple of others."

She nodded and turned to me, her bright purple eyes catching me off guard. "And for you, hon?"

"Water is fine," I replied, returning her faint smile as she moved away.

Jasper leaned back, a mischievous look in his eyes. "It seems you two can't get enough of each other, huh?"

I narrowed my gaze at him, feigning annoyance. "I thought we already had this conversation?"

He chuckled, running a hand down his beard. "We did. But I thought you'd be interested in knowing that Onyx couldn't stop talking about it."

As Jasper's words sank in, apprehension spread through my stomach. I tried to maintain a neutral expression, carefully concealing the surge of emotions beneath the surface. "Oh, really?"

Jasper was about to elaborate when I felt a pair of hands on my shoulders.

"Good morning, Great Falls community," Rayne announced from behind me, the closeness of his voice suggesting it was his touch.

"It's good to see you again, Rayne," Jasper greeted him as Rayne's hands left my shoulders and he stepped around the table.

Rayne wore a tight-fitting, deep blue, long-sleeve shirt that made his eyes stand out with an almost electric intensity. His gaze darted between us, filled with a spark of energy that seemed to enliven the surrounding space. His necklaces caught the morning light, adding a glint of silver to his ensemble. It was a familiar sight, yet something about how he carried himself made his familiar presence unique.

Onyx groaned slightly as he joined us, running a hand through his hair. "I apologize for how long it took to get back. Rayne insisted on showing me around."

His face's mix of irritability and grogginess pointed to an unplanned early morning pickup—clearly, he was not happy about the timing. Knowing he was far from a morning person, I couldn't help but find myself stifling a laugh at the thought of him having to manage Rayne's liveliness.

"Why didn't you have Riggs bring you?" I asked, watching Onyx slide the chair out beside me.

"What's the fun in that when I can drag the sleeping giant out of bed?" Rayne quipped, lowering himself beside Jasper. Onyx shot him a glare. "I'm kidding, you grouch," Rayne added with a playful grin.

I glanced at Onyx, amused. "We all know who isn't a morning person."

Onyx's hair hung loose and cascaded in raven waves, falling loosely to his collarbones—adding a rough charm to his appearance. The sunlight streaming through the windows highlighted the near-white hues in his eyes, adding to their mesmerizing depth. They seemed to darken as they met mine, a silent communication of our connection that spoke volumes without a word. His dark gray shirt clung to his frame, accentuating his muscular build and well-defined arms. Once he sat down, he positioned his chin on his intertwined fingers, his gaze shifting to the others.

"It's not that I'm not a morning person," he clarified. "I just don't enjoy *speaking* to people early in the morning, and he disregarded that trait the moment I arrived."

"You don't enjoy speaking to anyone regardless of the time of day," Rayne pestered, raising an eyebrow.

Onyx waved off the comment.

"Plus, you're famous. Didn't you know that?" Jasper winked, prompting a groan from Onyx.

"I'm sick of being famous. Can't someone else take the reins?" Onyx sighed, clearly peeved.

Rayne laughed, shaking his head. "Sorry, but I reject your request. That's the last thing I want."

"You and me both," Onyx agreed, leaning back in his chair. "But unlike you, I didn't have a choice in the matter."

Jasper's gray eyes flicked past us as Lila returned with our drinks. She set my water in front of me before handing Jasper his coffee.

"Good morning, gentleman," Lila greeted our new guests before asking, "What can I get the two of you to drink?"

"I'm good with water," Rayne replied, nodding toward me.

"Coffee with cream, please," Onyx said, rubbing his eyes before pointing at Jasper. "Unlike him, I'm not a sociopath."

I nearly choked on my water, stifling a laugh at Onyx's dry humor.

Jasper laughed, taking a long sip from his mug. "While that may not be entirely truthful, I can't deny some of my mannerisms."

Lila smiled at their banter, nodding before heading back to the kitchen. "I'll be right back with those drinks and the breakfast we are serving this morning."

She pivoted, walking away, and Rayne's eyes locked onto her

the instant she turned her back. Onyx groaned beside me as he noticed Rayne's intense gaze. "Oh my hell, Rayne, you dog."

Rayne dragged his stare away from her disappearing figure and met Onyx's amused look. "I am no such thing," he defended, a faint smirk playing on his lips. "I am simply admiring."

"What he meant to say is it's been a while since he's gotten anything," Jasper cackled, earning a playful elbow to the ribs from Rayne.

"Bed feeling rather cold lately, Rayne?" Onyx joked as he folded his arms over his chest.

The sunlight played with the shadows in the space, somehow casting a golden hue over him. Its rays highlighted the sharp lines of his jaw and his jagged scar, which told stories of the battles he fought and survived. This flaw only added to his allure, an imperfection that made him uniquely him.

Rayne glanced at us, a sneer spreading across his face. He exhaled sharply as Lila's footsteps approached. "You're lucky, Oakes. I was about to humiliate you in front of the entire dining hall."

Onyx's gravelly chuckle made me smile. "I'd love to see you try, Cromwell."

Before Rayne could offer the last retort, Lila approached, providing a timely distraction as his attention shifted instantly. Her movement was almost ethereal, and her grace seemed to captivate everyone at the table, including me. She had a way of commanding attention without even trying, and Rayne was clearly not immune.

She set the water down first, an almost premeditated gesture as if she knew she had Rayne's full attention. Then she moved around the table, placing Onyx's coffee and homemade creamer beside him. He gave her a brief nod before pouring the creamer into his mug, turning the coffee a light brown before he took a sip.

Lila's petite frame disappeared for only a few moments before she returned with our plates, balanced expertly on her arms. She lowered the first one in front of me with a smile. "This morning, we have waffles, eggs, and fresh ham from the recent hunt."

The scents of the various foods intermingled and became nearly intoxicating as my gaze bounced across my plate. The sight alone could have piqued my appetite. Butter and syrup generously coated the golden-brown waffles. The yellow hue of the eggs hinted the cooks whipped them to perfection. A freshly sliced piece of ham provided a savory contrast to the sweetness of the waffles.

It was perfect.

"Thank you," we all chimed in unison.

"I hope you enjoy," she smiled, bowing slightly before returning to the kitchen.

I cut into the waffles, my fork gliding effortlessly through their layers. Once I took the first bite, my eyes closed in enjoyment as a groan of satisfaction slipped from my throat. The food within the community continued to starkly contrast the rations I had grown accustomed to within the Walls—bland, utilitarian food meant only to sustain. This meal was a reminder of the simple pleasures that existed beyond the confines, another moment of indulgence that felt almost surreal in its normalcy.

"Holy hell," Rayne exclaimed delightfully after finishing his first bite. "This is incredible."

"I think I can now officially say welcome to Great Falls." Jasper winked as he brought his fork to his mouth, savoring the food with a satisfied smile.

"Finger on the outside of the trigger guard, straight and flat." Rayne watched me closely as I adjusted my grip from where I usually placed it when handling my pistol. "Perfect. Now fire."

Squeezing the trigger, the sharp crack of gunfire echoed through the rustle of leaves and the faint whisper of wind the crisp afternoon air provided. Rayne and I stood before the tree that Onyx had marked for target practice a few days ago. Despite the recent rainstorms, the painted targets remained visible, their bold circles standing out against the bark. Under the weight of our boots, the damp earth was soft and spongy after the storm that graced us during the night. Overhead, thick storm clouds blocked the sun's presence, urging a light gray light to dance across the field.

Lowering the gun, I pointed it at the ground before flipping the safety on and holstering it back to my thigh.

Rayne had been adamant about ensuring I understood the safety protocols before firing a shot. He reiterated that his insistence wasn't a question of my capability with a firearm but a reinforcement of disciplined habits that could save lives.

"Right through the middle." Rayne whistled from his position a few feet from the tree. "A perfect shot."

I nodded, folding my arms. "It's as if you thought I couldn't blast a hole through someone if I needed to."

"No," he shook his head as he walked back toward me. "I reassured you that was far from the case. Many people can handle a weapon, but there's a difference between baseline knowledge and being able to do so efficiently and accurately."

I smiled as he approached. "I know. I was giving you shit."

"You're a hell of a shot, Carnell."

"Did you think I was lying?" The question came from behind us, and we both turned to spot Onyx, a jacket hugging his expansive frame.

Rayne rolled his eyes, looking at his friend. "You just couldn't resist staying away, could you? We're gone for about an hour, and you're out here pouting like a lost puppy."

Onyx shrugged, glancing between us before gesturing toward the tree. He ignored Rayne's playful tone, focusing instead on the target. "Let me guess, she nailed the bullseye?"

Rayne nodded, taking the hint and looking back at the tree. "Right through the middle."

Onyx turned to me, tipping his head slightly as a soft, quick smile crossed his lips.

"Is everything okay?" I asked, trying to frame the question with concern and not unnecessary prodding that I knew he'd only deflect.

He shrugged. "I'm just out getting some air. I figured I'd see what the two of you were up to."

"As if there is some expectation beyond training?" Rayne chuckled, glancing at his friend with a playfulness that I knew hinted at his flirtatious nature.

"No," Onyx responded quickly and curtly. "I said nothing like that. I took a walk and figured I'd come and see how things were going."

Something was off.

Onyx's demeanor was noticeably distant, and his body language betrayed a discomfort he didn't voice. He buried his hands deep in his pockets, his shoulders slightly hunched as if shielding himself from an invisible cold. His lips pressed into a tight line, and a subtle tension pulled at the corners, suppressing what might have been a smile. It was a noticeable, unseen shift since Rayne's arrival.

Rayne nodded, acknowledging the change. "Fair enough."

I glanced at Onyx again, catching his gaze only briefly before he looked away. I clenched my jaw, feeling the cold deflection reminiscent of the continually hostile days between us. It was as if we had reverted to being enemies, a barrier suddenly erected between us.

"If you were looking for a training update," Rayne broke the silence, "she proved herself beyond proficient with her bow, and then we moved to handguns. Based on her last shot, I'd also mark her off on that."

Onyx nodded, his eyes scanning me momentarily before turning back to Rayne. "Is that all you're covering for today?"

Rayne nodded. "Yeah. We'll move into snipers tomorrow, followed by more close-range weapons."

"Wait," I interjected, turning to Rayne. "I thought Onyx was instructing close-quarter combat?"

"He is. But per our agreement, he's sticking to hand-to-hand combat and leaving weapons to me. Trust me, you'll want to go into a close combat spar with him well-versed in handling." Rayne chuckled cheerfully despite the enmity in the air.

I glanced at Onyx, who once again displayed a gesture of indifference, the lack of amusement lacing every edge of his features. His nonchalance was frustrating, leaving me to wonder what was happening in his mind.

"Fair enough," I replied to Rayne, trying to brush off Onyx's aloofness.

Rayne gave me a knowing look, silently acknowledging the odd shift in Onyx's behavior.

He clicked his tongue, "I believe Jasper wanted to run a few things by me before I got comfortable for the evening."

"Are you staying the night?" The question slipped out, laced with surprise.

"Yeah. I figured I'd stick around for a few days to help with your training." Before expressing my concern, he added, "Don't worry; the others are handling things back at the Capital for me."

I exhaled, exchanging a glance of thanks with him before he shifted.

"So, we're calling it for today, then?"

He nodded. "We'll pick up here tomorrow after breakfast. I need to figure out what our lovely, needy analytic wants with me."

I clenched my jaw, detecting the white lie in Rayne's casual explanation. His sudden departure felt contrived, a convenient excuse to leave Onyx and me alone. There was an understanding buried in Rayne's gesture, a knowing look in his eyes as he patted Onyx on the shoulder. As Rayne headed back towards the community center, his footsteps fading into the distance, the space between Onyx and me seemed to stretch, filled with unspoken words and unexpressed emotions.

As soon as Rayne's frame disappeared behind a building, I turned to Onyx. "Now that he's gone, will you tell me what's on your mind?"

Onyx licked his lips and finally looked down at me, a shadow passing over his eyes. "Did you mean what you said?"

I raised an eyebrow, taken aback. "What are you referring to?"

"After we kissed, did you mean what you said?" His voice was low, laced with an uncharacteristic vulnerability.

I frowned, trying to recall the exact words. "I'm going to need more specifics."

"That you're not as interested as I am?"

Confusion flashed across my face. "Where did you get that idea?"

He merely shrugged, avoiding my gaze as he dug his hands deeper into his pockets.

"Onyx." I stepped closer, refusing to allow him to retreat. "I never said that. What is bothering you?"

He exhaled heavily, keeping his eyes fixated on the horizon. "I guess I overanalyzed it, so don't worry about it. It was stupid anyway."

"No," I insisted, closing the gap between us. "I will not pretend something isn't bothering you or simply ignore it. You can talk to me."

Another shrug.

Frustration flared up inside me.

Before he could react, I pressed my lips to his, the contact soft yet charged with electricity. The kiss was a silent but powerful connection, a wordless communication that spoke volumes to our intertwined souls. It mirrored our first kiss, filled with an unspoken longing that neither of us could deny.

As I drew him closer, Onyx's body seemed to melt into mine, the tension in his shoulders easing. Turning to me fully, his fingers gently cradled my face. I deepened the kiss, the steady drum of his heartbeat beneath my hand a reminder of our effect on one another. Onyx's grip on my jaw tightened, guiding my head to the side and deepening the kiss further. He inhaled deeply, a low, primal groan escaping his lips as I pressed against him, our noses brushing in the intimate exchange.

My lips slowly pulled away from his, lingering for a moment. His eyes were dark with a hunger that mirrored my own.

"You can do that anytime you want."

I smiled, raising my eyebrows. "That would be too often."

He bit the inside of his cheek, his eyes never leaving mine. "And you think that would bother me?"

I averted my gaze as I shrugged. Before I could fully back away, his hand met my chin, lifting it and forcing me to meet his gaze.

"I believe I asked you a question, Sweetness." The rasp in his voice hinted at the desire clear in his tone.

"I don't know." I locked eyes with him. "Like I said, you have played hard to get since the beginning and have made it seem like you're nothing more than disinterested."

He shook his head, chuckling. "That is by far the furthest thing from the truth."

"Which part?" I asked, tipping my chin with the query. "That you play hard to get?"

"That I am disinterested," he clarified as his voice softened. "I've been more than intrigued by you since our first encounter, Astrid."

I brushed off the latter part of his statement, knowing there was a far deeper explanation to the pull between us, and playfully smirked. "So, you're admitting that you play hard to get?"

He rolled his eyes, nuzzling my face away. "I never said I don't. Did I?"

We both laughed, the tension easing between us.

Onyx ran a hand through his hair, and I couldn't help but feel a pang of longing and desire. Yet, another part of me feared commitment when faced with the guilt of all I knew and the secrets I kept.

"At least you're prideful enough to admit it," I teased, trying to lighten the mood.

He traced his tongue over his lips, a contemplative look on his face. "I guess it's something like that."

"I'm curious," I started, shifting the course of the conversation. "What was the first thought that ran through your mind when we ran into each other on the rooftops in Region Three?"

He smirked, a mischievous glint in his eyes. "That you would be easy to kill."

I punched him playfully in the chest, eliciting a genuine laugh. It was a sound I hadn't heard in a long time.

"I'm joking," he reassured me, his voice softening. "I thought you were beautiful, and I admired how you threw yourself in front of someone you cared for."

I winced at the memory of Radley, shaking my head. "I should've let you blow his brains all over the rooftop. If I had none of this—"

"You couldn't have known that," he interrupted gently, though my body quivered with his coax. "As much as we both harbor guilt about what happened, you couldn't have prevented it. Hold on to that."

I looked down, taking a deep breath. The memories of that night—Gael raising the gun at Imelda, the helplessness, Onyx's screams—were still fresh wounds, even with months separating us.

"There were minor hints toward his alliance," I murmured, hugging my waist. "I was just too blind to see them."

Onyx stepped closer, wrapping me in a comforting embrace. "I see the moments your mind wanders. The light in your eyes dims, and you become distant. It's like an instant switch to drowning in inescapable memories—instances where your mind circles what happened and attempts to curate solutions for what could have been different. I know the feeling because I live there and have experienced it many times. It happened to me during my service. It happened when we thought we lost Rayne. And it happened with Imelda.

"I will not lie and tell you it gets easier because it doesn't. It just gets more manageable. There are still nights I have nightmares over what I did years ago, things I wish I could undo. But the first step in getting past it and moving forward is forgiving yourself. You knew your intentions stepping into this community, and I don't believe you held ill will toward us, even as an ex-Venturer."

Onyx had a way of seeing through me and understanding some of the guilt and shame that threatened to sink me beneath the turbulent waters I worked to navigate. His reassurance reminded me there was potential for healing and redemption even in our brokenness. On the other hand, his acceptance made me question my motives—was I seeking forgiveness for something inevitable or using him to soothe my conscience?

As I leaned into him, I realized the walls between us had begun to crumble. The two of us were no longer enemies but two people finding comfort in each other's presence with a connection that went beyond levels of comprehension.

The draw was undeniable, and so was the reason it existed.

THIRTY

As I wandered the community's streets, the vibrant autumn leaves created a tapestry of various colors along the gutter line.

Each step I took sent a satisfying crunch through the air, and I couldn't help but admire the change. The sun, veiled by thick, dark clouds, fought to cast its light, illuminating the light fog that clung to the distant mountains like an eerie veil. The air was crisp and refreshing, a perfect blend of warmth and chill, while the scent of rain lingered—a perfect day curated to refine the skills I'd masked as unfamiliar.

I knew Rayne was waiting for me, as he had been for the past few days. Our training sessions had become a ritual, evolving from the basic handling of firearms to the nuanced dance of close-quarter combat with weapons. We began with simple sticks, crudely fashioned from branches scavenged from the tree line, slowly transitioning to the elegance and precision of swords and knives. Despite my initial skepticism of *who would wield a sword in this modern, shattered world?* Rayne had been adamant. He believed in preparing for the unexpected in a landscape where survival was a daily battle, and threats came in all forms.

Over five days, I learned to wield each weapon to near perfection, though I'd made it clear that I wished my skills would've developed quicker. Rayne, being the kind-hearted soul he was, encouraged my ability to adapt to each lesson.

As I rounded the last building that obscured our makeshift training field, I saw Rayne standing there, arms folded, waiting as usual. But this time, he wasn't alone.

Onyx was with him.

He'd pulled back his raven hair, exposing the full breadth of his powerful shoulders. He stood in black sweatpants, his shirt discarded, leaving his muscular frame fully visible. His tattoo, however, was far more notable. It wrapped around his left arm. Its lines flowed over his shoulder and across his back, mixing with the scars that marred his skin. It was a sight that was both intimidating and mesmerizing, a lived testament to all he had experienced and the intricacies of his past.

The sunlight that momentarily broke through the cloud cover cast him in a heavenly glow. His appearance was striking—a fallen angel stripped of his wings. Yet regardless of the beauty, as the distance between us closed, I felt a lump form at the base of my throat.

"Good morning, sleeping beauty," Rayne called out, peeking around Onyx's imposing figure. "Glad you could finally join us."

Us?

Onyx turned to face me, his piercing blue eyes meeting mine with an intensity that rooted me. His well-defined muscles were now entirely on display, bathed in the stark light that highlighted every scar and contour. I'd seen the strain in his T-shirt sleeves as they barely contained his biceps and the strength in his forearms whenever he rolled up his sleeves. But this—this was different.

"Good morning, Sweetness." His graveled voice contrasted the soft smile he extended.

"Good morning."

"Finally crawled out of bed, huh?" Rayne teased.

I shook my head, smirking. "You're too much of a morning person, you know?"

"That's an understatement," Onyx chimed in, turning his full attention to me, a predatory hunger gleaming in his eyes. "Are you ready for your final test?"

Glancing between them, my suspicion heightened. "What is that supposed to mean?"

Rayne chuckled, picking up on my wariness. "We've been training you to meet our standards as ex-Command Officers. Now, it's time to see how effectively you've learned."

"So, what?" I raised a brow. "Show off my proficiency with each weapon?"

"Not quite," Rayne replied, grinning. "This is what all your training has been leading up to."

Onyx's eyes met mine, a mischievous glint in them.

"You want me to face off against *him*?" I gestured toward Onyx skeptically. "No way. There's no way in hell this is happening."

Onyx chuckled. "Is there something you're worried about, Sweetness?"

"Worried about facing off against you? The one that every living human fears? The one that is known for his expertise in hand-to-hand combat?" I shot back with exasperation. "Yes, I am worried. I would be absolutely psychotic if I weren't. Are you joking?"

Rayne laughed, shaking his head. "If we didn't believe you could stand your ground, we wouldn't put you in this situation."

"Says the guy who set me up to fail multiple times this week just to make a point."

Rayne shrugged, looking at Onyx. "Even if I wanted to mess with you, he wouldn't allow it. Not at this level."

My gaze shifted back to Onyx. He smiled when our eyes met, a hint of concern softening his features. "I want you to give it everything you've got, Astrid. Fight me like your life depends on it."

"I don't want to hurt you," I admitted, though I was the only one who knew the depth behind those six words.

"You won't," a voice called from behind us, and I turned to watch Jasper approach.

"Ah, our referee," Rayne said, chuckling.

Jasper continued, "I'm here to ensure you can fight without any concern of injury."

"How?" I asked, confused.

"Aerokinetic," Onyx explained. "Jasper can manipulate surrounding air and create force fields to prevent lethal blows."

"He'll only step in for deadly attacks," Rayne clarified, his lips forming a tight-lipped smile. "We don't want Onyx to kill you, but we do want to prepare you for the actual threats the Capital will pose. They train every soldier there to kill. While we'll be fighting alongside you, there may be times when we're distracted and can't use our abilities to protect you."

"You need to be able to protect yourself," Onyx said, a note of concern in his voice. "At least until one of us can step in."

"Let me get this straight," I started, my gaze moving between them uncertainly. "We are about to go at one another, and the only one who will prevent my inevitable death will be Jasper?"

"*Our* inevitable deaths," Onyx sarcastically clarified.

Jasper nodded, drawing an exasperated sigh from me.

"Precisely," he confirmed. "So punches, kicks, and non-lethal attacks are fair game. But no abilities."

Onyx's expression remained impassive, as if the rules held no significance. It was a mask he wore well, honed through years of rigorous military training and countless opposition.

I took a deep breath, trying to calm the anxiety bubbling inside me. This was inevitable. It was a test I needed to pass before the mission to the Capital could proceed. Before any of them would allow me to go, and even though I knew my capabilities, there was a line between unleashing them and keeping myself shrouded in the shadows I walked behind.

"Take your positions," Jasper instructed, stepping to the side-lines with Rayne. "It's time to get this show on the road."

Onyx walked past me with a purposeful stride, each step

demonstrating intention. As he approached the opposite side of the makeshift ring, I couldn't help but count the steps it took for him to get there.

Five... Six... Seven...

Taking another breath, my mind raced, replaying every move and countermeasure Rayne and I had practiced.

Eight... Nine...

Onyx turned to face me, a soft smile playing on his lips. It was an expression that held a promise of challenge and a battle that would push us both to our limits. His eyes displayed recognition that we were about to cross a line from training partners to adversaries all over again.

We stood on the brink of a trial by combat, where skill, strength, and perhaps something deeper would be tested. Only ten steps separated us, a narrow distance that felt vast with the weight of apprehension hanging in the air.

"Here are the rules," Jasper's voice cut through the pressure consuming me. "Weapons are allowed, and they're scattered around the area. There are no firearms, just close-range knives and other blades. You two will fight until one of you submits. The goal is survival. Remember, lethal blows won't land, but fight as if they could."

Rayne gave me a thumbs up as if attempting to level my nerves—a teacher encouraging their trainee.

"It sounds simple enough," Onyx shrugged, turning his eyes back to me. "Are you ready, Sweetness?"

My heart pounded at his words and the realization that we were seconds away from being pitted against one another. The Most Wanted man alive and...

"Begin." Jasper's order came before I could reply to the man across from me, who rushed toward me on cue.

Shit.

Onyx threw a right punch in my direction, his movements swift and precise. Instinctively, I planted myself into the stance he had drilled into my muscle memory. The countless hours of practice came flooding back, guiding my actions toward instinct. I shifted my weight forward, sliding my left arm along Onyx's forearm, feeling the solid corded muscle beneath his skin. My arm glided up to his elbow, deflecting the force of his punch.

As my foot slid back slightly, my hips followed the motion, allowing me to harness the momentum. I wrapped my left hand around his elbow, pulling him closer. I knew brute strength wouldn't move him, so I elected to use his own force against him, pivoting smoothly. As I dropped into a slight bend, I aimed to slam my elbow into his exposed side, channeling all my energy into the strike.

Just when I thought I had an opportunity to land a solid hit, Onyx's left hand shot out, wrapping around my arm unrelentingly. He ripped me off the ground and, with a casual flick of his wrist, tossed me through the air. Time slowed, my surroundings blurring before my body connected with the ground.

The impact knocked the breath from my lungs, pain radiating up my back as I struggled to gather oxygen. Dazed, I lay there, attempting to roll onto my side.

"Ah, shit." I groaned, placing my hands and knees beneath me.

Before I could gather myself, a heavy boot slammed into my stomach, driving the recollection of air I gathered from my lungs. The intensity of the blow spoke of practiced precision, a move perfected through countless confrontations. I whimpered, curling in on myself as the pain radiated through me, my vision blurring at the edges. Each breath was a struggle, my body fighting to overcome the assault.

"Get up, Astrid!" Rayne called from the sideline. "Your life's on the line!"

I shook my head, opening my eyes as I spotted a glint in the grass. A reflective glow off of something...

A knife.

I lunged forward, grabbing the handle just as Onyx prepared to launch another attack. He smirked at me from his reflection in the polished steel of the blade, a taunting reminder of his power.

Watching his every move closely, I rolled sideways, narrowly avoiding the downward arc of his foot. The blade was my only chance to even the odds, and I clung to it like a lifeline.

His foot connected with the ground I had been lying on seconds before, the impact sending tremors through the earth. I pushed myself up, my body protesting with every movement. A slight hunch in my posture betrayed my pain, each breath an uphill battle. My mind raced to catch up with the flurry of action, processing the blows I had taken and the looming threats of those undelivered.

Onyx took his place across from me and smirked in my direction. "Might I say, I'm quite impressed. Most opponents of mine would've been incapacitated by now."

"You're a prick, you know that?" I hissed through clenched teeth, continuing to level my breathing.

"Yours, that is." He glanced at the knife in my hand, his unexpected words throwing me off.

"Focus, Astrid! Don't let him take advantage of you!" Jasper's warning ripped me from where my mind wandered as Onyx closed the gap between us.

This time, he swung a powerful left hook. I barely had time to react, instinctively ducking beneath the path of his fist. In one fluid motion, I flipped the knife in my hand, positioning it so the spine rested securely against my forearm—a technique to protect my hand while maximizing control.

With a burst of adrenaline, I took decisive steps forward, lunging beneath Onyx's extended arm. The knife cut through the air, finding its mark across his right thigh. The fabric of his sweatpants gave way with a sharp tear, immediately followed by the distinct sensation of the blade slicing into flesh. It was a clean cut, precise and controlled, its serrated edge biting into him just enough to draw blood.

A guttural snarl escaped Onyx's lips as the knife met his skin, an instantaneous and raw expression of surprise.

I spun on the knee I'd placed behind him, using the

momentum to propel myself away. My foot planted firmly, and I twisted my body, channeling all my strength into a kick aimed at his back. I thought I had him for a moment, but Onyx moved with a fluid grace that belied his size.

He spun around abruptly, almost as if he anticipated my move. His right arm snaked around my leg, trapping it against his side with unyielding strength, effectively pinning me in place.

"Gotcha." he winked as he looked at me.

Time seemed to slow as I watched the thin line of blood seep from the slash on his thigh. His expression remained unreadable, a mask of concentration and control. Before I could react, Onyx's hand moved to my planted foot, gripping it with a firmness that left no room for escape. He easily hoisted me off the ground, a curse slipping from my lips as I realized what was coming. The world spun around me, and I crashed into the cold and unforgiving field for a second time.

He left me breathless with the impact as a wave of agony rippled through my entire body. The force was greater than before, and for a moment, everything faded.

But unlike the first time he tossed me, he remained on top and undeniably in control.

Shit.

Onyx didn't hesitate.

He positioned himself between my thighs with a fluid, practiced motion, straddling my hips and pinning me down. His weight pressed heavily against me, a stark reminder of his domination. Desperation clawed at my chest as I tightened my grip on the knife. I swung it towards him as he reached down, the blade slicing across his forearm with a clean cut.

He growled in response, a deep, resonant sound that drew a grin across my lips. The crimson line appeared almost immediately, blood welling and descending his arm. A single drop splashed onto my cheek, warm and wet, contrasting with the coolness of the ground beneath me.

"You have got to cut it out with the damn blade." His bright eyes locked with mine, hair falling to frame his face as he glared at me.

"What, you don't want to look like a perfectly carved jack-o'-lantern?" I swung for him again, but the length of his fingers coiled around my wrists and pinned them above my head.

He leaned down, licking his lips slightly as his face fell inches from mine, a husky response following. "I could get used to this view."

Butterflies.

My core tightened at his words, and I tried to shake them off when I realized our position.

His hand grazed my fingers, his touch almost gentle as he tried to disarm me. He was careful, attempting to pry the knife from my grip without causing injury. But there was a purpose to his movements beyond just disarming me. As his fingers worked against mine, his hips shifted upward slightly, seeking leverage. It was a subtle movement, but enough to disrupt my focus. His words continued, a stream of distractions meant to throw me off balance, but he also distracted himself in trying to divide my attention.

It became a lapse I could exploit.

I acted on instinct, knowing I had only a split second to seize the opportunity. I bucked my hips upward with all the strength I could muster, feeling the shift as he momentarily lost his balance. In that instant, I wrapped my right leg around his left, locking it in place. The movement pinned him, giving me the leverage I needed. With a determined thrust, I pushed myself up toward him, using the momentum and his body weight to roll us over. The world tilted as our positions switched, and suddenly, I was on top.

With the knife firmly in my hand, I applied pressure to his throat, sensing Jasper's protective barrier. The cold steel kissed his skin, a reminder of the lethal edge held at bay by an invisible force.

Onyx grinned as he looked up at me, raising his brows. "I

could get used to this view as well. The blade is an impeccably added touch."

My cheeks flushed, not just from exertion but from the intimacy of our position. I became acutely aware of the sensation of his body beneath mine, the hard planes of muscle pressing against me. His earlier comment, playful yet suggestive, echoed in my mind, and I swallowed hard.

His eyes, filled with a predatory hunger, tracked every movement I made. A loose strand of hair slipped from my braid, tracing a path down my cheek. Onyx's gaze followed its descent, his eyes darkening with something unspoken. He swallowed, the subtle movement causing the knife to shift ever so slightly against his throat. His tongue darted out to wet his lips, a gesture that seemed almost unconscious but charged with tension.

It felt like it was just the two of us in the field, everything else vanishing entirely.

All the problems.

All the fighting.

All the damage.

The darkness and hidden truths.

Everything.

The sudden sound of clapping shattered the charged silence between us. Startled, I turned my head to see Jasper standing with a broad smile, his approval clear. He nodded, silently acknowledging the unexpected outcome.

Beside him, Rayne was a bundle of barely contained excitement, practically bouncing on his feet like a child. The contrast between their reactions and the intensity of the moment I had just shared with Onyx was jarring, serving as a reminder that not only had it been a battle of skill but that I'd passed.

The rush of realization flooded me, mingling with the surged connection I felt with the man beneath me.

I coerced Onyx into submission.

"Nice work," he announced from beneath me. "I can't say I

was all that focused, though, so you definitely had the upper hand."

I looked down. "Whatever you need to say to keep your ego from crumbling."

Winking, I pulled the blade from his throat and spun it between my fingers before sliding it into the empty holster on my thigh. The one I had equipped myself with for an expectation for further training today, only to be met with something else entirely.

"Nice work, Astrid," Jasper spoke as I pushed myself up. "As for you..."

"Me?" Onyx looked at him, cocking a brow as he pushed himself into a seated position. "What about me?"

"That was so half-assed." Rayne laughed slightly. "Half-assed or distracted, it was hard to tell."

My attention moved between them as they spoke, landing on Onyx, who shrugged. "There's no way in hell I'm going to put one hundred percent into a fight against her."

"Why?" My second question came with ease and a bit of defensiveness. "You don't think I could stand my ground?"

"I believe you could, but you have also seen only a sliver of what I am capable of."

"I *have* seen what you're capable of." I scowled at him, clenching my jaw. "*Plenty* of what you can do, actually."

"Not with hand-to-hand." He shook his head and pushed himself up, towering over me. "Before my kill count skyrocketed after the Fall, I had another tally—one from my time in the military. Technically, it was two separate counts. One for weapon-based engagements and the other for hand-to-hand combat. To give you an idea, my hand-to-hand count was significantly higher, and I was known in the ranks for my efficiency in close-quarter combat."

He paused, allowing the gravity of his words to settle. "My reputation made me the go-to trainer for many in the ranks—Command Officers, soldiers, and even specialized operatives trained under me. They never trained under me out of their own desire, but because those in command ordered them to. I became the benchmark for what to expect in a fight, and yet, despite that, there has never been a single training exercise where I've gone all out, even against highly skilled Command Officers. I never showed the full extent of my abilities because it wasn't necessary and allowed me to keep a few secrets up my sleeve."

Rayne rolled his eyes, "Per his words, I've only ever experienced seventy-five percent, and that nearly killed me."

I bit my cheek at his admittance.

Two separate kill counts—one from conventional military engagements and another from hand-to-hand combat. The latter was far more chilling. It wasn't just about taking lives but overpowering and executing skilled opponents with his bare hands. He thrived in chaos and built his reputation on his ability to dominate any combat scenario, ensuring those around him knew all he could do if anyone dared to cross that line.

The knowledge that men he'd trained during his time in the ranks were likely still out there made it even more daunting. He'd molded them with his expertise, teaching them to be ruthless and effective soldiers capable of killing without needing to leverage anything more than their knuckles. Logically, I knew that even though they reflected his teachings, they'd been equipped with a fraction of his prowess but remained dangerous to those incapable of standing their ground.

When standing against Onyx, I was only as vulnerable as I wanted them to think I was.

"Eighty percent for me," Jasper admitted, his eyes rolling slightly. "And I was in the medical ward for two weeks afterward."

"What the hell did you do to them?" I looked at Onyx, who was brushing a few pieces of grass from his bare stomach.

"They asked for it; I only did what they requested."

I returned to Jasper and Rayne, who met me with a mirrored shrug.

"You're masochists. You realize that, right? Why the hell would you willingly ask him to kick the shit out of you?"

"There's nothing quite like looking Death in the eye," Rayne smirked in response to my question.

Onyx raised his eyebrows and said, "An understatement again."

Death.

During his military service, it became a title that carried a weighty reputation and a legacy of fear. Earned through his combat prowess and effectiveness on the battlefield, it followed him even after he left the military to join and lead the Rebellion.

It was a mark of his skill and the darkness that clung to him, a reminder of the countless missions he undertook and the lives he irrevocably changed. Yet, it was just one piece of the complex puzzle that made up Onyx's past.

The things he did while serving—each mission, each life taken—left an indelible mark on his soul. It wasn't just the actions but the moral compromises and innocence lost along the way. There were decisions he hadn't forgiven himself for and ghosts from his past that haunted him as they would any empathetic human. I often wondered how many of those lives weighed heavily on his conscience, a burden of one stream of guilt he carried.

During his military service, the nickname might have been a badge of dishonor at the time, a reminder of what he had done, often under orders and perhaps against his own will. It was a title that likely brought shame, a constant reminder of the monstrosities he was capable of. It was a symbol of honor and defiance, marking his commitment to avenge those wronged by corruption.

But that nickname had taken on a new meaning in his current role within the Rebellion.

Rayne exhaled deeply, cutting through my thoughts. "I could use a drink after that."

"You could use a drink?" Onyx let out a graveled chuckle. "As if you were doing anything."

"I was worrying about Astrid's survival." He glanced at me, a slight grin gracing his lips. "She's rather enjoyable."

"You were worried about her and believed I wouldn't uphold my bargain to prevent anything from happening?" Jasper followed quickly, playfulness in his tone. "You have no faith in your superiors, do you, Rayne?"

"Superiority is dead and gone." Rayne looked in his direction and shrugged nonchalantly. "Besides, if we are going to throw rank around, we would both be kissing the ground he stood on." He jutted a thumb at Onyx.

"Please do not put your lips anywhere near my feet. I don't want the title of superior *ever again*." Onyx shook his head, waving them off. "Those days are long gone, so let's keep them that way."

"Alright, if you say so, *Captain*." Jasper winked, glancing between his two friends before glimpsing at me. "What do you say, Astrid? Care to join us?"

I nodded my head, "Please. I need something to settle my nerves after that bullshit you all just put me through."

The three of them cackled in harmony as they exchanged looks with one another before we began making our way back to the center of the community and away from the makeshift ring.

The ring where I held a win over Onyx.

The ring that had witnessed the beginning of all that would follow while concealing the essence of all I was.

THIRTY-ONE

We discussed enjoying beverages at the café, but the group quickly shot down the suggestion.

For one, it would have been about noon if time were tellable. Rayne jutted at Jasper, stating that if his people saw him drinking that early, it may pose some questions. These were all jokes, of course, but the judgment wasn't something any of us wanted to risk. Not when Jasper was working to recover the trust of his community members after the attack. Second, we all desired privacy, likely because of the heightened possibility of conversations arising that surrounded the infiltration, which was to be kept quiet.

For now.

Jasper dropped a pitcher of beer onto the large table in the center of the mission debrief room, sliding a stack of cups beside it. "Beverages secured."

Rayne reached across the expansive oak, sliding one cup from the stack. He grabbed the pitcher and filled it to the brim before slipping back into his chair. "Praise the lords."

I followed suit, tugging from the towering stack and freeing a cup of my own before pouring the golden liquid into it. But unlike Rayne, I only filled it up about halfway. I pressed my back into the chair as I took a sip, sighing.

"I hate beer, but this will have to suffice." Rayne's eyes peered over the brim of his glass as he watched Jasper take his turn. "Where the hell is Oakes, anyway?"

Jasper huffed a chuckle and took a swig before responding, "He went in for a quick healing session since Astrid showed him no remorse with that knife. And then to change, of course."

"Dressing to impress. I see." Rayne sat up, pressing his elbows into the table as his eyes fell on me. "I say we play a game of truth or truth while we await his arrival."

Jasper cocked a brow as he took back a larger mouthful of beer. "You're just admitting that you're a nosey bastard."

As I set my cup down, I shrugged. "I'll play. I have some questions I'd like answered as well."

The corner of Rayne's lips curled upward at my agreement to sign my life away without knowing it. He shifted again, grabbing his cup and leaning back in his chair, getting comfortable before lifting his eyes to me again.

"Ladies first."

I focused on the scar that hugged his left pointer finger. "How did you get that?"

Jasper sucked in air between his teeth. "Oh, she's going right in."

Rayne looked at it and then back at me, his expression unreadable. He set the glass down deliberately and then tucked his opposite hand into a fist. Confusion washed over me as I watched him push himself away from the table, his slow and deliberate movement making my heart drum against my chest.

He stood, his tall frame casting a shadow over us as we remained seated. My eyes followed him as he grabbed the hem of his shirt and, with a smooth motion, pulled it over his head. The action left him shirtless, the soft light from the room highlighting the contours of his bare skin. His light complexion seemed almost to glow under the illumination, revealing the powerful lines of his physique.

"And he's going in too," Jasper groaned as he looked at his now bare-chested friend, taking a longer swig from his glass. "If this is how this is going to go, I will need far more than one pitcher of beer."

Rayne's build was strikingly similar to Onyx's, marking their shared background. Muscles rippled across his arms, sculpted and defined, continuing across his chest and shoulders. The well-developed muscles of his abdomen created a sharp contrast with the shadows that deepened the valleys between each contour. My gaze traveled over his form, taking in the unexpected sight.

And that's when I spotted it. The scar that commonly tucked itself under the long-sleeved shirts he wore didn't stop there.

It began on the inside of his left forearm, its jagged path traveling upward. Crossing diagonally over his bicep, it seemed to defy the natural flow of his skin. The wound straddled his flesh, its lightness contrasting the color of the surrounding tissue. As it reached his defined shoulder, the scar became a significant, raised blemish. The mark seemed almost intentional, as if someone had tried—and failed—to carve a circle there. It was evidently a starting point, a deliberate disfigurement marking the entry of an attack.

From there, the scar grew even more intricate and harrowing. It traversed his chest; the tissue raised and lighter before continuing down the right side of his body, trailing along the length of his torso. It finally ended just before reaching the line of his pants, leaving an unsettling, almost unfinished impression.

The depth and extent of the wound spoke volumes, telling a violent story of survival. Seeing it left me near-speechless and rolling in the discomfort of my prodding, the jab an indelible reminder of the Rites Rayne had endured.

"Holy shit." The words escaped me in a near whisper.

Rayne's sky-blue eyes studied me briefly before he spoke. "I'm sure you recall our conversation about me being thrown into the Eradication Rites?"

I nodded, my eyes tracing the lines of the scar as I followed the pattern up and down his body for a second time. My mind attempted to draw conclusions about which portion marked the beginning and which pointed to the end.

"Essentially," he raised his arms, pulling the shirt over his head and back down the length of his body, covering the expansive injury before sitting down again. "It came down to me and one other in the Rite I was a part of. I tried to talk sense into every person I encountered during my time there, but no one seemed to want to listen, regardless of my blatant admittance of working for the government and having knowledge that none of them did.

"I lacked any desire to battle against any individual placed in my round, but I wouldn't be standing here today if I hadn't. Near the end, it was me and one other survivor. The government bodies monitoring the Rite clarified they wouldn't let us out until there was one winner. I didn't even learn his name before he attacked me. He wielded a large blade, and while I tried to talk him off the ledge of attacking me, he stabbed me in the shoulder." His fingers went to the raised scar he'd just displayed. "Then he filleted my chest as if I was some animal and worked his way down my side.

"I ended up retrieving the dagger I found during my trek of survival and stabbed him in the chest. He used his blade to re-enter the same wound channel." His fingers were again at the cicatrix on his shoulder before tracing down his arm. "As I worked mine deeper into his chest, he attempted to use the same technique used during his first attack. Luckily, the cut wasn't as deep because I caught him off guard. We both ended up collapsing around the same time, and I figured that my life had ended at that moment. But somehow, someway, I ended up surviving."

Jasper looked at his friend, shaking his head. "Gods, Rayne."

"I don't want sympathy or sorrow." His words were slightly

cold, even though I knew it was far from his intention. "I did what I had to do to survive, just as we all do in this hell-forsaken world we live in. And that's what it came down to when we stood in opposition. His blood, as well as many other innocent people's, covers my hands, and that's something I will have to live with for the rest of my life."

Exhaling deeply, I grabbed my cup and took another drink. Part of me wanted to apologize for immediately targeting him with such an intimate question, but I knew he'd block out my attempt.

I forced the liquid down my throat, biting back any expression that expressed my distaste for it. "I guess that would make it your turn."

The smile on his face before he displayed himself to the two of us returned. "You and Onyx, what is the story there?"

Jasper nearly choked on his alcohol, covering his mouth with the back of his forearm as he glanced in my direction.

My cheeks burned slightly as I lifted my hand, drawing circles around the brim of my cup. "We met back when I was a Venturer in Region Three. My prior counterpart and I were on a mission, and we came across Imelda, Onyx's previous partner. We tried to run her down, and Onyx came to her aid. And from there, the rest is history."

Rayne leaned forward, his elbows grazing the table. "I love a little backstory and find it adorable that you feel I didn't already know." My contorted expression drew a smile worthy of exposing one of his dimples. "But I am more curious about *feelings*. Considering how you interact, there seems to be something there."

"Oh, for hell's sake, Rayne." Jasper cut in, "Is that truly any of your business?"

"I mean, Onyx is one of my best friends. So, I would say yes." He beamed at me before speaking again, "Care to share your level of interest in the hard-headed, stubborn piece of shit?"

I grabbed my cup and downed the rest of the remaining golden liquid. Rayne was interrogating me for an answer that required courage to begin—liquid courage, anyway. Part of me felt I owed it to him, considering he willingly answered the question I posed. I exhaled deeply, placing my empty glass back on the table as my stomach completed a one-eighty.

I wasn't sure if it was the nerves I attempted to simmer or the beer I worked to drown them in, though it was likely a mix of the two.

"If you're asking if I find him attractive, the answer is yes."

"Who doesn't? Attractiveness is honestly an understatement with that asshole." Rayne shrugged as he took another drink, eyeing Jasper out of the corner of his eye before posing another query. "Are you two seeing one another?"

"No. I wouldn't say it's gotten to that level yet."

"Yet?"

I groaned, running a hand through my hair and rubbing my temples. "He's been playing hard to get since day one, and I can't figure out what he wants or how he sees me. Even though I've confronted him about it multiple times, and he's tried to reassure me, nothing concrete ever comes of it." I knew I should've stopped talking, but the words kept spilling from me. "I find him attractive and enjoy being around him. So, if you're asking for truthfulness, then yes, as I said, I am interested in him even if he doesn't feel the same."

Jasper chuckled, drinking from his cup again without uttering another word.

Rayne ignored him. "Wait. You're saying you don't know how he feels about you?"

I watched Jasper's eyes widen as soon as the question came from his friend. "Rayne, I don't think that's any of your business—"

"To be disclosing?" Onyx's voice came from the doorway, and my stomach rotated another half-circle.

I glanced over my shoulder, surprised to see him standing there with the quietness of his arrival.

He wore a Prussian blue T-shirt that clung to his upper body, stretching over his biceps as if struggling to contain the strength beneath. Dark wash jeans sat comfortably on his hips, contrasting with the shirt's vibrancy. His hair remained styled in its usual way—half pulled into a messy bun while the rest cascaded down in loose waves.

His powder blue eyes focused on Rayne with an intense, unreadable expression. But as his gaze shifted to me, something changed. The hard edge softened, a flicker of warmth breaking through his icy exterior.

"I'm hoping I didn't miss much." He dodged the conversation that we had been having. Either not wanting us to know what he had heard or having barely missed what I had admitted.

I hoped it was the latter.

"Glad to see you finally make an appearance." Jasper looked at him as he made his way toward the table.

Multiple chairs remained open since only four of us occupied the space. Rayne had positioned himself on the right side of the table directly across from me. Jasper, as usual, sat at the head, exuding his quiet authority. I sat on the left side, leaving the spot opposite of Jasper still empty.

As Onyx walked past that vacant chair, I watched him with growing curiosity. His imposing frame moved with purpose, and instead of taking the empty seat beside the coppery-haired male, he approached the chair beside me. He reached out, his hand gripping the backrest with casual confidence. With a swift motion, he pulled it out and settled into it next to me.

The proximity was palpable, and the surge he wrought jolted my entire body.

Rayne raised his eyes in my direction, a smug smile growing before he shrugged and took another drink.

"Don't stop your conversation on my behalf." Onyx grabbed the last cup from the center of the table and poured himself a glass. "I'm sure Rayne has been prodding into personal details, as that is what he is best at."

Rayne groaned, "You didn't come here to be a grumpy mood killer, did you?"

Onyx let out a graveled chuckle as he leaned back. "Nope. I came to enjoy the conversation, so feel free to continue."

"I believe it was your turn?" Jasper questioned, his gray gaze settling on me. "To ask one of us a truth?"

Onyx laughed again as he drank. "See, I knew prodding was taking place."

Rayne waved a hand in his direction as he swallowed another mouthful.

I looked between the three of them, considering who I wanted to pose the following question to before I returned to Rayne again. "How many women have you slept with?"

As soon as the words left my mouth, Onyx choked beside me. His shoulders shook with the effort of suppressing his amusement. The sudden motion almost caused the drink in his hand to spill as he battled to maintain his composure. He swallowed hard, forcing the liquid down before licking his lips, utter enjoyment lacing his expression.

Rayne let out a long breath, clearly entertained by the situation. He leaned back in his chair, a relaxed posture that signaled his ease with the conversation. With a calm air, he lifted his feet onto the table, crossing them casually. His left hand came up, fingers spreading wide as if preparing for a show. Holding his cup precariously in his right hand, he freed his index finger just enough to count. He tapped each finger on his left hand in turn. The motion was slow and filled with teasing anticipation, as if he was savoring the moment and the reaction it would elicit.

"My hell." Jasper rubbed his eyes with his thumb and pointer finger. "If we ask him to count, we could be here all damn day."

"If he knows how," Onyx spoke as he looked in his direction.

Rayne shrugged. "To be honest, probably too many."

"Valid answer," I laughed.

Rayne glanced between the three of us, contemplating his next victim. His eyes landed on Jasper. "When was the last time you got laid?"

I held back a laugh as I watched Onyx's eyes widen at the question. "My hell, what is this, a sex addict anonymous group?"

Jasper rolled his eyes as if unamused by the question, "Last night."

"What?!" The synced query came from both Onyx and Rayne, who looked at each other in disbelief before casting their attention back to him. The differed tonality spoke of varying levels of jealousy and intrigue.

"I don't understand why the two of you are so surprised."

"Who?" Onyx prodded, clearly in need of an answer.

Rayne retorted playfully, "Now, who's prodding?"

"Oh, shut the hell up, you're curious too."

My smile spread as they bickered, pressing Jasper for an answer. He took a drink from his cup and shrugged. "I don't want to disappoint anyone here."

"What the hell is that supposed to mean?" Rayne's brows pulled together. "Did you pull someone into bed that you regretted and just don't want to admit it?"

"Regret? No." Jasper glanced in his direction before casting out his blanket statement, "You act as if your puppy dog eyes don't give you away, Rayne."

Onyx chuckled as he set his drink down, "He's not wrong. We can pick up your horny radar from a mile away, just based on one look."

"No one asked you, prick." Rayne's barked rebuttal flew in Onyx's direction before he turned to fully address Jasper once more. "What camp member are you sleeping with? Isn't that against the rules to some degree?"

"Like a boss sleeping with an employee?" I asked, adding myself to the conversation. My contribution to the chaos-infused teasing seemed to draw a softened smile from Onyx, a piece of it tugging on my heartstrings.

"Yeah, like that!" Rayne motioned a thumb in my direction. "See, she understands what wavelength I'm on."

"You are that godsdamn curious?" Jasper raised his cup to his lips and took another swig.

After finishing it, he set the glass on the oak table with a soft thud. The solid sound seemed to shift the room's atmosphere, drawing all attention to him. He leaned forward, his eyes locking onto Rayne's with an intent focus that hinted at their playful rivalry. The edges of his lips curled into a subtle, knowing smile that spoke volumes more than words ever could. He was clearly gearing up to deliver a response that would drive home his point while offering a touch of smugness.

"Lila."

"The waitress? Considering the looks exchanged over the table during breakfast, I had a feeling." Onyx raised his eyebrows as a grin spread across his lips. "Oh, poor Rayne, thinking he had a chance."

"You asshole." Rayne narrowed his glance in Jasper's direction. "I had my eyes on her since we sat at that table."

"Oh, I know you did; it was blatantly obvious. It makes it even more hysterical because we have been seeing each other, off and on, for the past few months." Jasper cocked his head slightly, seeming to come up empty-handed on deep feelings for the woman they discussed. "For once, a female didn't have her eyes on you, which I know is mind-boggling. I will say that I appreciate your approval, though."

He winked as he finished his sentence, and I bit my cheek to keep the smile from growing even more expansive. The shock that spread on Rayne's face because of the reply nearly sent me over the edge.

"You snide bastard." Onyx laughed, his shoulders bouncing with a gesture of indifference. "I'm surprised, yet not at the same time."

"You two act as if he isn't attractive." I motioned in Jasper's direction and lifted a brow. "If it counts for anything, he's fine as hell. I don't know why you're both shocked he's getting laid."

"For starters, thank you for the compliment." Jasper bowed in my direction, his hand resting against his strong chest. "It's probably because neither of them has gotten laid in months. Honestly, when was the last time either of you hounds fooled around with anyone?"

"That's beside the point." Rayne waved him off, trying to avoid the question.

"Isn't this truth or truth?" I asked, glancing in his direction and leveraging the fact that he had been the one who desired to play the game. "I believe it is Jasper's turn, considering you happened to ask him the last question?"

Rayne scoffed at me, "You know, I liked you—"

"It's been over a year for me," Onyx answered with monotonality, indifferent about his admission.

His two friends glanced in his direction, eyes wide. Onyx shrugged as astonishment crossed their faces, another key sign of which he remained placid and careless in his answer.

"How is that even possible?" Rayne questioned with genuine curiosity. "With how women look at you, there's no way you have gotten nothing in a year."

"You think I'd openly admit that just to humiliate myself for fun?" Onyx chuckled as he took another drink, lifting his pointer finger in his friend's direction. "I swear on my mother's grave, it's been over a year."

"I can't say I'm surprised," Jasper chimed in, raising his hands as Onyx gave him a look of disapproval. "Not in a bad way; you're just selective about who you sleep with, unlike *some* people."

Rayne rolled his eyes as he threw a middle finger to Jasper, who returned the gesture with a profane one of his own.

I mustered the nerve to tease him as I cocked my head in his direction. "So, in other news, your right hand has become your best friend?"

"No hesitation. She just called you the hell out." Rayne

laughed loudly and shook his head. "Oh shit, dude, she's coming for all of us."

"You'd be correct, Sweetness, except," Onyx glanced out of the corner of his eye at me, his lip tugging upward slightly. "I think you'd remember from our sparring session that I am, in fact, left-handed."

I laughed softly at the playful correction he tossed my way. His words were lighthearted, but there was a sincerity in his tone that made the moment feel genuine. Looking into his eyes, I noticed the subtle crinkles at the corners, a heartwarming confirmation of the expansive smile that coated his face.

My interest in him was more than just curiosity—it was a cautious exploration of the possibilities beneath our interactions. And the fact that he seemed indifferent about admitting the truth —whether it was about a past event or a simple detail—felt like a quiet revelation. It hinted at comfort and trust as if he had silently acknowledged my place within his tight-knit circle.

"Rayne?" Jasper looked in his direction as he raised his glass, pointing at him. "You can continue to run from the question, but you know the game's rules. You won't be getting away with not answering."

He groaned as he slid his empty glass forward. "You're that desperate to know about my sex life, huh?" He grabbed the pitcher again, filling his cup to the brim before slumping back in his seat. "Six months."

Onyx chuckled deeply as he looked at him with feinted sympathy. "And you haven't passed away. By gods, how is that even possible?"

"That's what I was about to say," Jasper tacked on immediately, the two continuing to poke fun at their friend. "I thought that if Rayne went longer than a few days, he would turn into a toad or something."

"Ha-ha. You two are hilarious." Rayne brought the cup to his lips as he took another drink, draining about half of the liquid with one swallow. "Truly, your jabs are so incredibly original."

"So your hand has become your best friend, too, huh?" I teased, smiling at him. "Looks like you and Onyx are riding in the same boat, then."

Rayne returned my tease with another middle finger, making the gesture with his free hand as he took another drink, which made me laugh even harder. The other two followed suit, and we meshed together in joyful harmony.

"She didn't ask for a demonstration, you know?" Jasper countered as he leaned forward to grab the pitcher and pour another glass.

"We don't need to know what you're doing in bed at night, especially here." Onyx wrapped his hand around the cup and lifted it to his lips, parting them to allow the liquid to pass.

As I watched him take a sip from his glass, my thoughts drifted to the few times our lips had met. Each memory was vivid, his lips both gentle and rough, a perfect contradiction. There had always been a restrained intensity in those moments, as if he was holding back and afraid to cross an unseen line. From the very first day we met, I found myself both fascinated and frustrated by his elusiveness, even though it made me a hypocrite in being so.

I pulled myself out of my thoughts before others noticed my internal monologue and questioned its contents.

More specifically, one person in particular.

Rayne released a soft sigh as he leaned back in his chair, setting down his empty cup. His legs remained perched on the table, similar to how I had seen Onyx in the past.

"We really have to go to the Capital and do the damn thing, huh?" Compared to where we were, the question was a harsh snap back to reality.

While we joked, basking in banter and laughter, the thought of the world we lived in and all that awaited us had drifted.

For once, everything had felt decently normal.

No secrets.

No lies.

No masks.

Jasper exhaled deeply as he rubbed a hand down his face. His fingers brushed against his beard, a contemplative gesture that mirrored the thoughts running through his mind. He glanced down at his empty glass, the faint traces of liquid clinging to the sides cueing into his contemplation to pour another.

"Yeah, sadly, we do."

"What's your time frame?" Onyx leaned back beside me as he folded his arms over his chest. "And what are your expectations as far as numbers go?"

Jasper flicked the cup forward, disinterested in having another drink as he spoke. "Considering Astrid has cleared our expectations, we could go as soon as tomorrow."

"Shit," Rayne hissed as he ran a hand through his hair, the word revealing where he stood on the planned trek.

"But," Jasper matched Onyx's posture in his chair, "it would look bad on me as a leader to vanish without a word of what's happening while those I serve are still healing from the prior attack. And I feel it would be just as damaging for you, Rayne."

"Wasn't the agreement to do this infiltration to retaliate for what they did to the Rebellion communities?" The question fell from me as I glanced between the two of them.

Jasper nodded. "Correct, it is, which is why I want to explain that to everyone. My people deserve to know about the operations in the Capital and our plans to infiltrate their bases to make a statement about what has happened. On top of that, we truly don't know how this mission will end."

"Don't even speak that shit into existence." Onyx snapped from beside me, his words practically a snarl.

Jasper shot a look in his direction. "Do you mean to tell me you are now a Foreseer?"

Onyx clenched his jaw, his fingers closing around the width of his biceps to contain the retort he wished to utter. "I'm not doing the smart-ass remarks, Jasper. We aren't sitting here and speaking any of that bullshit into existence. We will stick together, successfully infiltrate the base, and all of us *will* survive."

A long breath came from Rayne as he attempted to steer the conversation elsewhere. "As far as men go. What are your plans there?"

"Us four and your crew." Jasper's response was brief and to the point, knowing Onyx wouldn't merely forget his suggestive statement.

His reply hit me, disbelief following as I looked over at him. "Eight of us, that's it?"

"What, you don't believe in what we can accomplish?" Onyx teased as he glanced at me. "I'm confident I could decimate their operations alone if Jasper would allow it."

"Not happening." Jasper shook his head. "Regardless of how badly you desire to go in there alone, I wouldn't allow you to put yourself in a situation that risky and dangerous."

"As if he wasn't among the highest-ranking soldiers before the Fall happened. And now is the Most Wanted and powerful," Rayne retorted as he threw his hands up in an expressive shrug. "Add a little rage on top of that, and it's the perfect cocktail to demolish them in the blink of an eye."

"That's beside the point, Cromwell." Jasper's words were sharper and more militant as he glanced between the two men. "I don't care what the desire is or how capable Onyx is; he won't be tackling this alone. I've selected the eight of us for this mission, and I'm not changing my mind, regardless of the arguments you attempt to throw in my direction."

I looked at Jasper, drawing his focus from them, even if just momentarily. "I know that the eight of us are more than capable. Part of me figured you would have recruited some men you trusted to aid the infiltration."

"Each community has already lost people; we don't need to add to those numbers. I know damn well that if we go in there too heavily footed, it will yield a graveyard." He stroked his beard as he continued, "The tighter and more formative the group is, the higher the likelihood of a success rate. We have individuals who specialize in tactical approaches, not only from prior experience but also as far as abilities go. That is why this isn't a one-person operation. We can use the two teleporters to get us within their facilities and Raven's invisibility for stealth. Leveraging one another's abilities, expertise, and knowledge will be the least risky route for us all."

"So essentially, you want us to stage an attack from within their infrastructure?" Onyx nodded, his lips curling in approval. "Not a bad idea, Bandell."

Jasper raised a brow at the use of his last name as if it brought back memories of the time the three of them served together. He smiled before speaking again, "Since the plan is to go in hot and heavy, attack from within, and cause as much demolition as possible, I have discussed building various levels of explosives with Lila."

"You mean to tell me she knows how to make bombs?" Rayne looked at him in pure astonishment, groaning as he dropped his head. "You really swooped in and snatched a winner from right under my nose, didn't you?"

Jasper chuckled, "Something like that."

"It sounds like we are just waiting on leadership then, so the two of you should get on your shit and tell your people what's going on. The longer we wait, the more likely we fall under their noses for suspicion. Hell, for all we know, they could be planning another attack on the communities as we speak." Onyx pushed his chair backward as he stood beside me. "We don't know what information Radley has openly disclosed to them."

"That's likely an understatement." Jasper ran a hand through his hair, the auburn strands contrasting against his freckled skin. "We will schedule a plan to infiltrate in a week." He glanced to his right at Rayne. "You can head out tomorrow to secure things and provide your people with orders during your team's absence."

Rayne moaned in annoyance, "This is why Onyx held the title over us when we were government puppets—leadership shit is far from what I signed up for."

"I led you for years and would think you would have learned

something during your time in the ranks. You know what your people want, how they operate, and how to disclose the information you *know* needs to be disclosed. Use what you learned and gained while serving alongside me and leverage it. The reins are in your hands, whether or not you want them." Onyx looked over at his friend, the finality of his words holding far more weight than surface-level interpretation. "Steer the horse accordingly, Rayne."

THIRTY-TWO

Seven Days

I rubbed my eyes and rolled over on the cot, the familiar stiffness in my limbs greeting me as I stretched. The early morning sunlight filtered through the curtains, casting a soft golden glow on the walls and creeping across the floor to dance over my bare skin. I threw off the blanket and sat up, savoring the warmth as I winced at the tenderness that clung to my muscles.

Gods—I was sore.

I hadn't realized how much effort it had taken to fend off Onyx.

I kneaded the side of my neck, my muscles protesting with a sharp ache that reminded me of yesterday's exertions. A sigh of relief escaped me as my thoughts drifted to the previous day's events—the battle with Onyx, the game of truth or truth, Jasper's infiltration plans, and an evening spent helping around the community. Every mundane task started to feel grounding, offering a small semblance of normalcy amidst the chaos.

I swung my legs over the side of the cot, feeling the strain in my thighs as I stood. Maybe taking on a patrol shift after a near-death encounter wasn't my wisest decision. The persistent muscle spasms were proof enough, and I was sure Jasper would lecture me about it if I brought it up.

Muttering a slew of curse words under my breath, I hobbled to the other side of the room. I hastily put on my undergarments, jeans, and a shirt before gathering my hair into a messy bun and leaving my room.

The space Onyx and I shared was small, but it suited our needs.

I had refused to take the larger of the two rooms, feeling it was unnecessary and insisting that Onyx keep it for himself. Convincing him had been a battle, but eventually, he caved.

I padded down the hallway toward the kitchen, careful not to disturb the morning stillness. Considering how late he had been out, I wasn't sure if he was awake and wanted to avoid being the one to interrupt his slumber. Rounding the corner, I found my answer, my breath stalling in my chest as I took in the sight before me.

He stood with his back to me, his hair tousled and wild, the intricate tattoo on his shoulder blade stark against his pale scars. Each blemish told its own story. I couldn't help but admire his raw reality. Each mark reminded me of the battles he had endured and all he'd overcome.

My gaze lingered a little too long on the only piece of clothing he wore—a simple pair of briefs. Heat rose to my cheeks just as Onyx turned, catching me in the act.

"Good morning," I managed, quickly shifting my eyes to his face.

"Morning, Sweetness," he replied, his voice rough with lack of use. "How'd you sleep?"

It was as if casual conversations in his underwear were part of our morning routine.

"Decent," I sidestepped him, trying to avoid glancing at the undeniable length beneath the fabric. "I'm sore as hell from yesterday, so thanks for that."

He chuckled, the sound rich and deep. "It was a successful session. Though that doesn't mean your soreness isn't warranted."

"I was relying on some level of immunity to the aftermath," I mumbled, reaching for an apple on the counter. "Let me guess, you feel fine?"

He glanced down at his thigh, where the cut from our earlier face-off had been. There was no trace of the wound—the rapid healing from whichever medic had helped him had erased it completely.

"Was I not supposed to?" he asked, a teasing glint in his eyes.

I bit into the apple, rolling my eyes. "You're a cocky prick. I hope you know that."

"You really need to get more inventive with your chosen insults." He leaned against the wall, blocking my path from the kitchen. "In a hurry to go somewhere?"

I chewed slowly, keeping my gaze steady and trying to push down the redness that threatened to consume my face. "Why? Do you want to spend time together?"

His eyes scanned me briefly, a smirk playing on his lips. "Are you prodding and testing the waters because that's what *you* desire?"

The deflection didn't come as a surprise—yet another question answered with his own query.

I scoffed, my eyes rolling slightly. "It wouldn't be a conversation with you unless you dodged every question by asking your own."

He laughed, his eyes never leaving mine. "I didn't realize today was going to be full of snide remarks from you."

"Why're you up?" I asked, overlapping his statement.

"I could ask you the same, though this conversation feels oddly familiar."

I shook my head. "Dodging again. I'm up because the sun was violating my face through the crack in my curtains."

"I told you to close them tighter," he said, shaking his head with a growing smile. "We can say I'm up for similar reasons."

"The true reason is that you just couldn't wait to see me," I teased, spinning the apple core between my fingers. "Let's be honest here."

"That would be one of them," he responded casually, cocking his head. "Speaking of, do you care to enlighten me on what you said to Rayne before I arrived for the worst game of truth or truth ever last night?"

Shit.

"Why would I need to tell you something you already know?" I shot back, hoping to successfully avoid choking on the apple.

Every grind of my teeth echoed in my ears. Onyx stepped closer, his eyes darkening as the space between us narrowed. The heat radiating from his body made my heart pound in my chest.

"Maybe I wanted to hear you say it yourself," he murmured, his voice low.

The words spilled from me. "Rayne asked about where you and I stood. I told him I was uncertain because of your constant inability to seem anything but disinterested. He pushed further and asked if I was interested in you."

Onyx reached out, brushing a loose strand of hair away from my face. "And I believe the answer to that question was a resounding yes?"

I dropped my chin, avoiding his gaze. "Something like that."

He hooked a finger under my jaw, pulling my gaze to meet his. His powder blue eyes scanned my features as if working to commit every one of them to memory. As soon as I went to shift the conversation, he leaned forward, his lips hovering near mine.

"Believe it or not, I have craved you ever since I saw you on those rooftops. Every inch of you drives me mad."

I laughed softly in disbelief, going to meet his admittance with a sarcastic remark, but he crashed into me, cutting me off with a fierce, unyielding kiss. The force of it pushed me back against the cold countertop, contrasting with the fever of our embrace. He pulled back just enough to lick his lips and smirk mischievously before diving back in, our lips colliding in a desperate dance. Each kiss felt essential, a shared intake of breath that became as vital as touch itself.

From the moment we met, a level of passion simmered beneath the surface for far more than just attraction. Being alone in the height of admittance, the dam of self-restraint finally burst, unleashing the entire reign of the emotions we could no longer contain. My mind sank back to the hunger I had caught in his eyes before, which became unmistakable in how his hands caressed my body.

My core tightened as I pressed myself closer. His left hand worked up my thigh, stirring a heat between my legs, while his right cradled my jaw.

Both of us held a deep-seated fear of intimacy shaped by the losses we had endured and the untold stories we shared that interlaced with underlying intention. The night we shared his bed awakened a desire I hadn't fully acknowledged, tied to something beyond simple intrigue. I knew Onyx struggled with guilt, keeping him guarded and reluctant to explore new relationships, and it was a fear I understood all too well.

I inhaled sharply, bringing my hands to the sides of his face and pulling him closer. I wanted to memorize his taste, his scent —a mix of sandalwood and eucalyptus—and how he felt against me.

His hand found its way into my hair and tugged gently, rocking my body with the surge our connection wrought. A soft moan escaped my lips as I felt the hardness of his arousal pressed against my pelvis—a physical manifestation of his desire.

A primal need surged within me, unleashed by the confirmation of his want. My hands slid up to his hair, fingers weaving through the dark strands as I tightened my grip. I pulled him closer, desperate to feel every part of him. I wanted him and needed him to need me.

"Shit, Astrid," he growled, pulling back just enough to speak. "Do you want me?"

In my heightened state, my mind could hardly process the question.

Yes, I wanted him.

I tightened my grip on his silken hair, silently answering. Our kiss deepened, and my movements became more desperate as I tried to convey my longing while chasing the high of our joining.

"Astrid," his voice was stern and heavily breathy with anticipation, "I need you to tell me what—"

I cut him off with another kiss, sliding my hands from the base of his skull to the back of his neck. I pulled away slowly, our lips parting reluctantly.

"I've wanted you for a while, prick. And that doesn't change now."

His hand met my thighs, lifting me off the ground and onto the countertop. His chin dipped, finding an opening to my neck as his lips brushed against the sensitive skin. "You want me to have my way with you? Is that what you've desired all this time?"

Biting my cheek, I retorted with equal tension, "I want you to take me harder than you have anyone else. Does that answer your question, asshole?"

He cursed under his breath as his grip tightened around my thighs, pulling me closer until his impressive length pressed against my core. It served as a potent reminder of the desire that simmered between us, making me ache with need. The wetness between my thighs became unmistakable, my body betraying the extent of my arousal. Instinctively, I wrapped my legs around his waist, and his lips found my collarbone. He kissed it softly before sinking his teeth into the junction where my neck and shoulder met, a searing sting assaulting my senses.

A moan, long held back, finally escaped my lips, and he continued his exploration, trailing kisses up my neck.

"Shit," I hissed, dragging my fingers up his back.

His teeth sank into me again, deeper this time, the intensity of the bite forcing my eyes shut. My body responded instinctively, arching toward him. His left hand glided over my thigh, tracing a path up the inside. The anticipation built with each inch, and my breath caught as his fingers approached my core. The fabric of my pants was the only barrier, a frustrating obstacle that heightened my need. A whimper escaped me, the sound a mix of desperation and desire.

Onyx pulled away from my neck, lifting his head to meet my gaze. His eyes were darker than I'd ever seen, a stormy blue filled with intense desire. A devious grin spread across his face as he traced the vertical seam of my jeans.

He taunted, "It's a shame your pants are in the way, or my fingers would be inside you by now."

"There's a solution to that," I replied, my voice deepening with craving and an undercurrent of frustration.

His tongue slowly rolled over his bottom lip as his eyes scanned my body. "Seeing you nude will likely be the death of me."

"One can only find out through trial," I teased with a playful smirk, tracing featherlike touches down his forearms.

With deliberate slowness, he returned the expression, reached for the bottom of my shirt, and lifted it over my head. He tossed it over his shoulder without a care for where it landed, his eyes exploring my exposed skin as his fingers trailed up my sides.

"Shit."

"That seems to be your favorite word," I smirked, tracing my hands up my waist to my breasts, palming them.

Onyx inhaled deeply, a low snarl escaping him. Without warning, he moved forward and captured my lips with his. The force of the connection pushed me back against the wall, my head meeting its frigid surface. His hands trailed around my back, unhooking my bra with practiced ease. Its straps slid from my shoulders as the garment fell, revealing more of my bare skin. His touch didn't stop there; instead, he trailed downward to the waistband of my jeans with urgency. With a quick flick, he unfastened the button, unzipping my jeans just as quickly.

He stepped back slightly, meeting my lips again before pulling away to create space between us. His mouth hovered over mine as our gazes locked, a devious grin spreading across his face.

"Would you prefer I taste you on the countertop or the bed?"

Shit.

Swallowing, I held his gaze. "I suppose it depends on how hungry you are."

In response, he wrapped his right arm around my waist as his left grabbed the bottom of my pant leg. With one swift tug, he yanked them off with perfected ease. His teeth nipped at my earlobe, evoking an inhale of pleasure from me, which yielded his grip to tighten—firm and possessive.

His hand started a slow journey up my nearly bare body, fingers brushing along the outer portion of my calf before traversing to my knee. They continued upward, crossing over to the inside of my thigh. A sharp inhale came from him as he reached the fabric of my underwear, his fingers gently caressing my folds through the thin material.

"Holy hell, you're soaked," he breathed into my ear.

A whine escaped me, a reaction to the sternness of his tone.

His fingers stalled, hovering above the bundle of sensitive nerves. "I want to hear you beg."

The desire heightened as he commanded for a second time, and my bottom lip quivered. "Please."

He chuckled darkly. "Please? That will not suffice. Tell me where and how you want me." His teeth nipped at my ear again as his voice plummeted octaves. "Beg me."

I wrapped my hand around his wrist, guiding his fingers to where I needed him most. He followed my lead, rubbing soft circles over the sensitive area, the friction sending jolts of pleasure through me.

"I want you," I whispered breathlessly, "to take me however and wherever you wish."

In response, his hand shifted under my grip, grabbing the side of the fabric separating us. With a swift motion, he tore it away, the cool air brushing against my heated skin. Before I could fully process the shift, his fingers were inside me, the sudden intrusion both shocking and satisfying.

I gasped loudly, his fingers sinking deeper and rotating upward. My legs instinctively tightened around his hips, pulling him closer as he pumped in and out with an unrelenting rhythm. His right arm gently lowered me onto the counter, then reached up to grasp my jaw, forcing my gaze downward to watch as his hand moved between my legs.

"Watch."

As soon as his command came, my eyes met his. The intensity within them made my breath catch. Then, as if under a spell, I looked back down. The sight of his fingers sliding out of me before plunging back in made me gasp even louder, my head tipping back to rest against the wall.

Onyx's hand caught my chin and yanked me back. "I said *watch.*"

I whimpered, struggling to maintain control as his hand continued its relentless pace. My legs trembled against him, each shudder a testament to the sensitivity of my body. Sensing my reaction, he picked up speed, his fingers twisting slightly as he added a third.

"Oh, shit, Onyx." My chest heaved as my hands looped around the edge of the countertop.

He maintained the relentless pace, the muscles in his forearm straining and becoming more pronounced with each movement. Hooking a finger under my chin, he urged my gaze to meet his.

"Cum for me, Sweetness."

His words sent stars dancing through my vision, my body tensing against him as a wave of bliss washed over me. I cried out in pure ecstasy, the sensation overwhelming, causing my legs to shake uncontrollably. One of my hands reached for his forearm, desperately trying to pull away from the consuming pleasure.

But there was no escaping it; my body was entirely at his mercy.

"Uh-uh." Onyx's hand released my chin, only to grab my

wrist, pinning it against the wall above my head. "I believe someone told me to take them however I wished. So you're going to sit here and do exactly that."

"Onyx, I don't think—"

"You can, and you will." His voice was firm as his fingers curled upward, grazing that hyper-sensitive spot again.

A loud moan burst from me, my head slamming back against the wall. At the height of my arousal, his fingers loosened before wrapping around my freed hand, trapping both above my head. His eyes bore into mine, narrowing with a mixture of dominance and desire.

"Shit, Onyx."

"Now, who has a favorite word?" he teased.

He ensured I felt every inch of the exit as he slowly withdrew from me. My juices dripped from his fingers, raising them in front of me to separate them slightly. His eyes never left mine as he brought them to his mouth, his tongue lapping along the length of his pointer finger with deliberate slowness.

My core tightened as I watched.

He pulled the last finger from his mouth and tipped his head to the side, hunger radiating off him. "You taste exactly as I expected you to—divine."

I gulped, watching him shift. His hand, which had pinned my wrists together, moved with him, pulling my hands down to my abdomen as he slowly sank to the floor.

To his knees.

"Luckily," he looked up at me from his position between my legs, "that was just the appetizer. And you, Sweetness, are a five-course meal."

He smiled up at me with an impish glint before he leaned forward. His tongue gently grazed the slit between my thighs, and a whine escaped me as I struggled to free my hands from his grasp. But his hold only tightened, his fingers gripping my wrists more firmly as he licked me a second time.

A moan burst from my lips with the third, more forceful and

deliberate. The sensation of his warm tongue exploring me sent my breath hitching. He teased my bundle of nerves with each flick, his nose pressing against my folds as he delved deeper.

Suddenly, his hand released my wrists, and before I could react, his fingers were inside me again. His tongue continued its exploration, drawing out an earth-shattering moan from my parted lips. Stars blurred my vision again as I reached for his hair, my fingers tangling in the dark strands and pulling him closer.

My climax was so close, the desire overwhelming every sense. My thighs squeezed around his head, uncaring of the pressure. A muffled groan from him vibrated through me, intensifying the pleasure.

Warmth flowed through me again as I chased the pleasure he delivered. "Gods, Onyx!"

His name was enough motivation for him to continue with what he had been doing. His fingers plummeted in and out of me as his tongue worked quickly to catch the juices that seeped from me, lapping them up as if it was his only source of sustenance.

After a few moments, he slowly pulled away, his tongue tracing his lips as he stood. His fingers slipped from inside me as he pushed himself to stand, the bulge in his briefs pronounced. Despite my recent release, the sight of him stirred a renewed desire within me, my core tightening at the anticipation.

His right hand braced against the wall above my head, while his left hand hovered near my mouth. His eyes flicked to his wet fingers, lifting them toward me.

His voice was husky as he locked his gaze with mine. "Taste yourself."

I opened my mouth, wrapping my lips around each of his fingers. My tongue swirled around them, savoring how I tasted on him. I pulled away lazily, lapping down each finger with deliberate intention as I met his gaze.

"Are you going to have your way with me now?"

I reached out, my finger gently tracing along his hardened shaft. He bucked slightly in response, a growl escaping his throat.

Instantly, he wrapped his arms around me, lifting me off the counter. My legs instinctively closed around his waist as he walked toward the hallway.

Just a few steps in, his lips found mine again, the kiss consuming and surging through me with immense power. Every connection demanded intensity, his tongue tracing the length of my bottom lip to request access. I quickly parted for him, granting him his unspoken desire. My hands dove into his hair, holding him close and savoring the numbing roar billowing in the back of my mind.

The feel of a door against my back told me we had reached his bedroom. The next moment, it was gone, and we crossed the threshold. Pressing my bare chest against him, I cupped his face, continuing to deepen the kiss. His muffled moans filled the space as he lowered me onto the bed, my back grazing the blankets. I bit his lip, pulling back slightly to meet his gaze.

"You're so stunning." His hand caressed my side as he positioned himself over me. "And I'm going to cherish every moment I have to admire you, no matter what it entails."

His eyes roamed over my bare body with a look of reverence, a smile slowly growing on his face. I couldn't help but admire him as he pushed himself away from me, his fingers trailing down to the waistband of his briefs. With a fluid motion, he hooked his fingers under the band, dragging them down his legs.

The entirety of his length ascended upward, hard and ready for pleasure. He was breathtaking, every part of him exuding a raw, masculine beauty. My gaze traveled down, taking in his impressive size as his fingers stroked his shaft.

"You're perfect," I gasped as I looked at him. "I want you, Onyx. Every inch and all aspects of you."

He stepped forward, positioned himself over the bed, and placed a hand beside my head. His lips found my cheek, pressing a gentle kiss there before trailing down my jawline. I exhaled deeply, tilting my neck slightly to grant him better access. He planted soft kisses along my chest as I tangled my fingers in his hair, watching as he descended to my breasts.

He treated the first with worshipful care, planting soft kisses around the sensitive skin. His other hand came up to tease the other breast, pinching and rolling the nipple. I tipped my head back, a moan escaping my lips at the dual sensations. He switched sides, giving my other breast the same attentive treatment. He kissed his way back up my chest and neck, nipping at my earlobe before pulling away, leaving me breathless.

"Show me how you want me to worship you."

I parted my legs for him, gently tracing my finger along my core as I held his gaze. "I want you on top of me, between my legs, so that I can admire you."

His knees hit the bed, and I brought my hand to my mouth, spitting into my palm before reaching out to wrap my fingers around his length. The act drew a deep, resonant moan from him, a sound that reverberated through my core and the very essence of my being. Desire surged through me as I stroked him a few more times, spreading my saliva along his shaft. I loosened my grip, leaning back and opening my legs to him fully.

He glanced at me and shook his head. "Such a beautiful sight."

He moved forward, guiding his length with one hand as he gently traced it down the slick slit between my legs. His gaze met mine, checking to see if I was comfortable and willing to continue. I nodded, giving him silent permission. He reached down, guiding himself into me with a slow, deliberate thrust.

A growl rumbled in his chest as he pushed himself fully inside me, his body lowering to press against mine as our bare skin touched. I gasped at the totality, feeling him fill me completely. Dragging my hand up, I pushed the hair from his face and pulled him closer, kissing him deeply.

He rolled his hips back, moving inside me at a slightly faster pace. Withdrawing, he entered me again, setting a steady rhythm as our tongues danced together. Our hips met with every thrust, the sound of our bodies connecting filling the room. My back arched off the bed, a deep moan slipping from my lips as he nipped at one of my hardened nipples, tormenting my senses.

He pushed himself upright, grabbing my thighs and spreading them wider. His eyes fixated on mine, watching me intently as he scanned the space between my legs.

"Gods, Astrid," he breathed raggedly. "I will never get enough of you."

His hands gripped my thighs firmly, pulling me closer as he reached around to the backs of my knees. He spread me even wider, leveraging my body to drive himself deeper. I felt him hit a spot that made my eyes roll back, a gasp escaping me as he sank even further inside me.

His hand slipped behind my head and forced my chin to my chest. "Watch."

I whimpered, looking down to watch his length slide out of me, glistening with my wetness. He plunged back in, a loud gasp leaving my lips as my brows furrowed in pleasure. He rolled his hips, and my eyes followed his hardened length before meeting his gaze again.

His hands met my hips suddenly, flipping me onto my side and lifting my left leg to rest on his shoulder. Without hesitation, he thrust back into me with a force that took my breath away. My back arched, and I reached out, clawing at his thigh as he continued to pound into me.

My eyes rolled back, my body shuddering against him as his hips continued their relentless rhythm. I gasped, feeling another orgasm building rapidly. He reached down, his fingers finding the sensitive bundle of nerves between my folds.

I whimpered, the sound spurring Onyx to quicken his pace. His fingers moved with precision, heightening the intensity of my climax. My legs shook uncontrollably, held apart by his firm grip, giving me no escape as he continued to thrust deeply until he reached his own peak. He plummeted from it, his chest heaving with deep, whimpered breaths, the sound of him soothing me throughout the wave of ecstasy that threatened to consume me—each sound we made conjoining just as we had on levels only I knew of.

Coming down from the peak I climbed to, he loosened his grip, slowing his movements as he allowed me to catch my breath. Lowering himself, he kissed me deeply, his thumb brushing against my cheek. I cupped his face, inhaling the earthy, sensual scent of him.

My lips parted from his as I sighed. "You're unlike anything I've ever experienced."

A graveled chuckle came from him. "Am I?"

I nodded as I kissed along his chest and up his throat before colliding with his lips. He groaned against me, his hands gently caressing my bare legs in a manner that suggested a check-in to ensure I was okay. It was a piece of him I admired after bearing witness to all the complexities that came with Onyx Oakes.

To some, he was a villain.

To others, he was a saint.

And I had the privilege of witnessing both sides.

Pulling away and panting, I collapsed back against the sheets. Onyx's warmth remained pressed against me as he lowered himself beside me. We lay in comfortable silence, our hearts beating in sync. The only sound was the occasional rustling of sheets and our labored breaths.

His hand traversed up my side, delicately touching me as though he feared he might break me. Once darkened with desire, his eyes softened to their powdered blue hue, holding something deeper—something that went beyond physical connection.

"You're beautiful," he murmured, brushing a strand of hair from my face as his fingertips lingered against my cheek.

I smiled, admiring the warmth in his gaze. "You don't look too bad yourself," I teased, still breathless. My hand found his chest, trailing over the familiar lines of his scars, each holding a story I had yet to learn.

He trapped my touch, his heartbeat detectable beneath my

palm. "I mean it," he whispered, his thumb brushing my knuckles. "Every time I'm with you, I feel like I've found something I didn't know I needed."

My chest tightened, his vulnerability cutting through the moment's intensity. I shifted closer, dropping my head to his chest and listening to the steady rhythm I had felt. Savoring his embrace, I lay there, locked with him, appreciative of all we had come to be with one another.

"You know," I murmured. "I don't regret anything we've done together."

His fingers traced gentle circles across my back, pulling me closer as he kissed the crown of my head. Without understanding the depth of my statement, he replied in kind, "Neither do I, my Sweetness."

We didn't need words. Instead, the shared existence of our warmth and breath provided insurmountable reassurance. The moments that made the chaos of our lives more bearable were the simplicities and shared connections. They were the quiet between the storms, where love, however fragile and unspoken, bloomed.

And I finally had it.

I finally had *him*.

But that was only the beginning of all I intended to obtain.

THIRTY-THREE

ONYX

Six Days

I gently peeled the blanket from my bare body so as to not stir Astrid.

She lay with her arms tucked under her head, the backs of her hands serving as a makeshift pillow. The early morning sunlight filtering through the room illuminated her skin, highlighting her beauty. The soft rise of her shoulders and gentle breathing pointed to her exhaustion, giving away her desperate need for a few more hours. Her lips parted slightly, a few strands of hair resting against her forehead, creating a picture of unfiltered serenity.

Gods, she was beautiful.

Running a hand through my hair, I freed the tangled strands that attempted to wrap around my fingers. My palms met my eyes for a few circles as a deep exhale left me. My body shifted toward the ledge of the bed before standing quietly. With a delicate efficiency, I pulled the tousled blankets up and around Astrid's body, tucking her into their warmth.

She sighed, tucking her hands under her chin. The child-like gesture was endearing, but her timeless beauty shone through. I leaned down and gently kissed her temple, a tender smile playing on her sleeping face. It was a moment of pure affection she wouldn't witness. My gaze lingered on her as I moved from the bed, mindful with each step as I left the room.

I positioned myself in front of the bathroom mirror, the rooom was attached to the space I reluctantly claimed as my own, per Astrid's insistence. She had decreed that I take the largest room, even though I had protested its necessity.

I placed my hands on both sides of the countertop and glanced at my reflection, exhaling deeply.

Did the encounter of the early morning entanglement we shared *actually* happen?

My mind began mapping out the entire day prior. The morning had started unexpectedly intimate, a moment shared with Astrid that I had long fantasized about. Following our time hunkered down together, the rest of the day had unfolded as usual —lunch shared with Jasper, followed by a quick supply run that earned a disapproving scowl from Astrid. Upon my return, she was in the café's kitchen with Lila, helping with dinner preparations. The evening progressed with a few drinks, per Jasper's demand, ultimately leading to Astrid and me in my room.

Together. Again.

I glanced down at my naked frame as a groan escaped me. "Gods, Onyx."

Were we intimate again? I hadn't been that drunk that I forgot, had I?

I shook my head, running another hand through my hair as the memories came flooding back.

We had played a game of strip poker that left us both bare, the playful tension thick in the air. Despite the desire to continue exploring her body, we spent the rest of the evening cuddling and savoring the rare moment of peace and intimacy stolen by the turbulence of our world.

Thank the gods, I wasn't so drunk that I couldn't remember another moment with her.

As I concluded the previous day's excursions, I pushed myself away from the bathroom countertop and turned on the shower. The limitations of the community's generators meant I would only have a few minutes of warm water if I were lucky. The lack of time to undress saved me precious seconds in the brief warmth.

Stepping into the stream, the water cascaded over me. I closed my eyes as it washed away the lingering effects of sleep, providing a fleeting sense of comfort. Inhaling deeply, I attempted to clear my mind of the darker thoughts that taunted me during quiet moments.

I walked a gray line between the water and the recollection of the exchange, my traumas threatening to pull me under. Counting my inhales, I focused on the sound of my breath and the memories of yesterday morning. Honing in on Astrid's breathing and the way she looked down at me as I knelt between her legs. Reminding myself that it wasn't—

"Shit," I gasped as the cold water sliced into my back, nearly ripping the air from my lungs.

The temperature change threw me even closer to the edge of no return as I cussed a few more times. Two minutes passed faster than I expected, or perhaps I had been too lost in thought to notice.

The memories I had worked for years to bury threatened to surge from the deepest parts of my subconscious.

I grabbed the handle, turning the water off as the air breathed a path of goosebumps across my skin. Cursing under my breath, I grabbed the towel from the door handle, wrapped it around my waist, and made my way into the room. I took another glance at Astrid's sleeping figure on *my* bed. Her chest continued to rise and fall in regular patterns, her position unchanged, both a clear sign she was long gone and not returning anytime soon.

Swallowing, I pulled a pair of briefs over my thighs, noticing the deeper scars that marred my skin—the blemishes, physical reminders of my past, both seen and unseen. Astrid had never mentioned them, never recoiled or showed discomfort at the sight of them. She seemed to see past my exterior, accepting the man I was and the history I carried. I shook my head, pushing the unsettling thoughts away as I dressed quickly, slipping into pants and a shirt from the dresser.

Drown them. Bury them. Prevent their surge.

Avoiding looking at myself in the mirror and facing the man burdened by the weight of his memories and fears, I grabbed a hair band from the counter. As I tied my hair back, the monster beneath the surface stirred, creating an immediate feeling of unease.

With one last glance at Astrid, I gently kissed her forehead and ran my fingers through her hair in a coaxing embrace before leaving the room with one thought on my mind.

Drown them. Bury them. Prevent their surge.

***

"You realize she's going to kill you for leaving without telling her, right?" Jasper raised his mug to his lips as an auburn brow cocked in my direction.

I swallowed the hot liquid, its bitterness rolling down my throat before I set my cup down. The two of us sat in the makeshift café, most of the open seats having yet to experience the press of warm bodies against them. The sun hardly started its creep over the horizon, meaning that most of the community members were still deep in their slumber, leaving Jasper and me as the only two patrons.

"She was out cold when I woke up. She deserves some rest." My answer came swifter than I intended.

The knowing smile on his face only seemed to grow with my response. He took another sip of his drink, his eyes never leaving mine as he intently studied me.

"Oh, for hell's sake, Jasper." I folded my arms over my chest, the sleeves of my henley bunching with the movement. "Is there something that you'd like to say?"

"Are you going to tell me what happened the other morning,

or would you like me to fabricate my own story?" He prodded as he set his mug down on the table we shared.

I leaned forward, placing my elbow on the table and rubbing my eyes with one hand.

From the beginning, Jasper had been the one to instantly pick up on my feelings for Astrid. He had called out the tension between us, labeling it as accurately as I'd felt drawn toward her since the beginning. It was strange and unexplainable, but it was something I'd accepted, and ever since we'd agreed to share a space, Jasper had been waiting, watching, and probing to get the answers he sought.

The all-knowing analytic. Gods help us all.

"Exactly what you expected." I pushed myself away from the table as my back connected with the chair. "I will not sit and describe everything to satiate all of your fantasies."

He threw a pout in my direction. "You're no fun."

"No fun for not providing you with material to drool over? Gods spare me." I grabbed the handle of my mug again, raising it from the table. "You've never let go of the threesome ideation, have you?"

His smile grew as he shrugged, glancing at me. "I guess you could say that."

I shook my head, taking another long-needed drink before returning it to the table. 'You never cease to amuse me, Jasper. All of these years that you've been a community head, with women fawning over you, and you have yet to pull two of them into your bed to satisfy your craving."

He cocked his head slightly. "I believe you know the reasoning behind that all too well, my dear friend."

He was right. I did.

Years ago, when we were both Command Officers, Jasper had made it known that having a threesome was on his bucket list. But it wasn't the typical fantasy one might expect from an alpha male like him.

No, he desired to have another woman and *me* in his bed.

I smirked at him as I tipped my head to match his gesture. "There's something fun about forcing the anticipation of it all and making *you* ponder the various possibilities."

The banter between us was familiar, a dance of unspoken desires and shared history. There was a mutual attraction, an undercurrent of interest that neither of us had acted on—at least not *yet*.

"I *anticipate* the three of us would have the time of our lives," he shrugged as he leaned back slightly. "But you continue to be a snide minx."

I rolled my eyes. "It's called waiting for brewing anticipation to crack."

"Yeah, yeah. It'll shatter eventually." He winked and waved me off, a smug grin spreading across his face.

For a moment, silence settled between us. Jasper's eyes softened, the usual sharpness in the gray hue replaced by something deeper. The contrast of his black shirt seemed to highlight the intensity of his gaze, making it all the more captivating.

"Is everything alright?"

Drown them. Bury them. Prevent their surge.

"Yeah, everything is fine. Why do you ask?"

He leaned forward, placing both of his arms on the table. "You should know that after years of us knowing each other, I can tell when you're up to your elbows in bullshit. Just as much as I can sniff out when you feed me a lie."

Now, it was my turn to wave him off. I wasn't getting into this.

Not now.

Not here.

"Onyx."

"Jasper." His name was a practical snarl between my teeth as I narrowed my brows. "Not here."

"No one—"

"I said, *not here.*" I lowered my voice to a whisper in a snapped warning.

He raised his hands in my direction, showing he wouldn't push—at least not in the space I demanded him not to.

"Finish your coffee; we're going on a walk."

I exhaled sharply, shoved the drink forward, and stood abruptly from the table. The conversation felt futile, knowing that Jasper's gaze would continue scrutinizing me as I attempted to finish. Sliding the chair neatly under the table, I pivoted and exited the building, aware of Jasper's silent presence trailing behind me.

We walked in silence, the only sound being the steady rhythm of our footsteps. The community center's buildings faded behind us as we approached the outskirts. My eyes lingered on the area where Astrid trained, the faint circle still visible on the tree to the east. The rustling of leaves in the autumn breeze and the soft slap of grass against our boots filled the crisp morning air, starkly contrasting the storm brewing within me.

I briefly closed my eyes, inhaling deeply and trying to force the rising tide of emotions back down. Stepping into the stream of water earlier, I had unwittingly unleashed a torrent of memories and thoughts, rising like an army of the undead to haunt me. Given the dark nature of my past and the world we lived in, it felt fitting but also a mockery of all I was.

For some reason, the intimacy of the previous night had heightened everything. It felt like allowing myself to be vulnerable had stirred up the shadows and secrets I'd worked to bury. After so long of keeping those parts of myself locked away, the floodgates had finally opened, unleashing the internal storm that waged within me.

As I clenched my jaw, I took a few more deep inhales, knowing that once we broke the boundaries of the community, he would fire questions at me.

"Are you ready to talk?" Jasper spoke from behind me, his words cutting through my mind and confirming what I'd anticipated.

"Talk?" I turned around to face him. "About what?"

He answered my question with a shake of his head. "Like I said, Onyx, I can tell when things bother you. The two of us have worked alongside one another for years now. We experienced loss and every dreadful nuance in between together. And as much as you wish I couldn't read you like a book, I can. Between your mannerisms to the dark circles under your eyes," he paused as he inhaled deeply. "You haven't looked like this since—"

"Since what, Jasper?" My question came out harsher than I intended it to.

"You want me to set you off? Is that what you want?" His gaze narrowed on me. "You've held shit in for *years*, Onyx, years!"

"And since when has it become your business to tell me when or how to release what *I'm* going through?" I bared my teeth at him, feeling my power spiral beneath my skin, threatening to take control.

"Since we shook hands and joined arms as partners—as *brothers*. Since we agreed to have each other's backs until the day we died."

His answer hit a part of me, loosening the chains in the depths of my subconscious.

"Since we escaped the hellscape they imprisoned us in!"

Memories bubbled.

I shook my head and inhaled deeply to ground myself.

I needed to reel it in; I had to regain control. My footing faltered, and I slipped closer to releasing the monster within me—a monster that was never an option to let loose. I had worked tirelessly to protect everyone, not just from the external threats of the government but also from the danger I posed.

The danger that was Onyx Oakes.

I exhaled, but it was far more shuttered than the last, the line I rode thinning by the minute.

Jasper pushed harder. "We made oaths the day you accepted your position within our ranks. The promise that we would walk by each other's sides through it all. And that is why I'm standing here in this field with you and asking what the hell is bothering you."

Jasper paused beside me and the sudden snap of wind swirled around us. He had placed a barrier. It was his way of ensuring our conversation remained private and undetectable to others.

A wall. Not to keep others out but to keep the two of us in.

To keep me in.

My breathing quickened as I felt the power within me drum through my veins, building with a towering swell that prepared its crash. Every attempt to drown out the thoughts and memories was failing. The walls I had constructed meticulously were closing in, threatening to collapse.

The walls—The walls—The walls.

Shit.

"You want me to push you over the edge? Is that what you need, Onyx?" Jasper barked over the wind that nipped at me.

My breath caught in my throat, only continuing to force itself out of me in rapid bursts—everything was devouring me.

The memories.

The pain.

The torment.

"Stop..." It was a practical whisper, a warning not to push any further.

He knew the depths of the darkness I kept locked away, hidden behind bolted doors within the deepest parts of myself. I could feel the world's weight pressing down on my chest, toying with my stability and sanity. My body trembled, caught in the struggle to decide which reins to keep hold of.

The internal monster I imprisoned just as *they* once confined me or the need to remain hardened in the face of emotional anguish.

My abilities or my memories.

"I should have never let you leave," his words were delicate, a soft coax lingering behind them as he shook his head. "I knew that as soon as you stepped out of the community that day, you would only continue to bury the wounds you have so desperately tried to escape from."

"Stop..."

"You don't want anyone to see you; that's something you haven't wanted ever since we met. All that time ago, when I rescued you from your burdens and you joined the ranks as a recruit, part of you assumed the worst when you got close to people, and I know why that is. I've *known* this entire time, Onyx."

This couldn't be happening.

"I know that your mother's death is something you have blamed yourself for since that day. The first time the two of us got to know one another, it was a piece of information that you offered up about yourself. Once you confided in me with that level of vulnerability, I knew that I could not and would not allow the darkness from your past to swallow you. Not when I acknowledged the depths of the abyssal blackness we would experience together. Your shadows are not something that will ever be capable of scaring me away." His voice whipped around me like the wind that he wielded. "Onyx, you haven't looked like this since Vix."

The world cracked beneath me, and my power surged uncontrollably as soon as he spoke her name. The darkness and obscurity of guilt and regret oozed from every pore of my body. Memories crashed into me, forcing me to my knees. The intensity of my abilities, combined with the battle against my subconscious mind, was overwhelming, shattering my will to control myself.

There wasn't enough oxygen in the world to match what I needed.

Drown them. Bury them. Prevent their surge.

No matter how hard I tried, I couldn't level myself.

The memories replied as a cacophony of everything I desperately tried to forget. They forced their way to the forefront of my mind, clawing out of my subconscious and tormenting me as vividly and painfully as they did the day they occurred.

I had to regain control. Somehow, I had to leverage against this overwhelming force. I had done it before; it had to be possible again. But here, at the community's edge, the risk was too significant. Lives hung in the balance, and I couldn't afford to lose myself like this. Not now, not when so many depended on my restraint.

I couldn't hurt others.

I couldn't—

Her green eyes locked on mine as she smiled, her freckled cheeks lifting in response.

"You're insane; you know that right?" Her radiance danced over me as she looked down at the picnic blanket under the starry night sky. "How cheesy can you get, Oakes?"

My last name rolled off her tongue with ease, and it was a relief not to hear my title thrown in front of it. With no rankings involved, the last few months had been blissful as she and I got to know one another. Our time together was infrequent, happening sporadically in my bed, her bed, and elsewhere. The way her bare skin had felt against mine the first time that the two of us had decided to lie with one another continued to be something I'd never tire of. Her laughter echoed through the bunkers at headquarters, disregarding titles as she bossed me around, which constantly brought a smile to my face.

The way she saw past and beneath me in ways that I didn't know were possible.

I threw the thoughts to the deepest parts of my mind, locking them away. At this point, I had no other option. I had to bury them.

She tossed herself onto the blanket and stretched her pale legs before her, gazing at me under dark bangs. "Don't tell me you brought me to the woods as a change of scenery for intimacy. You realize you do enough, always."

An inhale shuttered from me as bile built in my throat. I couldn't bring myself to answer her question, not after seeing the files. Not after seeing the proof. Not after receiving an order.

An order.

"Onyx?" Hearing my name on her lips made me think of how it sounded between kisses in every other instance.

I couldn't do this.

Tears stung the edges of my eyes as I inhaled, briefly closing them.

Her face was there—her laughter, her radiant and beaming smile, how she danced around me, the smell of her skin, the feel of her arms around me, and her lips on mine.

I tightened my grip around the gun holstered on my hip and raised it in her direction; before she could say another word, I released the safety and fired a single bullet into her skull.

I was drowning.

I had to be drowning.

The memories of Vix hit me like a freight train, sudden and overwhelming. The rush of bile surged in my throat, and tears burned my eyes, threatening to spill over. My breath came in rapid, shallow gasps, too fast to regain control. I was too far gone and beyond the point of return. No matter how hard I tried to reel myself back in, the chains had been unwound, delving deep into my subconscious and dragging out each buried memory with brutal force.

I was too deep in the recollection that I didn't want to be in.

Jasper's lips moved, but the wind created a muffled barrier that drowned out his words. The surrounding sound around me echoed, intensifying my panic and pushing me deeper into the abyss in my mind. The sense of reality slipped away, replaced by the vivid, harrowing scenes playing out in my head.

"Get off of him!" I struggled against the government agent as he slammed me into the wall, the tang of blood immediately evident.

Jasper's voice radiated off of the tunnel walls, his screams echoing toward me even as they dragged him away. The scuff of his shoes was apparent as his frame vanished around the corner with two soldiers, every cry and plea dying out the further they took him.

"You've been a part of it all!" I battled with all of my might against the soldier who held me, trying to break free.

Gael's voice came from behind me as he rammed his knee into the back of mine, forcing me to the ground. "And I don't regret any of it, Oakes."

"You motherfucker! You're going to tell me you agree with this?" My knees burned, but I shelved the feeling.

"Agree with what's necessary to ensure we don't face global collapse?" He wrapped his hand into my hair, ripping my head back toward him. "Yes, I do."

"They ordered me to kill Vix for manufacturing this virus! They ordered—"

"To put a bullet in her head so she couldn't disclose any information about it? Because she was a supposed traitor of the government for creating such a concoction?" A gut-wrenching laugh came from him, interlaced with humor and a darkness that belonged to someone else. "Just a bit of insight, Oakes. They ordered her to create that virus. It was an executive order per the President's request. He fabricated the files that you viewed regarding her betrayal. I mean, we had to give you enough leverage to kill the woman that you loved like the trained, obedient soldier you are."

Tears blurred my vision, and my mind immediately returned to all the moments I had shared with her—the memories, the laughs, the intimate moments.

The— The— The—

A gasped sob came from me as a scream of rage unleashed itself from my lungs, "I will kill you! I will kill every single one of you, even if it's the last fucking thing I do!"

Gael chuckled, the soldier behind me keeping hold regardless of how hard I tried to escape. "Is that so? I think it's also important to know—"

No, there was more.

There couldn't be more.

"When they did a sweep of her room to clear out her space after you completed your assigned duties, they found a pregnancy test."

No.

"It would seem that."

No.

"You may have had a child on the way."

No. No. No.

"Not only are you responsible for murdering the woman you loved, but you also killed your child." His hand met my shoulder as he knelt beside me. "I've wanted to tell you for a while now, but I suppose right now is a good enough moment. Congratulations, Oakes."

His taunting laugh was the last thing I heard before he shoved my head under ice-cold water.

I couldn't breathe.

I couldn't do this.

Not anymore. I couldn't handle it anymore.

"Please..." My chest shuttered as a cry tore from my throat, the warmth of tears progressing down my cheeks. Their salty taste lingered and reminded me of my utter helplessness.

"Don't lay another hand on her..." My hands trembled as I held the knife in front of me, standing between my parents, with my mom positioned behind me.

My father cocked his head. "Or what, you'll stab me?"

I tried to swallow my fear and stabilize the hand holding the blade, but it seemed useless.

My mom gently held my shoulder. "Onyx, just listen to him."

"I think your mother is on to something, son."

"Don't fucking call me that." I snapped at him, straightening my arm as he attempted to reach forward, forcing him to rear back. "Get your shit and get out of this house!"

"You're only seventeen years old. Do you really think it's a good idea to threaten me?" He grinned, amusement glinting in his life-less stare. "Think about your future and all that you could throw away by doing so."

"My future involves you getting the hell out of this house and never coming back!" I took a step forward, keeping my mom behind me. "Get your shit and leave!"

"Onyx." My name came pleaded off my mom's lips.

I couldn't bear to look over my shoulder at her, knowing that taking my eyes off of him could put us in danger, as well as the fact the bruises that coated her skin from the beating she had received before I had gotten home would greet me. It had been like this for months, ever since his visits to the bar became more frequent, even in the mid-morning hours.

"Listen, punk." I heard the ground protest as he took a step forward. I backed up to my mom and extended my arm again. "Put the damn weapon down. I will not hurt either of you."

"Get the fuck out of this house." I snarled between my teeth, "Before I gut you like the pig that you are."

"Fine." He put his hands up in surrender as he glanced between us. "If that's what you'd like me to do."

A breath of relief escaped me, and I lowered my guard momentarily.

A mistake.

My father's hand was quickly around my wrist, slamming me into the doorframe so hard that I felt my spine protest against the force. The knife clattered from my hand and onto the floor, and my eyes immediately went to my mom.

"Run." The words were a practical whisper but an order none-theless.

Her gaze bounced between me and my father as he wrapped a hand around my throat. Shaking my head, I placed my hands on his forearm, attempting to pry him away from me.

"Run, Mom!"

She looked at me once, tears in her eyes as she glanced at the knife on the ground. She ducked down to grab it, but he was faster.

I watched, remaining pinned to the wall by my throat as he slammed his foot into the side of her head and sent her tumbling down the tiled staircase. The sound of her body hitting the ground flooded through the silence that clung to the air.

She had to be okay...

Please, gods.

A puddle of blood began forming beneath her head, horror seeping through every ounce of my body.

My father's eyes moved from her and back to me. "Look at that. You made me kill her."

A surge of wrath rolled through me, and I unleashed a rage-filled scream that had never torn from my throat before. As I threw my head forward, my skull collided with the bridge of his nose. The sickening crack echoed through the house, followed by a string of curses as he struggled to pull himself back together.

I glanced down the hall, my eyes narrowing at the glint of the knife. Amidst the chaos, it sang to me like a siren, and I bent down, wrapping my hand around its hilt. The cool metal kissed my skin, serving as an anchor in my brokenness. I exhaled deeply, trying to steady my racing heart and chaotic thoughts.

Various profanities slipped through his lips; his voice sharpened with anger. Pivoting, he charged at me, his glare mirroring the wrath I felt. I raised the blade, feeling the cold resolve wash over me, and with a swift, unyielding motion, I drove it deep into his throat.

My vision reddened, rage rushing through me as I glanced at my mom's lifeless body at the base of the stairs. I turned back to him and ripped the knife from his neck, watching in cruel satisfaction as he collapsed to the ground. He struggled through gurgled breaths to clutch at his throat, crimson pooling beneath him. Its metallic scent filled the air as darkness consumed me wholly. I glanced at the blade in my hand before looking back at him, our eyes locking as horror spread through his gaze. Straddling over him, a scream of wrath and sorrow ripped my throat apart as I raised it before plunging it into the center of his chest.

Over.

And over.

And over again.

"Onyx!" My name was a distant call. "Onyx!"

As each rasped breath racked my trembling body, my throat ached. The turbulence within me subsided, allowing my heavy breathing to level minimally. The thick fog of torment slowly dissipated from within my mind. It felt as if I lost myself in a dark and twisted place far from reality and only just returned.

And my head...

Shit.

"Onyx!"

Again, my name. But from who and where, I wasn't sure.

Suddenly, I felt hands on my shoulders, firm yet gentle. A sharp gasp escaped my lips, like the breaths of desperation I released far too many times after being submerged. I could finally breathe, no longer drowning in the torment of my mind.

Jasper stood before me, pure concern etched every edge of his face. His brows pulled together as he glanced at me. "Onyx."

"Jasper." His name was a breathy response as my eyes met his.

Before I could formulate any response, he pulled me into his arms. The embrace was tight, with one arm resting against the back of my head as the other rubbed soothing circles on my back.

"Shit, dude." He didn't let go of me and elected to continue his coaxing. "Wherever the hell you just went, *never* go there again."

While Jasper's hug provided a steady comfort, it also allowed me to notice how violently my body shook. Wrapping my arms around him, I clung to the sensation of his touch, a shuttered sob falling from my lips. I inhaled deeply, attempting to ground myself, and focused on the familiar scent of cinnamon and cedarwood, basking in everything that was his presence.

The doors in my subconscious slowly closed, sealing off the demons that escaped. Yet, amidst it all, Jasper remained and kept me from losing myself entirely.

Standing in silence, we clung to one another as if our lives depended on each other's touch. His body's warmth soothed me, and the rhythm of our synced breathing slowly brought me back. The pounding in my head remained, dulling to a manageable throb but insistent nonetheless.

"I'm sorry I pushed you there." Jasper's apology cut through my focus as he slowly pulled away. Given the hesitation in his movement, it felt like he believed I would plummet back to where I had been if he adjusted too quickly. "I didn't mean to drive you into your darkness to the point it consumed you."

"It's fine." I slowly pulled away from him as I glanced around at our surroundings.

The field.

Away from the community.

Away from all the people.

And along the—

"What happened to the tree line?" I shifted my attention to the foliage that had once surrounded the community, creating a natural barrier beyond the constructed one.

"You destroyed it in whatever the hell that just was."

"What do you mean I destroyed them? There's nothing left?"

As I looked around, everything remained in a steady state of eerily calm, my unleashing seeming to not have bothered anyone. I blinked once, attempting to digest what I was looking at, but nothing shifted—there was no evidence of the trees that once surrounded us. An absence of destruction lingered, but the billowing power surge remained. The lack of debris or fallen branches was almost surreal, speaking to a level of my abilities I had yet to bear witness to.

"That's exactly what I mean." Jasper's voice came from behind me. "You decimated them entirely and wiped their existence from the face of the Earth. I've seen you do it to individual people or *things* before, but never..."

His words faded into oblivion as I examined the opening in the once dense forest, the miles and miles of trees gone as if they'd never existed, and I was the cause.

The ability surge was something I'd experienced a handful of times, but a piece of me couldn't help but ponder if there was something other than my memories that triggered it.

Or *someone.*

THIRTY-FOUR

Six Days

I awoke to a palatable tang on my tongue and a surge that assaulted my senses.

It was a sensation I knew all too well that had become familiar during my ventures with Radley—the distinct, electric feel of a power wielder tapping into their reserves and unleashing upon anyone within range. The mere taste of energy crackling through the air was almost tangible. Mind racing, I sifted through the possibility of what the swell of power could mean, specifically fixating on the night *they* attacked the community.

I shifted, rolling onto my side as my hand searched Onyx's side of the bed, hunting for his body and any level of confirmation, but I came up empty-handed. His side was vacant, the blanket neatly tucked around me, a silent testament to his absence. I pushed myself upright, the sudden movement making me acutely aware of my nakedness. The memories of the previous night's strip poker flashed through my mind, a bittersweet reminder of our fleeting intimacy.

Rushing from the bed, I wrapped a sheet around my naked frame and walked toward the window. Positioning myself beside it, I peered out cautiously. My eyes scanned the sidewalks, noting the piles of leaves that lined them as if pointing to some unseen destination. The trees' bare branches swayed under the bitter morning breeze as the sun peered beneath the dark clouds, casting momentary shadows across the community. Yet, despite the charged air, members continued their activities, oblivious to the undercurrent of power brewing around them and through the core of my being.

My eyes frantically swept the area again, hunting for anything or anyone that would explain the sensations I felt. With an uptick this intense and noticeable, I would've—

My heart hitched as my gaze drifted towards the training grounds where I had spent time with Onyx and Rayne. Someone had breached the thick vegetation, which served as an additional layer of security around the community. A massive hole gaped the tree line, spanning the length of a school bus and disappearing into the distance.

"Holy shit." My words were a near mumble as I stared at the sudden change.

The answer was clear enough.

I knew who was responsible.

JASPER LOOKED at me as he remained seated, his arms folded over his chest, one leg casually propped on the other knee. His black boots caught the light, gleaming faintly.

Like the one Onyx and I shared, Jasper's space was practical and sparse, yet it exuded a surprising sense of comfort. The kitchen tucked behind Jasper was minimalistic, leading down a hallway to two rooms—one his, the other of an unknown designation. Despite the apocalyptic conditions, Jasper's living quarters were unexpectedly tidy and well-kept, a testament to his disciplined nature.

"What the hell do you mean, an incident?" I remained standing, my foot drumming on the wooden floor beneath it.

Jasper groaned, rubbing a hand down his face. "That's not something I think he'd like me to discuss with you."

I narrowed my eyes in annoyance. "So Onyx's power surged and blew a literal hole through the tree line?"

His shoulders raised, "Essentially."

I sighed, "Where is he?"

Jasper looked at me, leaning forward as his arms uncurled from each other. His elbows planted home on his knees as he rested his chin on his intertwined hands. "If you prod him about what happened, it will not help the matter."

"Jasper."

"Astrid." His pointer finger raised under his chin, aimed for the hall. "I'm giving you fair warning."

I glanced between him and the lengthy walkway that led to the bedrooms as the faint sound of a chain jingling bounced between the narrow walls.

"First door on the left." Jasper's voice cut through my distraction as he peered at me under his brows.

I blew out a breath, the soft chime of metal links drawing my attention once more. Steeling myself, I followed the sound, one foot in front of the other, closing the distance to the unknown room within Jasper's space. My hand wrapped around the doorknob, and I slowly pushed the door open. The jingling grew louder, spilling into the hallway with repetitive percussions.

The room was a veritable armory, covered from floor to ceiling in militant gear. Guns of every shape and size lined two of the four walls, interspersed with knives and longer blades, arranged with an almost artistic precision. The array was both intimidating and awe-inspiring, a stark reminder of the world we lived in and the man who led the community. Maps and detailed plans adorned the remaining walls, a testament to Jasper's thorough nature. My eyes swept across the room, finally landing on the source of the rattling—a matte black punching bag suspended from a chain in the ceiling. Positioned in the room's center, it allowed ample space to maneuver around it.

In front of the bag stood Onyx with his back toward me, his fists consumed by a deep midnight blue wrapping.

I watched as his back heaved, and he drew in a lengthy breath, throwing two back-to-back punches at the bag. An indentation formed from his fists as the chain rattled in protest, pleading for him to let up. His shirt lay in a heap on the ground, revealing the sweat that coated his skin. The scars I had noticed previously ran shoulder to shoulder, the light blemishes making themselves known. Some sat higher than others, while their counterparts sank into near lulls. I gawked at his muscled traps connected to his neck, the view unusual due to his preferred hairstyle. But since the entirety of it had been spun up in a bun near the base of his skull, that changed, and I appreciated it more than I'd care to admit.

He sent three more punches into the bag, each harder than the last, as sharp exhales came between his teeth—focused breaths he had taught me during our sessions together. Every movement he made was decisive, the muscles in his back and upper body flexing and releasing as if timed perfectly.

This wasn't a practice session.

This was an emotional release.

Four punches followed, nearly sending the bag through the wall behind it. He switched his stance, shifting his weight with a fluidity I knew too well. There was no hesitation or sign of a preferred side, just as he'd demonstrated during our sparring sessions. I held my breath as he raised his back knee, planting his foot firmly on the ground. His hips rotated with perfect coordination, and his movements were seamless.

There wasn't a chance that he gave me everything he could have during our face-off because if he had, I wouldn't be standing here.

I had yet to see this side of Onyx.

The one known to have separate kill counts. The one designated for solely and precisely this—a lethal fighter.

He executed a spinning back kick in one swift motion, his left heel connecting with the bag with a resounding impact. The force was enough to snap the chain holding the bag, sending it crashing to the floor with a loud thud, echoing in the near-silent room. Onyx landed gracefully, his left foot steady on the ground as he leveled his breathing, the intensity of his workout leaving him momentarily breathless.

The power and precision of his kick were undeniably jarring. It displayed a lethal skill that could have quickly dropped any opponent.

"You just had to break my bag, didn't you?" Jasper's voice came from behind me.

I turned slightly to glance over my shoulder at him. He stood casually, his hand gripping the top lip of the door frame as he leaned into the room. A soft smirk played on his lips, his eyes flicking from me to Onyx. His gaze held a knowing glint, an unspoken acknowledgment that I had just witnessed a side of Onyx that few ever saw. The room's tension was palpable, charged with the weight of unspoken words and hidden truths.

On many fronts.

Onyx's shoulders rose and fell as he worked to replenish the oxygen in his lungs. His back remained turned to us, the muscles still tense beneath the sheen of sweat. He released a long, slow exhale, and something within him seemed to settle.

"You're the one who gave me free rein."

Jasper chuckled, "You've been going for two hours, dude."

"Two hours?" The surprise flooded my question as I spoke.

The sound of my voice must have caught him off guard. Onyx spun on his heel, his powder blue eyes locking onto mine before shifting to Jasper. There was an intensity in his gaze, something dark and elusive that I couldn't quite decipher.

Loss?

Fear?

Unease?

"Astrid, " he smiled at me, and the shadows seemed to vanish once his eyes found me again. "I'm glad to see you're awake."

"I woke up to a godsdamn hole blown through the tree line and rolled over for you nowhere to be found." The weight grew in my chest as my mind returned to that night. "Do you realize what I thought happened?"

"She's admitting that she's a worrywart." Jasper chuckled playfully even though my words were far from. "Sounds familiar."

Onyx looked at him before his brows softened. "I'm sorry. I should have woken you up and told you where I was going. I was more focused on letting you sleep because that seemed to be the first time in a long time that you fully rested."

My heart softened at the sincerity of his words.

Jasper said, "I told her you had a power surge that decimated our second barrier."

"What happened?"

The shadows crawled out momentarily, and I watched him withdraw slightly. "Memories. They're unimportant, though."

"You can't sit here and write it off as unimportant when you wiped gods know how many trees from existence."

"They aren't important." His words became sharper and more defensive, a cloak to whatever he hid.

Everyone knew Onyx for his tight control over his abilities, so seeing him lose his composure hinted at something deeper and more complex. The scars he carried weren't just physical; there were wounds within him that ran much further than the surface and beyond the plains of Imelda's death. He had buried parts of himself, fearing the consequences of exposing them to the world.

But Jasper had been there and had seen it all unfold. He was the one who had pulled Onyx back from the brink, the anchor that had grounded him when his demons threatened to take over. Jasper was the only person Onyx trusted enough to reveal his darkest parts, marking the auburn-haired male as the keeper of his secrets.

The realization ignited something within me; if I could get Jasper alone, perhaps I could learn more about the shadows that haunted Onyx and the intricacies he refused to share.

I lifted my gaze to Onyx, meeting his eyes steadily. I wasn't looking at the man who had shared an intimate moment with me just days ago. Instead, I saw the hardened figure I had first encountered on the rooftops in Region Three—the one who had shut himself off from the world, veiled in mystery and fear of being truly known.

I took a deep breath. "If you don't want to tell me, that's fine. I won't force the conversation."

His head bobbed in my direction as his eyes shifted to Jasper. "I'll get a new chain and hang it back up for you." His toe nudged the downed bag on the ground.

"Tell me why you just nudged it like it was a dead person." Jasper cackled, his eyes rolling as he shook his head. "It's not a big deal. I can take care of it."

A soft smile spread across Onyx's lips at the sound of his friend's laugh. He raised his eyes to the two of us again; some level of return was there as the shadows stepped back. "Likely because it would be a dead person."

"Such a lovely reminder to never get on your bad side." Another joke came from the male positioned behind me.

"And a simple reminder that you truly didn't give your all in our one-on-one." I shook my head as I gestured to the black mass on the ground, "Which I'm grateful for because I'd be that bag if you had."

Onyx let out a soft laugh, which seemed foreign to him for a moment. He cleared his throat slightly before electing to speak once more. "You wanted me to run those plans to Rayne, right?"

An exit plan.

A way out of the spotlight for the time being.

Jasper ran a hand through his hair, his large frame leaning against the door jam. "I would appreciate it if you could do so."

The perfect leverage for me to get Jasper alone.

"Considering we are six days out from infiltrating, I'll make it work." A forced smile tugged at the corners of his mouth. "I would like to rinse off beforehand if you'd be so kind as to allow."

There had never been a time when Onyx indulged in long showers. They were always quick, and I couldn't help but wonder if it was merely a practical decision because of the limited hot water supply or if it spoke to something more profound. Perhaps the act of lingering too long, allowing the water to wash over him, brought him too close to the brink of vulnerability—a place he wasn't ready or willing to go.

"It's likely a good idea; one can only imagine what conclusions Rayne could put together if you showed up like that." Jasper's playfulness continued, though the depth of his jeer went beyond a simple insinuation. "You're welcome to do so here or back at your place, whichever suits your fancy."

Onyx released the binding on his right hand, followed by his left, unwrapping both as he tossed them onto the desk on the northern wall. In what seemed to be the same movement, he bent down and grabbed his shirt off the ground. I observed him closely; how he presented himself had always been eye-catching, but after seeing what he could genuinely do, it extended beyond that.

"You have the plans here, right?"

Jasper nodded.

"I'll rinse off here then."

A snide grin fell on the auburn-haired male. "I promise I won't peek."

Onyx rolled his eyes, nudging a gentle fist into his shoulder before he wrapped an arm around me. His lips connected with my forehead, and I felt his grip tighten slightly.

As if he never wanted to let go.

***

I looked down at the map spread across the oak table, the tablecloth barely visible beneath the intricate web of markings and notes. The dim lights of the mission debrief room cast long shadows over the surface, adding an air of significance to the already tense atmosphere. Jasper worked incessantly, pinning plans on the wall in front of me. They were the counterparts to the ones he had handed off to Onyx earlier, who had left the room with a determined expression and a sense of urgency.

The countdown until our infiltration had only caused the knot in my stomach to grow.

I swallowed, pulling myself from the spiraling thoughts that threatened to consume me. My eyes focused on Jasper's flannel shirt, watching it stretch and relax with his movements as he pinned the last piece of the plan to the wall. The fabric tightened across his back, revealing the outline of his muscles, then loosened as he stepped back to assess his work. It was a mundane action, yet it held a weight of finality as if cementing the plans in place made the mission even more real.

"Is it interrogation time?"

My brows pulled together. "What do you mean?"

"I know you are curious about what happened with Onyx. I could see it on your face when you set foot in my space, and that look only remained after watching him in action." A hand stroked his beard as he continued, "He's working through some things, but he won't be this distant for long. Just give him some time to plant his feet in reality.'

"You saw what happened, right?"

A simple nod.

"And you can't share that with me?"

He shook his head as a *tsk* snuck between his teeth. "That is something that I will refuse to do. I know Onyx well. He and I made promises to one another that I will uphold until the day that I die. I have witnessed Onyx through many phases of his life. He and I have known each other since he was eighteen years old, and the first day that he stepped foot in the barracks, I knew there was something special about him.

"He had already experienced grave loss; I could see it in his eyes. The darkness you see now and the darkness you saw during your first encounter with him is a near match of how he came into the ranks. I promised myself that once he and I got to know one another, I would do all I could to protect him. No matter the cost. With time, that darkness lifted, but something else would happen as soon as it seemed to burden him no longer, and he would fall back into the depths of his internal abyss.

"It has been a battle to bring him out of it for nine years. There is a part of him that is so conditioned by those experiences, those losses, that his mind automatically assumes that is the result. He fears that once he has something good and life has graced him with it, he will lose it. You witnessed that happen to him firsthand with Imelda, and all that you need to know is that it is not the first time he has experienced something that painful. Life has been unfair to him in a multitude of ways and stripped him of things he loved more than anyone can comprehend. He has faced situations that created such heartbreak that would have cost any other person their life.

"And yet, he still battles. He still pushes forward with his head held high, regardless of all they've taken from him. Even though so many have labeled him a monster, I think you can see it now, Astrid. How he is far from all they've painted him to be." His eyes lifted to meet mine, an undeniable sense of love apparent within the stormy hues. "He is just a male who has endured more pain than anyone could bear to think of. He is a male who desires to feel loved to the magnitude he loves. And he is a male who loves you and is so damn fearful of that."

And I was afraid too, but for reasons of my own—and my guilt would undoubtedly be the thing to eat me alive.

THIRTY-FIVE

ONYX

Five Days

The early dawn air burned my lungs, each breath a reminder of the autumn chill. The sunrise bathed the mountains with a soft, rosy hue. Vibrant colors shimmered in the clear sky, marking the start of a new day. Cheerful chirping and other wildlife sounds gradually broke through the stillness of the early morning hours, accompanying the awakening world.

When I left our shared living space, the streets were eerily quiet. Not a soul stirred among the community members, which wasn't surprising given the early hour. My thighs burned with exertion as I ran laps around the field where Jasper and I had stood yesterday. Each time I passed the gaping hole in the once lush, green expanse, I couldn't help but examine the decimation I had wrought.

As the day of our mission to the Capital approached, the hours of sleep I got were dwindling, each night shorter than the last. The shadows of my subconscious prowled restlessly, waiting to be unleashed. Since the decision to infiltrate, I had walked a fine line with myself, aware of the volatile nature of the power I kept suppressed. This was one of the main reasons I had volunteered to go alone, hoping to mitigate the risk I posed to those around me.

But Jasper wouldn't ever allow it, and I knew that without him having to vocalize. I had to accept that only five days remained until we'd follow through with our plans.

Five days before I was about to lose—

"Onyx!" The sound of my name pulled me from the darkness that blanketed itself around me.

My eyes shifted from the targeted path before me to where the voice had come from—a voice I knew well.

As I rounded the field again, I spotted Astrid standing at the edge of the sidewalk, her presence a beacon amidst the frosty morning and the chaos in my mind. Her multi-highlighted brown hair caught the wind, the strands dancing in the bitter air. A smile tugged at the corner of her lips, her hazel eyes meeting mine as the vibrant gold ring around her pupil seemed to pulsate.

She went beyond the definition of beautiful.

Slowing myself to a walk, I approached her, not realizing how much space I had crossed while drowning in my thoughts.

She reached up, tucking a loose strand of hair behind her ear. The gesture was endearing and something I admired about her. Her other hand stayed tucked in the pocket of her oversized hoodie—my hoodie. The material engulfed her frame, the hem settling just above her knees.

"I hope it's okay that I borrowed this." She glanced down at the deep green fabric before lifting her eyes back to me, "I heard you leave and wanted to make sure that you were—"

Before she could finish her sentence, I closed the distance between us and pressed my lips to hers. The kiss was gentle at first, a soft connection that quickly deepened as she leaned into me. Her body pressed against mine with a hunger that mirrored my own as she rested her hand on my chest, my heart drumming beneath her touch. My fingers found her hip beneath the bunched fabric of the hoodie, pulling her closer as I inhaled the comforting scent of lilac that clung to her.

It was a silent exchange, a mutual understanding of the solace we found in each other amidst the chaos. The world seemed to fade away, leaving only the warmth of our embrace and shared breath.

Every aspect of me wanted every façade of her.

She was my everything.

I felt her lips slowly leave mine as she smiled softly, leaning in and placing her forehead against mine. "Did you miss me or something?"

I couldn't help but grin as I closed my eyes, savoring her presence. "I wanted to apologize for yesterday."

"Apologize?" Her brows furrowed with genuine bewilderment.

Sighing heavily, I opened my eyes to meet her gaze. "For how distant I was. I was gone for most of the day, and I don't want you beginning to think I'm avoiding you."

"I don't." She gently stroked her thumb across my cheekbone, her soft skin bumping over my growing stubble. "Why would I ever think that?"

Gods, this was stupid.

"I don't know. I'm just... I'm sorry." I shook my head, attempting to pull myself away but being unsuccessful. Her hand on my cheek kept me there, refusing to let go.

"Stop apologizing." She gently kissed my top lip, followed by my bottom. "We are all dealing with this mission in different ways. Honestly, I would be lying if I told you I wasn't terrified of how this could play out."

She saw through me.

She knew.

"Onyx, I understand. You aren't alone in that and no longer have to be. No aspect of you scares me; not an ounce of you could push me away. You don't have to drown alone; I don't want you to. I see how you are with those around you and want to give that back. At the very least, you deserve to know you're worth it, but I genuinely feel you deserve that and more. You can lean on me. You can turn to me when you feel you're drowning. And just know that I see you for all you are and all you fear."

She pulled away momentarily before her vibrant, multi-colored gaze found mine.

"Everything is going to be okay. We will get through this together and with everyone by our side. We are going to make our mark on history and show all of them what we stand for. I'm honored to do that with you. I'm beyond grateful to have met you on those rooftops and to be standing here in this field you completely obliterated." She laughed softly, her nose wrinkling as the harmonious sound escaped her. "And I guess I came out here to word-vomit all of that. But there was something far more important that I wanted to get off my chest. I've wanted to tell you it for a while, and this may be a leap into the dark—I love you, Onyx Oakes."

Time came to a standstill when the words fled from her lips. Her confession clung to the air, echoing through my mind repetitively. It had been years since I heard those three words spoken with such depth and sincerity.

My breath became stagnant in my chest, and I couldn't stop myself from falling into pure admiration for her. Having spoken her truth, her gaze shone brighter. The mixture of greens and blues in her irises beautifully complemented the dark lashes framing her eyes. They were a mesmerizing blend of colors, reflecting the complexities of her soul. The small scar on her brow told a story of resilience where she had faced danger and survived. It was a mark of her strength and a reminder that she fought fiercely for what she loved.

The details of her beauty were ones I wished to ingrain into my memory because, at any point—

"Onyx?"

I blinked, planting myself back to reality.

Those three words resonated deep within me, stirring

emotions I had buried long ago. They could stop the world from spinning and halt time.

"I'm sorry." I shock my head as I guided my fingers across her hip again, grounding myself with the feel of her.

She smiled, shaking her head. "Didn't I just tell you to stop apologizing?"

My jaw tightened as I took in her features once more, each detail more vivid than the last. There wasn't enough time in the world to truly capture her essence, to appreciate all that she was worth and all that she would give.

I loosened the breath I held, a sharp exhale following. "Can you repeat it?"

She cocked her head, slightly puzzled. "Repeat it?"

I felt my smile grow as my chest tightened. "Yes, repeat it."

"Onyx," She giggled, "You're going to have to be a little more specific because I just dumped a whole feast of words on a plate for you."

"What did you say at the end?"

"That you completely obliterated the field?" she teased, nudging me backward, "No, but seriously, those poor trees didn't stand a chance."

"Try again."

She lowered her chin, bringing her attention back to me and away from the leveling that I had caused. "That I love you, Onyx Oakes, you prick."

My name on her tongue and the selected term of endearment that came after those three words caused my body to surge with a newfound resilience.

I ran my tongue along my bottom lip, closing my eyes momentarily as a soft, almost disbelieving laugh escaped me.

The illumination she brought forth with her radiant light was blinding, casting away the doubt and fear that consumed me. The weight on my shoulders seemed to dissipate whenever she was near, and the world became less daunting, all because of her.

My Sweetness and my Illumination.

"And I love you, Astrid Carnell." My response came easily as if carved in the stonewalls eons ago. "My Sweetness."

Her grin only grew as she tipped her head slightly, examining me. "I'm sorry, but say it again."

I chuckled as I rolled my eyes. "Okay, now you're just doing it to pester me."

The joyous laughter that spilled from her lips with my tease seemed to mend my broken parts. Yet, even though everything felt right for what appeared to be centuries, a part of me continued to hang on to a level of weariness.

She lured me in with reasons that went beyond mere attraction, lust, or love, and that was becoming more undeniable every time she was near me. My abilities surged in response to her essence like a sailor fell for a siren—dangerous and unrelenting—but I'd gladly keep stumbling for her.

A SCARRED HAND clasped my left shoulder, pulling me from my reverie. I looked up to find Rayne standing beside me. The overhead light cast a soft glow and created a halo effect around his head.

As if that was even a possibility.

"Hello, friend." He grinned slightly, his taunt sinking its claws into the pestering I knew I was about to receive. "Slap my ass and call me Sally, but you seem radiant."

Jasper choked on his coffee, bringing the back of his forearm up to his mouth to wipe away what had spilled. "My hell, Rayne."

Riggs glanced between the two of us as he rolled his eyes. "I'm not sure what side of the bed he woke up on this morning, but this is how he's been."

"The usual side," Jasper and I responded in unison as we looked at Rayne's escort.

"You know, Rayne. I thought that women escorts were more your style?" Astrid's voice came from the end of the table as she looked up from her nails. "I didn't imagine that you had a thing for men."

"If we are going to talk about having a thing for men, why don't we hop on that train that Jasper has been trying to get Onyx in his bed with another woman for *years?*" Rayne lifted a brow, his smug grin spreading. "Or perhaps solely Onyx with the excuse of a woman joining them to heighten our ex-Captain's intrigue."

Jasper choked again.

"For hell's sake, put the coffee down." I shot the retort in his direction before looking at my brown-haired friend. "If you're jealous, you could just say so."

Astrid raised a finger. "To be frank, having two of you in bed would be a *ride.*"

Thankfully, Jasper had set his mug down at this point.

I shot a look in her direction, catching her eyes. She responded with a casual shrug, the notion a half-assed apology mixed with a hint of mischief. Recognition nonetheless, even though sharing a moment with the two of them would be a moment of a lifetime and something I'd craved for far longer than any of them realized.

Rayne's eyes bounced between us when I looked in her direction because of her remark. I watched as the gears clicked into place. His brows raised as the smile only grew.

"He's going to detonate; you realize that, right?" Jasper spun a pen between his fingers, keeping himself occupied while his caffeine was on hold.

"I'm waiting." I leaned back in my chair, kicking my boots on the table.

"Is it officially official?" His blue eyes darted back and forth as if he couldn't keep tabs on the two of us fast enough despite us sitting near one another.

"Has this been some type of bet or something?" she laughed softly, finding humor in the excitement. "Neither of you have faith in him, do you?"

"Oh, we do; he's more than capable of securing a woman." Jasper set the pen down as he leaned back to match my posture. "The real gamble is whether it's just a one night—"

"Fling." Rayne clicked his tongue on the roof of his mouth. "Let's go with the more gentle term."

"Coming from the womanizer." I jutted an elbow into his thigh, practically knocking him to his knees.

He cursed under his breath as he grabbed the back of my chair to stabilize himself. "Now, who's jealous?"

"You two are literal children." Jasper questionably reached for his mug again, the break from his daily beverage long enough. "I believe we are here for a reason, aside from banter."

Astrid glanced in our direction. "These two, in a room without bantering?"

A steep request.

Rayne pulled the chair out next to him before plopping into it, his long-sleeve gray shirt riding up a bit.

"I didn't realize we were getting a strip show, too." I lowered one of my legs and placed it between his, kicking his chair back slightly.

"If you want me to get naked, just say so." He snickered as he batted my foot away, "Per Jasper's dying request, I made an appearance today, so the least you could do is thank me."

I shook my head as I smiled, bringing my other foot down toward his chair again, but he caught it between his hands as he cocked a brow in my direction.

"If I didn't know better, I would think you were flirting with me."

"No," Astrid said, "If he's flirting with you, it's full of scowls and cussing."

Jasper choked for a third time.

I rolled my eyes as I pulled my foot away from him. "Stop pestering me, and I'll leave you alone, attention whore."

"I'll be your—"

"Alright, enough." Jasper raised his hand as he pulled himself together. "Are you two truly going to be able to communicate effectively while we are infiltrating?"

Rayne scoffed as he brought a hand up his chest. "I am *offended*."

A purebred drama queen.

"You've seen both of us on the front lines; you know how we are." I shot a pointed glance in his direction, hinting at many of our memorable missions during our time in the ranks. "We can be professional on rare occasions."

"Professional?" Astrid looked at me as a grin began slipping across her face.

I knew exactly where her mind was going.

"Oh, you two slept together." Rayne bounced a finger between us. "I can smell it."

Jasper dropped his elbows on the table and placed his head in his hands. "Gods above.'

"He's a little slow; we've learned over the years." Riggs motioned down at him as he kept his position against the wall. The yellow lighting in the space cast a shadow over his neck tattoo.

Rayne huffed, sliding deeper into his chair. "I don't know what you're talking about."

Precisely.

Jasper raised his head from its position and said, "Alright, now that you two have finished sniffing each other's asses like hounds, can we actually get into the reason we are all gathered here?"

"Please." I lifted my foot over my knee and pressed deeper into the chair.

"The plans I sent you, Rayne, include all the details this meeting will cover. I hope you had the time to review them so that we can cover tabs on both ends."

"Your belief in me as a leader is minimal." Rayne shifted, nuding Jasper playfully. "Of course, I reviewed them, jackass."

Jasper sneered as he continued, "We have spoken multiple

times about attacking from the inside, and I have devised a plan that allows us to do just that without engaging."

"Of course, he has to make it sound like some spy-level shit." Rayne tucked his arms behind his head. "We take the bombs that Lila crafted, plant them in different areas of the base, and detonate them as soon as we leave. See, I just covered this meeting in one sentence, and here he is thinking I reviewed nothing."

Jasper glanced at the ceiling, stroking a hand down his beard as he rolled his eyes.

"If it's that simple, why do eight of us need to go?" The fair question came from Astrid as she leaned against the arm of her chair.

"Because nothing ever goes as planned," Jasper spoke under his breath, his words carrying a weight only Rayne and I knew about. "The eight of us are going for the sole fact of us being prepared *if* shit hits the fan."

"Speaking it into fruition." Rayne jutted a thumb in my direction. "I say we send him in there and let him demolish the place."

"I've tried." I looked in his direction before glancing out of the corner of my eye. "He won't allow it even with an arm twisted behind his back."

"It's not happening." The harshness in Jasper's voice spoke volumes. "Drop it."

Rayne raised his hands before pointing at the mug to his left. "I think you need some more of that, stat."

Jasper brushed him off. "We will leverage Onyx's and Riggs' teleportation abilities to get us to the Capital, saving us the headache of traveling. Once inside their Walls, Raven's cloaking will keep us hidden as we maneuver through the buildings. Between the three of us," his hand moved from himself to Rayne and me, "we can navigate the space with ease."

"I could close my eyes and walk those halls." I sighed heavily, running a hand through my hair, which earned a concerned glance from Astrid.

"That's exactly my point." Jasper turned, his back facing us, before he pulled out a rolled and bound paper. His fingers freed the string from around it, moving it across the table.

The white blueprint sprawled before us, consuming the typical map that had acted as a tablecloth for as long as I could remember. My eyes scanned the layout, immediately recognizing it.

Floor plans.

"How did you get these?" I laid my hand across them and lifted a brow at Jasper.

"I might have stolen them when we fled," he shrugged indifferently as if the act of doing so couldn't have cost him his life. "These are the base blueprints where they've laid out each floor in extensive detail."

I forgot how massive the base had been—we were putting ourselves in a land mine waiting for one misstep.

"The labs are on the top floor of the building, and we are going to lay multiple charges there." Jasper's hands moved over the blueprints as he spoke, pointing out key areas with the confidence of a seasoned leader. Even though Rayne and I were already well-versed in the details, every word he uttered carried the weight of authority.

"How many charges do we have?" Rayne pushed himself up from the chair, taking his place beside Jasper at the head of the table.

His demeanor completely changed, as if someone had flipped a switch—the side of him that rarely made a front.

His playful nature had always been an outlet for him, given that he had grown up in a military family and was raised around the rigidity of protocol. He was more than capable of being in a position of power, but he despised following in his father's shoes and turned down promotions because of it. Yet he excelled in every aspect, shunning the mantle of authority and choosing to present himself as someone who knew nothing. It was a clever façade that hid his true nature—he was lethal in his methods and unwavering in his commitment to protect those he cared about.

A mask.

We all wore them.

"She crafted twenty," Jasper responded almost immediately. "One for each floor, which leaves eight behind that will be utilized for the lab alone."

"The personification of going out with a bang." Astrid leaned forward as she examined the mapped spaces as if downloading the information and storing it somewhere.

"That was the goal." Jasper stood up, folding his arms over his chest. "The best-case scenario is we get to each floor without getting overpowered, plant the charges, and get the hell out of there."

The sealed door of my subconscious cracked open, the shadows peering out.

"And the worst case?" Riggs chimed in from his unchanged position.

"The worst case is we get overpowered and have to fight out of there. If it comes down to that, we will unleash all we can to avoid getting captured." His attention landed on me, and so did the emphasis of his words.

As we discussed the contingency before, I knew what he was referring to—a last-resort scenario that left no room for error. I was our final line of defense, the hidden weapon we hoped to never have to use. The government curated me to be their monster, a perfectly crafted weapon, and if things escalated to that point, I would unleash it without a second thought.

They'd wanted me for years, and I was more than ready to give myself away to the monster that crawled beneath my skin.

THIRTY-SIX

ASTRID

Four days

I shifted my right foot behind me, feeling the familiar texture of the flattened grass beneath my boots. Taking my stance, I inhaled deeply, sweat and anticipation filling the air. Across the makeshift ring, my gaze locked onto my newest opponent.

Raven had braided her hair, two intricate twin strands cascading from the crown of her head. The tight weave accentuated the shaved sides of her head, revealing an intricate flower design etched into the left side and a delicate script on the right. Her gaze bore into mine as our eyes met, holding a steely determination absent during our last encounter. There was something different in her demeanor, an unmistakable fervor that set my nerves on edge.

"I would be lying if I said I hadn't been waiting for this moment." Rayne chimed in from the sidelines, earning an elbow from Onyx, who stood beside him.

"Ladies, this will be an all-out battle between you." Jasper cut off their bickering before it had the chance to begin, "Of course, I will put up a shield around each of you to ensure that all blows remain non-lethal."

"Lame." Rayne's retort yielded a glare from me, which he met with a mocking smile.

"If you don't shut up, I will—"

Jasper interrupted Onyx, entering the conversation. "Oh, don't you worry. You two will get your turn."

Rayne chuckled deviously. "Good, I've been waiting to kick his ass for years."

I glanced at Onyx, catching him faintly rolling his eyes before returning my focus to Raven. Her stance was impeccable, speaking to someone who'd trained alongside the best for years. While I had held my own against Onyx, the memory of his powerful punches reverberating through the punching bag left me questioning if they'd accurately gauged my capabilities, and the seriousness etched on Raven's face told me she wasn't here to hold back—she was here to win.

"The rules are simple." Jasper spoke again, "Incapacitate your opponent by whatever means necessary. The first one to accomplish that wins."

"Easy enough." Raven's words contained a soft venom as she raised her hands to protect her face.

Mirroring her stance, I raised my arms, taking a steadying breath. I had trained with the best, yet I couldn't help but feel the weight of Onyx's reputation hanging over me. The uncertainty of her fighting style, coupled with the intent eyes of those joining us on the mission to the Capital, created an atmosphere full of expectation.

"You've got this." Onyx's voice rebounded in the back of my mind, catching me off guard.

I groaned a little as I shook my head.

"She tends to lift her right elbow when she throws lefts, which happens to leave her wide open." He paused momentarily, and I could hear the smile between his words. *"Just a little piece of information to put in your back pocket."*

I wasn't sure if his words of wisdom were classified as cheating, but they were sound advice—information I already had the upper hand in.

Before I could contemplate further, Jasper's hand shot up, signaling the start of the match.

Raven wasted no time, closing the distance between us with appalling speed. She aimed a kick at the center of my chest—a blow intended to double over an opponent. I blocked it instinctively, the impact reverberating through my forearms. Inhaling sharply through barred teeth to stifle the pain, I stepped aside and feigned a kick with my left leg—a move drilled into me by Onyx.

Raven's eyes narrowed as she recognized the fake. Before I could adjust to her shift, she launched into a barrel roll, her body twisting mid-air as she avoided my attack with perfected fluidity.

This was going to be more challenging than I thought.

"Again, pay attention to her strikes. A side shot will catch her off guard." Onyx coached, his graveled voice rolling through my subconscious with unfiltered ease as if we were one and the same.

She landed gracefully, barely missing a beat, and pivoted on her right foot. Her left leg followed in a powerful spinning roundhouse, and the persona I wore forced me to take the impact as a surprise. I braced myself, bringing my arm and knee to meet one another, preventing the damage from her blow. Her shin collided with my leg, sending a zap of agony throughout the leg I'd used to defend with.

I'd have taken Onyx's sound advice if she would stop throwing so many damn kicks my way.

As her right foot slid back into position, she grinned and raised her arms defensively. Her confidence became palpable as she extended the challenge to me.

"You've got some sturdy blocks." She complimented, continuing to analyze me.

"I guess you could say the person who trained me had somewhat of an idea of what they were doing." I aimed my pester at Onyx, grinning slightly.

"Rude."

I laughed a little under my breath, knowing the minimal truth behind the statement and the overall advantage I held if revealing my entire hand was an option.

I lunged forward, launching a hard front kick aimed at her midsection. True to form, she swiftly blocked, her body shifting to the right with a slight hop. Continuing to keep my mask of innocent rookie plastered to my face, I allowed her retaliated attack to land. Her elbow drove into my upper thigh with a force that nearly buckled my leg.

Biting down to stifle a groan, I forced myself to remain upright. Raven closed the gap between us once more, and I tracked her, noting the tightening of her right fist.

An attempt to deliver a punch while she believed her landed blow had distracted me.

Sure enough, her torso twisted, and her right hand shot towards me. Pivoting on the ball of my right foot, I raised my arms, deflecting her punch just in time as a perfectly trained beginner would.

"Beautifully executed." Onyx's voice returned with hummed praise, *"I'd be lying if I didn't say you looked—Right. I probably shouldn't cause that level of distraction, although it is tempting."*

Intrusive asshole.

I closed the distance between us in a heartbeat, my right elbow leading. Forcefully, I shoved Raven to the side, using my momentum to trap her right arm beneath my armpit. The maneuver stunned her momentarily, and she ripped back against me, but I held on, restricting her movements. She tried once more, and I constricted harder, feeling her muscles tense as she struggled against my hold.

"Now is your chance. Lay her out, Sweetness."

I brought my back foot forward and planted it behind her right ankle, ripping her body toward me as her legs seamlessly vanished from beneath her. She grunted heavily as she hit the ground, and I followed suit. Throwing myself over her, I straddled her hips and raised my fist. Before I could react, I felt the tip of a blade rest against my side, its pressure enough to nearly draw blood—a flawless demonstration of the minimally dangerous woman I wanted them to believe I was.

"Checkmate." She grinned at me, her words a bit winded from the impact.

A groan escaped my lips, more out of surprise than pain.

"Incredible." Jasper's deep voice filled the air. "Your fighting has gotten top-notch, Astrid. We'll call that one a draw, all things considered."

With a deep breath, I released my hold and pushed myself up, extending a hand to Raven. She accepted it without hesitation as I pulled her to her feet. My gaze shifted to the crowd gathered around the makeshift ring, each bearing an expression of their own, but their acknowledgment was notable across the board. Onyx's eyes met mine, his face breaking into a warm smile as he nodded in approval.

Raven shrugged off the eyes as she turned to me. "Nice work. You leveraged some great moves against me." She smiled at me and sheathed the dagger behind her back before dusting herself off. "My only advice is to assume that every opponent you face is armed in some capacity."

I nodded, even though it was a piece of information I'd known for years. "Thank you for that. I appreciate it."

"Of course," she continued, her words softening with a sympathy-infused compliment. "You handled the back-to-back kicks like a champ. Most of my opponents take one and are down for the count."

"I don't doubt that for one second." I laughed, dipping my chin humbly. "Your attacks are no joke."

"Likely for the best when we are out in the field." She gripped my shoulder before glancing down at my leg. "I apologize in advance if I bruised your thigh. If you need any level of healing, feel free to take me up on it any time."

"Thank you."

Jasper cleared his throat as he spun to look at Onyx and Rayne. "I believe we have the duel of the century up next?"

Rayne chuckled as he stepped forward, casually removing his shirt. The action revealed a chiseled physique, every muscle rippling as he brought his forearm over his chest for a quick stretch. The movement was fluid and almost graceful despite the scars that marred his body. Each proved to be a testament to the battles he'd fought and survived—the Eradication Rites, only one of many.

He cracked his neck to the left. "Finally."

"Oh, get over yourself, Cromwell." Onyx followed suit as he pulled his loose-fitted gray t-shirt over his head.

The sun breaking through the clouds fully illuminated the expanse of his powerful build. His hair sat in its usual tied-back position, accentuating the sharp angles of his face and the taut muscles of his upper body. Every scar, every line on his skin, seemed to speak of the experiences and wisdom he held—both from before the Fall and after.

He was a warrior stepping into battle.

"Same rules apply, there—"

"No barrier." Rayne smiled as he peered at his auburn-haired friend. "Thanks, Dad, but it's unnecessary."

"What he's saying is he really wants me to kick the shit out of him." Onyx took his place on the right side of the ring as he delivered a grin of his own to his opponent.

"No, what I'm saying is I want you to feel every hit that I throw in your direction." Rayne raised a brow as he slid his left foot behind him, pure enjoyment radiating from him. "And the bruises on your ego when I'm finished with you."

"You talk a lot of shit, Rayne. Let's see if you can back it up." Onyx mirrored his stance, smirking snarkily. "Last I remember, I wiped the floor with your face and ass during our sparring session."

During my training with him, I quickly learned to navigate Onyx's orthodox and southpaw stances. In observing the two, it became apparent that Rayne specialized in the latter. As Jasper had forewarned, this fight would be a genuine test of skill and a demonstration of techniques they'd honed throughout years of experience walking alongside one another.

Jasper grunted in disapproval. "Fine, but abilities are off-limits. I don't need the two of you blowing this community apart."

"Fine by me." Rayne rolled his shoulders forward, readying himself as he completed his stance. "I won't need them."

Jasper raised his hand to cue the start of the fight, and I saw a grimace cross his face, hinting at his expectation of the fight's outcome. "The last thing I will add is a plea not to kill one another. We do, in fact, have a mission to execute in four days."

And with that, his hand dropped.

In mere milliseconds, they were in front of each other, moving in a tango of strikes and counters I had never seen before. The speed and precision of their movements were mesmerizing, the two waltzing together in a deadly dance. It was nothing like the training I'd undergone with Onyx or the grueling drills of Venturer boot camp. They met each attack with an equally adept defense, creating a nearly hypnotic rhythm as their flesh collided.

"Holy hell." A murmured voice followed the sound of Rayne's fist being blocked by Onyx.

Mykel stood beside me, the stark white of his hoodie contrasting against his warm complexion. His admiration for Onyx had become undeniable, but there was something different in his deep, coffee-colored eyes as he witnessed his leader face off against the world's most formidable opponent with uncanny ease.

My focus snapped back to the fight just in time to see Rayne block an all-too-familiar spinning backkick that had previously destroyed the punching bag in Jasper's living space. Its sheer force sent Rayne skidding slightly, a curse slipping from his lips as he fought to regain his footing. Onyx seized the opening, moving with feline grace as his lips curved to match. He pivoted, throwing his body weight into Rayne and tackling him to the ground, a resounding thud marking their connection.

"He's screwed," Everett breathed. "Frankly, I'm impressed that he held his ground for this long."

"I'm not." Riggs' deep voice cut into the conversation as we watched Onyx straddle Rayne, his seconds behind him, colliding with the center of Rayne's face. "Rayne is more than capable."

Each of us cringed, watching as Onyx's fist came down again. He aimed for the side of Rayne's face with a strike intended to assert dominance and remind him of his former rank rather than inflict damage. Based on the expression on Rayne's bloodied face, it was unlikely he'd hold the same consideration.

In a sudden, fluid motion, Rayne pivoted his hips and bucked upward, attempting to unseat Onyx. The raven-haired male straddling him held firm, riding the thrust with the practiced ease of a seasoned fighter. The look in Onyx's eyes encased respect and admiration for his friend beneath him, becoming a silent acknowledgment of their shared history and the complexity of their relationship.

"Tap so I don't have to damage your pretty face further."

Rayne refused, rolling onto his side and bringing his left arm around Onyx's neck before throwing him off. His transition was seamless as if he'd rehearsed endlessly. He landed a punch on Onyx's ribs, a deep groan of pain following from the male who'd lost mount. Rayne forced him face-first into the ground, his fingers digging into Onyx's hair to flip him over. Before Onyx could react, Rayne delivered a punch, harder than the previous ones, directly to his cheekbone.

Onyx snarled, a string of curses slipping from him as he spit out a mouthful of blood. With an imperceptible shift, he twisted his hips to the left, sweeping his legs beneath Rayne. Within milliseconds, his legs slammed into Rayne's chest, sending him sprawling onto his back and knocking the wind out of him. Rayne gasped for breath, the sunlight highlighting his bloodied nose and the rapidly forming bruise beneath his eye.

Okay, maybe he had been rougher than I had anticipated.

There wasn't any time wasted as Onyx grabbed the knife that had been on Rayne's person and placed it to his throat.

A clear victor.

"Record time, Rayne." Jasper piped in as Onyx moved off him, grabbing his hand and heaving him off the ground in one pull. "You stood your ground for nearly twenty minutes."

Twenty minutes?

They had been fighting for that long?

Onyx spun the blade with precision before pressing its pointed edge against his palm. Then, he offered the hilt back to Rayne in an apparent gesture of respect between friends and former soldiers. Rayne nodded, offering a cheeky grin. His long fingers curled around the knife as he slid it back into its hidden sheath.

"I thought we'd be picking up your broken face off the floor and dusting it off before we glued it back together." Everett retorted as he folded his arms over his chest, watching the two of them.

Rayne let out a manic laugh, wiping blood from his nose before aiming his response at multiple people at once. "And you didn't have faith in me.'

"I never said that, nor did I doubt for a moment that you could hold your own against me. We used to spar constantly when we served, and you stood your ground then. The real question was just how long." Onyx shrugged, smirking as his friend's winter blue eyes rolled backward. "I'm glad to say that I'm not disappointed, and it's noted that you've put in *some*work."

Rayne delivered a hard punch to Onyx's shoulder in response to his backhanded compliment, eliciting a hearty laugh from the latter.

As they moved toward the group, my eyes swept over Onyx's body. His bare chest glistened with sweat, the remnants of their brawl etched into the dirt and grime clinging to his skin. The sun seemed to catch the perspiration just right, casting shadows that danced along the contours of his muscles. A fresh bruise was already forming on his ribs where Rayne's punch had landed, a faint yellow hue marking the spot. Similarly, his cheekbone bore a similar discoloration, the beginnings of another slow-spreading contusion.

Rayne caught my attention as he pranced to the circle's perimeter. Blood continued to trickle down his nose, stubbornly defying his attempts to wipe it away with the back of his arm. The maroon streaks of his life force contrasted with the earthy tones of his skin, mingling with the sweat that traced rivulets down his chest. The greenish-yellow bruise under his right eye marked Onyx's numerous strikes that Rayne had somehow taken without protest.

"Nice work, both of you." Jasper looked between them. "But after that shit, I need a godsdamn drink."

Rayne let out a deep and harmonious laugh, the sound rolling through the group as he nodded in agreement. The others joined in, their camaraderie clear as they walked alongside him, nudging him to start their playful banter. Onyx stepped to my side, his comforting presence immediately decipherable. I glanced up at him with a soft smile, taking in his well-earned battle marks.

"Gods, you're a mess."

He cocked his head in my direction, the lighting catching the scar that rolled across his beautiful face. His icy eyes snagged their well-renowned glint. *"Your* mess."

"My *prick."* I corrected, my smile growing as I wrapped my fingers around his and tugged him with me as we followed the others.

THIRTY-SEVEN

ONYX

Four days

The whiskey burned the back of my throat, leaving a trail of heat as I lowered the glass to the table. I exhaled deeply, the familiar sensation grounding me, providing a momentary reprieve from the storm brewing in my mind.

The countdown to our trip to the Capital had begun, and the weight of potential outcomes pressed heavily on my thoughts. I pushed the glass forward, signaling for more, as Jasper observed me from behind the café countertop. He held the bottle in his hand, a silent understanding passing between us.

"Another?" He tipped his head to the side in consideration. "This is your fifth shot, dude."

I flicked the glass with my pointer finger, sliding it forward again as it rattled against the wood. "Another."

Rayne shifted in his chair, his movements intentional. The bruise under his eye had spread, a dark gradient reaching across his cheek and toward the edge of his hairline. It had been a while since I had gone hand-to-hand with someone, and knowing I still had that capability brought a strange sense of comfort.

He swallowed his drink before lowering it. "Is there something you'd like to talk about?"

I groaned, pressing my thumb and pointer finger into my eyes as Jasper poured more of the caramel-colored liquid. "Nothing is wrong."

Rayne threw his head back, tucking his hands behind it. "Right, and Jasper isn't bisexual."

The comment drew a laugh from me and a near scoff from Jasper as he leveled his gaze. "Getting him to open up is like getting a goldfish to walk on dry land." He slid the fifth glass forward. "I've tried to get him to talk, and he brushes me off every time."

"It's not a brush-off." I grabbed the glass, knocking it back as the liquid's scorch began its heated wake. "It's me not wanting to talk about it."

"That, my friend, is what we call a brush-off." Rayne glanced at me, lifting a brow as his mask of leader slipped to the forefront. "You realize that going into this mission with a clouded mind will only put all of us at risk, right?"

His words cut through the quiet, striking a chord deep within me. They prodded at the fissures in my subconscious, stirring thoughts I had long buried. This reminded me of the countless times I had sat on the other side of the desk, counseling soldiers under my command. I wore the title of Captain, a mantle of authority and responsibility back then. More than once, the soldier who confided in me had been the shaggy brown-haired man sitting beside me—Rayne.

If anyone understood, it was them.

The seventeen-year-old boy in me, untouched by the ravages of loss, longed to confide in them. It was a complex feeling of fearing vulnerability but needing to be seen wholly. There was a time when grief hadn't hardened me, when an internal wall of steel didn't silence my emotions. That life felt like a distant memory, almost as if it belonged to another person. The man who now sat at the bar in the Great Falls community was entirely different, shaped by the harsh realities of a world that had fallen apart.

A ticking time bomb.

"It's Astrid, isn't it?" Rayne's words were like ice-cold water as they ripped me from my depth of thoughts. A level of rage crossed me, my jaw tightening at the mention.

Jasper seemed to sense the shift in the atmosphere. I watched as he shook his head, a subtle gesture that told Rayne not to push further. But Rayne was unyielding. His blue eyes locked with mine, a determined glint in them. The corner of his lip curved upward, a clear sign of his intent to pry the truth from me, regardless of the cost.

His voice narrowed slightly as he leaned forward in his chair, the alcohol detectable on his breath as he closed the gap between us. "Do I need to ask again to get an answer?"

My jaw feathered, popping under the tension.

Jasper groaned and grabbed the empty glasses from the counter, preparing for an all-out brawl between us. Which, based on the balls that Rayne had, was a likely outcome.

"I *told* you I don't want to discuss it." The words came from me in a warning hiss as I felt the fire inside me ignite, burning brighter with each passing second.

Rayne drew his lips together, his tongue crossing his teeth, before glancing away from me momentarily. But I knew he wasn't done; he never backed down that easily. "I'm thinking that someone is paranoid because they enjoy another person's presence."

"Rayne." His name was another warning from Jasper.

He raised a hand, a simple gesture showing that the conversation was far from over. My jaw clenched tighter to hold back the words and emotions threatening to spill out, but it was becoming a futile effort.

"Did you explain the cause of the scar on your face?" Rayne's question was simple yet pointed, and my ears began to ring as I contemplated all my faults and failures.

"Rayne." Jasper attempted to get him to stop prodding, but it was no use.

"Have you told her about your escape from the bunkers we housed for years?"

Inside me, dark flames flickered, urging me to release them. For nearly ten years, I had kept these emotions locked away within a fortress built to suppress their intensity. But now, they were banging on the doors, demanding to be set free. My demons demanded unchecked freedom to consume everything in their path.

"Have you told her why you are as powerful as you are?" Yet another query that drew me closer to the edge of my oblivion— my abyss.

"Rayne." This time, his name came from my lips, a near growl constricting it.

"How much does she *not* know about you, Onyx?"

"Rayne, I think that's—"

"No," Rayne snapped at Jasper before turning back to me. "How much have you held back from Astrid for fear of her seeing you as this monster that you think you are? Based on the look on your face, I can tell that the answer to each of my prior questions is no. So let me ask you this, Onyx. What is the reasoning behind not telling her the truth of what she already knows?"

I was afraid of the truth.

The room suddenly felt too small, unable to contain the boil-over of emotions that taunted me. The walls seemed to close in, the air thick with unspoken truths. I knew the answers to Rayne's unasked questions and had *known* them all along. But facing them meant confronting the monster within, looking him in the eye, and acknowledging his existence. It meant accepting the darkness as a part of myself, a truth I had long tried to deny.

"No," The answer was a near croak as I forced it, raising my eyes to Rayne. "She doesn't know about the cause of my scar, just as she doesn't know the truth about my escape or the reason for the level of my abilities."

"For what reason?" Rayne swung an arm to the back of his chair. "Is it because you are afraid to lose her or that she will abandon you like everyone else has?"

He was pushing a button, and I was too close to detonation.

"Rayne." Jasper slammed a hand on the table, the glasses rattling with anger. His gray eyes cast storms under his auburn brows. *"Enough."*

"Does she know about Radley?"

I closed my eyes for a moment, focusing on leveling my breathing. The tumult of surfacing memories threatened to overtake me. Still, I wasn't about to let go—not entirely—not now when the consequences of such a release were too familiar, too devastating.

I swallowed the tang of power I felt building in my throat as I answered him, "No."

"She doesn't have a clue that Radley served under you for two years before everything went to hell in a handbasket?" Rayne dragged a hand down his face. "Shit, Onyx. You still haven't told her?"

I clenched my fist, punching the bar with enough force to splinter the wood. "No. I haven't told her, Rayne. How could I sit her down, look her in the eyes, and tell her that the male she trusted for so long worked under me and acted as if he didn't know who I was when we crossed paths that day? That the reason that I nearly killed him on the rooftop in Region Three wasn't because of his threat to Imelda but because I have been hunting him down since this!"

I jutted a finger at the scar on my face as I sucked in a breath, and then it was all pouring out of me. I couldn't stop it.

"I didn't tell her the truth because the hands behind its cruelty belonged to the man she had trusted. She had known Radley for years and had known me for mere months, so there was no way she would have believed me over *him.* We are talking about the man who partook in my year of torture and the man that I scouted Region Three to *kill.* I saw him with her, and I didn't know what to do when he didn't acknowledge me; part of me had thought that maybe he had been a mindless asshole as I had once been. Or that perhaps what I believed was him during that year had been mere hallucinations, so I gave him the benefit of the doubt. Not only for myself but for *her*."

Another breath. I had to breathe because the moment I stopped, *everything* would unleash.

"I didn't tell her the truth about my escape from being held captive, tortured, and tested on like an animal because I didn't want her sympathy. She looks at me like I am *someone* worthy of being seen, not some lab rat or the output of a government experiment and torture. There are parts of me, memories, thoughts, ideations—things that I have tried so hard to bury, to forget about. I have worked so hard to let go of this darkness that shrouds me, the darkness they crafted to be, and I just can't. And I don't—I can't let her see that part of me."

I inhaled deeply, exhaling slowly, as I fought to maintain my fragile balance to keep myself away from plunging into a spiral of despair similar to what Jasper had witnessed.

"When she looks at me, she sees the scars inflicted upon me but overlooks them. She doesn't view the wounds *he* was responsible for as definitive factors of my character. She doesn't ask questions or prod me for answers about the causes behind them, and if I tell her...if I tell her he visited me during my time there. If I tell her he was the one who ripped Jasper away from me to face his punishment for claimed betrayal, all while Gael tormented me about—"

Vix.

I shook the thought of her out of my head.

"The way she sees things, not only with me but herself, will completely change. She trusted this male for years and confided in him without understanding who he truly was. He wore a perfectly curated mask around her since the first day they met and continued wearing it when we crossed paths. And while I wanted to confront him, while I wanted so badly to *kill* him, he was never alone. He was always by her side because he knew the second he left it, my hands would have been around his throat, and I would've sent him into the afterlife.

"So, I let it go and brought him here, confided in Jasper, and we agreed we would give him a chance to deem himself worthy of our trust. And he did; he proved himself not to be the person I thought he was, the male who frequently stopped by my cell and shackled me to tables per the higher-ups' orders. Then the day that I finally let it go was the day that he attacked the community..."

Silence.

Rayne looked at me honestly. His expression was not one of disappointment or disapproval but something else entirely—understanding.

My chest heaved as I felt the darkness that had burst from that door in my subconscious slowly withdraw. It was as if I had realized that I wouldn't give it the power to unleash itself and destroy the people Jasper and I had worked so hard to protect.

"You love her, don't you?" Rayne's question was softer, lacking the push that once existed.

I nodded, unsure if I could genuinely muster the energy to answer verbally, but I forced the words. "Nearly too much, and it horrifies me."

"I see it in how you act around her. The darkness that we know nips at you seems to fade whenever she is around you. It's almost as if that side of you finds peace and a place of acceptance for what you were and what you are now because she sees you without question or judgment." He reached forward, placing a gentle hand on my shoulder. "But she isn't the only one, Onyx. *We* see you."

The corners of my eyes burned as tears welled and the rawness of my emotions laid bare. It felt like every piece of me was exposed, as if someone had cut me open and dissected me for all to see. The dampness of a single tear kissed my skin, tracing a warm path down my cheek before falling to the ground. Another followed, and I let them. Each drop was a silent acknowledgment of the weight I carried.

"I can't bear the thought," My voice broke as I spoke, the emotion taking hold as I sobbed through the words. "Of losing her. I've lost enough. I've had everything I've ever cared for ripped away. It's the main reason I left the community for those years because I had thought that if I got as far away from Jasper as I could...I wouldn't lose him, too."

I drew in a shuttered breath and continued to let the tears that contained years of hardship, loss, and wrath fall.

"I had thought we had lost you, Rayne. And I couldn't even consider the thought of losing the last person I loved. Then I met Imelda, and she became another person I'd come to cherish. We understood and saw each other for what happened to us. And then..." I choked on a cry and shook my head, the pressure in my chest building to a near-unbearable level. "I lost my mom, the men I led as a Captain, and Vix. Each fucking death was my fault and is something I will never forgive myself for. I failed in all the ways I promised I never would, and that guilt is something that I will carry for the rest of my life. For hell's sake, I killed Vix without a second thought, even though she filled the insatiable hole inside me. I...I could have been a father."

Jasper wrapped his hand around my other shoulder, squeezing gently. It was a touch that could only belong to him— one that seemed to simmer all of my sorrows and guilt.

"And now, Astrid. She walked so clumsily into my life that it nearly feels flawed, and I never envisioned that things would get to where they are between us. But here we are. She sees me for who I once was, the man before all the loss, and looks at me with so much wonder. She sees someone like myself, responsible for so much annihilation, deserving of such love and compassion. And with this mission, I have been so beside myself, focusing on the worst probable outcomes." I raised my watery gaze to Rayne. "So, to answer your question, yes. It's about Astrid because I am so godsdamn scared of losing her, losing *any* of you, just like I've lost everyone else."

Rayne offered me a soft, understanding smile as he pushed himself out of the chair. He closed the distance between us, wrapping his arms around me and pulling me into a comforting embrace. His chest was a solid, reassuring presence, his chin resting on the back of my head. Jasper joined in, his hand rubbing soothing circles on my back.

They gave me a reason to keep going—a reason to live.

"Here's the beautiful thing about letting stuff like this go." His voice came gently through my sobs as he kept his arms folded around me. "Others can relate to that fact. From what I recall, a special someone whom I intensely looked up to during my service told me that. You are a good man, Onyx. You have always been, and I don't want you ever to forget that. The men that you led admired you for so many reasons, all of which were deserving. And while lives were lost then, you are not solely responsible. You aren't to blame for the situations you had no control over.

"You care so deeply for so many and see people in ways they cannot see themselves; you did so with me. And that is not a trait that many people have, let alone many would carry on with them after going through what you have been through. You have faced darkness, braved through it, and crawled out on the other side as a man still capable of greatness. So I don't want you to think for one moment that you are this monster they've labeled as. You are far from such a thing. You are a man who loves and deserves to be loved. A man who cares and deserves to be cared for. And a man who listens and deserves to be listened to."

"You are a man who deserves to have a fleet of people walking behind him and battling for what he believes in. Because when someone can go through what you've been through and still choose to forgive and have faith in the people who once hurt him, they deserve all the praise one could muster." He pulled away and smiled softly, rubbing my back as I looked at him. "I will always follow and support someone with those traits."

I swallowed, wiping away fallen tears, only for more to take their place.

"We will walk beside you in this lifetime and any other." Jasper's voice came from behind me, reminding me of his grounding presence. "You are a valiant leader, protector, and all-around a selfless man. You deserve to recognize the greatness that you cast on those around you and the love that you have. It shines brighter than anything I've ever witnessed; anyone who experiences it is lucky. We are lucky. And we will walk beside you in this infiltration and do our damndest to protect Astrid because we see how much she means to you and what she does for you. And you deserve that."

A soft, broken laugh escaped me, and my shoulders shook with unshed grief. Words failed me, and the weight of the moment was too great to articulate. Instead, I stood up and pulled them toward me in a tight embrace. For once, I allowed myself to sit with it all—the loss, the hatred, the consolation.

To feel and accept every part of myself.

My decisions, my mistakes, and my trials.

To relinquish control of myself with my two friends, whom I was lucky enough to call brothers.

THIRTY-EIGHT

Three days

Morning light danced across my skin, coaxing a groan from my lips. As I opened my eyes, I caught a glint of sunlight reflecting off the windowsill. Its blinding presence reminded me of Onyx's insistence on shutting the curtains tighter.

Tangled together in a few heaping bundles, the blankets engulfed my body in comforting warmth. I sighed softly, my gaze driving to the ceiling as I cherished the early morning symphony. The tree branches rustled faintly outside, mixing perfectly with an accompaniment of cheerful chirps. Yet it was the soft breathing beside me that brought a smile to my lips.

Slowly rolling onto my side, my eyes scanned over Onyx. He faced me, his eyes closed and lips slightly parted, deep breaths slipping between them. His bare chest gleamed in the morning light, marking him in a near-ethereal glow. Each of his features was mesmerizing and something I realized I'd never get enough of.

I reached forward and gently brushed a strand of hair from his face, savoring his beauty. My finger trailed along the line of his jaw just below his brow before slipping to his cheek. He groaned softly, stirring slightly as his eyes fluttered open. A sleepy smile crossed his expression, a soft greeting that made my heart sing.

"Good morning." I beamed as I continued to cherish every ounce of him.

"Morning, Sweetness." His voice was rough and unused, deeper than the usual crescendo.

A blush crept up my cheeks as I brushed a few more strands of hair from his face and leaned in for a kiss. Onyx responded with a mix of a growl and an exhale, wrapping his arm around my waist and pulling me closer. Our lips moved together, and I inhaled in his scent, a mix of musky sandalwood and something uniquely him. It grounded me, securing my feet in the present and making me momentarily forget about all the baggage I carried. I slowly pulled away, savoring the lingering taste of him and the feel of his marred yet perfect skin.

His eyes were still closed as he spoke, a deep hum greeting me. "I will never get sick of waking up beside you."

"Likewise."

He moved closer, resting his head on my chest, and I instinctively began stroking his hair. A sigh of contentment left him as his body sunk deeper into me.

The moment was a rarity, a mere fraction of time and stolen peace in its rarest form.

He hadn't been here when I returned from my run with Raven. Instead, he had left a note, letting me know he'd be spending the evening with Jasper and Rayne. It was a well-deserved night out for them to reconnect and unwind, but his absence left a dull ache of longing inside me. While the letter disclosed the array of things he had planned for me, I couldn't help but fixate on the final line he'd written. It had mentioned that waiting for him was unnecessary and that he would be home later.

Home.

My heart swelled as Onyx nuzzled into me, his breath warm against my skin. I had heard him come in last night, his footsteps stumbling and his voice slurring with curses as he struggled to remove his boots—a clear sign of his intoxication. I had listened as he crossed the room, sighing softly when he found me in bed. He kissed the side of my head gently before climbing in next to me, cradling me in his warmth before sending me to oblivion.

I had expected to wake up and find him fully dressed, ready for the day. But to my surprise, he had stripped down to his briefs, leaving his bare skin pressed against mine.

A sigh came from him, but not one that matched my feelings.

"What's wrong?" The question was quick off my lips as I looked down at him.

He raised his head slightly and looked at me, a weight present in the depth of his eyes before he rolled onto his back, out of my grasp.

No answer.

"Onyx," I shifted, propping my head on my elbow. "You know you can talk to me."

"There's far too much to talk about and far too little time." His words were monotone but housed a pained acknowlededgment.

"We have a whole day to talk as long as we start now." I pushed gently.

Silence followed, so dense that even the slightest sound would've been decipherable, and it was. Onyx swallowed as he lay beside me, his eyes hyper-fixated on the ceiling, hesitant to look at me.

What happened last night?

What felt like a century passed before he finally spoke. "There are a lot of things that you don't know."

A confession.

"I could say the same." I tried to iron out the apprehension in my words. "There is still a lot of learning that we have to do with one another, but you are the person I want to do that with."

"As do I. I wish to spend and experience life with you for as long as I draw breath. And I can also acknowledge that, while you likely have untold pieces of your own story," he paused for a second, a pained expression crossing his features. "It is unlikely you'd even touch the depth of what I have buried."

There had always been something enigmatic about Onyx, a quiet strength in how he carried himself. The stories about him whispered among Venturers and propagated by the government had painted a picture of a man shrouded in mystery and danger. They had branded him a threat, a villain. But I knew there was more to him than the rumors suggested.

He was a man full of secrets, and I was his mirror.

I watched as the muscles in his jaw feathered. "While I spent time with Jasper and Rayne last night, I noticed many things I have failed to mention—things that have sat on my conscience since we met."

He was *actually* opening up.

"I know that if I hold on to any of it any longer, it will deter my focus when we go to the Capital, and I can't risk that. It wouldn't only be putting myself at risk, but all of you. I swore an oath that if things were to go south on this mission, I would take the brunt of it. And if I go into the headspace I've been in, I can't guarantee I'd be able to execute that. I've needed to air the burden for a while now, and last night, I dumped some of it. But there is unfinished business with you and me, Astrid. I've realized there's too much to risk by continuing to walk the gray line between half-told truth and buried honesty.

"There are parts of me I have hidden from nearly everyone for fear of people seeing me for all I am. You are no exception to that fact. And equally so, there are things that others haven't been honest with you about. I will say that I am running a risk in confessing all of this when we are mere days away from the mission, but it's a risk I'm willing to take." He brought his hand to his face as he rubbed his eyes. "You may hate me after this or choose not to join us for the infiltration. Honestly, a part of me hopes telling you will yield both outcomes. For your safety."

"Onyx, there isn't anything in this universe that could make me hate you. We have all made mistakes and have our own stories, but that isn't something I'd judge you for." I commented, knowing the depth of my story was far from highlighted in innocence.

He looked at me, his eyes brimming with tears. "You can't say that without knowing the *truth*, Astrid. So give me this, and then you can decide everything. About *us*."

My throat tightened as my heart dropped with a building sense of dread.

He gulped as he turned his attention back to the blandness of the ceiling. I realized he did it to gather courage and that looking at me as he professed his truths was too much for him. There had been things to confess on both ends, and I'd known that for far longer than I'd let on.

"I killed my father when I was seventeen." He heaved a breath as the words began pouring out of him like a broken dam. "He abused my mom and me. And while I didn't have an issue being knocked around how I was, I couldn't handle another day hearing my mom scream the way she did during his beatings. I hadn't planned to follow through with it. I just wanted him to get his things and leave—to get out of the house and our lives, and now that I can reflect on that portion of my story, I know he never would have left. I hoped that something would change, but I lived in a fantasy where he'd continue his reign of terror, regardless of my mother's pleas and my threats.

"While trying to protect the two of us, my mom got distracted and tried to grab the knife that was knocked from my hands when he threw me into the wall. He was faster than I was at the moment and kicked her down the stairs. It wasn't just a rough tumble. He killed her in front of me. And the rage that came as a result, I hadn't experienced anger to that level before, but I lost control of myself. I drove that knife so far into his throat that there was no return; he bled out in front of me, and I felt *nothing*. I lost both of my parents on the same day because of monstrous actions, some of which belonged to me."

I wanted to hold, hug, and coax him into believing everything would be okay, but I knew he was far from done.

"They nearly sentenced me to life despite my actions being in self-defense. My father had gained a reputation in our community and with government officials, not as a soldier, but as a successful business executive. So when they found out I had killed them, it was a near-unanimous vote to put me behind bars. But a government official was in the room during one of my hearings; I'm still not entirely sure why he was there, but he was." A soft smile crossed his lips amid the recollection of gut-churning agony. "Jasper saw me, naïve and young, so full of loss and hatred, and recruited me. They agreed that if I signed my life away to serve, they wouldn't throw me in prison. I didn't look back and elected to walk arm-in-arm with Jasper into Special Operations.

"Jasper was only nineteen at the time and on the edge of becoming a Captain of our squadron. And at seventeen, I climbed the ranks faster than anyone had ever witnessed. I passed all of my tests with flying colors—endurance, academic, physical —you name it. There had been an ongoing joke that I would fall into a higher position if I weren't careful, and sure enough, it ended up happening. They promoted me to Captain, and Jasper gracefully stepped away from it after seeing my capabilities and deeming that I was far more equipped than he was. And I mean every word when I tell you I wish that hadn't been the case.

"Things were great until the point that they weren't. I was making good money. I had hunkered in with a fantastic set of friends—Jasper, Rayne, and others. However, the lives lost during some missions I executed still haunt me. Our unit handled executions of those getting their toes wet in government opposition— espionage, treason, and anything along those lines. We were the ones responsible for torturing, killing, and ridding of the bodies— a unit that served as a means of extermination. To ensure that those in power would remain, with no one batting an eye over it. There wasn't a day that I didn't experience an unnerving amount of guilt for what I was doing and ordering others to do, but what choice did I have? What choice did the seventeen-year-old who sat in that courtroom alone have?"

I had to remind myself to take a breath as he continued.

"I had a newer recruit join us about three years before the Fall. Her name was Vix." I watched his chest heave, his voice breaking slightly as soon as her name was off his tongue. "We ended up getting close, and she looked at me similarly to you. She saw past my darkness and the horrible things I had been through, and I truly believed I had loved her. About two years before the virus emerged, those over me informed me she had committed treason. Those in power put together files to show that she was formulating a concoction against the government's orders that would inevitably yield mass destruction. It had been the same virus they turned around and used to decimate the world as we once knew it." He closed his eyes, a single tear rolling down his cheek and traversing the edges of his scar. "They ordered me to execute her."

"Gods, Onyx. I'm so sorry."

He shook his head. "She and I had been intimate with one another on multiple occasions, never really thinking twice about the consequences of not using protection. And when I executed her that night, I hadn't known that she..." He couldn't seem to get the words out as a stifled sob came from him, "...she was pregnant."

My stomach turned as soon as he whispered it, bile surging in my throat with the horrors he'd experienced.

They had manipulated him into believing she was the enemy, a deception that had led to tragedy. He had killed a woman he once loved, unknowingly ending the life of their unborn child. They stole not only his freedom but his chance to be a father and to have a family of his own.

I had to say something, anything.

As I spoke, I glanced down at the blanket, brushing my fingers over it as I held back airing my truth. "I know you've been through a lot, but, like I said, I'd never judge you for any of that." I reached for him, but he shifted away from me.

"I'm not done." His response came as a hardened deflection.

His decision to decline my comfort broke a piece of me as I looked at him, trying not to weigh too heavily on his choice. He was vulnerable, which I had known made him vastly uncomfortable.

"As I mentioned, there have been people who haven't been honest with you." He shook his head. "Myself included."

My heart thundered in my chest, beyond audible. It couldn't be that bad, could it? He had already expressed deep parts of himself that seemed nearly abyssal, so the lingering shadows couldn't be any worse than he'd already admitted.

"As you've heard, when Jasper, Rayne, and I tried to escape that day, it was when I found the truth about Vix's execution. We had thought that we mapped out our plan so foolproof that we'd be able to execute it with no issues. But that proved to be a massive mistake on our end." He bit the inside of his cheek, exhaling. "Soldiers intercepted us, Gael included in the count. From there, they held Jasper and me captive and conducted experiments on us, which led to the abilities we possess now."

My throat was dry, and I couldn't swallow, but not because any of it surprised me.

"They detained us for nearly a year and tortured us almost every day; at least, I can confidently say that about myself. The scars that you see on my body are from the time that I spent in the cells once used for criminals, and a lot of the things they did to me, I barely remember. But enough of the memories linger for a specific detail to remain that haunts my subconscious. Half the time, I question its validity because there were many occasions where I assumed what I'd experienced were hallucinations from the unbearable pain I sat through. I lost track of time and was ready to let myself die before they got their hands on me again." His words trailed, and I knew enough to fill in the blanks. "But there's something else, *someone* else in the story."

Someone?

Onyx shook his head, exhaling as if he couldn't stomach what was coming. "Radley."

A wave of nausea hit me, my stomach curling in on itself in response. His name was one I hadn't heard in months and was a part of my past I had fought to bury, just as Onyx had tried to leave his demons behind. But the memories of our time together, the lies, and the betrayal still lingered.

The one who—

"Radley served under me for roughly two years before they captured us." His admittance nearly made my vision blur, tears abruptly falling as my chest tightened. "He was one of many responsible for what I experienced during my holding."

His words faded.

I couldn't hear anything he was saying if he continued to speak.

This wasn't—this couldn't be true.

Radley had claimed minimal affiliation with the government, insisting that he had grown up in a military family but had chosen not to serve. His denials had been consistent, his demeanor earnest, but a part of me had always suspected otherwise. The look of feigned sympathy on his face, the slight raise of his brows, had always felt hollow to me. I'd known everything about him had been empty.

Lies.

My breathing became rapid.

They had *known* each other.

He had known.

The tears stung as I lifted my head and pushed myself upright, forcing myself to breathe.

Breathe—breathe—breathe.

"Astrid." My name came first before I felt his touch.

I batted his hand away from me before I pivoted to glare at him, my teeth baring together. "You *knew!*"

His brows raised in sorrow, sympathy, or something. Something that I didn't care about. Not because I felt betrayed by him, but because I'd known the entire time that something wasn't right.

I'd known all along, and somehow, that made everything even more convoluted.

Radley worked under Onyx, which meant that he worked alongside...

I couldn't breathe.

His words were a near whisper. "I'm sorry."

"Sorry?" I shook my head as my voice raised to a nearing shout. "All of you knew! You knew this entire time, and you refused to tell me! You saw me with him and said nothing about it! We were with you for weeks, and you said *nothing. Did nothing.* And not only that, but everyone else around you knew and followed your lead!"

My throat ached as the words came out of me with so much fire that I couldn't control them. It was anger directed at someone else entirely, and for some reason, I couldn't get myself to stop.

"You made me think and *believe* that you were trustworthy and actually cared!" I laughed in disbelief, the sound nearly as hysterical as I felt. "You just waited for the perfect moment, didn't you? To sweep in, play Prince Charming, and pretend you were the knight in shining armor. In reality, you had *known* what he was capable of and what he could do the entire time. How could you bear the thought of looking me in the eye and telling me everything was *fine* after what happened? When the whole time you *knew* who the monster was among all of us!"

My wrath didn't belong to me; the surge beneath my skin provided enough proof.

He inhaled, closing his eyes. I knew he was trying to contain himself, but I lacked sympathy, even though that was far from the truth.

"How *dare* you take my vulnerability and leverage it!" The venom spewed from me as I narrowed my blurred glance at him.

"How could I have told you?!" His voice boomed through the space to match my volume, "You *didn't* trust me! Can you truly think, for one moment, that if I told you at the beginning that he wasn't to be trusted, you would've believed me? I *wanted* nothing more than to tell you, but I knew no ounce of you would've taken my word. Not only that, but he didn't look at me as he had when I was his Captain; he looked at me like a stranger." He ran a distressed hand through his hair, trying to justify where he went wrong, but it wasn't him. It was me, and I was projecting. "When I saw him in a Venturer uniform with you, it made sense that he would serve. It made sense that he would still follow the govern-ment. And when he looked past me, I thought that he—"

"I don't care what you thought!" my voice broke as I looked at him. "You *lied* to me!"

The look on his face nearly shattered my heart just as the ire-filled words fractured his. I was nothing more than a hypocrite as uncontrolled venom spewed from my tongue, and the mix of pain and knowing on his face suggested that he'd anticipated this reaction.

And that hurt far more.

His gaze pulled away from me as he sighed. "I know, and all I can say is that I'm truly sorry."

"You are no different than him; you realize that, *right?*" I regretted the programmed words as soon as they left my lips, but I couldn't stop. "Regardless of knowing for sure if he handled your torture, you led him into this community willingly. You *knew* that he had been there the night that Gael interfered, and you *knew* the type of person he was and who he served. Logically, putting those pieces together, you *knew* who Radley was loyal to. And you still chose to bring him inside these walls. The walls of the people you say you vowed to protect!"

I tried to stop myself because I'd predicted what was coming —an attack so low and full of destruction. One that I knew would ultimately destroy him, but I couldn't slow the words as they spilled from me without my control.

"It's *your* fault the attack happened that night. It's *your* fault that Imelda is dead!"

The entire world cracked beneath me as I finished my sentence, my breath catching in my throat. In my heated rage, the unseen leveraged the one point I knew would hurt him deeply.

The night that he still hadn't forgiven himself for, the guilt that remained trapped inside him.

The nights I had spent with him, sharing words of reassurance that it wasn't his fault, all disintegrated at that moment.

His eyes said enough. With his brows pulled together, he shifted his gaze past me and ran a hand down his face, tears building and intermixing with a sense of betrayal. He pushed himself up from the bed, turning his back to me, saying nothing.

My chest ached as I sank back from my peak, realizing the damage I'd caused. I wanted to apologize, hug him, and reassure him I had meant none of it—that it wasn't *me*.

I understood why he did what he did, why they all had because I was doing the same. But it was too late.

A shuttered breath escaped me as the billowing surge swarming my veins dissipated, my thunderous heartbeat slowing to a near-standstill.

He bent down, grabbed his pants off the floor, and pulled them over his legs before reaching for a shirt. My heart sank even more at the regret fueling his movements, the anguish I had caused beyond recognizable. I could see the open wounds I had worked so hard to mend, completely unwind, and reopen.

All because of me.

He shoved his feet into his boots and worked to fasten them, tightening the laces before pushing himself upright and finally looking in my direction. The heartbreak that billowed off him made me practically crumble to my knees and reveal all the baggage I'd carried. The secrets that tangled all of us together in a web too convoluted for explanation. At that moment, I wanted him to hate me because I knew it would be far easier than this.

He clenched his jaw before speaking. "There was a piece of me that was so lost when I found you two on the rooftops that day. I reflected a lot on the pain I had caused people around me, people I loved. And when I saw the two of you together, when I saw him, I was ready to avenge myself for the damage he'd caused. But when I saw your face, the panic that overcame you at that moment, I knew I couldn't strip him from you." He swallowed, practically forcing himself to keep going. "I saw myself in you, the scared seventeen-year-old who wanted nothing more than safety."

I had to move. I had to apologize. I had to—

"So instead of killing him, I decided against it because I had already been responsible for so many deaths in my lifetime. I was trying to work away from that and become a better person, and I wanted to show that to Imelda. I wanted to show her that there was greatness in this world, regardless of how haunting it had been. Irrespective of the loss we had experienced and all that others had because of my doing. I saw your vulnerability, but most of all, your love for him.

"The moment we locked eyes, your expression brought back everything I'd worked to bury. The moment I watched my mom's fleeting attempt to protect me, resulting in her death. To the men who looked me in the eyes as they begged for their lives. To the night with Vix when I put a bullet in between her eyes, and she stared at me like her world had just crumbled. I saw and felt all the fear, so I spared him. Not for anyone else but *you*.

"So, it may be my fault that I saw some good in him. And it may equally be my fault for bringing him here and putting everyone in danger." His voice broke slightly, the tether between us fizzling to a barely lit ember. "And sure, it's my fault that Imelda lost her life at such a young age and in such a horrific way. But I *hope* if there's one thing you can see at the end, I did so for *you*, Astrid.

"The decisions that I made that day are ones I can't go back and re-trace, just as I can't take back the choice I made by keeping his truth from you. But part of me refused to rob you of that happiness because I had already done so with enough people in my lifetime. And maybe that makes me selfish, but I'd rather give people the chance to enjoy their solitude than completely strip it away from them."

He turned on his heel, reaching for the door handle. His hand tightened around it as I watched his shoulders rise and fall in breathy waves.

"Onyx." His name was barely audible off of my lips as I watched him pull the door open.

"I'm sorry for the damage that I caused you and the pain that I worked so hard to avoid. I'm sorry for keeping things from you because I refused to become that shrouded cloud again. I'm sorry for leading you to believe I'm *anything* like those responsible for the destruction you witnessed. And I'm sorry for all the lives I'm responsible for taking." He stepped through the threshold before the last sentence left him, forcing me to my knees. "But there isn't an ounce of me that is sorry for doing what I could to protect you. Nor is there a piece of me that is sorry for falling in love with you."

And with that, he walked through the door and shut it behind him as I knelt in his room.

I buried my face in my hands, sobs wracking my body as the weight of the past and present collided. Everything I thought I knew vanished, and only one thing remained—resolve forged in the crucible of my secrecy and promises.

THIRTY-NINE

Three days

I stood before the mission plans pinned to the wall of the debrief room, my eyes scanning the intricate details. Each blueprint, each marked route, burned itself into the darkest recesses of my mind. The facility's layout stretched across the oak table, obscuring the map beneath it. The walkways and hallways I had frequented etched themselves into my memory, reminding me of past missions and the dangers that lurked within.

I didn't have long

I knew Jasper was out on a mid-morning scavenge with a few of his trusted right hands and Rayne. The details of his planned scouting had come up during our conversation the night before, and that had only meant one thing—the window of opportunity was open.

I could act on my plan to go to the Capital—without them.

I was tired of leading others into catastrophe. Jasper hadn't objected to me going in alone because he doubted my abilities or commitment to the Rebellion. No, his hesitation stemmed from a deeper concern—he knew I would enter the fray with a score to settle, driven by the dangerous combination of rage and a sense of nothing left to lose.

But, at one point, it ceased to be a cause of concern.

Astrid had stepped into the picture and confessed her love for me, pulling me from those ideations. She helped pull me out of the darkest moments of my life when I felt like I was drowning. She looked at me with so much love and understanding, an expression I hadn't seen in years. I had known from the moment that I tackled her to the ground in the bunker the night of the attack that she would be different.

That she would make a difference, and she had.

She had brought warmth to my freezing hatred, a balm to my inner turmoil. She had seen the intimate parts of me, never flinching or questioning the darkness that threatened to consume me. Her unwavering support had been a lifeline, pulling me back from the brink more times than I could count. She'd been an immediate draw, a lure I couldn't quite figure out. She had been there during one of the gravest moments of my life and had somehow saved me from the abyss I had—

"It's your *fault the attack happened that night. It's* your *fault that Imelda is dead!"*

My hands trembled as I recalled Astrid's words and how she looked at me that morning. It had begun like a dream, lying in her arms, her warmth comforting against the cold reality of our world. But I couldn't stay beside her, burdened by the weight of my secrets and the darkness I carried. Revealing the truth would only bring destruction, and I hadn't yet fully comprehended the extent of the damage it could cause.

There was nothing left of me to destroy.

Once again, I became the shell of the man she had faced on the rooftops—the one who fought an internal battle every day, surviving only for the sake of Imelda. I was the one responsible for countless deaths, including that of a young girl whose bright eyes had once shone with hope. Now, I was a man with nothing left to lose, a dangerous edge sharpening within me.

The monster.

I cursed under my breath, snapping back to the present. My eyes flicked between the blue lines on the stark white paper. I braced my hands on the table, steadying myself as the floodgates of my subconscious swung open. I knew that if I didn't leave soon, I would only cause more harm.

I had done enough damage and left enough scars. It was a proven fact—everyone I crossed paths with somehow became tainted. No one who stood beside me would escape unscathed. The fire within me would inevitably consume them, leaving nothing but ashes in its wake. It was time I made the ultimate sacrifice for those I cared about. If I had to be the sacrificial lamb for the good of thousands, then so be it.

I couldn't allow this mission to continue. If any of them stepped foot in that facility, there would be only one outcome— Death—and the thought was unbearable. I had been the harbinger of danger for too long and couldn't bear to see it happen again. Fueled by enough reasons to avenge those wronged, I had enough rage for my last stand. I would be the one to step in front of the bullet, to take the hit meant for them.

I was the Wanted one, feared by the masses, and I was about to prove exactly why, regardless of what the outcome would mean for me.

I knew I had a few choices at this crucial juncture. A part of me wanted to disappear without a trace, to go radio silent and leave no hint that I had ever left the safety of the walls Jasper had built. Maybe then they wouldn't know where to look if they even deemed me worth the search. But another part of me knew I couldn't leave everything behind—the maps, the blueprints, the plans...

They'd follow me.

"Pull your shit together."

I ran a hand down my face, feeling the roughness of my growing stubble as I grabbed the blueprints from the table. I pivoted and began ripping the plans from the wall one page at a time, the paper shredding beneath my touch. The risk of Jasper and Rayne knowing about the facilities loomed large, but it was a hurdle I was willing to face. This was my choice, my burden to bear.

Hopefully, it was a large enough one to slow them down.

Everything I had ever done was for someone else. I wielded the knife that day to protect my mother. I joined Special Operations to help the world. I became a Captain to lead my squadron. I pulled the trigger that night to save humanity. I tried to see the best in Radley for *her* sake. And now, I would do this to save them all, even if it was the last thing I did.

I tried to force down the lump in my throat as I reached for the pad of paper on the table and a pen.

I knew Jasper would blame himself for this and come to believe he'd failed somehow. But the truth was, I was flawed and had to distance myself before I tainted their futures—before I placed any more burden or pain on the people I loved most, on the woman who seemed to consume every essence of my being.

It would be worth it.

I took a deep breath before I lowered my hand and wrote, allowing the stream of tears to begin.

FORTY

JASPER

Three days

I hauled the bag over my shoulder as I walked through the streets with Rayne by my side.

The sun crept through the dark clouds overhead, casting intermittent light on the buildings that lined our community. It had to be mid-morning, which meant we had likely been out scavenging for a few hours. Despite the passage of time, our haul had been more successful than expected.

The streets were bustling with activity as people moved about, their days having started an hour or two earlier. As we passed, I greeted a few familiar faces, heading toward the debriefing room to take inventory of everything we had secured.

But despite all our successes, there was something off.

I could feel it in the very center of my being.

Rayne groaned as he shifted the bag he'd elected to haul on his back. "Of course, you had to make me carry the heavier of the two."

"I think that's a delayed complaint, considering we are already back." I nudged an elbow into his side, and he scoffed in reply as we continued our pace.

Something was *definitely* off.

The bell that hung above the door chimed as Rayne slammed his body into it. "Yeah, well, I will complain if I want to."

Before I could reply, I halted, my eyes locking on the wall before us. The usual maps still hung in their customary positions, but the multiple pages of mission plans were *missing*.

As I took another step forward, the bag slipped from my hand and crashed to the floor. The blueprints I had meticulously spread across the table were also gone, and my stomach dropped as the realization hit me like a punch to the gut.

"What the hell..." Rayne said breathlessly as he turned to face the space, his bag released beside mine. "Where did it all go?"

I shook my head, suspicion and dread burrowing deeper into my chest. I crossed the room to the table, my steps quickening with urgency. The notepad that usually sat at the head of the table, where I kept detailed notes, was moved to the center, a pen lying haphazardly across the top.

No.

The weight in my chest intensified as I leaned over and snatched it from the table. Large, hurried, yet oddly neat handwriting covered an entire sheet. It was a script I knew well, one I had seen many times before.

Onyx.

Rayne's questions drowned out as I felt my knees buckle beneath me. Lowering myself to the chair, I began reading.

> *Jasper, A part of me already knows your reaction as you read this—a level of betrayal and Resentment that is justified. If anything, I hope it makes you hate me enough that you finally let me go, although I already realize that is far from possible. I know that every ounce of you worked to prevent this kind of situation, but I want to tell*

you that my decision to go against your orders has nothing to do with you and <u>everything</u> to do with me.

If we are being honest, it was naïve of me to assume that I would experience any level of solitude in my life. It just wasn't something the universe destined me to have. And I don't want to sit and wallow in my sorrow because that isn't what this letter is about. This letter is a thank you, the words I wish I could have given you myself, but I could never formulate them. You were the one person who saw my darkness and pulled me under your wing. I mean, for hell's sake, you rescued my sorry ass all those years ago, and I can genuinely say that without your guidance, I don't know where I would be.

Thank you for your greatness, kindness, and passion for helping others. For all that you taught me and all that you will continue to teach others. For the protection you give to the community you run. Thank you for simply being the man you have been for so many people and the man you were for me. There are pieces of you that are engrained in my soul and portions of myself that I am still coming to terms with when I think about us and all we experienced. Together. Now that we are past the sappy shit, because I know neither of us does well with it, let's get into the more serious matters.

As you can see, someone has taken the mission plans and blueprints. Not a traitor but me (although maybe I am one now?). There's no point in looking for them because they exist only as ash now. I also destroyed the bombs you had Lila make, and while I can feel your radiating anger as you read this, please know that I did this for all of you. My last requests are the following and are relatively simple. Do NOT come looking for me, no matter how badly you desire to. I am begging you to <u>live</u> your life. Live your life for me when I couldn't live for Imelda. Continue to lead this community valiantly and walk alongside the people who look up to you so heavily. Let Rayne visit frequently, as I know the two of you probably need that. And please, keep a close arm wrapped around Astrid and tell her how much I loved her. But most of all, please try to hold on and recall how much I love you. My decision to go through with this has nothing to do with any level of punishment for any of you. None of you have done anything wrong that has led to this moment. It may have been a long time coming when you look at the map of my life. And yeah, maybe it is selfish of me. But this is my final stand to keep you out of harm's way and ensure your safety while continuing to revolt against the government we once worked for.

I am doing this for the entire Rebellion and the future of it, for the people you lead so selflessly, and for every individual who has made a grave impact on my pathetic life. So thank you—time and time again. Thank you for all that you have done and all that you have ever been for me. Thank you for being an incredible leader and, most of all, an incredible friend. I love you, Jasper, and I hope you never allow yourself to forget that. Perhaps we will get another chance in another life that will, hopefully, be vastly different. Signing off, Onyx Oakes.

My breath caught in my throat, my eyes blurring with unshed tears and unshared feelings. My fist tightened around the paper, crumpling it slightly. Every effort I had made to ensure Onyx wouldn't go AWOL had been in vain. Every command I had given for this mission seemed useless now. Onyx had always been the type to follow his own path, regardless of the risks.

The weight of my failure crushed me, anger and frustration bubbling to the surface. My responsibility for Onyx's safety had begun the day he signed away his life in that courtroom, and now I had failed him. Despite my efforts to protect him and ensure he could live for himself, everything had fallen apart.

I forced myself up from my seated position at the table, wrapping my hands around its edge and flipping it onto its side. The chair behind me crashed to the ground, echoing my frustration. *"FUCK!"*

Rayne shook his head, realization crossing his face as his shoulders sunk. "Don't tell me that—"

"He took every ounce of our plan, destroyed it, and went off on his own." Rage fueled my response but failed to expose my disappointment in myself. "I should have *seen* this coming, dammit!"

I threw the letter to the floor, taking a deep, steadying breath. I knew Onyx had already left the community and was heading for the Capital. There wasn't time to sit and wall in defeat—I had to act now.

Rayne bent down and picked up the paper, carefully smoothing out the creases so he could read it. I paced the room, running a hand through my hair, my mind racing with everything I should have said but never did. As Rayne read, his face contorted to match the emotions that billowed within me. When he finished, he shook his head, tearing the letter in half and letting the pieces fall to the ground.

"No, fuck that." He looked up at me, his eyes filling with tears. "I *refuse* to allow him to step in there with some expectation that we won't follow him. That we won't battle *with* him and *for* him. He led us for years and stood by all of us during that time. If he is truly stubborn enough to believe that we won't hunt for him, that's fine. But I am not and *will not* stay here when I know he is out there on our behalf. Not after what he went through during that year, Jasper."

I dipped my chin in acknowledgment, glancing at the overturned oak table and the surrounding disarray. The explosion of my vexation could have been more detrimental if I'd tapped into the abilities I consistently kept under wraps. While the ire I held wasn't directed at Onyx, I couldn't help but find myself spiraling into an internal slew of self-deprecation.

I had assumed he was okay and had come to terms with his past, but the reality was he was still fighting internal battles. It struck me like a freight train—he had called me selfless, yet he willingly stepped into a situation with a known and highly inevitable outcome. I couldn't allow him to sacrifice himself for the rest of us. There were still things I needed to tell him, feelings I hadn't fully expressed. Settled with my decision, my hardened stare lifted to look at Rayne, and the command left my lips with ease.

"I don't give a damn about his request. We are going after him. Gather everyone. We leave tonight."

FORTY-ONE

ONYX

Eight hours

The fresh aroma of rain filled the air as it pattered against the surface beneath me, casting a gloomy veil across the horizon.

I pulled the hood of my jacket over my head and nestled myself among the shadows cast by the building I stood on. Hiding in the mid-morning hours would have been practically impossible during the spring or summer months, but the darkness brought by the looming fall storm provided the perfect cover. It all felt familiar, akin to the times I had served. Lurking in the darkness to fulfill a mission, leveraging the knowledge I had gathered—it all came rushing back as if it were second nature.

They'd constructed the Walls around the Capital's base with far more intention than other communities. During my past excursions to different bases, I had grown familiar with the concrete structures built for protection around their perimeters— effective in keeping out the atypical threats. But what stood before me under the tenebrous sky was a different league altogether.

Large steel slats shot themselves skyward, engulfing what they stood in arms to safeguard. The Walls were so high that even the tallest building I now stood on couldn't see inside them, the facilities inside containing far too many undisclosed secrets. I watched soldiers converse with one another at one of the fortresses' entrances, a massive metal gate working in tandem with its matching Walls. A military vehicle had stopped to likely exchange some level of clearance paperwork, a process that I was far too intimate with.

The entirety of it was well-guarded and protected against anything other than the unseen, looming threat.

They'd curated a false sense of security, believing their defenses would effectively keep many out, but they didn't account for an attack from someone capable of decimating their operation without setting foot inside.

A smile spread across my lips as I felt my power hum an internal symphony. Its energy pulsed through me, vibrant and alive, as if it were searching for something—a missing piece.

I had held back for the longest time because of the intensity of my abilities—depths I hadn't explored in years, the abyssal demon buried within me. The chains in the depths of my subconscious slowly released the monster they had shackled, the doors in my mind opening as the darkness seeped out. The person they had kept chained to tables and tormented for hours, days, and months on end was finally surfacing for retribution.

This moment had been a long time coming, and now that it had finally arrived, I allowed myself to devour its glory.

It felt like gears clicked into place as the hair on my arms stood in the onslaught of the merge. My grin continued to expand as I felt the pulsation of rapturous delight—pure ecstasy. The shift was almost instant, and my power snapped into place. A circular path of energy ran through me like an electric circuit, the thrum causing me to shudder slightly.

Not in pain, but *pure* satisfaction.

I directed my attention back to the soldiers below, observing their methodical movements as if the higher-ups had prescribed the same task to them for months. Each step was precise, with no room for error. The dark hue of their uniforms nearly camouflaged them into the Walls, but their movement helped me pinpoint their location.

As if they were chess pieces waiting to be moved.

I closed my eyes for a brief second, inhaling deeply as galaxies and eons flashed across my vision. I tipped my head back, relishing in the metallic tang that grew in the back of my throat, my power building within me. Pins and needles tingled through every part of my body as I let go completely. I savored the feeling of the rain on my skin before every ounce of me went numb to the intensity of my potential. The sneer on my lips solidified, and I opened my eyes, recognizing the undeniable release of emotions that was about to ensue.

It was time to *play*.

I brought my thumb to my pointer finger, and the second they made contact, the military vehicle at the gates collapsed—metal screeching and twisting before crumbling into a ball. Panic ensued immediately among the surrounding soldiers. I watched as they desperately clawed at the Walls, the structures designed to keep them safe, becoming an active force keeping them out.

The surrounding obscurity kept their enemy cloaked and hidden—kept me standing amongst them without their knowledge of my presence.

The soldiers, equipped with weapons to fend off attackers, stood no chance against me.

Their screams acted as a beacon for my attack, guiding me to each pinpoint location. My eyes traversed the outer barrier as bodies combusted in my path. Gruesomely painting the Walls, crimson blood started pooling on the sidewalk and asphalt. The rain worked to wash away the grotesque scene, the smell of copper mingling with its purity.

A chuckle escaped my throat as I watched in levity, my attention scanning the horizon for the next threat. A fleet of military vehicles, the community's primary means of transportation, came into view. The irony was palpable—if they worked so hard to keep themselves locked inside, why not make that a complete reality? They would realize the folly of their cowardice as they hid behind a steel fortress while I shredded through every safety net they believed they had one by one.

From where I stood, I raised a single hand, covering the Humvees entirely in my line of sight. The circulating energy within me thrummed with an insistent rhythm, a pulsating beat that seemed to synchronize with my heartbeat. Their metal exteriors vibrated violently, the tremors growing stronger with each passing second. In an instant, the vehicles disintegrated into dust, particles swirled and dispersed, carried away by the wind and rain, leaving nothing but an empty space where they once stood.

An uncontrolled, manic laugh fled from my lips as euphoria washed over me. I lifted my hands, facing palms up toward the sky, unable to feel the rain any longer. My gaze shifted from the dark clouds overhead to the steel fortress again. I had evaluated all outcomes of my attack and knew there was only one way forward. Accepting that innocent lives would be in the mix was a hard truth, but the evil inside the fortification needed to be eradicated.

I bent my arms forward, bringing my palms together as my brows furrowed in concentration.

The metal Walls folded in on themselves instantly, each end coming together and crushing everything inside. The deafening crash reverberated through the empty streets, its intensity causing discomfort even from forty yards away.

Once thought impenetrable, the steel snapped under the force of my power, collapsing entirely.

No screams, no knowledge of the attack—a peaceful send-off and the end of a destructive era.

The Capital base stood in ruination at my feet.

Inhaling sharply, I closed my eyes and began detaching myself from my more sinister side—the monster longing for destruction could finally rest once more. I relinquished the power responsible for such annihilation in mere seconds, feeling the tingling tendrils withdraw back to where they had come from. The chains restrained my internal demon, which had reigned for those moments, joining me in arms as it had in the past. The doors in my subconscious sealed off the darkness that had spread in those joyous moments, locking it away again.

Even though its undecipherable search continued for whatever missing link it hunted.

As I brought myself back to who I was, I felt the dampness of my jacket. The cold precipitation dripped against my skin, contrasting with the heightened pleasure of decimation that was finally satiated. I slowly opened my eyes, the entire horizon coming into view without interference from the artificial haven. Thunder cracked through the tar-black sky, grimly acknowledging the loss and destruction. The cloud cover rolled over the expanse, a dull contrast against the surrounding buildings and what was once a symbol of rulership. A large piece of twisted metal now sat in place of the once-glorious empire, the remnants a mere memorial of what once was and a stark highlight of what was no longer.

I rolled on the balls of my feet before shifting back to my heels, turning away from it all.

My years of serving and my allegiance.

The memories and the pain of them that haunted me.

Excruciating hours of torture.

Finally, buried and put all of it to rest.

I glanced over my shoulder once more, consuming all I'd freed before I grabbed the sides of my hood. I slowly lowered it, appreciating the cool rain against my heated skin. My foot connected with the ground, and before I could process anything further, a force collided with the side of my face so hard that I lost my footing.

My hands and knees slammed into the loose gravel of the rooftop as I grunted in pain. My right ear rang, and I spit out a mouthful of blood, struggling to lift my head and face my attacker. Before I could turn completely, a boot connected with my ribs, lifting me off the ground before I collapsed in a heap. The intensity of the kick stole the oxygen from my lungs as I forced myself to roll onto my back for a clear line of sight. A puddle greeted me, beginning to soak through the material of my hoodie.

"Well, well, well."

I heard the snap of electricity as I forced myself to swallow oxygen and level myself from the back-to-back hits. With sopping wet clothes, the baton stood a far higher chance of inflicting damage.

"Gael." His name came as a snarl as I clenched my teeth, fighting back the groan of agony that came with the movement to face him.

He wore a Command Officer uniform, one I recognized all too well. Its black camouflage pattern coated the entirety of the fabric. The suit's sleeves were rolled up just below his elbow, revealing burn marks on his left arm. A utility belt sat across his waist, full of various knives and ammunition clips for the gun strapped to his thigh. The holster on his hip, designed to house a baton, was empty, his gloved hand gripping it tightly. The overcast weather highlighted the contrast between the mahogany highlights in his hair and the brightness of his eyes. He spun the baton in his hand, cocking his head slightly, a sinister grin spreading across his lips.

"Not excited to see me, are you?" he cackled, the electricity seeming to join him in the taunt. "Don't tell me you are that naïve to think it would be that easy to take the central operations down?"

The power that surged through me moments before begging to drum again, the rain intensifying to a downpour in response. It seemed like the gods, if there were any, carved a moment in history for our confrontation. The numbing current within me grew exponentially as the memory of him raising the gun at Imelda and pulling the trigger surged to the forefront, taking me hostage from all I knew.

A scream of rage escaped me as I pushed myself up, my body no longer registering the pain from the blows. I launched myself into a sprint, slamming into him and tackling him to the ground.

My fist connected with the side of his face. The contact was insufficient to satisfy the hatred and suffering he had a hand in, and part of me knew the risk of getting this close when he wielded a weapon that could incapacitate me instantly, but I didn't care—not anymore.

I would kill him. Gut him alive and—

The baton's wave of electricity slammed into my side, forcing every muscle in my body into submission. The intensity of the shock jolted through me and seared my insides, causing a throbbing headache to begin at the base of my skull—a clear sign of its impact on my abilities. My grip on my power slipped from my grasp as I felt myself falling.

No. I refused to allow it to take me down. Not yet.

I raised my arm again, landing another punch squarely on his face. The baton remained pressed against my side, electricity still pulsing through me. I knew he had turned the knob to increase the voltage by the near-unbearable sensations flooding my body. Maintaining my position took every ounce of focus, and I allowed my rage to assist in my temporary upper hand. My knuckles split with the force of the punch as I recoiled and struck again. With each blow, I felt a small piece of myself return—a piece lost to the darkness and pain of the past.

Not yet. Not yet.

My vision darkened momentarily, then cleared—a warning that I was on the brink of passing out. Blood flowed from my nose as I raised my fist again, knowing my body was nearing its limit and adrenaline was the only thing keeping me going. I reached for a knife on his utility belt, understanding that my power was no longer a reliable asset.

If I couldn't use my abilities to my advantage, I would go down doing what they knew me for during my years of service.

I wrapped my fingers around the hilt, yanking it from its sheath. I twirled the blade before driving it deep into his side, twisting it to ensure the impairment was sufficient to get him to back off, even if only momentarily. The roaring in my ears nearly drowned out his scream of agony, but I basked in its undertones, savoring the satisfaction that rose in inflicting pain.

"Ah, fuck you!" Gael shifted under me, wrapping his foot around mine in an attempt to pin me.

But I was quicker.

I yanked my leg forward, freeing it from his grip, and drove my knee into the hilt of the knife. Pushing myself to stand in the same motion, my legs trembled from the residual electricity. I couldn't stop fighting, not with so much to avenge.

Not when I was making a stand for *her*.

I raised my foot, slamming it down onto the knife in Gael's side. The movement forced the blade deeper, eliciting another scream from him. I lifted my foot again and brought it down on his chest, feeling waves of fury consume me as I continued the relentless assault.

Again.

And again.

And again.

I had lost count of how many times my blows connected with his flesh, but there wasn't an ounce of me that cared—even in knowing what I did. My entire body shook, and I wasn't sure if it was from the wrath that consumed me or the electric current still waging war within me. A snarled breath escaped my lips as I looked down at Gael, a twisted satisfaction coursing through me as I watched him spit up blood. He didn't grimace in pain; instead, he smiled deviously, his teeth coated in crimson. Before I could fully grasp the meaning behind his expression, I felt the sudden surge of two electrical currents slamming into my body with unforgiving force.

They started on both sides of my neck, sending a paralyzing jolt throughout my system. My vision darkened as my knees slammed into the rooftop, only briefly returning when the intensity amplified. Between the first attack from Gael and now the dual onslaught from an unknown assailant, I was on the brink of losing myself.

My body convulsed violently as I collapsed chest-first onto the graveled surface, unable to catch myself. I tried to lodge a hand under my chest and push myself up to keep fighting, but it was useless. Every ounce of me was burning from the inside out, my brain unable to keep up or process anything further. A pool of blood formed beneath me, mingling with the rain and the dirt, creating a murky red stain that seemed to mock all I believed.

As my vision flickered in and out, I watched someone stride over the top of me. Polished boots were the first thing I saw before the person knelt, lowering themselves in front of me. I struggled to raise my gaze, my eyelids heavy and uncooperative. Between the flutter of my eyes, I spotted bright blue eyes and near-white blonde hair. The face came into focus slowly, a mixture of familiarity and dread washing over me.

Radley.

He smiled at me, some level of pity in his eyes as he chuckled deviously. "Long time no see, *Captain*."

I didn't have the time to mutter a response before he slammed the back of the baton into my face, casting me into the realm of unconsciousness.

FORTY-TWO

Four hours

The sting of cold water snapped through my body, pulling me from the darkness that had consumed me on the roof.

I wasn't sure how long I'd been out, but there had been enough time for someone to bring me back to the confines of my past. The water drenched my hair first, each drop falling from it like a tiny icicle against my skin. I realized then that they'd stripped my rain-soaked clothes from my body, the only remnants belonging to the briefs I wore. I gasped as goosebumps spread across my skin, my body shivering with the gravest wake-up call of the century.

I forced myself to open my eyes, blinking through the water that coated my face. My head throbbed, and the lights in the room only intensified the pain. Their fluorescent glow contrasted with the stark white walls, making them nearly luminescent. I recognized the space immediately—one I often frequented when I questioned captives during my time as a Captain.

They had taken me to an interrogation room in one of the

bases mere miles away from Capital's central location—clever bastards.

The metal squares overhead glared down at me as if they, too, recognized who I was. The matching table pushed to the wall on my right indicated that casual conversation was out of the question. Chairs that usually sat beside each other had been stacked and placed to the side. I lifted my gaze to the large window before me, where I knew people were standing and monitoring. My abilities nipped in response to the glares of distaste I could sense. That alone was enough to make my lips twitch upward.

My reflection stared back through the dark glass, my bare skin practically gleaming under the room's harsh illumination. I could see a bruise forming where Gael's foot had collided with my ribs. My arms stretched overhead, restrained with fortified steel, forcing me into immobilization. The shackles, conjoined and unyielding, made it impossible to shift from my position on the unforgiving floor. The bilateral zap of electricity pulsed through my body, stifling my abilities.

I scoffed under my breath slightly.

Gael lowered the bucket to the ground, responsible for my icy wake-up call. He glared down at me, nothing but heightened amusement on his face. "We've got a lot of catching up to do."

I scanned him for the injuries I had inflicted, only to come up empty-handed—there were no bruises on his face, no bindings to conceal a stab wound. The gratification I'd felt earlier vanished instantly as if it had never existed.

What the hell?

He sneered, "You look surprised to see me in good health."

"Truly an understatement," I replied bitterly.

"I think you'd be happy to know that we have an equal interest in killing one another." He laughed before shaking his head. "But sadly, he ordered me to keep you alive. It seems that there are greater plans underway."

"Truly, Gael, I don't give a shit." I lifted my head to look at him, my sneer growing. "The petty act you're putting on for me is pitiable. I came here for a reason, with full expectation of landing in shackles. So for the sake of both of us, save the stoic bullshit."

"Ah, the hardened Onyx Oakes and the mask worn as a byproduct of the Fall. I can't say I'm surprised by your demeanor." He ripped one chair from the stack and dropped it onto the floor in front of me before lowering himself into it. "Let's chat like old friends, then."

I had to swallow the aching growl to escape my throat, leveling my glower.

"For starters," He crossed his right ankle over his left leg, "I think we should talk about your downright stupidity thinking that the Capital base would've remained in its original location, all things considered."

"We had blueprints that showed otherwise."

"Oh?" He positioned his elbow on his thigh before dropping his chin into his hand. "Blueprints found where, exactly?"

There was no way they could have been this far ahead of us the entire time. The conversation was headed down a route I knew, my anger building in correspondence to the realization.

He studied my face before continuing, "I'm presuming that good ol' Bandell grabbed them when you guys left the Capital base all those years ago, correct?"

I only nodded.

"And I also recall someone whom you granted access to the community. Perhaps someone who may have been responsible for a minor swap."

Radley.

The desire to wrap my hands around their necks and snap them easily grew with each passing second. I lunged forward, but the chains above my head stopped me, and a stronger zap of electricity assaulted my body. My muscles tensed, every limb becoming instantly heavier.

A throaty laugh echoed off the walls surrounding us as Gael pushed himself back into the chair. "Your plan was a failure since the beginning, and none of you had *any* idea."

I would kill him.

I would kill all of them.

Forcing myself to raise my chin, I glared down my nose at him. "The plan that never got executed? I guess that makes your grand scheme as much of a success as ours."

His brows narrowed in vexation, which drew a laugh of amusement from me.

He quickly interjected, "I'm presuming you're here alone for a specific reason. Would you like to talk about that?"

He wouldn't bait me. I wouldn't allow it.

"I think it's pretty clear why I'm here." My eyes iced over as my brows pulled forward, my lips drawing themselves into a straight line. "To gut *Every. Single. One.* of you.*"

"Well, I can confidently say that is going just as well for you." A flash of mirth glinted in his eyes. "But if we are being truthful here, I know there's a deeper reason. While you may be reckless, you aren't stupid."

I clenched my jaw, trying to steady my breathing. He wouldn't get me where he wanted me. I wouldn't step off the edge of the cliff.

He lowered his leg and planted it directly in front of him, leaning back and tucking his hands behind his head, demonstrating his intent to stay while serving as a demeaning taunt.

"I'm sure we can dig it out of you if you don't want to discuss it." His foot tapped against the floor I sat on, pushing me to my breaking point. "If we base things off your track record, you have experienced a grave loss."

I closed my eyes, inhaling sharply.

"I mean hell, every time you've gotten close to someone, you've lost them. Either through death or them realizing your true intentions." His lip twitched, curling upward before faltering slightly. A light, olive hue flashed through his glower, only to be replaced as instantaneous as his words' continuation. "And if we cross reference what happened with the attack we unleashed and the recognition of Radley's betrayal..."

My blood was boiling.

"You're here because of *the girl*, aren't you, Oakes?"

The wrath surged.

He snickered, "You stepped into a situation you *knew* you stood no chance in over a girl? Aw, was it a big fight? Did she *finally* find out who and *what* you are, Onyx?"

I lunged forward as he delved past the surface, pulling at parts of me he knew would get a response. The electricity that hit me this time was more potent than before, immobilizing me as soon as it touched my skin. The jolt was strong enough to force my head back against the cement wall, a crack reverberating through my skull.

"A soft spot." I could hear the smile in his words, even though my eyes were closed. While I tried to cope with the throbbing that overlapped the existing pain, his talking persisted. "I told you I'd force it out of you."

It felt as if my skull were caving in on itself, the back-to-back currents wreaking havoc on my body. Every part of me ached in response to the paths they'd carved. With my heightened power levels, electricity wasn't just a weakness but my undoing.

A near-death sentence.

"You're not as lively as you were during your prior holding," he said, pure iciness coating his words. "The harmony of your screams and pleas during that year remain imprinted in my brain —in the best way possible, of course."

A gravelly chuckle escaped me as I forced the pain to the back burner. The sound grew in the room, bouncing off the unforgiving cement walls. My shoulders shook, my laughter continuing as I lifted my head and matched the intensity I'd unleashed on the rooftop, buried knee-deep in destruction.

"Are your pathetic taunts and jabs supposed to make me *feel something*? I truly thought your interrogation skills would've improved after all these years and that you would've learned something, but it would seem your capabilities of such things are pathetic at best." My lips settled into a sneer, and the prodding in my tone continued, "If you want to get me to feel some type of way, maybe be a gentleman and ask me to dinner first."

He pushed himself up from the chair in one fluid movement, with enough force to knock it to the ground. Metal and concrete collided, ringing through the room in a song that highlighted I had pushed *just* enough.

"Oh, a soft spot." I taunted.

Checkmate.

Within mere seconds, he was in front of me, his arm recoiling and fist beginning its journey toward my face. His knuckles connected with my jaw with enough force to rebound my head against the wall again. The pounding was becoming unbearable, but I wouldn't give him the satisfaction of seeing that.

His fingers were in my hair, ripping my head forward as he snarled down at me, speaking between clenched teeth. "If you think the torture you're going to experience this time around will be anything like back then, you're *poorly* mistaken."

I smiled up at him as I felt the crimson liquid drip from my mouth—a decent hit, but poorly executed. "I look *forward* to it, bitch."

His face contorted as he contemplated a retort, evaluating whether it was worth it—exactly as I hoped for. I knew that once I got into his head, he would continue to question himself.

"The look on your face when I entered the room was enough to give way to a level of wonder." He shifted the topic of conversation as he let go of me and stepped away, his eyes narrowing even more. "Needless to say, there are plenty of things even you don't know, Oakes."

My brows furrowed briefly, confusion contorting my ability to process the depth of his proclamation. I forced my surprise beneath the surface as he scanned my body as a means to intimate me, but it was a deplorable attempt.

I cocked my head, studying him. "I believe I already mentioned needing to take me to dinner first."

He opened his mouth to reply, but the door to the left of the large window creaked, indicating an unknown visitor. I bit the inside of my cheek to keep a groan from escaping me as I turned my head. The severity of the agony in my skull was beyond manageable, the edges of my vision darkening in response.

The black camouflage uniform was the first thing that caught my eye. A long leg stepped from behind the door, followed by a towering frame moving through the threshold. My eyes scanned the stature I was all too familiar with, and as I progressed upward, blue eyes narrowed in my direction. A lengthy grin caused the corners of his eyes to wrinkle.

Radley.

The sound of his footsteps fell closer as the gap between us closed quickly because of his rather lengthy strides. He peered down at me as his frame swallowed the light in the room. "I figured I'd make an appearance."

I knew I wanted to kill Gael; there wasn't a doubt in my mind about that. But there was a different level of desire with the male who stood beside him.

"How's Astrid doing?"

The depth of his words and the leer on his face were enough to pull me back to the ledge I had stepped away from. I tucked my legs underneath me and lunged forward, but the metal on my wrists immediately halted me. The cuffs dug into my sensitive skin, and the heightened electricity surged through me. I collapsed, my chest heaving as my breath caught in my throat.

My vision faded as my body trembled; the pulsing in my brain was excruciating. Every internal organ felt like it was scorching from the varying circuits of electricity. With each movement, the intensity heightened to incapacitate me, and it was working. The room itself was tilting, darkening, spinning. My stomach churned in response to the agony, but before bile could rise, I felt a tug on my wrists, forcing me to a standing position.

Right.

There was a track for chains that ran from each side of the wall and across the ceiling. It was installed to leverage different positions for uncooperative interrogation subjects. While I hadn't often used its functionality, it was a bitter irony that it was being used on me.

The joints in my elbows and shoulders protested against the movement as if I hadn't used them in months. Their screams made me question how long I had been unconscious when they first brought me here. My toes barely grazed the floor as they forced my body upright and to the center of the room.

Lovely.

"It's been a long time since the two of us have been in this situation, hasn't it?" Radley peered at me, eye to eye, and a grin crossed his face, saying enough.

I followed his question with a mumbled whisper—a lure thrown in the water, hoping the fish would bite. Radley exhaled in annoyance as he leaned forward, attempting to hear what I had mindlessly mumbled.

All according to plan.

I rolled my head back, accepting the pain it would induce, and slammed it into the bridge of his nose. He cursed in agony, quickly pulling away and lifting a hand to his nose as blood quickly coated it.

My head was throbbing—throbbing—throbbing.

And the room was spinning.

But now wasn't the time to slow down. I had minutes and knew I wasn't getting out of these cuffs, but I had to try *something*.

I swung my legs, leveraging my upper body from where my hands hung from the ceiling. On the route upward, I parted them just enough to wrap around Radley's throat and rip him from where he stood. I flexed every muscle in my thighs, constricting tightly with such force that escape wasn't an option, no matter how hard he tried.

The electricity hit me like a freight train, but there was too much I wanted to do, too much I had to fight for. Adrenaline surged as I continued my assault. Gael yelled something, but my focus was elsewhere. I watched as Radley's feet left the ground, suspended between my thighs, his hands prying at them as he struggled for oxygen. I commanded my leg muscles to contract further, locking my ankles together to solidify the hold. If I could breathe through the surge, I could get him unconscious.

As soon as the thought crossed my mind, another prick of current attacked my wrists. Signifying that they increased not just one but multiple notches. The burn and tingle nearly forced me to release, but I refused. Warm liquid trickled from my nose—blood—I was running on borrowed time. I knew my brain and body would be molten by the time they finished with me, but I refused to yield. If there was one thing I knew about myself, it was that I was as hard-headed as an ox, and I wouldn't let go anytime soon, regardless of the recognition.

The muscles in my abdomen roared for release as I kept myself in the inverted position. Radley thrashing against me. His size and weight were nearly enough to yank me from my rotation. My focus tunneled on battling against him, ignoring the cuffs as they bit into my skin and drew blood from my wrists. I inhaled through my teeth, bracing myself for another surge in the circuit, my muscles tightening in anticipation.

It wasn't the burning of electricity that passed through me next, but the sting of a deep laceration on my back. Almost wiping my vision from me, the drum of pain bounced between my eardrums. The outer edges of my sight dulled and returned just as I felt my muscles loosening their hold. Next came the sound of Radley hitting the ground, accompanied by his gasping breaths and muttered curses. The steel bindings sunk their teeth deeper as my body rebounded to its prior position. My toes touched the ground, its iciness barely enough to keep me conscious.

Then, the echo transmitted my subconscious mind back to the cells. An all-too-familiar snap dug its claws into the cement walls, and my heart sank.

A whip.

I swallowed a focused breath, desperate to keep myself present as the second blow came.

The tip of it tore through multiple layers of skin and muscle, an intense wave of agony seeping through me. My fists instinctually closed, my grip so tight I could feel my knuckles whiten. The pain was too familiar, blazing a hole through my mind.

Gael's voice came behind me as another strike collided with my skin. An unfiltered and uncontrolled cry escaped me. "Did you *truly* think that you'd be able to kill one of us?"

Radley cursed under his breath beside me, but I couldn't bring myself to address either of them, no matter how badly I wanted to. Not with the deep burn and sting pulsating down the expanse of my bare skin. I could feel a warmth begin its caress, blood following the pull of gravity.

My lineage, my ancestry, puddled beneath me.

Another crack and connection forced my body to tense as I demanded myself to swallow the resulting bellow. The char the whip left was already noticeable, another path of blood traversing from the gash in my skin. A relentless quiver racked my body, not because of the electricity's impact but because of the overwhelming throb that seemed to rattle my bones. I had proven, in that moment, that my will was impenetrable.

I wouldn't give them the satisfaction of hearing my screams. I wouldn't permit them to relinquish control over me—I had control over myself.

I was my own domination.

The room spun slightly, my hearing rolling through waves of presence and absence. Sight pursued as darkness consumed and receded like the ocean tide. I forced my eyes open for what felt like the millionth time, and Radley's face came into view. He had positioned himself directly in front of me, a near snarl present on his lips. On the surface, it was deep-seated resentment, but looking closer...

Sinister delight.

He went to open his mouth to speak but closed it in a tight

line, his cat-like grin building. My vision faded again, and the snap of the whip fileting my skin nearly drew bile from my throat, forcing me back to consciousness. It took every ounce of my focus to draw a labored breath as my eyelids fluttered—the agony becoming profuse. When I thought I had reeled myself back, Radley's fist slammed into my stomach with such force that breathing became impossible.

I gasped; the back-to-back hits were nearly enough to send me into limbo. The lack of oxygen did not center me, and darker memories resurfaced, wiping clean every thought in my mind. My hold on my will was weakening, slipping between my grasp with each crack of the whip.

I had stepped into this willingly, knowing that the most likely outcome was the one I was facing. Memories of the agony I had experienced in confinement during that year flooded back, but I had accepted this as my fate. While part of me wished I could turn back the moment the weapon of my prior torture reappeared, this was necessary.

Necessary to keep them safe.

Necessary to keep *her* safe.

The crack of the whip came again as I tried to pull myself toward an area of light within the darkness consuming me. I crawled for some salvation of hope as the walls around my conscious mind closed in, searching for the beacon of preservation.

Of redemption.

Of illumination.

FORTY-THREE

Four hours

The feelings that poured over me at that moment were few and far between. My heart seemed to come to a stall glancing between Jasper and Rayne as they held their position on the opposite side of the café bar.

Despite the emotional wave, relief twisted within me—Onyx was still alive, which meant there was still a chance.

"W-What do you mean?" The stream of words was a struggle to articulate.

Jasper ran a shaky hand through his hair. "Onyx took it upon himself to go to the Capital alone."

"He acted irrationally," Rayne chimed in from beside him. "We have spent the last few hours reconsidering the plans we had mapped out—the same ones that he destroyed to protect and prevent us from following him. But we are going against that request. We leave tonight, with or without you, at the first sign of sunset."

There was too much at risk.

He was at risk.

I nodded. "I am coming with you."

I had promised that I would accept Onyx for all he was, without judgment or preconceived notions. And once he had finally given me the opportunity, I had buckled. While my anger was valid regarding what he shared, I realized the varying reasoning behind it and the influences at play. There was a level of desired protection there, meshed with a logical standpoint for my beliefs.

Two extremely valid arguments.

Instead of listening to what he expressed, I lashed out, reacting from a place of pure denial but also fear. The words I had thrown at him were topics of conversation where he had confided in me. In a blinded rage, I had weaponized the things he had shared against me. I had taken every moment of intimacy that we had with one another and thrown it in his face.

Yet I had to keep him close for reasons beyond forgiveness or love.

Jasper bowed his head with some level of thanks before lifting it again. "I'm uncertain what happened between the two of you, but there isn't a doubt in my mind that he's doing all he can to fight right now. For you."

The lump in my throat grew as I swallowed the building unease.

"Regardless, he will be grateful for your decision to tag along." A minor smile made its way across Rayne's lips. "Once we rescue him, you can give him hell about being his knight in shining armor."

I laughed softly, shaking my head. "I'll have to keep that one in my back pocket."

We stood in silence for what felt like passing minutes. The only conversations belonged to the patrons in the space who were enjoying their meals—shared words ranging between daily duties and prior memories, a conjoining of present and past. There were minor rustles of jackets as some of the community members dressed themselves again to brace the chilly afternoon air. The movements and the resistance of chairs on the epoxy flooring made it seem that the café preferred that they stay.

I was the first to say, "What about the others?"

"We informed them." Rayne responded quickly, "The four of them are back in the debrief room, ensuring we have all the equipment required for the mission."

"Might I add," Jasper leaned against the countertop, "we are going in without the explosives that Lila had provided."

I ran a hand down my face. "He truly took everything he could, didn't he?"

"It wouldn't be him if he hadn't." Rayne folded his arms over his chest as he slumped back into the barstool. "His hardheadedness and selflessness have always landed him in the worst-case scenarios."

"That's an understatement." Jasper and I chimed together.

I untied my stained apron, folding it over the side table. I didn't regret my decision to join Lila in the café. Something was soothing about giving back to the community members on this level as if I was serving in some undefined manner to make up for the destruction Radley had caused. Yet, each act of service also held an agenda, a step closer to the justice I sought.

"Before we came over here," Jasper's continuation of the conversation withdrew my attention from my thoughts. "We had spent some time taking inventory of our collected weapons. Between what our community has and what Rayne has provided, I'm not terribly concerned about our success on this mission."

"The biggest concern is where they are keeping him." Rayne leaned forward, bracing his elbows on the wooden surface.

"There are a few possibilities." Jasper bounced his words off of his friend's. "Not only is there a chance of him being held within the innards of the Walls, but there are standby locations outside. Essentially, they created them in the chance of a successful infiltration. If he's housed in one of those, it will make our mission ten times harder."

"Because they're well guarded?" The question came to me immediately.

"Because they are unknown." Rayne lifted his head, his winter-blue gaze darkening. "They established them after the Fall and as a safety measure once those who worked for the government departed. The only reason that I obtained this piece of knowledge is because of an interaction I had with a government official before I killed him."

Well, that was one way to put it.

"Different sites surround the Walls of the main Capital base. They are unmarked to keep them disclosed and unknown by survivors, especially those who belong to the Rebellion." Rayne's hand lifted to anchor his chin, his fingers trailing along the edge of his jawline. "If we can get close enough, Onyx may pick up on our energies. If he can, there is a chance we can reach him telepathically and determine where they're holding him. While it may not be exact, the simple description of his surroundings could be enough to guide us in the right direction."

Differing locations, all unmarked, meant that to make things clear cut for deliveries from other communities, the buildings that were leveraged were plausible to be vastly different. And the only way to leverage that fact would be to select structurally inconsistent locations to the point of easy detection.

"You two are geniuses; you realize that, right?" I smoothed a hand over my apron, ironing the seam.

Jasper went to respond, but Rayne quickly cut him off; instead of being met with a snarky, atypical response, a unique energy radiated from him. It was a side of him that rarely fronted and one I only witnessed once before.

Valiant leadership.

"We accepted the responsibility to serve our communities and their inhabitants. This is a demonstration of our dedication."

Two hours

I GLANCED down at the array of weapons on the large oak table. The elected map continued to serve as a protective barrier, a stark reminder of the thin line between life and death. The soulless display seemed to gaze back at me as if there were some living aspect within the cold metal—a silent mockery of their power.

"Pick your poison." Jasper clasped a hand on my shoulder. "However, I feel this would best suit you."

I watched the length of his fingers wrap around the riser, the strings of the compound bow snagging slightly on his dark clothing. He positioned it in my direction, the grip directly in front of me. My lips moved into a soft smile as I reached forward, tightening my grasp on the weapon and pulling it from his hold. A part of me wanted to linger in this moment, to reminisce about how he handed me the bow with such belief and admiration, much like my brother used to. But beneath the nostalgia, a distinct satisfaction brewed, knowing each step neared closer.

"Bitchin'." Raven nodded in approval in my direction, fastening a holster to her thigh.

"I would have to agree with him." Rayne moved the sling from his assault rifle to the center of his chest, the gun draping itself over his back. "You sure know how to handle a bow."

Everett sat in one of the chairs, sharpening a large hunting knife. His attention seemed fixed on the blade, but I knew he was keenly aware of every word spoken, waiting for his moment to engage. His hand moved with such intricacy along the sharp edge; one wrong move and—

"Whatever you do," Rayne nudged him playfully, "don't mess it up, Daughtler."

Another noteworthy last name.

Everett groaned, looking up at Rayne under his contrastingly dark lashes. "You're a real pain in the ass. You know that, don't you?"

"He doesn't only know it," Riggs slid a clip into his rifle before focusing on the two of them. "He embodies it."

"You know, logically speaking, I should probably take offense." Rayne holstered a pistol on his leg. "But I'd be lying if I said I was."

"That's because you lack—" Everett's response got cut off immediately.

"Not surprising." Mykel laughed as he fastened his utility belt. "We all know you live to be a thorn in everyone's side. And we also accept that without your presence, we'd all be lost."

"As if." Everett stood, wiping a towel along the blade gently before spinning it between his fingers as if it were the hundredth one he had handled.

Rayne threw an arm over his shoulder, tugging him in tightly. "You know that without me here to harass you, you'd be the gravest man in existence."

My eyes scanned the room as the rowdiness subsided. There was something about the way they interacted with each other. The way each one carried themselves suggested previous military experience—from their ease with weapons to the casual yet playful banter. As I continued to observe the taunts thrown back and forth, my eyes halted on the auburn-haired male I had paid little attention to until now.

Jasper wore a dark, assassin-style hood, his hair a stark contrast against it. The long-sleeve material nearly blended into the dark pants that hugged his legs. Combat boots sat fastened intricately on his feet as if the process had been drilled into him. A collage of knives sat snugly on his waist in the utility belt fastened there. It was a near replica of the one Mykel wore, but it looked vastly different on him. Two paired pistols sat in holsters on his thighs, a third visible on his right hip. A blade not as long as Everett's ran the length of his left thigh, stopping about midway. He'd strapped the largest rifle up for selection across his chest as he helped Raven with minor adjustments to her gear.

There were so many similarities to Onyx that it nearly made my knees buckle. The way Jasper held himself seemed to shift entirely at that moment, and my view of him altered in response.

He no longer wore the mask of a leader but one of a warrior.

Rayne swayed into me, his arm colliding with my shoulder. "I believe there is a saying out there. Something like, take a picture; it will last longer?"

I tightened my fist, throwing a punch into his chest, which was greeted with a deep laugh. Regardless of the callout, my eyes hadn't shifted from their position.

"I've never seen him—like that."

Rayne chuckled softly, "There's *a lot* you haven't seen from Jasper."

His words clung to me with such tautness that their repetition seemed to rebound through my mind. I knew there were pieces of Jasper I had yet to uncover, similar to Rayne. But I hadn't realized his capabilities as both a leader and a soldier. That fact proved he had more versatility and depth than he let on.

"Jasper is capable of a lot of things." Rayne continued beside me, "There is a reason the Officials deeply respected him at nineteen and why they granted him rights for recruitment so early in his career."

"Well, if he's that well-versed, why didn't he involve himself in training me?" I felt as if it were a fair question.

"He puts on the mask of being this intellectual and analytical individual, which he is, don't get me wrong. But he leverages that side of himself to mask the depth of all that he is truly capable of." A sinister grin, full of knowing, crossed his lips, "Think of a joker in a stack of playing cards—more times than not, it is used to mirror other playing cards, not having a direct meaning aside from being an extra. But there are some games when the joker can become one of the deck's most valuable assets. Depending on the game, it is sometimes the most damaging."

It was all beginning to make sense. There were so many pieces of each that I had yet to experience, Onyx included. But there was something entirely different about Jasper's unknowns.

"That's Jasper," Rayne chuckled. "That is why most refuse to get on his bad side."

"I don't blame them." I inhaled deeply as I glanced again toward the auburn-haired man.

I watched him smile at Raven, his hand gently touching her shoulder as he nodded in affirmation. I had seen this side of him countless times with various community members—the side that radiated warmth and assurance. The man whom many looked up to for the inner strength he possessed, whose very presence inspired confidence and hope. His ease of leadership was evident in every gesture, every word, and the way he carried himself with a quiet, unyielding resolve. His promises were not mere utterances but commitments etched into the core of his being. He looked into people's eyes with a deep understanding that spoke volumes about who he was and what he was capable of.

And how nothing would stop him from doing what he desired.

Rayne exhaled deeply, pulling me from my state of examination. I looked at him, noticing his hand looping around the pistol on his thigh as he pulled it from its holster. Its dark coloring glinted under the overhead light, a few pieces contrasting with its shadowy hue.

He aimed it at the ground, ensuring the safety was engaged before passing it to me. "Here."

I looked down at the weapon, which mirrored beauty and horror, before raising my attention to him. "What?"

"Take it." He nudged the gun into my right hand, grabbing my left and gently wrapping my fingers around the grip.

"I can just get another from the table—"

"There isn't another gun like this." He softly removed his

hands from mine as its weight fully sank into my grasp. "This is the one thing that I kept from my time serving."

"Rayne, it's *yours* then. I couldn't possibly take it from you." I attempted to return the weapon to him, but he refused, lifting his hands.

"Gods, it's no wonder you and Onyx get along so well." He shook his head as his arms returned to his side. "Just stop and listen to me."

I glanced between the gun that seemed to mold itself into my grip and the brown-haired male standing beside me. His face was full of recollection, his brows drawing together as he gazed at me. It was as if this moment had been something he had been waiting for, carefully timing its execution.

"That was the pistol I chose when I joined Special Operations. It was a similar scenario," he motioned to the table in the center of the room. "We picked the weapons we were most drawn to and comfortable with. As soon as my hand connected with it, I knew that there would be many things I did with that gun, which was an understatement if we are honest.

"That pistol is responsible for a vast amount of death. And if we are being truthful here, lives that likely didn't need to be taken." He shook his head, his eyes closing briefly as his throat bobbed. "Many of them were moments I wish I could take back; nearly all the scenarios haunt me to this day."

"So you're passing your burden on to me?" I jokingly cocked a brow as I looked at him.

He chuckled as he shook his head, "My hell, you've been hanging out with me too much, haven't you?"

"Something like that." I beamed.

"Asshole." His grin and comment forced a mirrored reaction from me, "While there could be double reasoning behind me handing it off to you, the answer is no. It's entirely different from that."

I caressed my thumb along the length of the grip, its smooth texture pressing against my skin. Some of me wanted to provide comfort for this departure, knowing the variability in its journey.

"The night when Onyx, Jasper, and I worked to escape," he looked down at the pistol before easing his gaze back to me. "We entered a vacated room, one that Officials deemed as uninhabitable, for what reason we never found out. The men trailing us were hot on our tails, and the door that connected that room to the route we were taking to the underground tunnels was blocked. I knew that time was the only thing that would allow the two of them the chance to escape. Onyx, especially because he was the one they wanted the most. The President's obsession with him was never something we fully understood. And as you know, I stayed behind to fight back and buy them enough time to flee. But what you don't know is that I used that gun to do so."

I felt my stomach sink slightly.

"I'm not giving it to you as a weighted burden. I am *gifting* it to you because you deserve to be the one with the weapon already responsible for saving his life once." He gave me a soft smile, a singular dimple gracing his cheek. "You are going to rescue him, Astrid. You already have."

I reached forward, wrapping my free arm around his neck and pulling him toward me. He gently wrapped his arms around me, kissing the side of my head as his hand worked circles around my back. There had been no other way that I could have thought to express how much this notion had meant to me aside from this.

Something about it burrowed itself into my memory, knowing what we were about to do. The differing ways I had experienced their care and support had become something for which I was immensely grateful. How they accepted me and granted me a chance to exist alongside them, remaining here after all that had happened—was beyond appreciation.

I shared the memories with them, growing since stepping foot in the community. The laughs and loss that we had all shared had altered me entirely. All of that was what I now clung to as my last hope of retrieving Onyx alive. But an army walked behind him—

behind each of us when faced with hardship. The things this group would do for one another were truly indescribable. Yet, amidst unity and shared purpose, things lay hidden, biding their time until the moment was right.

I swallowed as I tightened my arm around him, a wave of determination flooding through me as a simple response followed—but encased with depth and meaning.

"Thank you for everything, Rayne."

FORTY-FOUR

The steady drum of rain against my hood worked to drown out the emotional rush in the back of my mind.

Thunder roared in unison as lightning cast its pattern overhead, displaying power and destruction. The dreary skies that wept spoke to the betrayal within the cityscape, expanding before us as if even Mother Nature was mourning all that once was. While the storm attempted to wash away all that had been lost at the hands of a known evil within humanity, the setting sun glared beneath the inky horizon.

A beacon of hope.

My bow bounced against my back as I took my place beside Jasper at the lip of the graveled roof where Riggs had teleported the seven of us, knowing it would put us in direct sight of the Capital Walls.

Instead of being met with a towering, fabricated structure, we lowered our attention to a crumpled pile of metal. The leftover destruction pointed fingers toward what once was a bustling community, housing those responsible for the apocalyptic condi-tions we were all forced to live in. It looked as if a towering giant had made an appearance, molding the once-standing community into a giant steel ball—like a mere piece of pottery clay.

"Gods," Rayne spoke beside me, his hood pulled up to conceal his features. "He really knows how to make a statement, doesn't he?"

Jasper let out a wordless exhale as he kept his eyes cast on the demolition before us. Numerous bodies lay scattered visibly around the perimeter, and near replicated piles of metal sat beside each flanked side. He had unleashed an attack on all means of escape, trapping those inside helplessly while Death had its way with them.

Onyx had come with a vendetta.

A score to settle.

"His power level is unlike anything I've ever seen." Awe-struck, Raven's words came as a mere mutter.

"It's nothing you *want* to see," Jasper replied sharply, a level of concern buried in his tone. "There are things that Onyx is capable of that no one can even wrap their mind around."

I witnessed his abilities demonstrated a handful of times, but *nothing* to this extent.

"I've got something." Mykel cut through nature's pitter-patter, and I shifted, turning in his direction.

He knelt on one knee, his fingers wrapping around the hilt of a knife. A flash of lightning rolled through the sky, glinting against the blade. He pushed himself up before moving in our direction, flipping the knife in his hand and passing it to Jasper.

I watched his eyes traverse the blade, paying close attention to the etched details. "It's Gael's."

"Bastard," Rayne spoke through clenched teeth as he stepped up to obtain confirmation.

I leveled my gaze at Jasper. "That means that Onyx was on this roof at some point. Likely when he unleashed his attack."

Jasper nodded, slipping the knife into the only empty position on his utility belt. It was as if part of him had known he would find one of Gael's weapons here, desiring to use his weapon against him as a final statement of opposition.

The gravel protested under Rayne's boots as he turned back to the horizon, examining for any indication. "Well, since Onyx completely decimated the Walls, that leaves us with what we had concluded—he's hidden somewhere in the satellite locations."

"They're all within a few blocks of here, " Riggs said next. "According to the government agent we interrogated, of course."

"It was a reliable interrogation," Rayne stated smoothly, a bitterness clinging to each syllable. "He couldn't have lied, even if he wanted to."

"Wait." Jasper put a hand up. "During our time serving, Onyx secured access to a building on the northern perimeter of the Walls before everything went to shit. They used as a housing unit for interrogating suspects."

"You think they would keep accessing it?" Rayne glanced over his shoulder, his arms tightly folded over his chest. "Especially considering that Onyx had been there in the past?"

"But none of us had." Jasper continued, "It's a plausible assumption, considering he was the only one out of the group granted access."

I chimed in, "Wouldn't it be the easiest thing to do, considering they're so strung up on not diverting from their original plans if it isn't necessary? It's an already established building for activities that they partake in, and Onyx was the only one out of the three of you who knew of its existence. There is some level of mind game that comes with leading people to *think* they would completely abandon all prior government-affiliated buildings."

"She has a point," Everett said, looking from me to the others. "If they can lead people to assume they shifted locations, then the likelihood of those buildings being infiltrated decreases. They essentially camouflage themselves with the nuances of assumption."

"So, say that—" Rayne went to express his thoughts as the sound of a walkie-talkie cut off the conversation entirely, a static male voice following.

"Orion unit, do you copy?"

The only thing separating us from whoever it belonged to was a single expanse of the brick wall, which was easily maneuverable. The crunch of multiple footsteps forced the gravel beneath them to roll, pinpointing their location. Mere feet separated us, the grace of the persistent rainstorm the only thing preventing them from recognizing our presence.

"We copy," a more perceptible male stated. "The ten of us are taking routes through the downtown buildings; so far, there is no sign. The Crux unit is coming from the south end, and Ursa is closing in on the east. We plan to rendezvous just outside the evacuation zone."

They were clearly on the prowl for something and that *something* was us, which meant they knew we were here.

Rayne smirked as he and Jasper exchanged a simple glance, conveying what was to follow.

Before I could react, Raven stepped forward, gently placing a hand on my shoulder. The energy coursed through her fingertips, becoming detectable as a gentle hum that spread through my body. Her power was subtle but undeniable, with a faint metallic tang lingering in the back of my mouth. She extended her reach to the other three, enveloping us all in a shroud of invisibility, her presence weaving around us like a cloak.

Jasper and Rayne kept their backs to us as the rain continued to fall, a clear sign that neither of them would miss our presence for the time being. My eyes shifted between them, the pure power pulsating between them nearly enough to take my breath away.

Two Rebellion leaders, friends, and prior soldiers coming together to make a stand against all that faced them.

"We act according to plan—don't be brash or stupid," Jasper warned Rayne as he lowered the hood that concealed him against the elements. His auburn hair seemed to glow with the sunset as it worked toward its vibrant descent.

A laugh followed, but it did not belong to the brown-haired male who had gifted me the gun that now sat snugly against my right thigh. Instead, a familiar and harmonious sound practically brought me to my knees with an influx of guilt. It was a sound I hadn't heard in what felt like a lifetime, and the memories it evoked were almost too much to bear.

Rayne lifted his hands, pulling his hood down to reveal raven-black hair tied in a loose bun at the base of his skull. He cracked his neck to the side as he glanced at Jasper. The strong profile of a beautiful face, a deep scar crossing it in the distant light, came into view. "Let's get this party started. Shall we?"

Onyx's voice.

A final display of Rayne's abilities.

Jasper lifted a hand, bringing his fingers to his lips, and let out a loud whistle.

The reverberation of quick movement came from the other side of the wall, and soldiers worked quickly to flock to the noise. Two of them cleared the corner, raising their guns as they came to a halt—apparent bewilderment clouded their expressions.

Rayne lifted a hand, Onyx's hand, a smile present in his words. "Surprise assholes."

Before either of them could react, the wall behind them fractured. The sudden explosion left no room for error, its devastation immediate and brutal. Bricks flew into the men with such force that they nearly wiped out the rest of the unit that followed the original perpetrators. Blood coated the rooftop as the chaos ensued, pieces of bodies scattered alongside the debris.

Jasper took a single step forward, his hands opening at his sides as a giant funnel took shape overhead. The circular motion drew in on itself rapidly, intensifying the surrounding wind. It wasn't only a surface-level display of his abilities but a direct attack by the element he wielded as it shifted and formed rapidly.

Shit.

"There's no way in hell he is about to cast a tornado onto this rooftop, right?" Mykel looked between us in a slight panic. *"Right?"*

The funnel progressed in size, growing with immense power as lightning permeated it. My eyes widened as I watched its advancement, the tip of it nearing the rooftop as the sky seemed to retaliate alongside the man so many underestimated. The wind whipped around us as it built in strength, Jasper and Rayne remaining in their positions as if unfazed by the decimation they were causing.

The male responsible for the earlier communication fumbled with his walkie-talkie. "Crux and Ursa units, do you copy? We need backup! The suspects are on—"

I hadn't even felt myself reach for the pistol on my thigh or step from Raven's grasp.

Positioning behind Jasper and Rayne, I raised the weapon at the male, attempting to provide intel to whoever sat on the other line. Without hesitation, I pulled the trigger, and the gunshot echoed around us as he collapsed to the ground, blood pooling beneath his head.

While I lacked abilities like theirs, it wouldn't prevent me from fighting alongside the Rebellion.

The soldier that stood beside him glanced between his now-dead Captain and me just as another rounded the corner. I watched as both rifles lifted in my direction, a part of me having already accepted that it would come down to this. I raised my pistol back at them, my finger gracing the trigger as the firefight started.

The symphony of gunshots began as the others pulled out their weapons to provide covering fire, the remaining soldiers pushing back against us. The tornado overhead continued its descent, working to divide the differing groups. I focused on the male who seemed to be in second command, trying to avoid the concern for the destructive storm overhead. I exchanged bullets with him, each shot reverberating through the tension. One of my bullets found its mark, piercing his shoulder. A slew of curses fell from him, and his hold on his rifle slacked, providing me the perfect opportunity to finish what I'd started.

Before I could land another headshot, Jasper pivoted and rushed toward me. The sudden change in his position threw me off guard, his arms wrapping around me before I could fully comprehend what was happening. With me in tow, he continued with rapid succession toward the lip of the rooftop.

"Hang on tight, Carnell!"

I didn't even have a chance to breathe before the two of us were free-falling off the building, the unforgiving asphalt below getting uncomfortably close. The wind whipped past us, and my heart pounded in my chest.

"Are you insane?!" I constricted myself around him with a near-death grip, which he responded to with a simple chuckle.

A sudden updraft followed, catching us mid-air as the rapid descent ceased. The feeling of plunging to my death abruptly stopped, but my heart continued to drum with immense force. I dragged my eyes away from Jasper's chest, gazing at the road beneath us.

We hovered just above the street, suspended as if some invisible force held us.

Were we...flying?

I lifted my head to Jasper, who glanced back down at me with a glint of amusement in his gaze. "Figured I'd give you the opportunity of a lifetime."

"Next time," I breathed between words, "Give me a heads up so I don't nearly shit myself. Please and thank you."

He chuckled as he pointed toward the building. "I had little choice."

I moved my attention from him toward where we were located mere seconds ago. The entire funnel had encased the structure, wrapping itself around it. Its wind speeds ripped the building apart, shredding bricks, steel, structural members, and other parts like paper. When comparing it to the manner of another tornado that would leave a pathway of its terror and decimation, this one held its place—entirely still, as if this building was the only thing it needed to feed its appetite.

"Holy shit." The reckoning before me continued as I spoke. "For the longest time, I thought you could only make force fields."

Jasper groaned, his arms still tightly wrapped around me as the two of us began our descent to the ground below. "You're lucky I didn't drop you for that insult."

"I will murder you."

"If you were splattered all over the asphalt below, that wouldn't be an option," he said, his grin growing as I glared in his direction. But he simply changed the subject. "You know, I'm not sure if I should feel slightly offended that you assumed I wasn't capable of much or proud of myself for maintaining that level of mystery."

"If mystery were your goal, you should be proud." My eyes couldn't help but explore our surroundings as we remained over forty feet off the ground.

The sunset seemed to glint against the material that made up each standing structure. Regardless of the Capital being the home for the planned apocalypse, it still faced the destruction that followed. Multiple sections of the surrounding buildings concaved on themselves, leaving their innards to wear the elements. Many shattered glass windows told wordless stories to those who hadn't been involved. The foliage had traversed inside as if trying to bury the city's filth. Upon examination, the immense irony of Jasper unleashing the funnel reemerged—he only added to nature's annihilation, all humanity once fabricated crumbling in her grasp.

As I tried to absorb it all, I felt my feet connect with the earth, and the urge to collapse entirely against it heightened. The comfort of its presence beneath me was a level of coaxing that I hadn't realized I needed. My eyes scanned the city streets, and before I could ask where the others were, Rayne's unit appeared in front of us, and relief flooded my senses.

"I'm going to ask that you give us a heads-up the next time you decide to release a multi-vortex tornado in our presence." Mykel leveled his attention at Jasper.

Jasper shrugged, his lips tugging themselves upward. "My bad."

"I hadn't realized you were capable of *that* power level." Raven breathed, "I thought we were goners up there."

"You and me both." I jutted my response toward her as I slid my gifted weapon back into its holster.

The sound of feet landing on the concrete behind us drew my attention from them as I looked over my shoulder. My breath caught in my throat immediately, even though I already knew who was beneath the disguise.

Raven hair glinted in contrast against the setting sun, a couple of loose strands falling to frame the face I'd come to admire. The jagged scar progressed in its usual manner, its lighter complexion highlighted. The smile that crossed his face belonged to him, every single aspect. But I knew it was a mere illusion, a replication of the man my heart ached and yearned so deeply for.

The man that the seven of us were here to save.

Before I could savor any more of him, every feature shifted until Rayne stood before us again. "Damn, Jasper, you went for it, didn't you?"

"I told you beforehand that I wasn't holding back." Jasper grabbed his hood, quickly pulling it back over his head to shield against the everlasting rain.

Rayne followed suit, a grim smile appearing as he walked toward our group. "I figured you'd save a show like that for the finale."

"Who's assuming I don't have more up my sleeve?" Jasper shook his head, smiling back at him as he placed a hand on his shoulder.

A gentle reassurance to himself that everyone was still okay.

"Have you had any luck connecting with Onyx?" Rayne aimed her query at Riggs.

The chestnut-skinned male shook his head to answer, "No. I even tried to tap in telepathically since we were deeper in the city. No luck."

My stomach sank slightly as my mind wandered to the possibilities behind the lack of response. I had brushed aside all the worst-case scenarios and focused on the one that could yield that outcome—he was unconscious. The thought brought a sliver of hope amidst the torrent of fear and uncertainty. It was better than imagining the alternatives, each darker than the last.

"Well, that leaves one option at this point." Rayne exhaled deeply. "We rip apart this city until we find him. We don't have any other option."

"We are running on time at this point." Jasper brushed his damp hair back under his hood. "I'm not entirely sure what they want to do with Onyx, but the longer we wait, the greater my fear of what awaits him becomes."

"He's an unstoppable force." Mykel looked between them, his words expressing some consolation.

"Even an unstoppable force has a weakness." Everett moved from his position beside Raven, stepping forward.

It was as if we had been standing in a minefield, and one minor movement was the triggering point. As soon as the shift happened, the sound of targeted gunfire ricocheted between the buildings that surrounded us.

Not from a single source.

But many.

FORTY-FIVE

ONYX

Shackles dragged across the concrete floor, waking me from wherever I had faded off.

My slip into unconsciousness had not guided me to a dreamscape but to a place of pure darkness. It felt like part of me didn't deserve to step into a realm of peace; instead, I remained lost in my own abyss. The relentless actions inflicted on me likely caused me to fade into a plane beyond this one, but a healer brought me back. Even though the session granted total health, the absence of agony left me questioning the validity of what they put me through.

The surrounding room made me feel like I hadn't woken, its shadows swallowing me whole. The darkness sent me to where I had just returned from, a repeated horror at recognizing where I had been. There was a brief question about whether I had fully ascended, but I knew that was merely what I hoped for. There was an ease in fleeing torture with Death, but it wasn't a likely scapegoat for me, not with Gael and Radley behind my imprisonment.

Death would never grant or meet me with ease.

I shifted from the position I sat in, a throbbing tug stopping me in my tracks as my back protested against the movement. I inhaled sharply, the tang of blood present on my lips. Some level of affliction weighed down every ounce of my body, making it nearly impossible to move my limbs. The presence of an electrical path wreaking havoc was notable, and my lungs burned with every breath. My wrists were not only raw from electrocution but also from battling against the unforgiving metal that encased them.

Everything ached, and I couldn't help but find my mind wandering to the pain I'd experienced during my imprisonment, its infliction caused by the same tormentors. It felt like the universe wanted to mock everything I was, having achieved freedom to live in a world where no one was truly free, landing in their hands once more. It was pitiful how humorous it was that my life had resulted in a full-circle punishment for something even I didn't know. Then again, all my faults and failures were worthy of it. I deserved to be punished for the lives that fell at my hands, and the cold floor beneath me reminded me of that.

Or so that's what it all felt like since proof was no longer present.

I wasn't entirely sure how long I had been unconscious or what had happened in the time between. It was like assembling a jigsaw puzzle with pieces that didn't belong to it—an utter nightmare and impossible to solve. I lifted my head, a flash of lightning sparking in the distance beyond the minor cutout in the barren room I sat in. The sound and smell of rain were the only things keeping me conscious as I tried to focus on leveling myself.

Every aspect of my brain was clouded, muddled by the never-ending currents that had violated me. Minor trembles rolled through me as if to act as a brief reminder of how bad it had been. My mind had pondered the possibility of how long I would remain in this room or what the result would be. But logically, I knew that there was no end.

They would keep me here as long as they wished.

This was where I would die, in a concrete box under the control of those who I had tried so hard to stay away from.

My chest tightened at the thought, my fists closing in on

themselves as I forced myself to swallow the emotion—it was useless. Tears burned the corners of my eyes as a shuttered sob left me, and I brought my legs toward me. Sadness wasn't the only thing that filled the cries that practically fell from my lips—regret, anger, and imprisoned wrath all mingled together. I slammed my fist down into the concrete floor beneath me, my knuckles splintering on impact as my chest heaved. I lifted my hand again; another collision with the ground was enough to ingrain this moment into my mind, each strike a desperate attempt to hold on to some semblance of control.

All I could hold on to were memories of them—of *her*. Getting out of here was no longer an option, at least not alive. My decision had wholly swallowed my chance with her and the relationship we could have developed. I had sacrificed it all for the hope of their safety, for the slim chance that they wouldn't have to endure what I was going through now.

By my mistake.

But it wasn't a mistake; it was an effort to keep them as far away from this as possible. The thought of them having to bear what I had been through in the past handful of hours turned my stomach on itself. I couldn't let them suffer this fate. My imprisonment, my torture. It was all worth it if it meant they remained free, untouched by the horrors inflicted upon me.

This was worth it.

Their safety was worth it, regardless of what that meant for me.

I rested my head back against the wall, tears continuing to fall in unison with the sound of the rain pattering outside the cell they locked me in. Each droplet on the window seemed to echo my despair, a symphony of sorrow that matched my turmoil. The shuttered sobs from me worked through the tiny window and into the stormy night. My lungs protested as I released a rage-filled scream that was immediately swallowed by a clap of thunder overhead.

I was done fighting.

FORTY-SIX

ASTRID

The surrounding architecture attempted to absorb the back-to-back reverberations, the echoes bouncing between the concrete jungle where we stood.

The abrupt attack left no room for backfire. Multiple engines added to the distress as men began filling their way into the street. They all wore dark uniforms, a pattern of camouflage covering them. They ignored the destruction from the funneled cloud they passed, raising their rifles in our direction.

As soon as the first gunshot went off, I watched as Rayne slammed himself into Everett. The force of the movement took the two of them to the ground behind a cement barricade. The rest of the group worked to take cover, an immediate separation occurring between the seven of us, which was likely exactly what *they* had wanted.

"Get down!" I felt Jasper's arms around me before we came into contact with the asphalt seconds later, a slight sting nipping at my elbow that had collided with it.

The gunfire remained persistent as he forced the two of us behind a vehicle, directing me where to stand to avoid the streamed attack. The bullets ricocheted against the metal frame, their deadly shells penetrating it with sickening ease.

We weren't going anywhere anytime soon.

"Shit." Jasper hissed between his teeth as he attempted to peer around the corner of the car, a spark reeling him backward.

They had us pinned and unable to retaliate.

My mind frantically scoured the attempts to get us out of there alive. The only option that remained was to leverage the abilities that the others held, especially considering what Rayne was capable of when he—

"Raven!" Everett's call for help was panic-stricken and enough to rattle my concentration.

I shifted to my right, focusing on where he sat with Rayne, and my heart sank immediately.

Everett's hands pressed tightly against his leader's stomach, but they quickly became stained with deep crimson. Determination laced Rayne's pain-infused expression as he tried to wave Everett off, a futile attempt to show that he was fine when it was the opposite. There hadn't been a second thought when Rayne had thrown himself in front of his counterpart to protect him from the inevitable. His will to risk himself for the chance that those he cared for could survive reigned true, just as he did the day he and his two closest friends had tried to escape.

I realized that the distraught call at that moment was for the one person capable of healing.

The one person who could save his life.

The same person trapped behind a cement wall and shrubbery just outside a towering skyscraper as repetitive gunfire rained down on all of us.

"Rayne, you stubborn asshole, don't you dare die on me!" Jasper's heightened apprehension became detectable as he bellowed over the gunfire.

Rayne let out a wheezed laugh as he looked over at the twelve-foot gap separating us. "Threatening me even now, Bandell?"

"It's not a fucking threat. It's an order."

Everett's eyes landed on us, connecting with me for a few moments longer. Fear pulsated in his gaze as he realized Rayne's selfless sacrifice. As he processed, every second seemed to stretch into eternity, the weight of it pressing down on him with a suffocating intensity.

"What do we do?" His words were soft, barely audible of the pops and cracks that continued to echo around us.

Jasper leaned back against the car we had taken shelter behind, his eyes closing briefly. The heightened power that drummed off of him sent a familiar tang to the back of my throat. It was a near match to what I had tasted the morning that Onyx had caused the trees to vanish seamlessly—he was opening the door to the true depth of his abilities. The surrounding air seemed to ripple with the force of his energy, a tangible shift that made the hair on my arms stand on end.

His secrecy was finally coming to a close.

He opened his eyes, his grey irises mirroring the eye of a hurricane, encapsulated with a white hue and pure wrath. "I'm going to give you one order—run once I reach one. Got it?"

I nodded, watching as the storms intensified within his building glower.

"Raven!" His voice boomed over the bombardment of shells. "You're going to have seconds to move from where you are. Do you understand?"

"Copy!" Her answer came immediately, anticipating to move from where she stood at the drop of a hat.

"Three."

Rayne let out a breathy laugh, a croak coming from him as blood coated his teeth. "You're a godsdamn lunatic, you know that, right?"

Jasper merely smiled, "Two."

I positioned myself on my hands and toes, matching a runner's stance. Gunfire faded around us as we focused on Jasper's order. The world slowed as adrenaline pulsated through me, and every muscle in my body coiled, ready to act at the signal.

"One."

When the countdown ceased, an immediate updraft occurred

so suddenly that my braid opposed gravity. The shift in the air surrounding us took a sharp left before cutting right and heading directly for the skyscraper towering over the street. It was as if the air obeyed Jasper's command, instantly reshaping the battlefield.

I tucked my feet under myself and sprinted, the sound of shattering glass and fracturing structural members following. The soldiers attacking us seconds ago had ceased fire as they turned their attention skyward to where the upper levels of the building seemed to hide in the clouds. I followed suit once I had positioned myself behind the barrier, resting my hand on Rayne's shoulder in reassurance, his bloodied form a stark reminder of all that was at stake.

The top half of the building was severed diagonally with such ease that you would've never guessed one man was responsible for the displayed decimation. The ear-piercing squeal that followed indicated that the upper section, no longer connected, was beginning its rapid descent. Gravity became its best friend as the once-stable structure plummeted, heading straight toward the soldiers stationed below.

"Holy shit..." My breath caught in my throat as I watched it surge downward.

I spotted Raven as she leaped over the lip of the cement structure she had been hiding behind and rushed towards the four of us. The chaos of the moment seemed to blur everything except her determined figure. She had mere seconds before the decapitated building would crush her and the men who battled to keep us at a standstill.

The other two of Rayne's men remained unaccounted for as the city rained down on us in the onslaught of Jasper's rage.

FORTY-SEVEN

ASTRID

Raven slid beside me, her breath hitching as the skyscraper collapsed to the city streets below.

The impact shook the ground beneath us, sending a tremor through our bodies as debris flew toward us. I quickly tucked myself behind the cement barricade, the roar of destruction assaulting my ears. The asphalt cracked and splintered from the force, and the shriek of twisting metal invaded my senses until the inhumane noise finally ceased. My ears rang in protest, and the silence that followed felt almost as oppressive as the chaos.

"Woo-hoo!" Mykel laughed from his position where Jasper and I had just been, glancing over in our direction. "Talk about a way to make an indent on humanity."

Rayne laughed weakly, "Gods, you're so stupid."

I watched as Raven shifted her position, leaning forward and motioning for Everett to lower his hands. Her focus was far from the destruction surrounding us, fixing on the man who had led them for years. There was something profound in her eyes, intense assurance with an underlying level of affection.

Her palms were near pinkish red, and tendrils of light ascending her forearms made my mind wander back to the clinic where Elowen explained the color differences between healers.

"Users whose abilities center solely around healing emit a blue, green, or purple hue when channeling them."

The berry hue was a testament to the fact that Raven wasn't solely a healer but a dual wielder. She took a deep breath, her shoulders rising as her eyes closed. The color grew more vibrant, pulsing with energy. She focused intently, channeling her power as her hands hovered over the wound in Rayne's stomach. The bleeding halted almost immediately, the glow from her hands reflecting in Rayne's eyes as he watched intently.

"Lucky for you all, you have a healer on hand," Jasper said, sitting beside me. His eyes scanned the surrounding area to ensure that no soldiers had survived his attack.

"Pretty nifty, isn't it?" Rayne pushed himself upright, which earned a hiss from Raven.

"For hell's sake, stop moving."

I laughed, looking over my shoulder at Mykel, who made his way over to us. His eyes seemed to tally each of us before he stopped, his brows narrowing slightly.

"Where the fuck is Riggs?"

A smile spread across Rayne's face as he obeyed Raven's command. "In the time we've spent together, he's learned to seize opportunities. I might have encouraged him to use the chaos to his advantage, to see if he could determine where they took Onyx."

"You snide bastard." Jasper kicked Rayne's booted foot as he shook his head. "I should've known."

Rayne shrugged in amusement. "Considering he abandoned us, I'm going to conclude that he could pick up on his energy."

"So, that means he's alive?" The relief was far too prevalent in my inquiry.

Rayne looked at me. "You think that stubborn asshole would die that easily?"

"There's no way Onyx would give them that level of satisfaction." Jasper cut in as he glanced over his shoulder. "His will is nearly impenetrable. Giving in to the two men he hates the most would be the last thing he'd *ever* allow himself to do."

Relief flooded me, a weight lifting off my shoulders. The alleviation I felt was not just for the success of locating him but something else entirely.

He would stop for no one, and neither would I.

Raven leaned back on her heels and looked at Rayne. "Okay, *now* you have permission to move."

As he pushed himself up, groaning slightly, he threw her a pointed grin. "Apologies for the holdup. We can resume destroying everything in our path now."

Everett threw a punch into his shoulder once he was standing. "If you do any stupid shit like that again, I will take it upon myself to kill you."

"Is that a threat or a promise?"

Jasper huffed a laugh, shaking his head as a leveled glare came from Everett. "The best plan of attack would be to continue our progression through the city, especially since we likely have soldiers on our heels because of the mess I made."

"The fact that you completely severed the upper section of a building speaks to your level of love for me, doesn't it?" Rayne winked, taking a moment to fully recognize what Jasper had accomplished during his time of need.

After witnessing Jasper's capabilities, I knew he would and *could* decimate entire cities for the people he loved most. His injuries on the night of the attack on his community made sense now. The combined power of Jasper and Onyx would have left nothing standing if he hadn't held back. They would have annihilated every government official attempting to breach the gates.

He had proven that.

"Something like that." He merely shrugged as he took a step forward. "They seem to be stationed in the north since most of their operations have stemmed from there."

"Which could be where they're holding Onyx." I motioned

toward the clear obstacle in our path. "All things considered, they'll have to reroute."

"And so will we." Rayne's eyes moved between the buildings. "If we can stick to the alleyways and potentially the rooftops, it may give us an advantage."

"Or it may put a target on our backs." Everett countered, "Who's saying they don't have men stationed at vantage points? It would make sense for watch duties."

Rayne snapped as he pointed to the whitish-blonde-haired man. "Touché."

"The alleyways aren't a bad idea considering they connect to the sidestreets." Jasper motioned to the nearest one. "We'll have to stay on our toes the entire time. Given how hard they've worked to remain hidden, they've likely scattered traps throughout this city."

"Alright, we stick to the alleyways and use our abilities if we encounter any soldiers. If a less visible attack is possible, we'll take it." Rayne chuckled softly as he pulled his hood over his head, not to shield himself from the rain but for another purpose entirely. "As far as I'm concerned, going in with a bang is what these assholes deserve."

WE CREPT through the side streets, keeping our footsteps as light as possible. Shadows cloaked the city streets, and the overcast sky loomed overhead. While the rain had ceased, the thick clouds blocked any light from the moon, plunging us into near darkness. Our eyes gradually adjusted, making the dim light manageable.

I had my bow drawn, an arrow notched and ready should the need arise. Jasper walked beside me, his finger on the trigger of his rifle, the safety off. After seeing what he could do, I wondered why he even bothered carrying it.

My gaze shifted to the others. Raven stayed close to Rayne ever since she healed him, seemingly prepared to throw herself in front of him if necessary. Meanwhile, Everett and Mykel maintained their positions on the outer edges of our formation, weapons drawn and ready for action.

Most of the walk had been quiet—almost too quiet. They explained that the higher-ups worked to eradicate the Runners from the city to ensure the safety of government officials. According to Rayne, many of those responsible for the outbreak's aftermath remained here, ranging from high-ranking government officials to scientists. Their protection became a top priority, and assigned soldiers were tasked with eliminating any potential threats entering the city while continuing to work alongside those in power.

"I hadn't seen the President since about a month before our escape," Jasper broke the silence beside me. "But I believe he's somewhere within the city, executing orders and taking part in the Eradication Rites."

A humor-filled laugh left Rayne. "Oh, he is. He made a very notable appearance when I was there."

Everett scoffed in disgust.

He continued, "There have been rumors that he and his posse essentially keep power wielders as pets."

"Servants would be better terminology." Raven shot back at him.

"He and other higher-ups infiltrated cell blocks, looking for individuals who 'aligned most with their needs.' They took them back and forced them to submit to their every beck and call," Rayne said, spinning a knife in his hand. "It wouldn't surprise me if the President wanted Onyx all to himself, considering the methods and routes they took to manufacture him into what they wished he'd become."

"I'd love to put a bullet in his head." Jasper's response came through clenched teeth. "What they put Onyx through is inexcusable."

Rayne turned in his direction, walking backward as he spoke. "I think incapacitating him and allowing Onyx to combust his internal organs one by one would be the best means of revenge. He doesn't deserve a painless death."

Part of me wanted to know what had happened to Onyx under the President's orders, but I would allow him to share that with me when he was ready. Regardless of not knowing the details, I firmly believed every government official responsible deserved unbearable endings.

"Is it too grotesque to say I'd love to behead him and play a game of kickball?" Mykel's question came from behind us with a playful, yet serious, undertone.

"I think that's a fair statement." Jasper nodded in his direction, a level of approval present in the movement.

"It'd be a sweet game." Rayne chuckled. "I would put far more *oomph* into my kicks than I did in grade school."

Jasper made the motion of a dropkick, throwing his hand over his brows and pointing off in the distance. "Home run."

His reenactment drew laughter from the entire group as we continued our route through the city. It hadn't been long since we departed from where the firefight had started, leaving the resulting demolition as a symbol of our presence. Since we reconvened, Riggs still hadn't reappeared, which concerned me. I couldn't help but wonder if his attempt to retrieve Onyx had failed, and now not one, but two, were captured. I tried to hold on to the hope that they wouldn't have any issue with a successful escape if he could get in and out.

The rise of Rayne's hand abruptly stopped my racing mind, signaling us to hold our position. He motioned for us to move to the right side of the streets we explored, and we obeyed. I stepped over the curb, pressing my back against the brick wall of the structure beside me. There was a minor gap between Jasper's position in front of me and where I stood, an alleyway acting as a divider between the two portions of our group.

Rayne, Raven, and Jasper stood at the front while Everett,

Mykel, and I closed the back of our line. I scanned the dark landscape, searching for the reason behind the unspoken order. The silence was unsettling, especially after Rayne promptly ordered us into our positions. It was as if we all held our breath, waiting for a sign of what he had seen.

A flashlight illuminated one alleyway only a few feet away from us, cascading through the darkness.

"We are clear." The male's voice was uneasy as he spoke. "There were no survivors from the attack. We swept the area, and the vigilantes had already fled."

The walkie-talkie cracked momentarily before the response came through. "You have an order. Find them."

A recognizable voice, one that I had heard many times before.

Its hoarse nature and authoritative undertones belonged to someone of high standing. My mind raced, sifting through memories and digging through the files stored within my subconscious to identify the familiarity.

"I knew it. Bastard." Jasper snapped from in front of me, his voice a near whisper. His response was enough to confirm what I had anticipated.

The voice behind the walkie-talkie belonged to the man that many had longed to kill.

The President.

"Copy that," the male retorted. "We will sweep the rest of the city for their location."

Another crackle followed, agitation and satisfaction weaving through his response. "They are power users; ensure you are mindful of their capabilities. While they will pose a threat, the height of their abilities won't scratch the surface of what Oakes is capable of. Now that he is subdued, there truly isn't anything that stands in our way."

I would kill him.

"What about the girl?" The question was simple but recognizably pointed in my direction.

"You know what to do."

The two men in front of me emanated a ripple of power, a blend of rage and heightened protection. Their stance conveyed that the unknown threat wouldn't have an opportunity to act without overcoming the obstacle they presented. While I appreciated their protective instinct, something in me shifted—anger roaring through my veins.

I wasn't the one who needed to be saved.

I could stand on my own, and I would prove it to anyone who doubted otherwise. My purpose and intention were clear, and every piece of shit who questioned my resolve would quickly learn about the destruction that followed me.

"Copy that."

Inhaling deeply, I tightened my grip on my bowstring and raised it. I aimed for a car parked just outside the alleyway from which the male's voice had come.

I would show them *exactly* what I was capable of because, like the others, I held secrets that benefited me far more than even those I aligned with realized.

My fingers released the string, sending the arrow soaring toward its target—the gas tank of an idle vehicle. While I knew the likelihood of it containing enough fuel for an entire commute was low, there could be just enough residual to achieve the outcome I had discussed with Lila.

Explosives.

The arrow lodged deeply into the side of the car, the sound of its impact drawing the attention of the men lurking in the surrounding darkness. Their voices grew louder as they approached the source of the noise. Jasper shot me a look of uncertainty, which I met with a confident smile.

I watched as the first man, likely the one conversing on the walkie-talkie, came into view. His frame emerged from the alleyway, his uniform similar to those we had encountered before, clinging tightly to his body. As soon as his foot touched the sidewalk we were sharing, the fuse within the arrow ignited the flammable liquid—detonating the gas tank.

A bright flash preceded the combustion, and the entire vehicle erupted into flames. The force of the explosion knocked the man back into the corner of the building, where he collapsed, fire quickly engulfing his unconscious body. I pressed myself tighter against the wall as the heat from the blast swept towards us, then receded, a stream of cursing following.

"I believe I said something about going in with a bang, didn't I?" Rayne smirked in my direction and nodded in approval, a smile tugging on the corners of my lips.

Everett stepped forward as two men emerged from the alley. They quickly pivoted and aimed their rifles at us. Before they could pull the trigger, two ice javelins hurled in their direction, impaling both men.

"Still got it." There was a slight chill in the air as he spoke.

He lifted a closed fist in my direction, the two of us knocking our knuckles together as he bowed his head in my direction—a sign of mutual respect.

"Let's kill these assholes." Rayne nodded at Mykel as he leaned against the wall. "Show them what you've got."

Mykel took a minor step forward, his hands at his sides, his attention fixed on the burning car before us. The oranges and yellows of the flames illuminated his face, revealing the shift in his eye color. As he advanced, his irises, once a caramelized brown, turned nearly white. The car protested slightly before lifting off the ground, all by Mykel's doing. He inhaled deeply, moving the vehicle with ease towards the alleyway opening, where more soldiers were gathering.

Jasper lifted his hands to his face, positioning them palm to palm with a sliver of a gap between them. "Let's light them up, Astrid."

I nodded at him as I pulled another arrow from the quiver on my back, sliding it into position and leveling it at the levitating car. Out of the corner of my eye, I saw Jasper blow a powerful breath into the space between his palms, causing the fire to grow exponentially, its destructive wake reaching deeper into the alleyway.

"Now."

I released the string without repentance, aiming the arrow directly at the bottom side of the vehicle as Jasper held his position. Upon collision, a second explosion followed, and the flames intensified to match, a mix of reds joining into the coloring. The heat was enough to cast warmth down my entire body while the fire crawled through the entire side street and launched itself skyward. The sweep replicated that of an oven, rippling horizontally before moving up the perpendicular bricks—cooking anyone who stood beneath them.

"Burn." My words were a near whisper as I watched the fire progress to the surrounding structures, completely engulfing them. The crackle of the cataclysmic progression illustrated its expansive reach. A radiant hue cast a bright light through the streets, signaling our presence to anyone aware of the commotion.

I lowered my bow when a steady clapping streamed from the side street that had separated us. The sound grew louder, the luminosity from the explosion gradually revealing the concealed figure.

"You know," The familiar voice was enough to draw bile to my throat as the unforgiving, icy blue eyes came into view first. "Your bow skills have always been impressive."

A near growl escaped me as I locked eyes on Radley, his all-too-familiar camouflage suit clinging to him in a close replica of his Venturer uniform.

"Kill him." Rayne's snarled command followed, the click of a safety interrupting.

"Ah, ah, ah." Gael's response was quick, near demeaning, as he lifted his gun to the back of Rayne's head. "I say it's in your best interest to stand down, Bandell."

My hand tightened around the grip of my bow, my knuckles whitening. "You realize we took down *groups* of soldiers? Do you really think the two of you stand a lasting chance against us?"

Radley tipped his head back, laughing. "It's adorable, truly. That you even *believed* you could walk alongside them."

"Watch yourself." Jasper sneered as he looked in his direction, but they brushed past his warning.

"Those who wield abilities are a separate breed within humanity, and here you are, trying to align yourself with them. You so desperately sought a connection that you reached out to those who aren't even like you. While they may have accepted you, it still doesn't suffice or bridge the gap," he said, shaking his head at me. "You're pathetic, Astrid."

Jasper stepped forward, halting as a gun pressed against the back of his skull. I shifted my gaze slightly past him to see countless soldiers emerging from the shadows, one by one. The number was far greater than we had encountered since arriving here, growing with each passing second. It was as if they had crafted our arrival to suit their needs, waiting for the perfect time to launch their attack.

With the growing numbers, it became apparent that if any of us moved, they would unleash their firing squad. Unlike Onyx, who could infiltrate someone's mind, we didn't possess that level of power.

"So you're admitting that you and your men hid in the shadows until it was safe enough for you to interfere?" Rayne retorted, his question directed at the man behind him. "It's not only pathetic how big of a coward you are, Gael, but so incredibly amusing."

Gael's brows narrowed as he glared at me from behind Rayne, his jaw tightening. The gun pressed firmly against Rayne's skull was a clear sign he would pull the trigger without hesitation, creating an injury even Raven couldn't fix.

As I continued to observe him, his lips curled into a devious smile—one I had seen many times during our training together and within the Walls of Region Three. The same smile that signaled he had a rebuttal, one he deemed damaging enough to fuel his sadism.

My eyes moved a fraction too slowly, catching the glint of a second gun he retrieved from his waistline, aiming it in my direction. My mind flashed back to the order given in the alleyway—per the President's command, they knew what to do. Gael would stop at nothing to destroy everything Onyx cared about, starting with Imelda and working through each of us, even if orders opposed that.

I swallowed at the realization that the gun's position would sever my abdominal aorta, which would require immediate attention. But such care wouldn't be possible with soldiers flocking around us and the dire circumstances we faced. Even if Raven begged, it wouldn't be an allowable request. While I briefly considered dodging the attack, I knew it was futile. The minor gap between us didn't give me enough time, and I wasn't faster than a speeding bullet.

I inhaled deeply, my mind racing through memories—from the second Onyx landed on the rooftop to the night we were intimate to the moment I met Jasper and the acceptance he granted me. From Rayne's initial hatred to the hug we shared when he gifted me the gun at my hip—every passing second with each of them had been worth it. Standing beside them and fighting alongside them felt like a familial bond I hadn't realized I needed after mine was so easily stripped away.

My purpose went beyond the surface, the bonds we had formed, and the battles we fought. And while I wasn't one of *them*, they accepted me as such.

The sound of gunfire snapped me out of my memories, yanking me back to the present. My body jolted with the inescapable fear coursing through my veins. The intense anticipation of pain made me unaware of the passing seconds since Gael fired his weapon. I closed my eyes, bracing for the inevitable agony of Death.

An undeniable surge of power grew behind me as the lack of pain persisted. I inhaled slowly, opening my eyes to see Gael standing behind Rayne. Rayne remained motionless, an ever-growing smile spreading across his face as his gaze focused just past me.

I swallowed again, still reeling from the lack of agony that I should have been feeling. Gael's face twisted in horror and shock as his eyes followed Rayne's gaze. I looked down at the space between us and saw the bullet, still spinning with immense velocity, suspended in mid-air, refusing to move forward.

A gentle hand rested on my shoulder, a comforting touch I was far too familiar with. The graveled voice that followed undeniably belonged to the man we came to save, causing my knees to buckle and tears of relief to line my eyes.

"I hope I'm not too late, Sweetness."

ACKNOWLEDGMENTS

Congratulations—you made it to the end, even with the numerous twists and frustrating turns. However, I can't promise the next book in the series will be any better (in fact, it will likely be worse). I would apologize, but ultimately, I am not sorry for the angst.

My ultimate wish was to share this story with the imaginations and minds of others. Writing has always been a form of escapism for me, and creating worlds with characters others can relate to or find comfort in has been equally enjoyable. I relate to a particular character heavily in this book (if you know, you know), and I hope you were able to find similarities or comfort in some of them as well.

To my husband, JJ—for supporting me in writing and pushing me to pursue every dream and vision I have ever had while supporting my inner child and her most prominent dream. I could not have done this without you.

My parents—for being there through the lulls and highs of life and reminding me I can do whatever I set my mind to. For pushing me to consider sharing this story with others and being my #1 fans. Thank you for teaching me how to fight for what I wanted and never back down in that pursuit; you have given me the willpower of Onyx and all he stands for.

To my grandma—for begging me to send you a copy of this novel and always valuing my imagination and thoughts throughout my life. Thank you for showing me an undying level of love that many of the characters in this story yearn for.

To Mads who took the time to read this story since its inception and listened to the numerous ideas I threw in their direction. While, at the same time, screaming at me for my decisions and the paramount moments these characters went through. I honestly would not be here without your endless support and encouragement.

Thank you to my beta readers, who sent me reactions and remained engrossed in the story, choosing to give it a chance and see it through to the end.

And to all the other friends and family who have walked alongside me on this life journey, regardless of the trials and hardships that have arisen from the shadows. Every one of you has guided me toward my path of illumination.

As many are wondering, the beautiful cover designs are from Sophia and Jazzy. If there are any artists I could recommend, it would be them. Sophia and Jazzy brought my ideas and visions to life to create the visual representation of this story for you all.

My heart goes out to Indie Forge and all the incredibly talented and supportive women who started a company to give back to the indie community. Your tireless work and commitment to me and my novels means the absolute world to me, and I genuinely don't think I can thank you enough for taking a chance on me.

And to you, the dear reader, thank you for joining the Rebellion and standing for all you believe in. I hope you've enjoyed the first novel in this series, and I can promise that the next one will have you screaming and likely tossing your book across the room while cussing me out. Though, if it weren't that way, I wouldn't have done my job as a writer.

Enjoy a glimpse into Onyx's past and the story from his perspective in *The Abyss*.

A Glimpse into "The Abyss"

THE ABYSS

783 days until the Fall

Working with the government didn't mean agreeing with their methods.

My approach often clashed with standard protocol, but they accepted it. When they forced me into the role of a Command Officer, my capabilities quickly became apparent. The respect I earned allowed me to navigate the typical bureaucratic red tape, with those in power often overlooking my deviations from the norm with an understanding that the results I delivered were worth the leeway.

As the room's atmosphere remained thick with obedience, I focused on the photograph in the file I held. The overlapping triangles in the image seemed to stare back at me, an eye at their center fixed in a penetrating gaze. Geometric shapes encased the image perfectly, with the two triangles intersecting seamlessly at their apex. Concentric circles surrounded the eye, with the outermost ring featuring a pattern of dots. The meticulous design was near perfect, creating a focal point that demanded attention from any onlooker.

"It's the same symbol," I said, gazing at the two men across from me. "When we were in Caracas and executed our targets, Cassius Denali had an identical mark on his neck."

Gael Adler, one of the President's right-hand men and a high-ranking Command Officer, allowed a slight grin to form. "Which was what we presumed you would tell us."

"Where exactly did you come across the person who had it?" Jasper, who I commanded to accompany me to this meeting more for my sanity than out of necessity, leaned forward as he asked the question.

"We uncovered conversations between men within our ranks working to establish some type of rebellion against the President's orders," answered Aiden Vernox, the other man in the room.

Aiden was as well-known as Gael within the elite circles of the government's power structure. He'd built his reputation on a foundation of cold efficiency and unwavering loyalty to the President, holding a powerful position within the inner circle. His responsibilities went beyond simple advisory duties, making him the executioner of anyone deemed a threat to the administration's security. His unique and crucial role made him indispensable, unlike many other high-ranking officials who could be replaced or rotated out with little disruption.

His presence alone sent a simple message: any challenge to the established order would face persecution by his hand.

"Cassius mentioned something along those lines," I said, snapping the file shut and sliding it back across the table. "It seems there are men within our ranks forming alliances and committing to defiance. But what exactly are they opposing?"

There was a moment of silence, a palpable sense of something left unsaid.

"Generalized discontent," Gael replied, halting the file's progression with his fingertips. "Overall disagreement with McKinley's methods of leadership."

Aiden exhaled, adding, "It's similar to Andrei's situation. They're attempting to establish connections with other regions while stealing and leveraging internal information. It's a threat to national security."

Leaning back in my chair, I folded my arms over my chest. "While I hate to sound like an asshole, what exactly do you expect us to do about it?"

Gael chuckled, his gaze turning almost predatory. "Are you sure all your men are trustworthy?" His eyes shifted subtly toward Jasper, a deliberate gesture that set my teeth on edge.

I shook my head, a warning in my glare.

Gael was well-respected within the ranks and had collaborated with us on multiple missions. His expertise was undeniable, proven time and time again. Despite our professional interactions, something about him always set my instincts on edge—as if there was something more to him than what remained at the surface.

"You're not going there, Adler," I warned, my fists clenching involuntarily as we locked eyes.

His grin widened, deepening the lines around his emerald eyes. "It's a fair question, considering the circumstances."

I opened my mouth to retort, but Jasper intervened, raising a hand. "Respectfully, I made an oath when I signed on as a Command Officer to serve the greater good and protect humanity alongside our leadership."

"Didn't we all?" Gael shrugged, unfazed by the building tension. "But oaths don't mean shit when we have men going against them left and right."

A sharp snarl escaped my lips as I slammed my hand on the table, pushing myself up. "If you're going to sit here and accuse my men of treason, then I'm throwing the ball right back in your court." Leaning forward, I closed the space between us, my voice dropping to a hissed whisper. "Where were you when we went to Caracas to take out Andrei and his followers, Adler?"

His smirk didn't falter as he laced his hands behind his head, leaning back in his chair. "I believe Aiden can provide an alibi for me, but if you must know, I was attending a dinner with senior officers to discuss the very issues we're presenting now."

I scoffed, feeling the heat rise in my chest. "And I'm providing an alibi that my team was with me in Caracas, each of us responsible for the bloodshed that day. If they were working with the enemy, why would they have pulled the trigger on those they established allegiance and rebellion with?"

Aiden cleared his throat, sliding his chair back. "We apologize for the frustration. We are merely doing as ordered—crossing t's and dotting i's. Surely, you can understand the necessity."

Jasper stood beside me. "If you need proof, feel free to search us for the tattoo mentioned in the file, but I assure you, you'll come up empty-handed."

As Jasper's words faded, my focus remained locked on Gael. His eyes held an unsettling gleam as though he took pleasure in the discomfort he caused. His manner mirrored too closely to that of the President, every subtle smirk and tilt of his head pointing to a man who thrived on manipulation.

Gael finally rose from his seat, followed by Aiden. "We just want to ensure that our best officers are walking alongside us, not against us," Gael said, his voice smooth and composed. "If someone threatened your team members, you'd do anything to protect them, wouldn't you, Oakes?"

My jaw tightened as I forced down the retort on the tip of my tongue. "You're correct."

Gael grinned and dipped his chin before they moved in unison, pushing their chairs back and heading for the door. Aiden paused as they reached the threshold, glancing back over his shoulder.

"We appreciate your service and are doing everything possible to protect you. Thank you for your time and cooperation."

For the first time, I met his gaze directly. His hazel eyes contrasted with Gael's, lacking the same predatory amusement and reflected a deeper, more serious emotion—caution. It was as if he was trying to convey something he couldn't speak, a silent warning left unsaid.

Aiden turned and exited the room before I could delve further into his expression. Gael followed closely behind him and cast a final look over his shoulder. The sneer on his face was unmistakable, a silent challenge that would hang in the air long after he was gone.

"In case anything changes, you know where to find me," Gael stated insincerely.

I watched them disappear into the hallway, the russet highlights in Gael's hair catching the light one last time before he vanished into the darkness.

They were like the two sides of a coin—one oozing concocted confidence while the other hid in the shadows of caution.

As the door closed behind them, I exhaled slowly, trying to process the interaction. The room felt colder, the echo of their presence still palpable, and my mind raced to understand why.

They had come with questions, but it felt like they left with more than just answers.